Peter Dillon h[illegible]ulti-track career in theatre, tv, film and academia. He has written plays for northeast England theatre companies, scripts for tv's serial drama *Emmerdale* and wrote the feature film *The Other Possibility* for Pinball Films. He co-produced *An Angel Passes By* for Wildcat Films, which won the Golden Spire award at the San Fransisco Film Festival. He won an RTS award for the BBC2 documentary *River Racing*.

Through membership of the Shoetree Arts group, formed to explore the rich history of Heaton – a suburb of Newcastle upon Tyne where he lives – Peter has been involved in producing films, music events, theatrical productions, and exhibitions.

The Driver is his first novel.

First published in Great Britain in 2025 by ARP 43 Publishing.

Distributed in the UK, US, Canada, Australia, and other territories by Ingram Spark.

Any errors are the responsibility of the author.

ISBN 978-1-0369-2726-4

ARP 43 PUBLISHING

THE DRIVER

PETER DILLON

ARP 43 PUBLISHING

To Roma;
lovely coffee
All best wishes

Peter.

To Joan Dillon [Min]
1920 – 2011

‘I’m backed up in a dark corner
and I don’t know who’s hitting me.’

The Dark Corner, 1946.
Screenplay by Jay Dratler and Bernard C. Schoenfeld.

CHAPTER ONE
GREECE 2010

Duncan was in agony.

His skin was on fire. He could bear it no longer and stood up. The receptionist ran the tip of her biro down the column of names. "I'm sorry, Mr Connor, we already have so many waiting."

At least she had said his name correctly; most people added an O.

A man, probably sixty-something, wearing a blue beanie, sat arms outstretched. He was leaning back against the wall on a wooden chair, its two front legs in the air.

"Are you familiar with the motion picture 'My Darling Clementine', in which Mr Henry Fonda takes the part of the Sheriff Wyatt Earp?" He spoke in an American accent stained by a life-long addiction to tobacco.

Duncan shook his head.

Beanie rammed his chair down on the tiled floor, every echo reverberating painfully through Duncan's body.

"Christ!"

"He won't help yer," laughed Beanie, now on his feet. "Mr Fonda got the girl alright, but only after a shave and a dance at a church consecration." He leant forward. "One of the director's, Mr John Ford's, finest."

Duncan could still taste Eleni's kiss. But was she missing him? Was she even thinking about him? She had to be… But why hadn't he heard from her? He checked his mobile.

Nothing.

How in heaven's name had things got to this?

"Hey, O'Connor!" shouted Beanie.

"There's no O, never has been, never will."

"The hell I care. Someone to see you." Beanie stood aside and a woman in a white coat beckoned Duncan. "Count yourself lucky, boy, most of us have to wait."

Beanie helped himself to an olive from an elderly woman sitting on a bench.

Duncan was led into the surgical room, where a tall doctor with dyed hair leant against a desk, flicking through a medical catalogue. He spoke in Greek to the woman, who left, closing the door behind her. Then, working from the feet up, he took in his latest patient, interest only stirring at the abrasions round the neck and the distinctive black eye.

Duncan gently removed his denim jacket. "Do you speak English?" he asked.

"Not so much."

Duncan lifted his sweat-soaked t-shirt over his head, but it stuck. Unable to see, fearful of more agony and aware how absurd he must look, Duncan was marooned.

"I cut."

Two flourishes of the scissors followed.

"A sacrifice." The doctor, proud of the word, dropped the t-shirt into a bin.

Duncan's torso was covered in red welts; his skin had crinkled and blistered into several clusters forming ridges of bubbles. Lower down his abdomen, a series of dark-coloured blemishes of different sizes resembled an abstract painting.

"There's more."

He dropped his jeans to the floor revealing thighs and legs pockmarked with numerous gashes – some leaking – plus alarming, yellow-coloured growths the size of golf balls. The doctor gestured him to turn around. An array of blotches and suppurating red cuts ran down to his heels.

Duncan sat down on the couch.

His body exposed to the air tingled uncomfortably and his head throbbed.

"Fucking hell."

"Fugging 'ell," the doctor laughed. "Fugging 'ell…"

A swell of vomit surged into Duncan's throat, and a projectile flow into the t-shirt bin looked odds on. But just as quickly the spew subsided, leaving a vile taste in his mouth. He pointed towards the water cooler.

"Ice?" asked the doctor, filling a polystyrene cup.

They could have been in the taverna next door.

The doctor re-focused on the bruised eye and the corrugated neck. "How do this happen, please?"

"An accident."

Humming softly, he lifted Duncan's chin with his forefinger and inspected the abrasions.

"Aaaaarggghhhhh…" Duncan's restless insides threatened again. He gulped back some fresh gunk in his mouth and drank from the cup.

The doctor's gaze switched from the neck to the eye and back again, until reluctantly, it seemed, he stopped the examination and picked up a needle and a dish from inside a glass cabinet.

Duncan eyed the long needle. "Is this going to hurt?"

The doctor shook his head and, starting with the fiercest golf-ball growth, punctured each one, allowing dark puss to drain into the dish. Next, using cotton wool, he dabbed the blemishes with a liquid that looked like iodine, but mercifully didn't sting. At his desk, he wrote out two prescriptions.

"This one for insect bites, and this for – ah – sunburn," he explained, while Duncan pulled up his jeans carefully to avoid chafing. "You go this way for pharmacy." The doctor pointed out the window overlooking the square.

He opened a cupboard behind his desk, judged Duncan's size and chose a white t-shirt from a shelf.

"Oh, thanks." Duncan measured it against himself.

"No for fashion." The doctor pointed at the bin. "Instead."

"Suits me. Not exactly the last word in fashion, am I?"

"You will be better in some day – if no, I see you again." He pointed at Duncan's neck. "Be safe. Yes?"

Duncan guessed the doctor suspected he had tried to hang himself.

On the infirmary steps, beneath a grand archway, he took out his mobile. Still nothing.

A group of donkeys, saddled up, stood in a grove opposite the taverna, where the tables with gleaming white tablecloths had been readied for the day's business. The square, paved with chunks of marble, sloped upwards towards the pharmacy, behind which rows of houses were dug into the hillside that towered above the port.

What Duncan couldn't fit into the picture was the shadow of a young man who had dogged his progress since leaving the infirmary. Now this fellow–thin, angular, dressed in uniform – cut in front of him and spoke.

"I'm sorry, I don't understand," said Duncan, and as swiftly as his injuries allowed tried to pass. But the fellow stretched out his arms like a shepherd fencing in a runaway sheep.

"Police!" he said.

Whatever you do, Nikos had warned him, don't trust the police.

The policeman crooked his finger.

"No," Duncan spoke slowly the way people do when someone doesn't understand them. "I go to the pharmacy," and he pointed up the slope. "I am ill." He waved the prescriptions in the man's face and continued.

"*Ochi* [No]," insisted the policeman and grabbed Duncan's arm.

Duncan screamed. The policeman had seized a shank of bubbly sunburn. The pain shot down to his toes, then reversed to mingle with his hangover, and a torrent of vomit splashed over the policeman's shoes. Duncan reeled backwards against a low whitewashed wall.

The policeman stooped and carefully picked up the fallen prescriptions. For a moment it looked like he'd use them to wipe his shoes, but holding them gingerly, he read them.

Duncan gurgled and spat.

"Stop," said the policeman in English, as though he had command of Duncan's digestive system. Then he daintily slipped out of his shoes and pointed to the pharmacy. "I go. You, here."

As a well-travelled person, this was not how Duncan preferred to arrive in a new place, but it wasn't the first time he'd landed in disarray. But how did the police know? Who'd tipped them off?

Half an hour later, his arm had deepened in colour from an irritated brown to an angry red. He'd taken a tablet and applied some cream. He hadn't been arrested, but after interminable language difficulties, the policeman explained they'd like him to answer some questions.

In a cramped office, Duncan was told to sit down at a desk. A jug of water and a tumbler had been provided. Next to him was a stack of thin files. He distracted himself by looking through them. Each one contained a suspect's photograph and, he supposed, a paragraph or two of biography. He wondered whether they had a file on him, before he realised they were all of young women. The last file dispensed with written details, and contained only a gallery of shots mostly taken, Duncan guessed, without the suspect's knowledge. In the final picture, though, much larger than the rest, she had posed in complicated underwear. Admirable, he thought giving it a second glance, before returning it to the pile.

Then, wearing a light blue shirt and tie, dark blue trousers, and black highly polished shoes, the spitting image of his primary school teacher walked in. She had bright red lips and billowing dark hair. She sat down at the desk opposite Duncan and smiled. As a child he'd often dreamt about Ms Coleman, and now he understood why.

"Good afternoon," she said. "I'm Police officer Andrea Koutsikos."

"You remind me of somebody."

"Do I?" she replied, producing Duncan's passport from the desk drawer, and flicking through to his photograph. "You don't."

The policeman brought her a cup of coffee and hovered. She snapped out an instruction. He collected the files from the desk and, looking sheepish, quickly left.

"Duncan is a Scots name, isn't it?"

He nodded, adding, "The Connor is Irish."

He kicked himself. Do not on any account offer information. But the bewildering similarity between this woman and Ms Coleman was playing havoc with his emotions.

His default position was guilt. An interrogation offered a serious tussle between his desire to conceal and the temptation to confess. The latter option had the upper hand, and he cursed whatever higher order had landed him in this fix.

"Happy birthday," she said closing his passport. "For last Friday."

"Thank you."

"Did you have a party?"

Duncan blinked. She'd come straight to it. "A few drinks, nothing much really."

"Oh, that's surprising," she said. "Thirty is a landmark, don't you think?"

He shrugged.

"I'm sorry about your injuries, Duncan Connor," she said sympathetically, switching on a headlight-sized smile. "But so long as you're well enough, I'd like to continue."

He shivered. Ms Coleman had always addressed him by both names.

"Are you cold?"

She looked into his eyes – obviously thinking, you poor man, you're far from home, and suffering terribly, but once this silly investigation is over, I'm going to take care of you, and the first thing we'll do is…

"I'm ok." He traced his fingers gently over his arm, imagining it was her, or better, Eleni. If only Eleni would call, she could explain in Greek, and he could catch up on some sleep.

Officer Koutsikos produced a file from the desk drawer. So, he did have one.

"There is no record of you travelling on the hydrofoil. I'd like to know how you got here."

"I caught the supply boat."

The supply boat regularly visited the island. Duncan had spent part of the trip relaxing in an islander's new metal bath, and one of the crew had placed another islander's tree in a pot nearby to give him shade. It had failed.

She opened the file. "We've counted 195 euros, and of course the visa card."

"You can discount the card. It's just the cash."

"So, tell me about the supply boat," she said, and leant back like someone settling in to hear a good story.

"Well, I offered them my services."

"What sort of services?"

"I suppose you'd call it labouring. I helped them load up."

"All this time the supply boat has been coming here, so why did they need you?"

"I don't know. They probably didn't."

"Was there some special cargo that you had, perhaps?"

"No. Nothing like that."

"Did they pay you?"

"Not as such, but Captain Petros did give me a bottle of – well, I'm not quite sure what it was. There was no label and for my sins I drank it."

"Your sins, Duncan Connor. I'm interested in your sins."

"No, well, it's just a manner of speech really."

"Go on."

"I drank it. Simple as that. All of it, and it made me ill."

"Do you drink much?"

"No, I don't think so. I can turn it on and off."

"Do you drink when you're happy, or you're sad?"

"Both, I suppose, or neither… I don't know."

"Do you drink to forget?"

"No, not consciously anyway."

"Would you like a drink now?"

"I'm not an alcoholic, if that's what you're asking."

The policewoman leant forward. "Do you ever hear voices in your head?"

"Doesn't everybody?"

"What are yours telling you now?"

"How much you look like my primary school teacher."

"Ah," her eyebrows raised. "And did you have a crush on her too?" Her approach was bringing him to the brink, and it was taking him every effort not to fold. "Do you find people in general feel sorry for you?"

"I wish you did."

"But you're not really thinking about me, are you, Duncan Connor?"

His full name, once again.

"Ms Coleman was always far too old for me."

"Tsk, So, now we have her name." She smiled. "In an average week, Mr Connor, about how many times would you say you fall in love?"

"What?"

"Do you fall in love with every woman you meet?"

"No." But he conceded to himself she might have a point.

"So, you are discriminating?"

"I must say you speak very good English."

"Please do not patronise me."

"Certainly not. No, it's the line of questioning I'm finding rather odd."

"I take the holistic approach to interrogation. Have you ever been interviewed by the police before?"

"No," he lied.

Just tell her everything. Confess. She'll get it out of you anyway. Tell her the last five years… no, make it the last ten: they have been a waste of time. How you've taken wrong turnings, and maybe Eleni is just the latest, but she's not here because… well, why not?

Was it the bites, the sunburn, the herbal cream, Ms Koutsikos herself? Duncan thought he might be delirious. She left her seat and came round the desk towards him. "So by the time the boat arrived, you were ill?"

"Drunk. I wandered about, found a beach. It was hot, very hot, and I stripped off. Then I passed out, the worst thing. The mosquitoes spent the night biting the hell out of me and in the day the sun finished me off."

She leant down inspecting his eye. "This wasn't mosquitoes."

Her perfume lapped at his nostrils.

"I was working on a lighting rig for a music show." He looked up at her. "You know?"

She was still looking at his eye. "I know what a music show is."

"I was climbing up some scaffolding when one of the lights slipped and crashed into me. Smacked me right here."

"Really?"

"Yes."

"Where was this?"

"In Hamburg… Germany."

She returned to her side of the table and sat down again. "Who was playing?"

"Jennifer Lopez."

"Did she kiss it better?"

Duncan suppressed a laugh. "No."

"Tsk, you're lucky to be alive."

He nodded.

"So, you caught the supply boat, you got drunk, and you've come here. Why?"

Confident he'd weathered the storm he told her the story he'd prepared earlier.

"I'm on the trail of Simon Gray."

"Who?"

"He was a British playwright, who also wrote some very funny diaries. He used to visit Spetses on his holidays."

She called out, and the policeman came to the door so quickly he must have been listening. She spoke in Greek. He laughed and left again.

"Now, we have this, Simon – ?"

"Gray."

"Simon Gray and Jennifer Lopez; music shows; so much culture. You are a very sophisticated fellow."

"Well, I wouldn't go so far as to say that."

"Oh, come on, we're so honoured to have you here on our island," She deadpanned.

The policeman returned, laid out a map on the desk and pointed. "This Spetses," he said.

"Whereas" Officer Koutsikos' finger stabbed at another island. "This is where you are, Mr Connor, not Spetses. You are here."

"Oh?" Duncan felt foolish. "Yes, I see." He smiled lamely. "It's always good to know where you are."

"Unfortunately, you will have no chance of finding Mr Gray here."

"No, I won't anywhere. He died."

Her stare cut straight through him to the guilty marrow. "I don't believe a word you've told me."

As he walked down the corridor all he could hear was someone vigorously polishing their shoes.

Outside he checked his mobile phone again: nothing.

Somewhere there was a photograph of himself and J-Lo. They're both grinning at the camera, though her smile has a more practiced and professional look. Duncan had never counted, but at a guess there were around a hundred and fifty other people in the photo: the stage crew, the venue's admin staff, the security detail, and Ms Lopez's entourage. For the record, the photograph had been taken several years before.

Koutsikos had had him from her entrance: her smiles, sympathy and, undeniably her suspicion. But it was the mugshots she'd finally shown him that preoccupied Duncan: Mazarakis and Kafandaris, the unwelcome birthday party guests. He realised they were the two he'd nicknamed 'Combat Jacket' and 'Sunglasses'. He denied to Koutsikos knowing them, or ever having seen them before. There's an old saying that trouble comes in threes, but Duncan bucked the trend. For him, it was twos. There had been others before Mazarakis and Kafandaris. Diabolical duos, he'd called them.

He made his way through the narrow street bound on each side by whitewashed houses. However far he'd travelled over the years – his father would have said, fled – he wondered if he'd ever escape. Life he was now certain, moved in circles; the same patterns repeated over and over, until – what? A reckoning perhaps, but with whom? Which twosome to choose? Or else, it was himself. He was the trouble. He was the one who had to slay his demons.

The Port was a horseshoe-shaped harbour with the town built up on all sides. Shops and cafés stood on the wide marble quay, streets like gullies leading off to the squares behind. The residential quarters stretched high up on the rocky crags. Further still, beyond the tree line, perched a monastery. On a promontory peak, an old windmill stood guard over the harbour entrance.

In a show of muscular prowess, brawny multi-national crews tacked their racing yachts towards the open sea. Zig-zagging between them sped the taxi boats ferrying sightseers to the other little ports, hotels and sunbed-packed beaches along the island's coast. Moored to the quay were the floating monstrosities, the 'fuck off' yachts, signalling their owners' empire-sized wealth. Liveried staff emerged from the galleys, trays piled high with food and drink for the guests, perhaps a princess and her courtiers, while their host in the captain's cabin conducted his nefarious business with Wall Street or a Dacha on the Steppes. Another million made. By comparison, the indigenous fishing smacks, Euro pop blasting from the wheelhouses, resembled the relics from the island's seafaring history.

Duncan, tucked beneath a café's awning, focused on the hydrofoil berth where the boats unloaded passengers from Piraeus. Every half an hour or so, cruise ships several stories high arrived to disgorge hordes of camera-ready day trippers, who clicked their way down the quay to spend two hours and at least 5 euros each in the range of shops: the tacky souvenir end to the downright expensive clothes and jewellers. Mingling with the longer stay visitors rattling down the gangplanks with their wheelie bags, they accounted for the island's economic buoyancy.

He had texted Eleni to make sure she got the right island, but he could miss her amongst the throng. Especially so with Beanie, the American patient from the infirmary, to distract him. Like a puppy nosing out a new chum, he surged passed the tables and joined Duncan. No sooner had he ordered an espresso and lit the remains of what looked like yesterday's cheroot, then he began his own interrogation.

"If you want the truth, I'm looking for peace of mind, but since I arrived that's been rather elusive."

"Hey, now don't you go philosophical on me," warned Beanie.

"Alright, let me condense it for you. How about, I'm lying low?"

He perked up. "Is it the law, the bad guys, or the ladies on your tail?"

"Come to think of it, I suppose it's a bit of all three."

"Then I'd say you've found the spot. All exits and entrances covered. But while you're here, any specialities you can add for the communal good?"

Duncan thought. "Yes, driving cars fast and a growing tendency to hit people."

"Ok, so what? You're James Bond?"

"No," Duncan laughed. "But maybe, Jack Reacher."

"Stop taking yourself so fucking seriously."

"Hey, go easy, I'm not feeling well."

"And you think I am? I was at that quack's too, but for argument's sake, I'll take you at your word. It's a no-car island, unless you count the dustcart. That's strike one. And I could list you any number of folks for a good beating, but I guess that don't square with any peace of mind, so strike two."

"I don't set out to give anyone a good beating. It's mostly self-defence."

"But the other party ends up on the floor, am I right?"

Duncan weighed it up. "They tend to, but I'm not here to brush up on my skills."

Beanie waved at a cadaverous figure in a dark coat, conspicuous on such a hot day. He carried a black briefcase and, after navigating a gaggle of cats, nodded at Beanie. His eyes, sunken in a pale skull, glanced at Duncan.

"Cutting the bullshit: if you're just washed up, then that's fine, you've made a good choice, you belong to a great tradition."

Duncan followed the briefcase man's progress as he joined the queue for the hydrofoil.

"Would you say there's any chance of redemption?"

Beanie chuckled and spread his hands outwards. "Hey fella…"

"Is that what happened to you? What's your story?"

"He's got a better one," said Beanie, pointing to the queue. "He was once the richest guy in Milwaukee."

Duncan assumed it was a joke but catching Beanie's expression, probably not.

"It's been a while for me." Beanie puffed on the cheroot, then, realising its day had gone, he stubbed it out and checked through his shirt pockets.

Duncan had become aware of a waitress taking her time clearing a nearby table. She turned and saw him watching her. She smiled, and he smiled back, and then he remembered the galley shots in the policeman's file. He looked again. Yes, he really had arrived in a village. And she really was making a meal of putting dirty plates and cutlery onto a tray… had she been listening? Was he being followed?

"Hell, damn."

"The way you talk, I think I'm in a movie."

Beanie laughed. "There was a time when I flirted round the edges of that sub-strata of the city of the Angels better known as Hollywood. Apart from a few walk-ons, no dice. I didn't have the whaddyamacallit." He clicked his fingers. "The ring-a-ding-ding, the shazam. But look out for me in TV re-runs; I'm the Jack Daniels in the bar scene. Ah, what the hell, I was a kid then."

Duncan wondered if he had ever come to the local sheriff's attention.

Beanie stood up and searched through his jeans pockets, but nothing doing. "You're going to have to excuse me, pardner."

While he headed inside the café, passing the waitress going in the same direction with her tray, Duncan considered who else might know his business.

The once-richest man in Milwaukee had boarded the hydrofoil. Another cruiser dropped anchor. Still no sign of Eleni… but there was always the next boat.

"You plan to stay here all day?" Beanie had returned. "Come on, time to check out my room," he winked.

"Really?"

"Hey," Beanie opened out his arms. "If a fella can't help a fella, where the hell are we?"

An offer Duncan could not refuse. Besides, the waitress was coming back. And Eleni? She could text on arrival – whenever that was going to be.

"Thanks."

"Don't hold your breath, it ain't the Ritz."

As they passed a group of tethered donkeys, Beanie stopped. "If you wanted to take the weight off, how about one of these fine beasts?"

From his perch by the corner of the Bank, a Donkey Man headed over.

"Glad to hear someone's got my welfare at heart."

"Is that what's meant by British sarcasm?"

"No, no." Duncan looked down at Beanie's feet. "You were limping, so…"

"Hey, let me tell you, these babies have hacked it all the way across the Navajo Desert – Sorry, Costas, no dice."

The Donkey Man sloughed off.

Duncan followed Beanie steadily upwards past the infirmary, the bustle of the Quay receding behind them. They climbed some narrow stairs by a carpentry shop. Despite the noise of roaring saws and electric drills, a large golden labrador slumbered in the doorway. Onwards up endless steps they fell in behind a donkey train carrying a range of household goods, including the bath Duncan recognised from the supply boat. They paused as the last donkey unloaded spectacularly and a man with a broom and a shovel fought a rear-guard action.

They arrived at a first-floor flat by a flight of wooden stairs. A kitchen and living room combination lit by windows on all sides, offering a fine view of the valley below. It was sparsely furnished with a sofa-bed and a couple of chairs – one in need of urgent attention. A guitar leant against the wall. Amongst the few paperbacks in a small bookcase sat a dog-eared copy of Hunter S Thompson's 'Fear and Loathing In Las Vegas'. Unless he had a treasure trove elsewhere, was this all Beanie had to show for his x number of years on the planet? The man wheezed as he tidied the kitchen worktop, and Duncan worried he was looking at himself in years to come.

His host led the way down a short corridor, passing the bathroom, and showed Duncan into the back room. A solitary window shed light on a mattress propped against a wall and a dark green trunk housing bedding. Only the bars missing from the window persuaded Duncan it wasn't a prison cell. A door opened out onto a narrow balcony, above a stone floor belonging to the occupant beneath, Beanie's landlady. Below the building the ground dipped where a scuzzy looking dog was chained to a eucalyptus tree. He was barking at some stray chickens who pecked at the overflow from his food bowl. Beyond, the ground rose steeply upwards to houses in jagged rows.

Duncan came in from the balcony.

Looking at the accommodation through Eleni's eyes, he was aware this would not do. But for now, beggars couldn't be choosers. In the long term, well, it was better to keep Beanie where he could see him. If nothing else, the man was a source of information. Duncan rescued a cheroot from the mantelpiece – perhaps the one Beanie had been searching for at the café. His host clamped it between his lips, the deal was sealed.

Except…

Beanie attempted to light the cheroot. Clint Eastwood never had this trouble. ("That guy's the ultimate bastard," he said, later. "And he's a Republican.").

"I don't know what your game is, and I couldn't give a shit, but I do want the lowdown on that new cop." In a surge of flame from his misfiring lighter, the cheroot caught fire. "I hear tell you and she had a close-quarters encounter."

Duncan might have laughed at the predictability, but it was disturbing. "Are you spying on me?"

"That's my business."

"What d'you want, a date?" and he waved his hand at Beanie's outfit. "I think you'd have to smarten yourself up a bit."

A cloud of foul-smelling smoke drifted across the room, which Duncan batted away.

"One thing you better know," said Beanie. "I would never swap chow with the enemy."

He clenched his fist and took a step forward. They eyed one another for longer than Duncan felt comfortable. Beanie, yet to refer to his new lodger's injuries, came closer, but his stare turned rheumy, and he lowered his fist "I just remembered your speciality."

"She's on a mission," Duncan suggested, and Beanie's eyes widened. "I don't think she's a regular, probably seconded from Athens."

"Now you're telling me."

Then it was Duncan's turn to fish. "Maybe she's on the trail of Golden Dawn?"

Beanie grunted a level deeper than his usual register and took a long pull on the cheroot. "What d'you know about Golden Dawn?"

"This and that."

"Damn it, if you're not a tight-assed son of a gun," he wheezed. "That where the shiner came from?"

Well done, Beanie, you've hit the jackpot. But Duncan didn't admit to knowing anything more about the bunch of far-right Greek nationalists.

Beanie pointed his finger. "So long as it's peace of mind you're after, you're welcome."

"Thank you."

"Make yourself at home."

Beanie left. Neither had learnt much.

As Duncan reached down to take some sheets and blankets out of the trunk, his stretched skin felt like it would snap. The prescription was wearing off. He sank to the floor. Last time he had suffered such pain had been at school.

He looked at his mobile. Again, nothing. Zilch. Zero.

What was the point? In his fevered mood he thought about leaving. Catch the first boat to anywhere and chuck his phone into the sea. After all, he was a past master at leaving places.

Later feeling not much better, but as thirsty as hell, he staggered into the kitchen. In the nick of time, he spotted a sign above the sink tap 'Drinking Strictly Verboten.' He poured himself a glass of mineral water from a bottle in Beanie's fridge.

He gulped down the water, glanced out the window and nearly dropped the glass.

Surely not. Was he seeing things?

A figure from the past was climbing the steep steps opposite up to a row of houses at the top.

CHAPTER TWO
NORTHERN ENGLAND 1995

BAM!

The gloved fist rammed into his mouth and dislodged his teeth. That's what it felt like, but there wasn't time to check. Another punch landed in his solar plexus and Duncan doubled up. 1… 2… 3…, he counted. The pain came slower than last time but was just as devastating.

It was fifteen years before his journey to the Greek island and, in what was to become a trend, Duncan found himself backed up in a tight corner.

"Fucking defend yourself, you twat!" spat Wright, standing over him.

"I'm – trying…" He could barely breathe.

Wright prised off his boxing gloves and pulled Duncan to his feet. "You're not good enough."

Duncan nodded. Over Wright's shoulder he saw Major Williams, the head of sports overseeing the construction of the boxing ring. In a fortnight's time, in front of a packed gym of pupils and staff, Duncan would step onto the white canvas, hedged in by the ropes and the four freshly painted red corner posts, for the first round of the school's boxing competition.

The portrait hanging in the school's dining hall of an old boy symbolised the institution's ethos. Lord Uxbridge, who had lost a leg at the battle of Waterloo, was an inspiring example of what King and Country expected. Character was forged in physical adversity. While many similar schools had long since dropped the outwardly visible signs of their 19th century values, or even medieval inheritances such as a barbaric boxing competition, Duncan's had not.

But he had a plan. He would fight the good fight and lose. Then, head held high, he'd leave the boxing ring never to return.

Meanwhile Wright, the captain of boxing and two years older than Duncan, put his gloves back on for another interminable bout of sparring. The same every Tuesday evening for the previous three months, and Duncan was black and blue.

On the day, he arrived as late as possible for his fight. The changing room resembled a battlefield medical station as warriors from earlier bouts tended to their wounds. One of these poor souls, his nose bleeding, handed Duncan a pair of sweaty leather gloves. A bell tolled. From opposite sides of the gym, Duncan and his opponent, Carson, bristling and flexing his arms, approached the ring through the crowd of boys eager for drama – best of all, a knock-out. Members of staff and school prefects, well clear of the blood, sweat and toil, sat above the fray in the balconies.

Referee Williams, in all white, called the boxers into the centre of the ring for a rules briefing. Duncan, undermined by Carson staring him down, missed every word. He returned to his corner, doomed.

Another bell, shrill and gut shredding, rang for Round One. The stool beneath him was whipped away and Duncan was alone – except for Carson, who strode towards him gloves rotating. Spectators sniggered. A nervous reaction before a massacre?

Then came the punch, a good punch, a body punch, thudding into Duncan's chest. It hurt, but triggered an unexpected reaction. So much for capitulation; rats to public humiliation: the primeval instinct to survive kicked in. Incensed that he'd been hit, Duncan fought back. Techniques from those hellish sparring nights sprang into action. He weaved, feinted, and then landed a perfect righthander on the tip of his opponent's chin.

Carson's eyes rolled. He slumped back on his heels in shock. Duncan's follow up volley of punches pinned his opponent to the ropes. Next, a right to the face, a left to the chest, another right, and shaping for an uppercut…

The bell rang.

The next round passed in a blur. Only seconds had gone, it seemed to Duncan, before Williams, without waiting for the judges' scores, raised his arm and announced, "Connor, the victor."

That night Duncan lay awake trying to understand what had happened. His bruised torso hummed, Carson's single impression, but it offered a clue. Carson had started it. In self-defence, Duncan had attacked and with that came an adrenalin rush, excitement unleashed in him. This was new.

Punch, punch, punch.

He sat up in bed. He was the same person he'd been before, but something else had emerged. A streak of menace had crawled out from inside. He supposed it had been there all the time, unacknowledged. But now he thought, how could these two sides of himself coexist? Weren't they in opposition, and wouldn't they fight for supremacy? Fight being the word. Sporting rules would keep him in check, but what about outside the boxing ring? What more could he do, he wondered? What more was he capable of? He had frightened himself. He lay back down and turned over; it was easier on that side. To hell with it, he'd won. No time for any more introspection, the next fight beckoned.

A repeat. An opponent only had to hit him, and they were toast. With each fight, a new respect was owed to him. Boys bunched around below his corner of the ring copied him. Duncan had not realised, but prior to every time he attacked, he tapped his gloves together.

A week or so after, praying to lose, he reached the final: his fifth fight. He looked up at the portrait. How did Lord Uxbridge feel on the night of 17 June 1815, knowing within hours he could suffer an agonising death or else a brilliant victory? If Duncan won, would he too be immortalised on the dining room wall? Dangerously close to buying into the school's tradition, a culture he had set himself against, he turned his back on Uxbridge. But there was no mistake, he really wanted to win.

Walking tall he stepped into the ring, surely the champ in waiting. To cap it all his parents, Pat and Beth were sitting in the balcony, his father wearing a big 'That's my boy' smile, while his mother looked in shock. Out of sight, out of mind was their usual reaction. Surprised as Duncan by his progress, they had driven the hundred plus miles that afternoon and booked into a nearby hotel. So, what could possibly go wrong?

Maybe it was the memory of his opponent Caldwell's outright semi-final victory. Referee Williams had stopped the fight. Perhaps it was nerves, or the presence of his parents, but exactly why Duncan started so badly was a mystery. Flat-footed, he shipped punch after punch and was reduced to the useless sparring partner-in-training he once was. His technique floundered, the trademark glove tapping a shadow of its former self, and the flurry of punches that had bamboozled his previous opponents were nowhere to be seen. Against this, Caldwell jabbed and ducked out of range, then stepped back in, punching at will. Was Duncan's inadequacy so blatant that Williams would stop the fight? Thankfully, the bell rang.

He trudged back to his corner. If he'd dared to look up at the balcony, he wouldn't have seen his mother. She had slipped out in tears, while Pat drummed his fingers along the balustrade. Below, Duncan could not avoid the worry on his supporters' faces. Opposite, Caldwell was sneering.

Victory was his.

What happened next could have come straight from the pages of a 'Boy's Own Annual' story. Wright poked his head through the ring ropes and whispered in Duncan's ear.

"If Caldwell isn't carried out at the end, report to my study."

A trigger better than an opponent's punch. On the bell Duncan, as if plugged into the electricity grid, surged across the canvas. His right glove clashed with his left, no fancy-Dan tapping this time, and in one punch banished the memory of the first round. Caldwell was caught cold. He staggered. Duncan followed with a fierce blow to the body, the next to his opponent's unguarded face. The bounce knocked out of him, Caldwell ran, but Duncan like an animal after prey, cornered him, landing punch after punch. His was the kill and he thumped Caldwell through the ropes. The referee urgently shouted, "STOP!"

The crowd, strictly against school rules, leapt to their feet applauding. Williams discouraged Duncan from milking it. Caldwell was led away by his seconds and, as a precaution, into the Doctor's care. Duncan had never felt more alive.

By the time he got to his parents' hotel, he was celebrated out. His fan club had smuggled in a crate of Carlsberg Special Brew and heralded 'Tiger' Connor. Still, he could tell, his parents greeted his victory with less than enthusiasm. Beth's only concern was that he'd survived.

"I won, Mum."

"You're not yourself. Hadn't you better see a doctor?"

"He's pissed," said Pat. "So perhaps we should wait until tomorrow."

"Certainly not. We'll tell him now."

In this drab country hotel that still served chicken in a basket, Beth explained that, against her advice, Pat had invested in a financial scheme, which she'd been convinced was suspicious. And now the company involved could not be traced.

"I'd prefer it if we focused on the future," said Pat.

"I bet you would."

"The remedy as I see it," Pat told Duncan, "Is that – "

"There isn't a remedy. The money's gone," said Beth. "You'll never see it again."

"In the circumstances," persisted Pat. "Your mother and I have agreed we need to make some savings – "

"Urgently. Sorry, Duncan, he has made a complete hash of this – "

"The first in line to go are your school fees." Pat let that sink in.

"Which means – "

"I have to leave?" cut in Duncan.

"I'm afraid so," said Beth, a consoling hand reaching out to him. "We explained all this to the headmaster this afternoon."

"Oh, that's fine. Yeah, great."

His parents, surprised, looked at one another. "I – we – thought you were happy here," Beth said.

"Honestly, I don't mind." Duncan was excited by the prospect of leaving. "Really, I don't. I'm sorry about the money, obviously, but you know, it's not like we're out on the street, is it?"

Pat nodded and looked at his wife.

"Not for the want of trying," she said.

"Think of it this way, you'll retire the champ," said Pat, clapping him on the back, their first physical contact since he arrived. Beth groaned.

Later he overheard his father. "Well, that went better than I expected."

"You're still a thundering idiot," replied Beth.

His parents' trip had not been to see him box. He could forgive his mother for disapproving of boxing; for months he had, too. His father? Well? Perhaps Duncan's victory in the ring had allowed Pat a temporary reprieve from his troubles.

As they drove him away down the school drive, he remembered arriving. They had dropped him on a dull early autumn afternoon at the black wrought-iron gates emblazoned in Latin proverbs. He'd stood there, suddenly alone, and daunted he'd looked up at the tall, gaunt school buildings. Later, he'd learned Beth had cried all the way home. Now though he was leaving as the conqueror, and the sun was shining. The taste was so much better. But then from the back of the car as he watched his parents sniping at each other, Duncan felt the slim family bond loosen a further notch.

CHAPTER THREE
GREECE 2010

After a sleepless night Duncan painfully hauled himself down the cobbled street to the island's smaller port. He'd scoped it on his arrival and, even in a drunken haze, had admired the little harbour's beauty facing outwards to a flank of the Greek mainland in the blue distance. As calm as the fleet of fishing smacks and taxi boats anchored below the low circular harbour stone wall looked, the prospect of casting off on the choppy sea beyond tempered his interest in a voyage. A waiter scraping the chairs along the concrete floor in the taverna overlooking the harbour jangled his nerves.

After inching his way back to Beanie's, he mashed a pot of weak tea and lay down on the mattress. The figure he'd seen the evening before climbing the steps opposite, he convinced himself was at best a case of mistaken identity, or an hallucination. Then he fell asleep. But not for long. His host, fresh from an all-nighter, bounded up the stairs to the bathroom and urinated with the power of a fire hose.

"Hey, Pardner, you awake?"

"I am now," groaned Duncan.

"Busted the asses off a bunch of limeys at backgammon." Beanie came to the doorway, fishing out a wad of euros from his back pocket. "Breakfast is on me. A chef I know does the sweetest omelette this side of Amarillo."

Duncan pressed his head into his pillow. Sweetest omelette this side of… you could not make Beanie up.

"Come on, Pilgrim, whaddya say?"

Duncan raised his head. "Kind of you, but I think I'll pass."

"Buddy, you look sick as a dog."

"We met at the Doc's, remember?"

Beanie dawdled. "See I can't figure whether it's somethin's wormin' its way through the brain matter, else it's just plain, good ole mechanical wear out."

Probably both, Duncan conceded to himself, and then carefully lifted his t-shirt.

Beanie whistled. He knelt, inspecting the sores, and grabbed the tube of cream Duncan had re-applied during the long night.

"That quack gives you this?" he said, tossing it over his shoulder. "You should've told me."

Instructing Duncan to stay where he was, Beanie shot off down the stairs. Duncan checked his mobile. Eleni hadn't called. He tried to doze off, but Beanie returned with a handful of light green leaves.

"Got the answer." He cut one open and a viscous liquid oozed into his hand.

"What's this: voodoo?"

"If these little cuties don't get you as right as rain by sundown, my name's not Archibald MacLeish."

"You're a Scot?"

"I have no allegiance to any nation. I am a citizen of the Earth. Born Glencoe, Illinois in 1892; died Boston, Massachusetts, 1982."

"You're looking well for a ghost."

"I must say your education's sadly lacking, pardner. I share my name proudly with the poet, and screenwriter of the anti-fascist film, 'The Spanish Earth.'

"You're right, but if you don't mind, somehow Archibald doesn't quite fit."

"Let's not go to war about that. Cary Grant was an Archie, first time round."

"Probably why he changed it. Are you from Illinois, too?"

"Salt Lake City."

"Christ, a Mormon to boot."

"Lapsed. Now lie back."

Duncan held up his hand. "Just so long as those haven't been lifted from someone's orchard. I'm in enough trouble as it is."

"Either I treat you or I bore your runty arse with the history of Mormonism from the time of the leader Brigham Young."

Duncan succumbed and shivered as the green liquid trickled into the cuts and weals on his racked torso. Beanie admired his handiwork, which had transformed Duncan's chest into a green-coloured slick.

"Michelangelo would've been proud."

"You planning to exhibit me?"

Beanie arose, rubbing his sticky hands. "Gunna come up as shiny and new as a baby's butt."

He produced a cheroot from his top pocket.

"Oh, no," begged Duncan. "Not in here."

"You ever seen the best film Eastwood ever made, 'The Outlaw Josey Wales'?" Beanie asked, returning the offending stick back into his pocket.

"No."

"Damn it to hell, boy, what have you been doing with your life?"

"Don't ask."

"Some great cheroot work, best I've seen on celluloid, but you've got to take Mr Philip Kaufman's contribution into account. He'd set up the whole style of the movie when he got shunted and Eastwood took over."

"I'll bear it in mind."

"Get better, buddy, and start living. What the hell are you waiting for?"

Only the pain had moored him, Duncan wanted to say, but Beanie had left "for one of the great breakfasts of our time".

It would be another twenty-four hours before Duncan stirred. As the cocks began their dawn chatter, he dared look. Some wounds were still visible, but the raw bruises were a shadow of their former selves; the bumps and sores vanished. Crucially, there was no pain. Eager to show Beanie he found him beneath a duvet, but when Duncan saw he was not alone, he withdrew thankful he had slept soundly.

In the bathroom mirror, his bruised eye and neck lacerations looked to have improved, too. Only one thing could top his newfound health, but there was nothing from Eleni. He did the next best thing; he thought about her.

Duncan had taken the afternoon off from working in Janni's 'souvenir' shop in the Monastiraki district in the centre of Athens. Time to plan his next move. Catching the tram up the coast, he hopped off at a spot offering a beach and a go-kart track. He wheeled round the circuit a couple of times, but even though he had not driven a vehicle of any kind for a while, his enthusiasm did not last. He put it down to his restless mood. He dipped into the sea. Afterwards he fell asleep on the beach, his future still undecided.

He was woken by a cry. He sat up and saw a couple in the sea and, running down the beach towards them, a woman in a black bikini. Duncan stood up.

The man in the sea was bent double, peering into the water. The woman beside him, a slim dyed-hair blonde, shouted, and the woman in black ran back up the beach for a towel. This was Eleni. Her costume, her cascade of dark hair, her voluptuous body: Duncan was captivated. She returned and helped as the man hopped out of the water. Attended by both women, he sat down and then lay back his foot in the air. Duncan, getting closer, saw a deep gash was bleeding heavily. A nail or a rusty can must have ripped his heel open.

"Can I help?"

The man, wiry, curly haired, in trunks a size too big for him, looked up at Duncan.

"We'll manage, don't you think," he said, as the women wrapped his foot in the towel.

Wiping a lock of dark hair from her eyes, Eleni stood up and, smiling at Duncan, said, "We've lost our driver."

"No, no, I'm driving," said the man insistently, and with the blonde's help got up on one foot.

"Don't be stupid. How can you?" replied the blonde. "You'll only make it worse."

Duncan guessed he did not want another man in the coop.

Eleni looked down at the bound foot and then at Duncan again, with that same smile. "If you can?"

"I'd be happy to," he said, avoiding the man's eyes boring into him.

Introductions all made, Nikos leaning on Maria limped up the beach, while Duncan, pleased to help Eleni strike their camp, followed.

"We'll take him to the hospital, but I'm late for university, I have to get back for a tutorial."

Duncan smiled to himself, remembering his dilatory behaviour during his student days.

Eleni decided Nikos would find it easier to keep his foot upright if he laid his leg across Maria's knees in the back while she sat in the front and gave Duncan directions.

Their car, patched up with a replaced wing, reminded Duncan of the aerodrome days and he drove like it. Snaking through the traffic, he switched lanes, overtook cars at twice their speed, and risked what the other occupants feared were head-on collisions. This beat the hell out of go-karting. As they tore along the three-lane Poseidon Avenue, narrowly missing a motor cyclist, Eleni screamed.

"Sorry," said Duncan, braking.

"No, no," she checked the clock. "I think we'll make it."

Nikos, his place usurped, was head down, but Duncan, glimpsing him through the rear-view mirror, suspected he was planning to get back on terms.

As they drew up outside Eleni's department building, she sat for a moment and with the others got her breath back. Then, smiling at Duncan, she thanked him and suggested they all meet again. Nikos impatiently held up his bleeding foot. She leapt out, and from the steps looked back at Duncan. He waved.

A gentler drive to the hospital followed and, once Nikos had been whisked away by a nurse, Maria confided in Duncan. She was a pharmacist's daughter, who had completed her degree. On the tip of bursting into tears, she fretted she could not find a job.

"It's so bad here, and I think it will get worse. You can never tell what people will do. They are so desperate."

Duncan's attitude had been 'you reap what you sow'; Greece's problems were mostly of her own making. But now he saw the European Union's imposed austerity on the Greek people had more to do with helping those who had already made a mint out of the country, thank you very much. The impact on Maria was no doubt repeated many times over. However willing Eleni maybe, his desire for her suddenly felt like a version of northern European oppression.

Nikos and Eleni, Maria told him, came from affluent families. He was an architect's son, her mother, a lawyer. Their relationship had reached an eddy. Eleni was studying for her PhD, but Nikos, the younger of the two, had spent a year on a student exchange at Manchester University, then returned and dropped out of his undergraduate course.

"What happened in Manchester?"

"He must have 'met' Friedrich Engels." Maria shrugged. "Let's say they share similar views, but Nikos is always likely to take everything further."

In search of a toilet, Duncan heard Nikos' voice. A door was ajar. Laughter, then a woman spoke. Duncan edged closer. Nikos was lying on a medical couch, his foot wedged into a young nurse's thigh while she wrapped it in a thick bandage, tightening and loosening her grip. He exaggerated his reactions and the nurse, grinning, slapped his wrist. Nikos held out his hand for more.

Later, the patient, wearing sunglasses, hobbled out with the aid of a walking stick. He shook Duncan's hand as if meeting him for the first time. Duncan suspected Nikos could be as charming or as malevolent as the mood took him.

The trio, Eleni, Nikos, and Maria, were properly a quartet. The fourth, Dmitri, an Albanian, worked in one of Athens' swankiest hotels. Eleni decided they should treat Duncan to drinks "at Dmitri's". Eleni insisted this meant dressing smartly, which Duncan saw threw Nikos into a sulk. She added the sweetener of celebrating Nikos' recovery. He'd abandoned the stick, and his stitches were due to be removed. Duncan found a snazzy frock coat that had once belonged to Janni's son.

"My parting gift to you," Janni said. He and his son were no longer speaking.

Families, thought Duncan, what a curse. Nikos' costume was solved by rummaging through his wardrobe at his parents' house. Maria had finally landed a job interview in Patras and left with their blessing.

Duncan could not wait for that evening.

CHAPTER FOUR
NORTHERN ENGLAND 1995

"For God's sake, answer, will you?"

Duncan had arrived at his grandmother Hannah's bungalow five minutes earlier. "Come on."

The front door was ajar, and despite shouting for her there'd been no answer. Anxiety increasing by the second, Duncan looked in the kitchen. Empty. The drawing room, too. Had she been burgled? An old woman living on her own, would he find her beaten up and lying on the floor? Was the burglar round the next corner waiting for him?

None of the above.

Her bedroom door was open. He went in and immediately left to call for help.

"Finally," he said, as Pat answered the telephone. "Gran's still in bed and she's a funny colour. You better get here."

Duncan tentatively returned to the bedroom and was astonished to find his grandmother sitting up in bed.

"What's all the fuss about?" she asked, pointing her glass at the bottle of Johnnie Walker whisky on the dressing table. "Come on, I need topping up."

Duncan poured her out a glug. "Hardly healthy, Dunc. Topping up I said."

He poured in as much again.

"Have you seen my gaspers anywhere?"

"I'm not sure you should be smoking in bed, Gran."

"I can do what I darn well like."

She had made a remarkable recovery from the crumpled figure he had found with her head on one side, her mouth lolling open. Her pale blue nightdress, her shock of white hair framing her parchment-lined face: she was very much alive.

"Where are you going?"

"To ring my dad."

"Sit down, I want to tell you something."

"Alright, I will, but just let me – "

"SIT DOWN!"

Duncan pulled up a chair beside her bed and listened.

It was August 19th, 1942. The call had come into the Ambulance HQ at the Royal London Hospital late in the afternoon. The survivors from a catastrophic raid on Dieppe in northern France were back. It had been a disastrous attempt by Churchill to test whether he could establish a bridgehead for an invasion on occupied European soil. At least, that was the reason they made up afterwards. Hannah believed It was a ploy to keep Mountbatten, who'd devised the raid, happy. Canadians, mostly, advanced across the Channel in the early hours and not only lost their way but had alerted a German cruiser. Arriving at dawn, they had disembarked onto the pebble beach: sitting targets for the German defences embedded in a cliff. The commanders out at sea, unaware of the slaughter, had sent in wave after wave of troops. Not for several hours did they realise the horror and retreat.

Hannah led a convoy of ambulances from East London to Waterloo Station. The men looked so young, just boys, many of them, younger than her. None spoke. Hannah and her colleagues collected the stretcher cases from the train. One boy, who didn't appear to be wounded, sat alone on a platform bench. He stared straight ahead, pale face, faint stubble on his chin, but it was the terror in his eyes that drew her to him.

"I could see the battle. See what he'd seen, horror beyond words." Hannah said. "He frightened me, worse than the dead, much worse. I was shaking so much I didn't think I could drive."

She had offered the boy a cigarette, which he'd taken, but she couldn't tell if he knew she was there. An officer promised her he'd look after him, but how could he? While the soldiers' shattered bodies stood a chance of healing, the damage done to this boy was incalculable.

"I didn't sleep for nights. He was on my mind for God knows… He still is. I thought about his mother too, the poor woman."

"D'you know what happened to him?"

But Hannah was faraway. Suddenly she came back, a new vitality in her voice. "Whatever you do, wherever you go, you've got to fight those fucking Nazis."

The F word came as a shock, but, more alarming, her mind seemed to have locked, and she was still fighting the war.

"You must never forget that plenty thought Hitler was a joke in 1929, but by 1933 he was in power. Ever see a flag with nationalism stamped on it: burn it. Anyone tells you they're a patriot: underneath they'll be a Nazi. On the right or the left, mostly right. Still out there, they are. Never let them get a grip."

She scanned the room. "Where's a Bible? I'm going to get you to swear on it."

"Gran, there's no need. I promise."

"You'd better," she said. "I'll be watching. Remember all the things we'd done in the 1960s, enlightened forward thinking, social reforms, and then look what happened."

Duncan was blank.

Hannah slapped his hand, "Good grief, boy, ten years later? Thatcher and Reagan."

"I know you didn't like them, but I don't think you could exactly say they were nazis – "

"We went backwards. However far we progress, there's always a reverse. And you mark my words each time the backlash will be worse."

She held out her glass. Duncan hesitated. "Come on."

Duncan poured; Hannah drank. "Never mind your father going on about Dieppe, I was the one who was there."

Born in the shadow of the Second World War, Pat had toured the battlefields and, keen to pass on his obsession, had taken Duncan to

Dieppe. To Duncan's embarrassment, Pat had complained at sunbathers on the beach: didn't they know what had happened here? They were trespassing on sacred ground. His haranguing was met by bemused silence. Father and son retreated to the casino – the invaders' objective, which not one of them had reached. They sat down and ate sandwiches. Afterwards, they visited the cemetery where the Canadian dead were buried. Each visit, Pat looked up the same names.

"Something I'll tell you about your father," said Hannah, pushing herself up in the bed. "Before he met your mother, he was an amorous sod. Tomcat, I called him."

To Duncan's relief, he heard the front door open, a shout, steps in the hall. Huffing and puffing, Pat arrived. He caught his breath, took in the scene before him, and glared at Duncan.

Hannah drained her glass. "Well seeing as the clan's all here, we'd better have a cup of tea."

As he waited for the kettle to boil in the kitchen, Duncan pondered why Hannah had told him her story. She rarely spoke of her war. She had driven an ambulance through a permanent fire: the London blitz from September 1940 to May 1941. One of the most dangerous places on earth. She'd learnt to smoke cleaning out the back of the ambulance at the end of each shift: "You can't imagine what it was like in there, but the old gaspers saw me through it."

He was in the hallway with the tea tray when he had his answer. Pat came slowly out of the bedroom shaking his head. Duncan returned to the kitchen and put the tray down on the table. Pat followed him and for a moment they both stood in silence. Then Pat clasped his son to him and held him tightly.

"You were right to call me," he said, on the brink of tears.

It was the closest Duncan had felt to his father in years. Pat, well-built, had lately seemed diminished, as if something or someone was slowly crushing him. His head, previously held high like the military man he had wanted to be, had sunk into his neck.

Pat pulled away and clicked his fingers.

"Just like that," he said and poured out a cup of tea without milk and took a sip. "D'you want to see her?"

Duncan had never seen a dead body.

"Nothing to be frightened of."

Hannah looked resplendent. She had slipped down in the bed and, as Pat put it, 'had conked out.'

She appeared so content Duncan was sure she would open her eyes and with a twinkle say, "Only kidding."

But she didn't. Memories that had haunted her all her life were over. She'd passed them on, and Duncan was proud they'd come to him.

Two spritely veterans from her ambulance days attended her funeral and he was pleased to hear his grandmother had been the leader of their gang: a courageous and honest friend. Yes, argumentative, but usually against the management. They had all been in love with the handsome doctor, but it was Hannah MacLeod who had snagged him, and a tragedy he had died so young. Duncan had never known his grandfather, only rejoiced in his name. Perhaps he, too, had been a boxer in his youth. Joan, one of the veterans, gave him a dinky model replica of a WW2 Austin K2 ambulance. Duncan's mouth dropped open; his eyes filled with tears. Cracks in the blue-grey paintwork had worn off somehow adding to the dinky's authenticity.

"Are you sure?" he asked Joan.

"God bless," she replied. "It'll keep you safe."

They embraced. Then he rolled the little ambulance round the palm of his hand, before clenching it tightly in his fist. He promised himself; he'd keep it always.

And there was more.

Days after the funeral, Pat opened Hannah's garage and led Duncan inside.

Pat started her car, a Volkswagen Golf GTI, which stuttered and choked, then died.

"Sounds more like the Admiral Graf Spee after the battle of the River Plate in 1939. And you know what happened to her."

"No, but I bet you're going to tell me."

"Took shelter in Montevideo and never came out again." Pat paused.

"Scuttled. Thing is Dunc – " he slapped the steering wheel " – she's left it to you."

Duncan had recently passed his driving test. "But I'm sorry to say, the only place for it is the knacker's yard."

"Hold on," said Duncan.

Within hours, a car-nut friend of Duncan's, Martyn Husthwaite, had taken a different view. A chubby fellow with pale skin, the sort of boy you would guess never left his bedroom, he had gone over the vehicle in detail.

"This one's got legs."

"Don't you mean tyres?"

Martyn kicked the flaky Dunlops and suggested he could get ideal replacements.

"Ideal for what?" asked Pat.

"We can give it something with a bit of a poke," said Martyn.

"She's well tuneable, GTI: rebuild the engine, tune it, fit a roll cage, fully lighten, uprate the suspension and brakes – "

"What's it going to cost?" cut in Duncan, pound signs spinning.

"Don't worry about that," winked Martyn. "I know people."

They re-christened the car 'Hannah' and housed her in a hastily patched up and waterproofed hangar at a nearby decommissioned aerodrome. And then the work started. Martyn, true to his word, begged and borrowed. The car was transformed.

Next, using sheet metal, tyres, and other filched detritus, they created a racecourse of chicanes, bends and a long straight stretch to the finish. Then they restored the control tower. Once the rickety staircase had been secured, the old operations room provided the perfect platform to watch the races. The remaining Nissan huts were used as refreshment stations, workshops, and storage space for spare parts. A place that once shook to the sound of young fighter pilots in their war planes roared to the discordant racket of a new generation, this time racers tuning up their vehicles.

Duncan had a yen for driving. In an article he'd read about Jackie Stewart, the World Champion had said that above the stink of petrol and oil; during a Grand Prix, he'd smelt freshly mowed grass. The car, the history and the added mystique of new sensations was a winning combination for Duncan. Hannah, he knew, would be proud he had revived the aerodrome, and he hoped he could share with Pat the thrill of a wartime location. At heart, they were all romantics.

Duncan proved himself on their handmade circuit and saw off most of the local track day-drivers. Dangerous, but intoxicating, racing matched for him the adrenalin rush he got from boxing. He longed to share his new passion with a girl at school, Abby Ranson.

CHAPTER FIVE

Sharing a classroom with girls had done untold damage to Duncan's powers of concentration. But that was more than made up for by the joy of sitting within touching distance of Abby Ranson. Her long hair smelt of fruit and her eyes flashed with possibility. Admirers were legion, but no boy had managed to penetrate the posse of girls that surrounded her. Among the fraternity, the talk was that Abby was seeing an older man who had a car.

Duncan could match this lothario in the latter category. Still, divine intervention was required or, on Earth, an adjustment of the local tectonic plates – if the geology existed. He didn't have long to wait.

While his parents had somehow explained Duncan's school switch to their friends, cancelling the Connor family's annually hosted bonfire night party in the park might have provoked unwanted speculation about the family's finances. Instead of paying waiters from the local Italian restaurant, Beth dragooned Duncan into handing round sausages on sticks and glasses of wine. Already a reluctant recruit, he endured his father's turn as the DJ for the evening.

The only option was to enjoy as much of what he was offering as he could. Duncan soon got the hang of it. Serving an elderly couple who commiserated about Hannah's death, he tried to explain how he had come up with a way of preserving his grandmother, which, no, did not involve cryogenics.

"I think that boy's a little touched," he heard the woman say, as she steered her husband away.

Duncan pirouetted elegantly, or so he thought, into the path of Abby Ranson. What luck! But the effort to remain upright unfortunately turned him cross-eyed.

"Are you drunk?" Abby grinned.

"Certainly not," he replied. "I'm dazzled."

She was holding a sparkler, which, as well as adding to her lustre, gave her a halo.

"Are you going to offer me something?" Abby relieved him of his trays and handed him the sparkler.

"Will it go off?"

She laughed. "Not before you do."

An old Beatles number ramped up: 'I Saw Her Standing There'.

Nice one, Dad, he thought, watching Abby sashay round the guests in a tight-fitting pair of jeans, her hair glowing in the light from the bonfire. Intent on keeping her in view, his sparkler fizzled out. He quickly grabbed another one to impress her. But she trumped him by returning with empty plates.

"For your information, the future is female."

He had difficulty keeping up. "D'you live round here?"

Abby's eyes looked heavenwards.

"I only ask 'cos I could pop round and learn about feminism."

"You can hardly say it."

"Doesn't mean I don't mean it."

"That sounds Irish."

"Well, I am," he said triumphantly. "How are you enjoying school?"

"Oh dear, I thought you were bright."

"Is this one giving you any trouble?" Posse member Rachel Crathorne appeared from nowhere.

"You grab one end, and I'll get the other. Not," said Abby, slipping her arm into Duncan's and guiding him away.

"Shall I compare thee to a summer's day? Thou art more lovely and more temperate," quoted Duncan.

"Mm go on."

He couldn't, but luckily – WHOOSH! The fireworks started.

Abby and Duncan found a cosy shelter.

"This is the very spot where the Bowling Green Pavilion stood," said Abby.

Duncan hadn't expected a guided tour.

"You don't realise the significance, do you?"

Duncan hopelessly looked around for clues.

"Local suffragettes burnt it down in 1909."

"Of course," he replied.

"Only a pair of galoshes and some trophies were saved."

The girl was a mine of information.

"God knows what I'm doing with you," she said, and kissed him.

The rest of the evening passed in a glorious fog, his abiding memory being of her lovely soft mouth. Any further investigation was resisted on the grounds that posse eyes were everywhere, so he proposed a surprise for the following weekend.

She was dubious when asked to meet him at an aerodrome, and one look at Hannah and a male squad switched to female alert did nothing to help. She was used to the cars most boys drove, but her favoured vehicles were less streamlined and more built for comfort. Acting co-pilot in a helmet was not her idea of a welcome surprise. But Duncan was convinced his driving skills would impress. A quick spin then something to eat, his treat obviously. After putting in such skilful service at the bonfire, he had negotiated a raise from his mother.

"Make sure you treat her properly," Beth warned. "And it might be an idea to find out what she'd like to do."

Abby was terrified. Beneath their helmets, Duncan mistook her screams of alarm for joy and accelerated faster through the chicanes. Next, he pushed the car to the maximum and skidded expertly round a stack of tyres, but it was too much for Abby who yelled at him to stop.

She was white-faced and shaking. "Open the door, please."

"But we haven't finished, we're not at the end yet – "

"Yes, we are. Where's the handle?" She demanded, operating the window control, which let in a gust of wind. "Open the door, will you."

Determined to retrieve the date, Duncan did so. But worse was to come. Dispensing with her helmet, Abby headed for the grass verge.

"Where are you going?"

"Home."

He ran after her and took her arm. She shook him off and was sick.

"Oh no, sorry. have you got a bug or something?

"No." she groaned. Then she was sick again.

The wind blew her hair across her face, and it became entangled with the vomit. Duncan tried to help but was refused. Cars whizzed by, racers leaning out of the windows jeering. He offered to drive her back to the hangar at no more than 20mph, but she was adamant: "I'll never ever get in a car with you again."

And for the next five weeks she refused to speak to him.

Duncan was distraught, and seeing her every school day doubled the pain.

He pinned his hopes on the end-of-term Christmas disco. The M.C., a student on teaching practice ignorant of their history, chose Abby Ranson and Duncan Connor to draw the raffle. Those in the know gasped, and some cheered crudely.

She wore a low-cut velvet top, a short black skirt, sparkly black tights, and her hair flowed in slow motion when she moved. The M.C., no doubt partial to Abby himself, made gauche remarks about 'glamorous assistants'. Hoots and whistles from the floor. The student hastily produced the hat. Duncan and Abby dived in for a ticket at the same time, and their fingers touched.

"You look fantastic," whispered Duncan. But she barely looked at him.

At the end, he took a deep breath. "Well, let me get you a drink."

"I've got one." She gestured towards a table guarded by her posse, who were craning forward to listen.

"I'm so sorry, I thought you were enjoying it, and well, I was wrong. In future I promise we'd never go anywhere near the aerodrome."

She turned away.

A friend, Ray, who had won a record token in the raffle, filled the breach. "Thanks for this mate, we're going to the pub after."

Duncan sidestepped a couple kissing and made for the exit. He was putting on his coat when Abby appeared behind him holding out her glass.

"I'd like a lemonade shandy, please."

It was going to be the best Christmas ever, and when she agreed to think about going out with him again, the New Year would be even better. He floated off to the pub, sank several beers, and fantasised about what exactly lay beneath Abby's velvet top.

CHAPTER SIX
GREECE 2010

Eleni seemed buoyed up by the air itself as, dressed in Kolonaki linen, she floated towards Duncan and kissed him on the cheek. Her laughter echoed from a distance as if caught by a gust of wind, and then suddenly was still. In the silence, they smiled at each other. For a wild moment he thought Eleni was on her own.

Nikos appeared round the corner. Duncan suspected he had deliberately held back, intrigued to see how Eleni greeted him.

They traipsed into the hotel beneath the gaudy chandeliers and the loud shout of money, a distant memory for most Greeks. Duncan had liked Dmitri on sight. Mid-twenties, fair hair, and a look in his eye that said, 'shape up if you want to be my friend'.

His guests took their seats at one end of the bar while he brought them drinks at a knockdown price. Nikos dramatically described how close to death they'd come.

"I was nearly killed for the sake of my foot."

Eleni and Duncan shared a discreet smile.

Dmitri clapped Duncan on the back. "That's his way of saying you did good, my friend."

They all chinked glasses, before Dmitri set to work mixing a cocktail for an overweight, middle-aged American.

"Hey baby," the American ogled Eleni. "You're sure as hell built to make a man happy."

He told everyone, whether they wanted to hear or not, the Acropolis was overrated, the food in the museum pig swill, and the hotel air conditioning inadequate.

Then he turned on Dmitri. "Hell, no, whaddya think you're doing?"

To the American's dislike, Dmitri was assembling the drink in the wrong order.

"Don't you dare charge me extra for your ineptitude."

"Certainly not, sir," Dmitri reassured him, and to each of his following instructions replied, "As you wish, sir, thank you, sir."

The longer he deliberately took, the American's demeanour darkened from red to sulphur. Duncan strained not to laugh, but Nikos steamed, his anger fuelled by the American continuing to leer at Eleni. At last, the drink – a vegetable garden in a glass – was complete and Dmitri, looking his customer in the eye, pushed the concoction across the marble top bar.

"Thank you, sir. I hope it chokes you, sir."

The American stared. "What did you say to me?"

As if talking to a child, Dmitri smiled. "I said, sir: thank… you… sir, … I… hope… it… chokes… you… sir…"

He was still smiling when he handed in his uniform, collected his jeans and trainers from his locker and skipped down the hotel steps for the last time.

As they headed for the exit, the American, drink digested, stood alone, hands on hips at the top of the hotel steps: an emperor of all he surveyed. Eleni tried to guide Nikos clear, but he pulled something from his inside jacket pocket and shoved it into the American's back.

"Woah," the man cried, falling forward down the steps, but remaining upright.

Nikos pressed harder. "It's a gun."

"Wha' – ?" The American raised his arms.

"Arms down, walk."

"I'm a citizen of the State of Mississippi – "

"Oh, my God," said Eleni. "Stop him!" She told Duncan.

"Me? I can't…"

As Nikos frog-marched the American away from the hotel, anyone might imagine they were dancing a mad-cap two step. Eleni had vanished. Duncan ran down the steps. Nikos and the American had disappeared.

Did Nikos really have a gun? He was on the point of asking passersby if anyone had seen – but how to frame the question? He came to a narrow alleyway beside the hotel. Halfway down, Nikos stood beneath a grey awning beside a large green waste bin.

"What are you doing?

Eyes ablaze, Nikos pointed a small silver pistol at Duncan. "Get back, I'll shoot."

"Help me, please!" came a frightened voice. "Call the cops!"

Hidden from public view by the awning and the bin, the American was on all fours amongst detritus and animal dirt, facing the wall. Nikos bent down and rammed the pistol into the crack of his bulging bottom.

"Full name, fucking faggot, or I shoot your arse to hell."

"Max Beauregard Richmond. Is it money? I've got money."

Nikos laughed and dived into Richmond's jacket pocket, taking out his wallet and a phone. He stuffed a handful of notes into his trousers and threw the wallet away. The phone followed.

Duncan froze; his head swimming with a memory from long ago. A schoolboy, Cunningham, bent over a chair, his face contorted in pain, weeping. He lent back against the wall and heard again the boy's whispered cry, 'Mummy…'. Then the tune of 'Three Blind Mice' thumped out on a piano hummed through his head. Next, frightened young voices faltering into song.

Nikos kicked Richmond's arse hard. Richmond's head cannoned into the wall. The American yelped, startling Duncan back to the present.

"Take off your belt."

"Jesus Christ! Please, no – "

"Face the wall!"

Richmond had tried to angle himself round. His forehead was bloodied.

"Take it off."

Richmond, shaking, undid his belt.

Nikos grabbed the man's trousers and yanked them down.

"No, please don't fuck me," he pleaded, and with one hand he helplessly tried to defend his naked bottom. "I've got kids and a sick mother."

Nikos pocketed the pistol.

Richmond whimpered; he was praying. A stream of piss now drizzled into view.

Nikos grabbed him by the hair and forced his head backwards, Richmond struggled to breathe.

"Repeat after me – "

Richmond gurgled.

" – I'm a fat, small-dicked bastard."

Richmond did.

"And the USA is the most stinking, corrupt country in the world. I spit on my flag."

Richmond got as far as 'world.' Nikos prodded him.

"Say it, American!"

"I spit on my flag," repeated Richmond, his voice reduced to a quaver, and weeping.

"Piss-arsed prick. Never come back here again." Nikos yanked Richmond's head back and pointed two fingers of his right hand into his eyes and mimed shooting.

Then he ran.

"Come on," he shouted to Duncan.

Richmond hammered the ground with his fists, any words obscured by his bleating. His piss, damned up by fallen rubbish, swirled into a pool. He tried pulling up his trousers, but they were drenched. Jowls wobbling, he lost all control, tears pouring down his cheeks. Duncan saw the child in the man.

"Can I – ?" he started, unsure what help he could offer.

Richmond ignored him.

"What's happened?" Dmitri had arrived. Surely this would be the final dent in whatever pride Richmond had left.

"Sorry," Richmond said, his voice a strained falsetto. "I'm very sorry,"

It was more of a plea than an apology. Then he gathered his trousers and his boxer shorts covering his lower half, he shuffled away. He picked up his empty wallet. Dmitri went after him with his shattered phone.

"No, no," said Richmond, unable to face him.

"This way, please," said Dmitri, pointing him towards a back door into the hotel.

Duncan pondered. How would this semi-naked man, his roots dug open so publicly, his humiliation so thorough, ever return to who he was? Better the police were never involved. An American and rolling in money; these were the only currencies this man valued, and neither had protected him. At home no one would know, unless one drunken night he told how in ancient Greece he had fought off a band of brigands. But later, alone in the darkness…

Duncan was drawn to the pool of piss. The tarmac would soon dry, but what had happened here would hover in the ether. Duncan knew that from experience.

"I don't believe in revenge," said Dmitri, who had returned, his expression sombre. "I should know."

"But they sacked you – "

"Where does it stop? I must go. Another bar job."

He told Duncan where he'd find Nikos. "I'll ask if they want any more help. Probably cleaning glasses, or something?"

"Thanks."

Dmitri had borne the brunt of Richmond's bullying and lost his job. Yet in the end he was the one who had helped him. Dmitri was the best of them.

Duncan arrived in Syntagma Square. Beneath a cloudless sky, he sat down on a bench and watched the soldiers in traditional Greek costume march up and down outside the parliamentary building. He was in a fairytale, one by the Brothers Grimm, perhaps. So why was he still here? What was he waiting for? Eleni? Who was he kidding; she was with Nikos. And what about her disappearing act? She must have known what might happen. Had she taken the cowardly way out, the pragmatic route – or was she just frightened? But what now? The thought of leaving was as enticing as ever. He stood up and left the square.

CHAPTER SEVEN

The silver pistol lay on top of the table.

"It belonged to my grandfather, he fought against the fascists," explained Nikos, adrenalin still running.

Duncan recognised the mood in himself.

"Don't you want to try it?"

Duncan shook his head. Nikos ran the pistol's barrel between his thumb and forefinger.

"It's not your penis," said Eleni.

"Ha, you should've seen his." He held up his fingers again, shortening the distance. "This small."

"You're so childish." She got up and went inside.

They were sitting outside a taverna, a short distance from Janni's old shop. The surrounding trees, their leaves sweeping to the ground; the soft talk of courting couples at nearby tables; the tap-tap of a computer keyboard; coffee cups; and the rich tang of sweets were all a planet away from the alley.

"Did you tell her what you did?"

"Mind your own business." And Nikos pushed his face into Duncan's.

"So, what is the English view?"

"How would I know? I'm not English."

"Don't be pedantic." Nikos sat back. "Come on, you've been travelling around Europe, presumably not blindfold, but I expect as good as."

"I'm sorry – very sorry what's happened to Greece, it's a disgrace –"

"NAAAH! That's shit especially from Britain," said Nikos, emphasising B-R-I-T-A-I-N.

"What d'you mean? I'd have thought you'd have it in for the Germans, before anybody else – " Nikos pointed the pistol at Duncan, who reared back. "Don't, you fool."

"I'll blow up, Berlin." He lowered the pistol. "You would've saved that arsehole, wouldn't you? Huh? And been the hero?"

"You're a prick, Nikos."

"And you need to work out which side you're on."

"The side of common decency."

"You call him decent?"

"No, but what you did isn't, either."

"Let me tell you something about the fucking Brits: it was them who screwed it up, 'specially Winston Churchill."

"What?" Duncan protested, "Greece?"

"Yes. Haven't you read any history books? And I don't mean British ones, not the Empire fuckers, not the Palmerston gunboats, we-ruled-the-world shit. The stuff about Churchill siding with the Nazis in the Civil War."

Duncan was bewildered. Where was Pat when he needed him?

"It's true," said Nikos, vehemently.

Duncan held his hands up. "Plenty of people can't stand Churchill, but siding with the Nazis? Come on."

Eleni returned.

"The man needs an education!"

"I'm sure Duncan knows as much as you." Eleni sounded bored.

"He knows nothing." Nikos bared his teeth. "I'm right, aren't I? All your time with your travelling, you're still in Rule Britannia. I bet you haven't even learnt another language. D'you know Greek? Huh! In my country, I must talk to you in English." He slammed the palm of his hand into his forehead. "I, Nikos, talk to you in English. You people make me sick."

The runt had him, and he knew it. "Instead of shouting at me, tell me."

Nikos smiled at Eleni, victorious. She folded her arms.

His thesis began in the Second World War when, he said, the Greek Resistance to the Germans had come from the left wing. But, as in all occupied countries, there were pro-Nazis and collaborationists. "Even in your Great Britain."

"Mostly the aristocracy."

"I'm glad to hear you do know something. The traitors in Greece betrayed the resistance members to the Nazis, who dragged fighters out of their houses and, in front of their families, murdered them."

"And in France, I think you'll find, particularly with the Jews."

"Ok, so everyone knows that. In Athens, they starved us – here, everywhere, bodies in the streets."

In 1944, the country dissolved into civil war, and Churchill, anxious that Greece did not fall into communist hands, sided with the right-wingers, the Nazi sympathisers, the collaborationists. And worst of all, no one told the British soldiers, who – confronted by resistance on the streets – thought they were shooting Nazis.

"In a situation like that surely no one knew who was shooting who," suggested Duncan.

Nikos shook his head, "Don't try and sugar coat it. People desperate for food, eating anything, none of it suitable for humans, they were starving, dying of malnutrition on the streets. You cannot imagine."

Duncan looked at Eleni, who nodded. But Nikos wasn't finished. He drew a line from the Civil War through to the Military Coup in 1967, when the right-wing Colonels took charge until 1974.

"'67, yeah. It was the Summer of Love, they call it, for you, yeah?" mocked Nikos.

"Before my time and yours."

"Yes, but I know about it; you don't. Thousands of us were imprisoned, tortured, and murdered."

"Us?"

"Yes, us. And the split goes on, between us on the left and the government stooges sucking up to Merkel. They're the grandsons and granddaughters of the collaborators, still here, still killing Greece – against us: we who love our country and want to save it."

"And is humiliating an American the way to do that?"

"Don't you judge me. Think of what your British did. Your army, your politicians. You have the worst reputation, the biggest slavers, you built an Empire on it. And remember, while we had great philosophers and democracy you were running around in animal skins and warpaint."

"I suppose that rusty nail or whatever it was is my fault too."

"Of course, from a British boat," Nikos mocked again.

"Dmitri doesn't believe in revenge."

"That's rich coming from an Albanian. Their country's drenched in blood feud, it's in their culture -"

"Come on, Nikos, "interrupted Eleni, "that's why he left, why he's here, he stands against it."

"Well anyway, who knows?"

Eleni snapped, "I do know."

"Something else for you to learn," Nikos pointed at Duncan.

"Thank you for the history lesson, very enlightening," said Duncan keen to finish the argument.

"Then get reading and show some respect."

"But it's got fuck all to do with what happened today, and you know it. The guy was making eyes at Eleni, and you couldn't take it."

"Hah!"

"Yes, hah. And while you were being little big man, it was Dmitri who suffered. He lost his job, or have you forgotten, playing your nasty games? And who was it that took Richmond back to the hotel? He's ten times you, or me."

"So, who else wants to make out with Eleni? Eh?"

Duncan flushed. "You have a beautiful girlfriend; you don't deserve her."

"Such a gentleman."

Eleni leant across the table, "Duncan, would you come with me, please."

Nikos raised the pistol, "Things could have been a lot worse for the fat man."

"Don't say that." said Eleni.

Nikos smiled. "Who knows what can happen?"

Eleni stood, holding her hand out to Duncan. "Let's leave him to play with himself."

Nikos pulled out some euros from his pocket and flung them across the table.

"Buy her dinner, on the American."

They stood outside an expensive dress shop. Eleni sighed at the display. "You mustn't think I'm like that."

"A woman wanting a dress; I hardly think that's a surprise."

Duncan wished he could buy her what she wanted. During his touring days when he had money, he always looked out for things to get Kathryn – though she had been out of reach then and still was. Now, even in front of Eleni, he realised Kathryn was never too far from his mind.

Duncan had expected to hear a list of Nikos' failings, but Eleni had made no mention since they'd left the taverna.

She linked her arm in his. "I don't depend on men to buy me things."

"What do you depend on men for?"

Eleni laughed.

"No, I'm interested."

"Honesty, truthfulness, thoughtfulness, kindness… Are you any of those?"

"Not me. No."

"Then I'm disappointed Duncan"

She skipped away from him and climbed up onto a low wall that surrounded a small church standing in the shadow of the cathedral. She pretended it was much higher than it was and stretched her arms out like a tightrope walker. "Will you catch me if I fall?"

"You won't fall."

"Don't depend on it," she said, stepping down.

"Why did you run away?"

"I was frightened."

"I'll tell you what he did,"

She put her hands to her ears. "He couldn't kill anyone, I know that."

Duncan wasn't so sure. What were Nikos' limits? He had asked the same question of himself. He gently pulled her hands away. "Be honest, Eleni. Is he, kind, truthful?"

"I love him."

Then she turned from him and looked back the way they'd come from the shop. "Which dress did you like?"

"Ask Nikos."

They were silent. Both maybe wondering if too much had been declared.

"You look very handsome in your frock coat."

He had taken the coat off and carried it over his arm. He smiled. "I can't begin to tell you how you look."

"Would it be indecent?"

"Very."

She took his hand. "You know how sometimes you can get caught, or stuck in a place?"

"I do."

"Well, then you have to think about it not so much as leaving, but looking somewhere else."

"Yes," agreed Duncan. "You're talking to a past master."

"Is it the same with you, with women?"

"Well, I'm on my own, so it must be."

"Tell me about what's in England."

"Torrential rain and gales, the last time I heard."

"There's a reason, I think."

"Well, however good it's been, I've never found a place I didn't want to leave."

He realised they'd walked in a circle. Round the next corner was the taverna where they'd left Nikos.

Eleni stopped. "Maybe she is someone you know, but you don't understand it yet."

"That's probably truer than you think," he said, avoiding her gaze.

"Then you have to stop asking questions."

"What do I do instead?"

"That's another question, so don't ask… You wait."

Eleni linked arms again.

"We were talking about you," said Duncan.

"Oh, I'm not so interesting."

Duncan laughed. "Don't you believe it." He faced her. "Is it a change you want?"

"I don't know," she glanced shyly at Duncan. "I really don't. I want someone to tell me."

"Now you're flirting with me."

She scrunched up her nose. "Do you like it?"

"What would Nikos say?"

She let go of his arm, her phone was ringing. She fished it out of her bag and answered it. Dmitri had got the job and there was another one going in a taverna – dishwashing a couple of nights a week. Eleni tossed her hair back and smiled, and then it struck him: maybe Dmitri was the one for her.

CHAPTER EIGHT
NORTHERN ENGLAND 1996 – 1997

When Duncan arrived home from the pub he was on a high from Abby's promise, but something had happened. His mother was in bed, sedated, his father in distress. That afternoon, Beth had driven home in tears and was inconsolable. Only when the police turned up had Pat learnt there had been an accident. Beth was charged with causing the death of Malcolm Gifford.

Perhaps it had been careless of Malcolm, an ornithologist who had been recording birdsong, to cross the country road where he did. Maybe the tall hedges obscured his view of Beth's car and clamped to his headphones, he never heard her. She took the bend at speed and scythed him down. No blame would ever be attached to him: neither from the court, nor the Connor family. How could it? What happened next was unforgiveable.

Beth had stopped, run back, knelt beside Malcolm's body, saw the terrible injuries to his head and panicked. She had returned to her car and driven off. The thought of Malcolm on that cold, hard road, far from his loved ones, dying alone to the sound of his beloved bird song, had hurt the Gifford family the most.

Billy Noble, a young farm hand putting out feed for cattle, reached the scene. He had witnessed Beth's rapid departure and memorised her registration number. Malcolm lay half on the tarmac and half in the ditch.

"He was a sorry sight, like," Billy told the police. "I couldn't tell whether he was dead or what, so I just called the ambulance."

The post-mortem provided no conclusive evidence as to how long Malcolm had lived. Had he survived, the prognosis was that his quality of life would have been nil. None of this was any comfort to his wife or teenage daughter.

Duncan had lain awake that night praying the winter sun had blinded Beth, or that she had slid on an ice patch and lost control. Perhaps a defect in the car, a loose nut had rolled free, jamming the steering wheel and denying her any chance of correcting her slalom into poor Gifford. But Beth had not explained why she left the scene.

A front of shivering cold ghosted into his bedroom. He sat up, convinced the road had re-routed through the house to haunt the Connor family. At dawn, he got up and looked out the window. A misty figure was trapped in front of a car bearing down on him. There was a cry… his mother, next door.

Beth's nights and days were tormented by the sight of Gifford's body being hurled into the air and then nosediving onto the tarmac. Next, his smashed skull, the blood leaking onto the frosted grass verge. She could not remember driving away. But the evidence was clear. The dent to the car, and a purple Christmas party hat, quivering in the breeze next to Gifford. This festive memento and the birdsong piping from his dislodged headphones had greeted the paramedics.

Malcolm's funeral was on the local TV news. He had written research papers for the British Ornithological Society and won special commendations from the RSPB. Duncan offered to switch channels, but Beth insisted on watching. The camera fixed on a teenage girl – all in black, which emphasised her blonde hair – following the coffin into the little church. The Gifford's daughter, Kathryn. The report said a woman had been charged in connection with the death. Beth left the room.

It was a bleak Christmas, but the Connors imagined nothing like as grim as the Gifford's. Beth got it into her head to visit them – 'for what?' asked Pat.

"Well, to apologise, of course. Say how sorry I am."

Nobody thought that a good idea. The local vicar called, but Beth refused to see him. She had never been a churchgoer and was not starting now. About to wish the family a happy Christmas, he thought better of it and, plonking his trilby back on his head, left.

They all agreed to forgo presents, but a 'gift' addressed to Beth dropped onto the mat. A jiffy bag full of shit wrapped in toilet paper. Duncan found himself thinking about how the shit had been transferred from its usual destination, and the hygiene issues involved. Had the person come far? Had they driven, a stranger, perhaps, or did they walk? Was it someone the family knew? He peeped through his bedroom curtains.

Pat spent Christmas day in the garden shed. A deluxe, insulated, powered-up office with filing cabinets, shelves, an electric heater, and a desk where he worked on his consultancy papers. Duncan never understood with whom and about what Pat consulted – except to know the oil industry was involved. But oil was not uppermost on Pat's mind. He had a question: where had his wife been on the afternoon of the accident?

On Boxing Day, Duncan escaped to see Ray, but Ray's parents, hovering with questions about Beth, cut his visit short. He returned to hear his father say, "I don't know any of our friends who live out that way."

Unseen, Duncan lingered in the kitchen doorway.

Pat sat at the table, while Beth, her back to him, stood at the sink peeling potatoes.

"Not our friends, no," said Beth. "It was one of mine."

Pat frowned. "Well, what's her name? Would you tell me that?"

Beth reached for a dishcloth, which she twisted in her hand. "It wasn't – it's not a woman." She looked at him. "His name," she confessed softly, "is Richard Patterson."

"Richard Patterson?" repeated Pat.

"You don't know him," she said. "He sells books. He's an antiquarian on the coast."

"Oh," said Pat, one mystery solved. "Well, that explains the direction of travel."

Beth put down the dishcloth.

"Have you been fucking him?"

Duncan gasped.

His mother spun round. “Oh, hello, I thought you were out.”

“I’ve just come back.”

“Did you have a good time?”

“Yeah, well, sort of.”

“And how are Ray’s parents? Did they – ?”

“That’ll do!” barked Pat, and Beth shuddered.

Duncan backed away. Pat pushed the door shut after him, but it jammed.

“I asked you a question.”

Duncan heard the scrape of a chair and then Beth spoke, but only as far as “I’m sorry” before her words were drowned in a howl that echoed through the house.

CHAPTER NINE

For the rest of the Christmas holiday, Pat avoided his wife, who spent much of her time with solicitors, while Duncan escaped by thinking about Abby. She was spending Christmas with her grandparents. He could not wait for the beginning of term. But anxiety overshadowed the day. Everyone would know about his mother.

On the look-out, Duncan headed to the railway tunnel where Abby and her friends smoked and gossiped. Ray rode shotgun, but in the face of trouble, Duncan was not sure he could trust him. After all, it was his fight.

"Guess who you want," slinked up Rachel Crathorne. "She's not here. She's not bothered with us anymore."

After enduring history taught by a man so gaunt a pupil's mother once left him sandwiches, and who insisted on calling him O'Connor, breaktime was Duncan's next chance.

The Common Room was bulging with pupils, the air thick with holiday gossip. At first, Abby was nowhere to be seen. But then he saw her taking a coffee cup from the machine. She stood up. She was smiling, but not at Duncan. Holding her hand was Trevor Ingleby. In disbelief, Duncan watched him kiss her on the lips. She let go of him while he collected some papers and a book from his pigeon-hole.

"Hello."

Abby turned, still smiling, but it faded. Her words tumbled out in a stream. "Oh hello, are you ok? I'm sorry about your mother and everything – "

"You said you'd go out with me."

"What? No, I didn't."

Duncan steered Abby into a corner, "Yes you did, at the disco."

"No, Duncan, sorry, I said 'we'll see."

"What's this?" Trevor came up behind them.

"None of your business, fuck off."

"Duncan, no. I should've told you, but what with your mother… I'm sorry."

That might have been the end of it, but for Trevor's condescending smirk, which had 'I've won, you've lost, now do one' written all over it.

Duncan lashed out and Trevor fell back and knocked his head against the post rack, his papers and books scattered. He tried to steady himself, but slipped down to the floor.

Abby knelt beside him. Trevor shook his head and then, with the back of his hand, wiped his mouth. He was bleeding.

Shortly after lunch, Duncan and his father stepped into the Head Teacher's office. Jessica Barwick, a sturdy woman in her fifties and dressed in Tory blue, explained she had taken the Connor family's 'misfortune' into account and understood the pressure Duncan might be under.

"This has nothing to do with my mother."

"I think it might be as well if you kept quiet, Duncan." Pat urged him.

"Just saying, I'm good with my fists, and if Trevor hadn't provoked me then – "

"Shut up," said Pat.

"Are you suggesting Trevor attacked you?" asked the Head.

Duncan jumped up, fists pumping together. "I'm wired like a cobra, primed to go off," and he shadow-boxed towards her.

Ms Barwick leaned back in alarm.

"No, he wouldn't dare." Duncan relaxed his stance.

"Sit down, Duncan," said Pat sharply. "He's just showing off. I'm sorry."

"I'm not." Duncan grinned at Ms Barwick, clearly shocked. "It's my temperament," he continued, and sat down. "My grandmother, maybe I get it from her."

"Unfortunately, my mother died," said Pat, as if such an explanation helped.

"She fought fascists all her life – "

"Right," interrupted Ms Barwick standing up. "Please leave my office."

"What? Why?" asked Pat.

"Your son, Mr Connor, has just raised his fist towards me."

"No, I haven't, not like that, I didn't. I wasn't threatening you."

"If you're refusing to leave, I shall call the caretaker to escort you off the premises."

"But you've asked me here to discuss my son's behaviour."

"I did, but neither of you are in an appropriate frame of mind – "

"It's not about Mum," Duncan pointed at his father. "It's him."

"That's enough," said Pat.

"It's his fault, always is. Greed, that's the trouble. He's lost all our money, which is why I'm here,"

"How dare you – "

"THE PAIR OF YOU!" shouted Ms Barwick.

Silence.

The Head Teacher strode round her desk and opened the door. "I shall put my decision in writing."

Pat and Duncan shuffled out and heard Jessica Barwick ask her secretary if there was any brandy in the drawer.

Pat walked ahead down the corridor. "Don't you ever talk about our problems, least of all in front of someone like her."

"Your problems, you mean."

"Fucking hell, Duncan!"

Some First Years scurried past, going "Ohhhhh!"

"You terrified the woman. It wouldn't surprise me if you got expelled."

"I didn't mean it."

"Precisely what Captain Nolan would have said."

"Who?"

"He sent the Charge of the Light Brigade the wrong way at the battle of Balaclava, October 25th, 1854."

Duncan sighed.

"One-hundred and seventeen dead, one hundred and twenty-seven wounded. If he hadn't been killed himself, Nolan should've committed suicide. Personally, I would have."

"I'll go back and apologise."

A door opened at the end of the corridor, and a large man in wellington boots stood aside for them.

They left.

Lying on his bed, Duncan read the letter suspending him for a fortnight and advising him to write to Trevor Ingleby and his parents apologising for assaulting their son. He scrunched it up. Beth brought him a cup of tea. "This is all down to me, isn't it."

"Will you stop it, Mum? It's not. I hit Ingleby, and I shouldn't have."

"What about the girl?"

He shrugged.

"Hadn't you better apologise to her?"

"I'm always apologising."

"It's something you'll get used to." Beth, her face drawn, her hands perpetually knotted around a handkerchief.

"I'm sorry, Mum."

While Beth's troubles put his into perspective, they did nothing to quell Duncan's anger with himself.

At the aerodrome, events threatened to repeat themselves. Andy Coxwold, who everyone thought was too large for the driving seat, was boasting how he had just recorded his best lap time ever.

Duncan couldn't resist it. "Race me and the best you'll ever do is beat your lap record."

"You're a fucking big 'ead, Connor," said Coxwold, going for Duncan.

Martyn Husthwaite quickly came between them.

"Hey, hey. No one's going out there like that."

"How about your mother, eh?" Coxwold sneered. "I hear she's a getaway driver."

It took Martyn and another competitor, Hutton, to restrain Duncan. Coxwold was told to leave, which he did, but left Duncan pumped up and demanding a drive.

"Are you sure?" asked Martyn.

He nodded.

"A couple of laps?" offered Hutton.

Martyn clapped them both on the back. "Easy does it."

The car was Duncan's sanctuary. He poured out his frustrations about his mother, Abby, and every damn thing he could think of, even Coxwold. His driving hit top form and, as it turned out, was scintillating to watch.

The winner was never in doubt, and he raised his fist in victory. Hutton drove off, an arm extended with a thumbs-up. Duncan was considering a further solo lap when he saw a fierce-looking group of rough-looking men, some in leather jackets, others wearing studded motorcycle boots, marching towards him. He jumped out of the car taking off his helmet.

"Duncan Connor?" one of them asked in a thick Scottish accent.

"Er – ? Who's asking?"

"Mick Cochrane," replied the Scot as his gang surrounded him, but most paying more attention to Hannah. Duncan, intimidated, was relieved a gaggle of drivers outside the hangar were watching. But if things turned nasty, the home crowd would be no match for these desperados.

"They tell me you're the one who set all this up."

"Well, I – me and my mate, we started it, but there's plenty of other people, too." Duncan indicated the hangar crew, some of whom were sloping off. He desperately searched in vain for Martyn – had this mob come to collect in return for favours?

"Impressive for a young fella." Mick gripped him by the shoulder. "And we've been having a look at you."

"Me? And why would you do that?"

"You're ready to step up," said Mick handing him a card on which was sketched a road winding through a hilly landscape, and a phone number. They were serious petrolheads. As a side bar to Donnington

Park or Brands Hatch, they tested their metal on B roads across deserted northern moors – if Duncan was interested? And with that, each one nodding at Duncan, they left him and Hannah. He was the only driver Mick had given a card to.

Back at school, he discovered Ingleby's provocative expression was not sneering condescension, but a nervous tic. However, offering a personal apology was outlawed. Duncan's punch and the inaccurate rumours that his ferocious father had threatened Ms Barwick, plus the Connors' eviction by the caretaker, persuaded everyone to be cautious. Pupils, heads down in the corridors, beetled by, and even teachers failed to acknowledge his raised hand in class. The cold shoulder, rather than confrontation, but then something else…

The initials CPC sprang up on lockers, desks, and several times in the corridors. Duncan hadn't taken much notice until, contemplating the literature written on the inside of a toilet door, he read CONNOR POSH CUNT. Not the Ingleby incident, nor his mother's case: they had chosen to go for his private-school background. The skills that had made him a champion and popular in the other place now isolated him.

He told Pat he wanted to leave. "I've made some mistakes, Dad."

"Yes, you have. But what this family needs more than anything is stability."

"Fat chance. Mum's going to prison, isn't she?"

He had spoken the unspeakable. Pat looked straight through his son.

Duncan got up and left the shed. Breathing in the dead air at home was suffocating him, and his rejection at school emphasised his loneliness.

But what to do? Mick's card in his wallet offered escape. It never occurred to him that racing across the moors might not be his best option. On the contrary, he would do almost anything to stay out of the house. Besides, he had the urge to drive even faster – as fast as he could go, and if it killed him, then it killed him. Challenged, he would say teenage nihilism was all the rage. Check out Kurt Cobain.

Everything had gone to pot. Duncan had imagined the family rot had set in after Hannah died, but now he realised it had started long before that. His parents had lived through the 1960s, for goodness' sake. Why the hell had they got married? Surely, they had known families were a busted flush. Perhaps they did, but only after he was born. Hah! It was down to him, then; he was the problem, the only child. He was done with families, and vowed he would never have one of his own.

CHAPTER TEN
GREECE 2010

A taverna tucked in behind Piraeus port: a rough, raucous, rowdy venue where bands played loudly enough to do the building structural damage. Dock workers, prostitutes, the poor, thieves, and gangsters partied here. Life stripped down to fighting, drunkenness and joy. A singer, Despina, in her fifties, whose voice could strip paint. Dmitri loved it. The pay was nothing like the hotel, but he could eat and drink as much as he liked, and there were no insufferable Americans insulting him. It was no tourist trap. Nattily dressed in a white shirt and dark trousers, Dmitri swerved between the packed tables, taking orders, dispensing drinks; all done with his mile-wide smile. Maybe it was this that led to his downfall. He was just too damned happy – and he was an Albanian.

The front of house chaos extended backstage, but Duncan did not love it. The characters, the ribaldry as far as he could understand it: yes. But no to the sweatshop work with the emphasis on sweat. Chained to the sink in a cramped kitchen, condensation streaming down the walls, he was up to his armpits in suds and slime from an endless pile of dirty plates. By the end of every shift, Duncan was pleading for mercy, but up against the double whammy of poverty and austerity around him, he reminded himself he was a visitor. Everyone else in the place was trapped. Families no longer able to feed their children gave them up to Social Services, who similarly couldn't cope; people who'd built up their small businesses, hoping at the very least to bequeath something to the next generation, woke up to the possibility of losing everything. The struggle to survive took up every ounce of their ingenuity and strength. Stretched beyond breaking point, the answer for some was to lasso a rope over a tree branch and hang themselves. The so-called First World in the 21st century.

As another stack of dirty plates slid into the grimy water, he questioned what the hell he was doing. Repeatedly, he scoured a plate, but the remains clung on. In frustration, he sent it spinning across the kitchen, narrowly missing cleaving the chef's head in two, and smashing into pieces against the wall.

The kitchen stopped, rare enough.

"Tradition, isn't it?" Duncan pleaded. "You know, Greek?"

Uproar.

Dmitri had arrived at the hatch in time to see the plate end its journey and raced round to pull Duncan out. They sped to the storeroom, and locked themselves in.

"Sorry, mate, so sorry."

"It's ok, sit down. I'll deal with it."

"It's my fault, not yours. You don't have to."

"I do, if you want your job."

He did not, but such concerns were secondary to staying alive. The chef was hammering the door off its hinges.

"The way this works," explained Dmitri, "if you go, I go."

"That's not fair."

"What's fair? That's got nothing to do with it."

"No, it's simple: they sack me, I go."

"You do, but I go, too. I brought you in."

The chef burst in.

Dmitri opened negotiations, only for the chef to underline the penalty by drawing a finger across his throat.

Then the cavalry arrived. Her first set completed; Despina used the storeroom to change. She had a Tina Turner-esque approach to costuming: vivid wigs, mightily short skirts, and tops that emphasised each curve of her body. During her rollercoaster life, she had kept in good shape and was happy to share. No one raised an eyebrow when, in view of the staff, she sometimes dressed or undressed. On the nights she sang, there was little or no floor space.

Despina represented the spirit of human kindness so lacking in the storeroom. The story of the dishwasher's plate juggling had run round the taverna several times, multiplying the number of plates in orbit and, in keeping with the man's unpopularity, exaggerating the chef's eruption to twice the size of Vesuvius. The chef's yen for Despina was well known. Plus, she had taken an interest in Dmitri that could not be described as maternal. Something had to give…

Speckled in sweat, she approached the chef, who was primed to explode. "You never get any sense out of a man," she said, "unless you despunk him first."

Dmitri provided the translation later, so for Duncan the eye-popping moment Despina opened the chef's trousers came without prelude. In a move ever-after known as a Chef's Special, she turned his direction from employment issues and, through a series of swiftly applied strokes of her hand, brought him to the boil. As goggle-eyed as any man who has had his dreams come true, the chef slid back onto a bag of flour in satisfied stupefaction. But Despina wasn't finished. After a quick whisk of a Kleenex, she clasped Dimitri to her bosom and demanded he pleasured her. Dmitri looking around him happily agreed, but later. Only minutes earlier, the problem had seemed insurmountable, but in Despina's hands Duncan was hard pressed to think of a better solution.

"What has the Britisher to say?" she rasped.

Ignoring for the moment he was consigning himself to more nights in the swill. "Thank you. I'm most grateful." And he added, "You are an unforgettable singer."

Despina beamed. "Silly boy, it only takes a woman." And she kissed him. Then, with a swish of her clothing, she changed for her second set, leaving the three men grinning absurdly at each other.

"I'm sure she didn't mean it," said Dmitri.

Duncan smiled. "I'm sure she did."

Despina's rendition of Ike and Tina Turner's 'River Deep Mountain High' that night went through the roof.

Away from sink duties, Duncan spent as much time as he could with Eleni and Dimitri, and much less with Nikos, who never missed an opportunity to deliver a lecture. He continually challenged Duncan's Anglocentric view of the world and, however much Duncan protested he was proud he grew up in an enlightened country, Nikos jeered.

"What's enlightened?"

"Well, it's most people's experience."

"You think? Try growing up Black in Birmingham or some city like that. There's nothing fucking enlightening about the police and the EDL beating you up every day."

"That's an exaggeration. Birmingham, Alabama, maybe…"

"No, it's not. Birmingham, UK. You don't even know about your own country."

"I bow to your great wisdom. You obviously know everything about everything."

"I look, I listen, I read, I learn," snapped Nikos. "Britain is in disgrace, calling Mandela a terrorist, while the Queen Bitch Thatcher gave shelter to a criminal torturer like Pinochet. And don't tell me it's not like that anymore: her love child, Blair, is a warmonger. You people still live in Empire days. Bastards! Nothing will change until you say sorry."

One day, Eleni complained to Duncan about Nikos. "I'm so angry with him for giving up his education, we fight about it. He can go to university and keep up with his political activity. Others do."

"What exactly is his political activity?"

"Meetings, and then more meetings to organise even more meetings. Then there's marching, throwing things at the police, I'm not – what's the word? – I don't disagree with him. I hate what has happened here, but I can't think about it twenty-four hours a day. We also must breathe, to live somehow," she threw her hands in the air, "or else we are lost."

Duncan reached for her, and she took his hand. They sat for a while on the university steps.

"I'm so pleased you're here."

"I don't seem to make much difference to him."

"Not for Nikos, for me, I mean." Then, as though she had admitted too much, she kissed his cheek and left for a lecture.

"I wish I'd been so conscientious," he called after her.

"Yes, you're another drop out," she said disapprovingly. Then her pretend frown broke into a smile. "Talk later."

Duncan was jubilant, but still he could not let his feelings go for broke. In his head nothing stacked up… but since when had his head held sway?

CHAPTER ELEVEN

Dmitri had helped Duncan move into his tiny flat. A simple task, as Duncan's belongings barely filled a rucksack. And now, late in the afternoon they made their way to Agios Panteleimon, the Afghan community base in Athens, where Dmitri had heard of some excellent shops for cheap fittings.

"I think Eleni is the girl for you."

At the sound of her name Duncan's heart skipped. "Honestly, I wish that was true."

"Well, it is."

"Apart from the fact she's with someone else."

"Oh, now that is finished," Dmitri's hand slashed through the air.

"I don't know – "

"I do. You, my friend, are the answer for her."

"Just supposing you're right, I'd have to stay, or she'd have to leave."

"And what – that is a problem?"

"I don't think it's me, you know. It's you!"

Dmitri laughed. "Oh, no, come on. I've seen you two together."

"And I've seen you. Don't deny it, you like her, too."

"Who wouldn't? But her and me? No."

A youth in a helmet on a moped crossed the road and cut in towards them.

"Hey!" shouted Duncan.

At the last second, the driver veered away, then circled round in the road, facing them.

Duncan stepped towards him. "What are you doing?"

"Leave it," said Dmitri.

"That was deliberate."

"Maybe. Come on."

Duncan stared at the rider, who gave him the palm of his hand. Then he revved his engine and drove off.

Duncan looked round for Dmitri, but he had walked away. He ran after him, and they walked on in silence.

Then Dmitri threw his hands up in the air, "Maybe I'll just have to leave."

"What d'you say? You have to leave?" Dmitri's sudden change of mood had taken Duncan by surprise.

"D'you have to go home, or something?"

"No, I can't go home. Never."

"What is all this? Why not?"

Dmitri took a deep breath, "My father got into a big argument with a friend. He was drunk, they both were. My father shot him."

Duncan stopped. "God!"

"Four deaths followed as revenge. If I hadn't got out, I'd have been the fifth."

Duncan looked at him, stunned. Then he remembered Nikos and Eleni referring to Albanian blood feuds.

"I'm sorry," he said feeling it was hopelessly inadequate.

They walked on.

"But I still don't understand why you have to leave," asked Duncan, and gestured to the moped rider who had stopped beside a couple of girls, and who were watching them. "Not because of them, surely?"

"Oh, they want me to go, but no, not them."

"Then who are you talking about?"

"You have to listen to me – "

"I am, I am."

"I've been followed home, more than once now." He held up two fingers. "Two guys, the same two guys."

"How d'you know they were following you?"

Dmitri gave a low laugh, "I know who they are."

"Well…?"

"Not by their names, I don't. They're Golden Dawn. They have assault squads who target people: Egyptians, non-Greeks, and you'll never guess, Albanians. Hah!" said Dmitri. "All the people they say are screwing up their country, taking their jobs. You have the same kind of these at your home?"

"The EDL Look, we can deal with this. I'll wait and come back with you, and pick you up the nights I'm not working."

Dmitri smiled. "They'll think we're gay."

"Think what they like."

"Another reason to hate me."

They walked in silence.

"Two guys," Duncan suddenly blurted out. "It's always two guys."

"Which two guys now?"

"It's a long story. Another time, maybe."

"I'll look forward to that."

Duncan laughed sourly. "Yeah."

"Don't tell this to the others, ok? Between ourselves?"

"But this is meat-and-drink to Nikos; he'll want to know."

"No, I don't want you to tell him," Dmitri insisted. "You mustn't. I don't want him running in and taking it over. Please."

"Ok." Duncan was not surprised that he had tired of Nikos.

"Promise?"

He nodded.

They arrived outside the shop, but it was closed. Dmitri checked they had the right address. They had, but then they saw that most of the other shops were closed. Instead of shutters, one shop had barbed wire across the window.

The moped rider coasted by sneering.

Behind them police were blocking off the road. Duncan and Dmitri turned a corner and walked into the square dominated by a large brown brick building with a dome on top: St Panteleimon, a Greek Orthodox church.

They were not alone.

Men with hammers and bags of nails slung from their belts were erecting a stage in front of the church steps. On either side of the square, people were setting up stalls. A woman propped up an awning with a pole, while beside her a man hoisted the Greek flag. Next to them, a family seated round a table drank from bottles and shared food. Opposite, two women opened metal crates and pulled out bundles of leaflets, which another woman arranged in a display. Children, shrieking and shouting, ran through the square playing tag, the moped rider slaloming between them. A boy trying to avoid capture was in danger of cannoning into the flag. A woman shouted at him and, his shoulders slumping, he joined her. A girl, jamming a cigarette between her lips, took his place.

"Is it a Saint's Day, or something?" asked Duncan, unaware Dmitri had moved away from him and was standing beneath a tree.

Suddenly, jarring guitar chords ripped out at top volume from a rock concert-sized speaker hemmed between the branches of Dmitri's tree. A smell of burning oil and wafts of smoke floated in the air.

Lines of men in semi-military formation – some carrying Greek flags; others holding lit torches shoulder-high – marched into the square. Each one was dressed in black from head to foot, their mouths open in a communal roar. Followers from the stalls, as if summoned to the altar, tucked in behind the marchers, and they shambled to a halt in front of the stage. The music died away and was replaced by the crowd's guttural chant:

"Αίμα... τιμή... Χρυσή Αυγή... Πατρίδα!"

["Blood… Honour… Golden Dawn… Fatherland!"]

"Τιμή, τιμή... Χρυσή Αυγή!"

["Honour… Golden Dawn!"]

On the stage, several banners slowly unfurled, each one bearing a swastika-like meandros symbol. The sky, as if in sync, turned an angry red. Duncan could not believe what he was seeing. It was as though he'd slipped through a loop in time, or he was watching an archive film. Neither was true, this was happening, it was real. Right in front of him. Where was Dmitri? Was he safe? Duncan couldn't tell. Jammed in by the crowd pressing towards the front, he was trapped.

On stage, a priest stepped forward, his white surplice a beacon against the blackness around him. He blessed the assembly through a microphone.

The crowd's chant changed –

"Νικόλαε! Νικόλαε!"

["Nikolaos! Nikolaos!"]

A pug-faced man made his way through the ranks. He was small but rotund and surrounded by bodyguards cut out of granite. Nikolaos Michaloliakos the Golden Dawn founder unhooked the microphone from the stand, and the chant reached a crescendo. The crowd stamped their feet and the square shook.

"Φίλοι μου, σύμμαχοι, Έλληνε..."

["My friends, allies, Greeks…"]

More cheers and salutes.

"Το μήνυμά μου απευθύνεται εισ όλους τους αριστερούς, εισ όλους τους Εβραίους, εισ όλους τους βρώμικους κομμουνιστές, εισ τους Γύφτους: ειδοποιώ υμάς ότι οι ζεστοί φούρνοι ετοιμάζονται. Πρέπει να αναχωρήσετε τώρα!"

["I have a message for all the leftists, the Jews, the scum Commies, the Roma: you are on notice, the ovens are heating up, LEAVE NOW!"]

Although Duncan did not understand the words, the flags; the ugly bellowing from the bubbling hatred around him told its own story. The square was thick with odium.

"Θα βυθίσουμε κάθε σκάφος που μεταφέρει μετανάστες!"

["We will sink boats carrying immigrants!"]

Duncan was gasping. He couldn't breathe, suffocating in the putrid air.

"Η Ευρώπη των Εθνών έχει γυρίσει, Εμείς είμαστε οι πρωτοπόροι μιας καινούργιας αυγής ενός υπερήφανου εθνικισμού. Η Ελλάς για τους Έλληνες!"

["The Europe of nations is back; we are at the forefront of a new dawn of proud nationhood. GREECE FOR THE GREEKS!"]

Someone tugged at Duncan's arm: Dmitri. A gap had opened between the bodies behind him. But Duncan's legs were as shaky as the rest of him.

The gap closed, and then he felt something sharp thrust into his stomach. A man wearing dark glasses was making him an offer he couldn't refuse. He looked down at the sprinkle of coins in an open tin. All he had in his pocket was a crumpled euro note, worth how much, he did not know.

Thinking of Hannah, he dropped it into the tin. He had betrayed her.

Dmitri dragged him away. A woman shouted; a man threw a fist at Dmitri. Angry at himself, Duncan lashed out and caught the assailant in the face.

An overweight thug swung round at Duncan, who squared up to him.

"Run," shouted Dmitri.

He did, and they both headed for the police blockade.

"Walk," said Duncan, more of a plea than a demand, his breath coming in spurts. "Less suspicious."

They slowed down.

The police showed no interest, other than helpfully removing a barrier.

"Stop, please," said Duncan. He leant against the wall beside the shop they had come to earlier.

"Not yet."

The moped rider was on their tail.

"Come on," Dmitri turned off the street.

Duncan stumbled after him into a cul-de-sac. Conveniently, a couple of bitter orange trees offered cover.

The moped rider followed and then stopped abruptly. The man Duncan had hit caught up with the rider, who cut off his engine.

"When will you learn to stop throwing plates and hitting people?" whispered Dmitri.

"Sorry."

"And apologising."

Duncan lifted his t-shirt. Where the tin had cut him, there was blood. He feared there would be more as the man ran forward shouting.

Shutters opened upstairs in a house opposite, throwing a shaft of light onto the orange trees. Duncan and Dmitri crouched down. A woman, poking her head out of the window, screamed unintelligibly. Distracted by her, the man shouted back. To Duncan's satisfaction, the man's face was smeared with blood. The woman upped the volume. Boiling for a fight with anyone, the man ran across and hammered on her door. Other faces appeared at windows. Outnumbered, the man, gesturing at them all and shouting, seemed to be taking on the whole street, until the moped rider scooted over to him. After a brief discussion, they left the cul-de-sac, the man still shouting.

Duncan cautiously moved out from behind his tree.

The angry woman still on duty turned her fury on him. "Thank you," replied Duncan.

Dimitri waved at her. "She's calling us perverts."

They peered round the corner at the blockade, where several policemen enjoyed a smoke. The leader's voice crackled in the distance.

"How do they get away with this shit?" asked Duncan.

A member from the crowd joined the policemen and accepted a cigarette.

"That's how," said Dmitri. "And why d'you think it's happening here on the church steps? You saw the priest up there. All they need next are seats in Parliament, and they'll get those."

Duncan shook his head. "The church?"

"How much did the Vatican stop Hitler? Not really, I think."

Another man arrived at the blockade.

Dmitri grunted, "Recognise him?"

Duncan nodded. The man in dark glasses with the tin.

"He's one of the two that have been following me," explained Dmitri.

CHAPTER TWELVE

When Eleni smiled the air cleared, the sun came out, and everything charged up to full colour. They had left Nikos in the queue waiting for the nurse to take the stitches out of his injured foot. How she swung her arms pretending to march far away from her grumpy boyfriend. Duncan wanted to nuzzle her sweet neck, carry her down the hospital steps, and kiss her beneath the palm tree. They walked, he didn't know where, he didn't care, and they talked and talked. She had read 'The Great Gatsby'. She loved Leonard Cohen – he had lived on one of the Greek islands in the 1960s, didn't he know, and written some of his best songs, 'So Long Marianne' and 'Bird on a Wire'. She promised to take Duncan to his house.

They had lunch beneath a lemon tree, and she told him where to get the best sausages in the world. "Edinburgh. The restaurant at the National Gallery of Scotland."

"How an earth d'you know that?"

Eleni's aunt lived off the Corstorphine Road, and as a special treat they once went to the gallery, but it was 'the most delicious sausages ever' that she remembered best.

They lost all sense of time and missed Nikos' calls. Later, Duncan wondered – hoped – Eleni had done so deliberately. Nikos was furious, but aside from telling him he was behaving like a spoilt brat, Eleni ignored him.

"I blame you," he sulked, turning on Duncan.

Eleni sniggered.

"Isn't anyone interested in how I am?" Nikos whined. "It was hell in there."

Eleni and Duncan replied at the same time and then dissolved into laughter, but Nikos persisted. "Who wants to see my scars?"

"Please," said Eleni, covering her mouth. "We've only just eaten."

Nikos looked stricken, or pretended to, and Eleni took pity, "You're better, my dear, that's all that matters."

They fell into a kiss. Duncan felt sick.

When it happened, it was not as bad as he'd feared. A part of Duncan, a large part, hated fuss. He blamed himself, though: he should never have told Eleni. The first thing he knew, his arms were hauled out of the sink's sludge, and he was blindfolded. He heard the chef chortling as he felt himself led out of the kitchen. All had gone quiet – then a guitar played the opening chord. His blindfold was removed. Despina, shining under her spotlight, led the band, and the packed taverna belted into a rousing Greek birthday song. The chef and the kitchen staff shuffled in, everyone eager for happiness in dark days. Eleni, Nikos and Dmitri, sitting at the front table, clapped and sang.

A large yellow cake, the number 30 iced in red on top, was wheeled in. Nikos and Dmitri shook Duncan by the hand. Duncan blew out the candles, then cut a slice and passed it to Eleni. She clasped him round the neck and pressed herself into him with an all-encompassing embrace. Despina shimmied over and, slipping her tongue into his mouth, reduced Duncan to his knees. Well, he thought, this made up for a lot of soap suds. The chef waddled next in line, claiming gratitude for baking the cake, and, to his delight, received a slow upward sweep of her hand over his hopeful genitalia.

"Men are so simply pleased," she smiled.

At the back of the room Duncan saw the two surly figures in black t-shirts. One wore a combat jacket, the other, he recognised, as the man with the tin and never without expensive sunglasses. After St Panteleimon, Duncan and Dmitri had done the rounds of bars and tried to drown what they had witnessed. Impossible. For days, Duncan had shuddered at the memory. No amount of mixing with relaxed and urbane Athenians enjoying a night out in Monastiraki or joining crowds of tourists at ancient sites could disguise what had happened only minutes away.

Dmitri had noticed these dark characters from their sewer often slipped into the taverna an hour or so before closing time. They drank and smoked, barely spoke. Some customers acknowledged them, but they preferred to be apart from the crowd. In their minds superior, but in truth, isolated in a septic bubble. Not even Despina's top notes could pierce their complacency. They gave nothing, and their presence sucked the air around them out of the room.

Dmitri's shadows, who since Duncan's appearance had kept in step behind them on the way back to the flat, were yet to make a move. The night being Duncan's, he wanted them to leave, but Nikos stayed his hand.

"It won't be worth the trouble," he said scanning the room.

Duncan was doubtful.

"Nothing would please me more, but I promise you," continued Nikos shaking his head. "Trust me, I know."

Late in the evening, the birthday boy came out of the gents to find Eleni in the corridor, a lovely smile on her face. "I haven't given you your birthday present yet."

"Oh, yes you have. I couldn't have wished for a better night, I really couldn't."

She came closer, her forefinger to his lips. "I know this isn't the most romantic place, but – "

She put her arms around him and kissed him gently on his lips, drew back to test his reaction, and then, pinning him against the wall, kissed him again: a kiss that lifted them out of the dingy corridor to a much sweeter place of their own. Duncan was in bliss. Eleni wanted him, and he wanted her.

There was a noise behind them. They broke apart.

She searched his eyes. "You must not worry about Nikos."

"No?"

She kissed him again. The sensation of her body curling into him and her delicious lips on his banished all else.

But then from the end of the corridor came angry voices. Under a swaying dim light bulb, Dmitri was on the wrong end of a beating. Duncan raced towards the fight, yelling at Eleni to get help.

He cannoned into Sunglasses and caught him off balance, then hurled him against the wall. He followed up with a volley of bone-crunching blows. The man withered and slid to the floor. But now Combat Jacket had Duncan by the arms from behind, and pushed him down onto the floor, pinning him there. Sunglasses crawled off towards the door. Duncan couldn't move. He felt the coil of a rope around his neck, tightening. He grasped for the rope, but it clawed tighter, pulling him upwards. He choked, eyes bulging. He tried to scream, but no words came; the rope burnt into his flesh.

Suddenly the rope loosened. Nikos, his arm round Combat Jacket's neck, had yanked the attacker back. Duncan had leeway and burst free, but still on his hands and knees struggled for breath. Above him, Combat Jacket was getting the better of Nikos. Just in time Duncan, grabbed the fascist and smashed him face first into the wall. Combat Jacket turned, blooded and bruised, and squared up to Duncan.

"He was stealing," he said in English.

"Liar," replied Duncan and drove his fist into the man's face. Combat Jacket reeled backwards against the wall. Duncan took him by his collar and marched him through the taverna crowd. The band's drummer opened the door and Duncan hurled him into the street. As luck would have it, Combat Jacket fell over Sunglasses, who had collapsed in the gutter, his pride and joy shades beside him. Duncan stamped on them. He turned Sunglasses over, rifled through his pocket and relieved the Nazi of a roll of Euros.

"Call it quits," he said. Combat Jacket tore towards him. He quickly stepped inside and slammed the door. The bass player jammed the bolts shut, and Duncan slumped down in the nearest chair.

Combat Jacket, hammering on the door, cried out insults. The drummer twirled his sticks and replied with a rising crescendo. There was only one winner.

With his fingers, Duncan felt the burning and bleeding lacerations round his neck. His throat was raw. The chef brought him a large Metaxa, which he swallowed in one. He tossed the chef Sunglasses' euros and ordered drinks all round.

Eleni cried. "Dmitri's bad, very bad."

Duncan stood up, but his legs buckled. He held onto the table and Eleni took his arm and led him to Dmitri, lying unconscious in the corridor. A pillow supported his head, and two kitchen staff were trying to staunch the blood pouring from a hideous gash above his hairline. Despina, wailing, held his hand.

Two paramedics hurtled in through the back door. Duncan found Nikos, bloodied, hunched in a corner, a towel around his head. "Are you ok?"

"They'll be back." he urged, "It's not safe for you here."

"Fuck them. Are you alright?"

"No, I mean it, we have to plan."

"Dmitri comes first."

Nikos, his face pale. "It's very bad."

Eleni shouted, "Come on, we're going!"

The paramedics had stretchered Dmitri into the back of an ambulance. Eleni jumped in beside him. Nikos leapt into his car and, driving Duncan, repeated his warning.

"Listen, Nikos, I'm not running away from those bastards."

"That sounds very brave, but it is also very stupid."

"Ever heard that phrase, "For evil to triumph, good men do nothing'?"

"You think a lot of yourself."

"Not just me, you idiot, us, all of us."

"Hey, I know the saying. Don't lecture me."

"It makes a change."

Nikos banged the steering wheel with the palm of his hand. "You did well, very well. I can't think what would have happened without you. But you must know they had supporters in there tonight. Some of them, your party guests, Golden Dawn followers."

He turned a corner skilfully.

"Nice driving."

"Yeah, you're not the only one." Nikos put his handkerchief to his mouth and cleaned off the blood. "Believe me, Piraeus is a stronghold for these people." They were catching up with the ambulance, its siren blaring.

"Many of them may not agree with what happened to Dmitri, but they'd soon point out the dishwasher. Your days at the sink are over."

"Dmitri thought they were following him."

"What?"

"He told me."

"For Christ's sake…"

"He told me not to tell you."

"When? You should have. We'd have got him out. The minute we know they've targeted someone – Shit!"

"Who is we?"

"It does not concern you. You're going."

If he had told Nikos, then what? Could he really raise this mythical 'we', a defence corps that sprang into action any time a Black Shirt entered the neighbourhood?

"Well, there's one thing for sure," said Duncan, as Nikos parked outside the hospital. "My grandmother would've been proud of me."

"That's something, then," sneered Nikos, in keeping with the jealous man Duncan had first met.

CHAPTER THIRTEEN

"He's right," Eleni agreed. "You will have to go."

She was lying on her side across several chairs in the hospital corridor, a polystyrene cup of coffee in her hand. Her face was smudged with tears. Tracking down Dmitri's sister, she had found two numbers, neither of which had been answered. She was reluctant to leave a message beyond 'please call me back urgently'.

In the operating theatre, Dmitri had slipped into a coma. The surgeons were pessimistic and even if they could save him, his quality of life would be severely compromised. The death of Malcolm Gifford came to Duncan's mind.

All they could do was wait. After receiving some medical attention, Nikos fell asleep. Duncan, a bandage applied to his neck, sat beside Eleni. He stretched out his hand, but she did not take it. "If I go, will you come with me?"

She sat up, "How can you ask that now?" She looked at him closely.

"You went pretty crazy back there."

"I think I had to, don't you?"

"Have you been in fights before?"

He wondered for a moment how much to tell her. "I won my weight in a boxing competition."

"Oh… I thought I was getting to know you."

"Well, you are. And there's more."

"No, don't. It frightens me."

"But he's right," he pointed at Nikos, head back, mouth lolling open.

"You can't have it both ways. It's a war."

Eleni shivered.

He put his arm around her shoulders, "I thought you wanted to escape?"

Eleni stiffened. "Like I said, bad timing."

He held up his hands, and left Eleni and Nikos sitting on opposite sides of the corridor, facing in different directions. His neck was sore. His hands hurt, the knuckles scuffed and flecked with blood, his right one numb. Maybe he should buy some gloves. He mooched towards a confectionary slot machine.

"Kafandaris!" An Asian nurse walked up the corridor, a file in his hand. "Kyrie Kafandaris," he shouted out again.

A chair scraped in an alcove and a figure shuffled into view: Sunglasses, with a bandage round his head. The orderly, stuffing the file under his arm, tried to remove the bandage. But Kafandaris pushed the man away. The nurse patiently tried again, but this time Kafandaris spat in his face.

Duncan picked up a chair and advanced. "Shut up, vermin." The nurse quickly stood between Duncan and Kafandaris, holding the Greek back with his arm.

Duncan put the chair down and gestured to it, "This is self-defence."

"Stay back, please," replied the nurse in English.

"He is not worth your time. Throw him out."

Kafandaris scowled at Duncan.

Duncan picked up the chair again. "Tell him please, I wish him all the pain on earth for what he's done." He had more to say, but Nikos, woken by the racket, angrily pulled him away.

"What are you doing?" protested Duncan. Kafandaris screamed at them. "What's he saying? Tell me."

"He's going to kill you."

Duncan turned back to Kafandaris.

"Leave it," shouted Eleni from behind Nikos.

He looked back at her. She was nodding her head vigorously. Reluctantly, Duncan put the chair down.

Nikos dragged him round the corner. "You fool, we'll have to leave. Security will be here in a minute."

"So?"

"They're on his side," said Nikos exasperated, "They'll lock you up, no questions. You'll end up like Dmitri."

"Stop trying to be brave," added Eleni, "because you're not."

They left the hospital, Eleni providing all her contact numbers at the ward reception desk to a sympathetic woman, Cristina, who had shaken her head in Duncan's direction.

Dawn was in sight when Duncan and Nikos, no longer speaking, reached Dmitri's flat. The door was hanging off its hinges.

"Careful," warned Nikos, pushing ahead of Duncan on the landing.

Another door along the corridor opened fractionally, and the fearful face of a young woman peeped out.

"Είναι εντάξει," said Nikos. "Είμαστε φίλοι του Δημήτρη."

["It's ok, said Nikos, "We're Dmitri's friends"]

"Tell her I share the – " started Duncan, but Nikos waved him aside.

The woman explained several men had been a few hours before. The flat had been torn apart, the mattresses ripped open, the larder cleared out, the cistern and the basin destroyed, and messages sprayed on the wall – the most pertinent was in English.

GREECE IS FOR GREEKS.

There was no sign of Duncan's rucksack, but, looking out of the window, on a rough patch below a fire smouldered.

Duncan squatted in the corner. All he had, he was wearing. Luckily, that included some money, his phone, his passport, and half a bar of chocolate.

"Shit," he said.

"By your foot," pointed Nikos.

On the floorboard, a clump of excreta, curled to a dark head. Duncan stood up smartly.

Nikos fished out his mobile. "I have to make some calls."

"Is this to the 'we' you were talking about?"

"The less you know the better, especially as it's about you."

"Then I really do want to know – "

"Start clearing up."

"What if they come back?"

Nikos looked around him. "What for? They're done here."

After Nikos left, Duncan tiptoed through the flat, careful to avoid any more deposited clumps, and sat on the window ledge.

He rang Eleni, waking her up. "Seems to be my day for getting everything wrong."

"Yeah, birthday boy," he heard her yawn. "You're screwing everything up. How is it?"

He told her. There was a long silence.

"Please don't give me a lecture, Nikos has already."

"No, I was thinking," and her voice broke, "Dmitri will never see it."

"Oh, God, what's the news?"

"No, no, nothing, but whatever happens he won't be able to live on his own – not to start with."

"I know." Duncan looked out of the window. "It's lovely to hear your voice."

"And yours. What's happening next?"

"Ask Nikos. I'm under strict instructions."

"Better someone keeps you in line." She sounded distant again.

"I'd prefer it was you," he said.

She clicked off. Duncan looked at the phone, held it to his ear again, but she really had gone. He stared into space, wondering. Was he unlucky, or did he go looking for trouble? Was he compelled towards violence? He'd certainly hurtled to Dmitri's defence. Once he'd thought his victories in the boxing ring had been an aberration, but perhaps what Eleni had seen was his true self. She was grateful for what he'd done, they all were, but it was ugly and frightening. There was no denying the shock on her face in the hospital. He'd hated the way she'd looked at him. He was a stranger to her. Sometimes he wished he could turn to the innocent days before he'd pulled on the gloves. But there was no guarantee this part of him would've stayed hidden, he knew that for sure. All it had taken was a spark to trigger him.

He tried to mend a mattress by stuffing handfuls of feathers through the rips and holes where the brutes had scored noughts and crosses with their knives. Using some gaffer tape he'd found in a drawer, he attempted to stitch the thing back together. Twenty minutes later and it was approximately the right shape, but he doubted it would ever be fit for purpose. In distress, he slumped down on the mattress, which bulged under his weight. Feathers trickled out of gaps he'd missed between the strips of tape.

He urgently patted himself down. His dinky ambulance was missing. Since his grandmother's wartime colleague Joan had given him the tiny metallic object, it had not only kept him in touch with Hannah, it had become as important to him as a St Christopher was to travellers. For comfort, he'd often taken it out and rolled it around in the palm of his hand. He tried to remember the last time he'd done so. Where had he lost it? In the fight? At the hospital? Even before that? Impossible to know.

There was a knock on what remained of the door. Michelle, the young woman from along the corridor, had made some coffee.

Her flat was much bigger than Dmitri's, in working order and far better furnished. Her sofa was a welcome change from the wooden floor, and a distraction from his anxiety over the missing dinky. She spoke good English.

"They got you?" asked Michelle, wincing at Duncan's injuries, his eye ringed black.

"I got them, much worse," he smiled.

"I'm so frightened. I wanted my fiancé to stay with me, but he will lose money."

Michelle was French and her fiancé, Kostas, who Duncan had spotted one morning, worked in a bakery. They had talked of leaving. This raid had brought that forward.

"They didn't come in here, did they?"

Kostas had gone out to see about the noise but they had threatened him with knives and chased him back.

"How many?"

"Two to start, and then one more. It was like storm troopers, yes?"

Duncan nodded. "Where will you go?"

"Toulouse. My mother is there. But Kostas, this is his place," she despaired. "Don't they realise they're driving out Greek people?"

"I don't think they realise anything."

She shrugged. "Stupid, but so many believe them. They run this place, the district, I think." She looked out the window. "My father would tell them. He was a big man, but he's gone now… How is your friend?"

"Dmitri. He's not good."

"Oh. He's a nice boy, I think."

Suddenly shouts from below, then pounding feet on the stairs.

Nikos was wrong.

Michelle sprang up. "Same as this morning."

She snatched Duncan's cup and ushered him into the bathroom.

"Lock yourself in," she told him.

They got closer, hammering on every flat's door. Duncan turned his mobile off and sat down on the toilet seat. He thought, Greece in 2010? How is it possible? His fists clenched.

They arrived. Duncan stood up and pressed his ear to the door. From somewhere Michelle had found the strength and shouted at them.

"Αρκετά με εσάς, παλιομαλακες! Με ξυπνάτε μέσα στην άγρια νύχτα και νασας πάλι εδώ. Να πάτε να γαμηθειτε !"

["I've had it with you bloody bastards. You wake me up in the middle of the night, and now here you are again. Fuck off."]

Duncan inched the bathroom door open. Beyond Michelle, he could see a man with thick black hair, and another head, shaven. Neither Kafandaris nor Combat Jacket, who he trusted was still hors de combat.

Black hair spoke, but Michelle interrupted –

"Μην τολμήσετε και ξαναμπήτε στο σπίτι μου για να με προσβάλλετε, ξεκαπιστρωτα γαϊδούρια ".

["Never ever dare come into my house and insult me, you wild donkeys"].

He tried to speak again but once more Michelle stood her ground.

"Ούτε η γαμημενη Μάνα σας θελει να σας ξέρει , αμόρφωτοι μαλακες! Χαθείτε απο μπροστά μου και αφήστε με υσηχη."

["Not even your fucking mother wants you, you ignorant wankers. Quickly, shove it up yourself and leave me alone."]

Delivered in a rising voice and ending with the door slamming shut.

Silence.

Duncan came out of the bathroom. Michelle, shocked by her bravery, was rooted by the door.

"I've no idea what you said," Duncan said softly. "But you've frightened them off."

"I was very rude," she said, and fell into his arms shaking.

"Come and sit down."

He steered her to the sofa, where she sat on the edge of a cushion.

"You were brilliant… Magnifique!"

She grinned like a child. "I told them to go fuck themselves."

Duncan cocked his ear and pretended to listen. "And that's exactly what they're doing."

She laughed.

"I'm going to write Kostas a note," he said, "and I'll say how fantastic you are."

"I am, aren't I?"

Her mouth was so dry he poured her a glass of water, which she swallowed in one.

"So, they were looking for you."

"Thank God, you invited me in for coffee."

CHAPTER FOURTEEN

Nikos found Duncan safe passage on a supply boat leaving Piraeus for the islands.

"People will give you away, 'specially when there's so little money around. Not as much as 30 pieces of silver." Nikos favoured waiting for his preferred captain's shift. But even with his man on side, he was at pains to tell Duncan his safety could not be guaranteed. "You know how dangerous it can be on ships… lots of water."

Duncan dismissed Nikos's big-man-of-the-world talk, but his gift of the gab had worked on his mother. He had lied to get Duncan a couple of nights at his parents' home in Glyfada, not far from the beach where they had all met. Duncan, a tourist, went the story, had been rolled by some unsavoury people in Piraeus. While the British Embassy handled the case, where better to stay than Nikos' old bedroom?

"If I'd told the truth my mother would have had a fit, and there'd have been no bed."

Duncan wondered whether Eleni had slept here. Had she and Nikos made love on these sheets? And where was she? Since the hospital he had not seen her. Nikos had tried to persuade her to come with them to his parents', arguing they trusted her – more than that, they loved her. But she didn't. Was she reluctant to go along with the lie? Duncan couldn't see why. Or perhaps she didn't want to pretend she was still Nikos' girlfriend. He hoped it was that. Why hadn't she suggested her place, her bed? He'd love to know the answer. Unless she was disenchanted with Duncan, and her bed was where Nikos spent the night? Tying himself in knots, he wondered whether he had dreamed the beautiful kiss in the taverna corridor.

Duncan couldn't keep count of the lies or bluffs rolled into the conversation with the Gambetas seniors. Rather than interrogating him, Anastasia Gambetas rhapsodised to Duncan about Nikos's ability to attract the right girl.

"We're working extremely hard to keep him on track," she'd said, putting the finishing touches to her appearance in the hall mirror. "I think we've got a real ally in Eleni," swivelling towards Duncan for confirmation.

"She's very nice."

"Are you married?" she asked in a tone that expected the answer to be yes, especially at his age. Duncan suspected she already knew the answer, and she disapproved. By the time she left for a meeting of the local culture committee, and before her husband's return home, Duncan was sure she had convinced herself her son was virtue incarnate, though he had been condemned as a bad influence. Unexpectedly, Nikos turned up next. No further news on Dmitri, but Petros, the supply boat captain was sailing the next day, bus times to the port and rendezvous provided.

"How's Eleni?" Duncan asked.

"I don't know, working on some assignment," Nikos slapped Duncan on the back. "Perhaps you should concentrate on what you have to do, Mr Connor." He pulled two hundred euros out of his pocket. "It's not so much, but it's to keep you going."

"But I thought – "

The night before, Duncan had overheard Nikos asking his father to lend him some money to pay off an irksome debt.

"For your help against the bastards. I will get you more, you'll see. Take it."

Duncan thanked him.

"Get your swimming trunks on, you're going to be a proper tourist."

"Why's it always me who phones?" he asked Eleni, as soon as Nikos had left.

"I'm busy."

"Not too busy to come and visit me whenever I get there?"

She knew the plan and promised to call as soon as she could.

"Safe trip," she said.

When he looked up, Mr Gambetas was standing in the kitchen doorway. "Moussaka, or perhaps we could go out?" Mr Gambetas suggested.

How Duncan would love a taverna, but retribution from Nikos wouldn't be worth it.

"Actually, moussaka's my favourite."

Mr Gambetas strode into the kitchen, took the moussaka dish from the fridge and removed the polythene wrapping.

"What's your opinion of the police in this country?" Duncan asked.

Mr Gambetas put the dish into the microwave. "In what respect? Their ability on point duty, or their success in catching criminals? Because I'm bound to say if you think they'll find the people who did that to you, I'm sorry to say, but it's unlikely."

Duncan liked him and wondered if Nikos underestimated his father. Surely he knew about his son's activities and guessed that the story of what had happened to his guest was fiction.

"I mean, how politically active are they?"

"As a rule, as a group in any country, the police are to the right of centre, and Greece is no exception. Individually, there are many who take it much further; much, much further."

"Do you find that acceptable?"

Mr Gambetas smiled. "No, of course I don't. I find any form of extremism – well, I'm against it, right or left." He offered Duncan a cigarette. Duncan declined. "Wise man," he said. "D'you mind if I do?"

"No, please."

He lit the cigarette, inhaled, and then exhaled a stream of smoke, which swirled upwards in the evening sun's rays.

He looked directly at Duncan. "What has my son told you?"

"He doesn't trust them."

He rolled his eyes. "Imagine."

"…I don't know – are you aware of your son's views?"

"When you began this conversation, Duncan, did you think you were asking me something, or telling me?"

"Well, to tell you the truth, over the years, I've had my own trouble with the police – "

"Forgive me, I'm not prying."

"No, no…"

"So, please answer my question."

Duncan wished he had never started this. "I suppose both," he replied.

"Right."

The microwave pinged. Mr Gambetas pulled out the moussaka, prodded it with a fork and then returned it, turning on the microwave once more.

"Of course, Nikos doesn't trust the police, any of them. They hold a different point of view. But – " and now he pointed at Duncan "I should tell you about my son." He shook his head. "No, that's not quite right. I should warn you. I don't know what plans you and he have made together, but he is a very manipulative boy. And if I were you, I'd take a step back."

He stared so hard Duncan dropped his eyes. "Well, I have seen how passionate he is, so I'm pretty sure I know what to expect."

"No." Mr Gambetas brought his hand down hard on the table.

"This is my point: you do not."

"I don't know whether you realised – I should thank you for the two hundred euros."

Mr Gambetas waved his hand aside. "Not enough to make too much trouble."

"It's for clothing, spare – "

"Mr Connor," he interrupted, "I do not have a crystal ball; I can't tell you what's going to happen to this country, or to my son. But what I do know is that for both, and this is my warning, it will get a whole lot worse."

"You're very worried."

"I'm shitting myself."

The microwave pinged for the final time.

CHAPTER FIFTEEN
NORTHERN ENGLAND 1997

It was a pale wintry afternoon when Duncan caught the bus to an old pit village. He got off outside the boarded-up community centre and walked a mile down the winding road towards the coast. He had asked Martyn to overhaul Hannah and ensure she was in tip-top condition.

"You know those guys are Kamikaze pilots, don't you?"

"And you're just jealous they didn't pick you."

Martyn had walked away. Duncan had winced. "Sorry, mate."

Martyn had kept walking.

Duncan made for the Hangar door.

"HEY!" Martyn had shouted. "I'll need the keys."

They'd faced each other. Duncan had smiled, threw them over, and left.

As he hunched his shoulders against a sudden chill breeze, he realised he'd arrived. A pot plant and a fresh bunch of flowers wrapped in cellophane marked the spot. A card in what Duncan was sure was in a girl's handwriting he read 'A wonderful, lovely, man passed this way. X.'

He walked on round the severe bend. The lane coming in from the left must have brought Malcolm Gifford onto the road, and his path led in a straight line to the still visible tyre marks, which ended abruptly. His mother would've had only seconds, less…

A horn blared and Duncan skipped onto the grass verge. A van loomed into view, and the driver acknowledged him. Any car doing more than twenty-five miles per hour as Beth must have been, and without blasting the horn, well… He slowly returned to the little memorial.

"Are you a relative, like?"

Billy Noble, with long lank hair and wearing a tattered Barbour jacket and wellington boots, leaned over an open gate.

"Well – "

"Aye. See, Ah've been watching youse. Terrible business, eh?"

Duncan nodded.

"He was just there." Billy pointed at the spot.

"You were here?"

"After, aye… Wey, I saw her, the driver, aye," he gestured up the road. "She was running up there for her car."

Duncan couldn't stop himself. "It wasn't on purpose – I'm sure."

"Going off was. Wey, she were trying to save her skin, if you ask me, more than likely." He nodded. "You wonder what gets into people's heads, don't yer?"

"If we knew that – "

"Aye, well, animals behave better."

Duncan braced himself, but Billy became more reflective. "You see summat like that." He was staring at the spot in the road. "I never slept after, you knaa."

"Like a lot of people."

"Aye, the birds on the recording, it was still playing. I can't hear the birds now, like, without thinking 'bout this." He turned away. Duncan thought it was to hide a tear. Then he saw the dog. The red setter came through the gate and sniffed Duncan. He pulled back as though the animal might tell who he really was.

"Excuse me," Duncan called out.

"You're alright, he'll not bite." Billy whistled and the dog bounded after him. Together they headed off into the field.

"You didn't have the dog that day, did you?"

"Eh?" Billy turned round. "The dog? This 'un? Na, not the dog, I was feeding the cattle. "

"No, I just thought – "

"Eh? You thought what like?" Billy came back to the gate. "Hey, wait now, you're not a copper are yer?"

"No, no."

Billy frowned. "Who are you, then?"

"A friend of the family."

He did not seem convinced. "I seen the family when they come, I did."

Duncan felt the imposter he was, and Billy suspected. But the man was more concerned with himself. "Listen, right, I've told 'em all I did. What I saw. Everything."

"I'm sure." Duncan looked up the road again.

"Looka, I didn't want to be here, you knaa." He raised his voice, insisting Duncan paid him full attention. "I just was. I come back here, least once a day. I cannat stop meself."

"I'm sure you did all the right things. You shouldn't have a guilty conscience."

"Right, aye. Didn't say I did, did I?"

"No, I'm sorry."

"Right. Well, I don't, but she should, that woman, the cunt."

Duncan blamed himself for riling the man. Billy had just said what many people would think. Duncan gestured as if to go.

"You best had then," Billy nodded and walked off. He looked behind once, the dog ran ahead. Both glad to leave the site.

But Duncan did not go. He checked the position of the tyre marks again. What if Beth had been avoiding the dog, and hit Malcolm, would that have helped in mitigation? But she had not.

At the little memorial it wasn't just the sentiment that struck him, but how much care had been taken. The lettering on the laminated card was richly coloured, and in the top right-hand corner there was a drawing of a kingfisher. He was sure Gifford's daughter had designed it, and then, with her mother, had stood on this same spot, adjusting its place in the tableau. He wondered how she was coping. How do you cope with this? He didn't think he was. Not that that would have been any comfort to them.

He stood back. On this minor road, the seasons would change and the years pass. They had, too, at Dieppe, now just another French holiday resort where gamblers played at the casino. But for the people who knew what had taken place on that pebble beach, and on this patch of road, their lives would never be the same.

CHAPTER SIXTEEN

Duncan nudged Hannah up to the starting line and looked over at his nameless opponent, who was behind the wheel of a frost white Fiesta RS Turbo. Small, but deceptively fast. The man wore a black helmet, highlighted with gold. His darkened visor masked him completely. Often drivers hid their identities, or even assumed new ones. Perhaps as a form of escape. Duncan understood he had joined that club. His rival, he heard, was affronted to be racing 'the new boy.'

"So, make sure you beat him," Mick Cochrane, who had made Duncan his protegee, smiled and gave him the thumbs up. Duncan was thrown back to the boxing final against Caldwell and the Captain whispering in his ear. He had known a lot about his opponent then, not least what he looked like, but what if this guy was a professional race driver?

Sweat trickled down Duncan's brow; unease gripped his guts. He looked ahead and tried to focus on a plan. Clinch the lead on the opening stretch before the steep drop down through a series of zigzag hairpin bends. Then beware; mistime any corner, and a terrifying plunge into the stony river far below threatened. In second place on the zigzag, the best route back was driving up an opponent's arse, breaking their nerve and forcing them into one of the gravel lay-bys. Plenty had done it, admitted Mick, but first time out, he did not advise it. Intimidating tactics were 'illegal', but who would intervene? 'Marshals' were deployed along the route to film the action on camcorders, but most disputes were settled by a punch up. Well, Duncan could acquit himself… but he dismissed the idea. Once across the narrow stone bridge over the river, there was a mile up a mostly straight incline to the flag. A racetrack, a universe away from the aerodrome. Martin's warning echoed: was this really where he should be?

High, bleak and vast, centuries before, the moor had been the scene of unspeakable savagery, where warring families had slaughtered each other for cattle. Later, the area had been earmarked as a sanctuary for the locals should Napoleon cross the channel. Pity the poor refugee; it offered little in the way of warmth. A harsh wind whipped back and forth, the rocky outcrops whittled into sharp edges, and in the hollows, the marsh was still deep enough to sink today's unwary hiker. The scars remained of an industrial era, a reminder of the subterranean excavation of lead and zinc. After that, drawn to the moor as a young man, the poet W.H. Auden was inspired to write 'In Praise of Limestone'.

Duncan had analysed the poem at school.

'this land is not the sweet home it looks,
Nor its peace the historical calm of a site
Where something was settled once and for all:'

Repeating the lines to himself, he wondered if they were some kind of warning, or a premonition.

The petrolheads had come here, not with pikes and lances, nor with pickaxes, but streamlined cars transported in converted horseboxes. Their organisation was military standard. Before each race day, volunteers armed with walkie-talkies put up official-looking diversion signs and closed the road, adding twenty to forty miles of journey time for unwitting members of the public. Once a police car had ventured along the route, but saw nothing more than a bunch of Harley Davidsons and bikers dressed to impress as Hells Angels. Duncan had not taken long to realise they really were Hells Angels. The local farmers were taken care of by a handsome pay off, or with agricultural machinery.

Then, at the flourish of a flag they were off.

Duncan made two mistakes, or three, if he counted allowing the Fiesta to squeeze ahead before the drop down. A blood-curdling scare on the first hairpin, when Duncan misjudged his speed and the skid that followed pushed Hannah's rear end over the edge, her back wheel spinning in thin air. For a split-second, Duncan felt an overpowering urge to let it go and plunge backwards down into the gorge. But no, he skilfully steered Hannah back onto terra firma.

He was again too fast towards a bend. How many times had his driving test examiner warned him? The prissy fellow would have had a pink fit to see him now. He could have kicked himself; he was repeating his first error. He had no right to win. Duncan skidded into the handily placed gravel patch, with the back end stepping out, causing him to slide sideways towards some spectators. He managed to collect it together and get back on the road, heading for the bridge. And over it. Ahead, his opponent understeered heavily through the final bend, giving Duncan hope. He downshifted and aced the corner. On the final straight, and seconds behind, but crucially he was gaining.

From the first time Duncan gripped a steering wheel he had felt at home. Not just driving Hannah: Duncan was in tune with any vehicle at the twist of the ignition key. Innate understanding or, as he liked to call it, knowledge passed through the genes from his grandmother of what a car could do, gave him an edge. The petrolheads had spotted in his performances on the aerodrome the quality in all good drivers – indeed, all good sportsmen – he had time. He was always a fraction ahead of his opponents.

Duncan drove Hannah confidently up the incline, closing the gap, pressuring hard. He flashed his high beams. It paid off: the Fiesta driver faltered, missing a gear, and in the final five hundred yards, Duncan swung past him and took the flag.

The plaudits poured in. He was the new hero, a solid gold, future champion.

"Generosity," said Mick. "It's unusual from this lot, so enjoy it. You deserve it."

There were no victory laps. The family tension building over months had caught up and now it overflowed. Drenched in sweat and shaking from head to toe, tears followed. But, sheltering behind a rock, instead of release Duncan felt hollow, the inhospitable landscape matching his mood. He did not know it, but he had a guard, hovering close. Mick never questioned Duncan: it was his business.

Later, walking across the moor, Duncan was envious of a curlew which broke cover and looped gracefully through the sky. In its swoops and dives, he saw true release. But if he had followed the bird's trajectory back down to the heather, he would have spotted something sinister. Amongst the crowd gathered round the finishing line, one competitor stood out. It was his defeated rival, who had not offered congratulations. But with his back to the races and his identity still obscured by his helmet, he was tracking Duncan's every step.

CHAPTER SEVENTEEN
1997 – 1998

One evening after another successful drive on the moor, Duncan reversed Hannah out of the converted horsebox on the empty aerodrome. Pat arrived in his sleek new black SUV. How Duncan hated the pomposity of those cars, unnecessary in an urban environment, but the argument that followed would not concern his father's vehicle. While Duncan parked the Golf in the hangar, Mick shook Pat's hand and enthused about his son's driving skills. Next Mick produced a camcorder. Too late, Duncan cut in.

"Thanks Mick, but he's waiting for you."

Although the driver in the horsebox cab was happily eyes down in the 'Sunday Sport', Mick took the hint.

"Ok, next week, same time, yeah?" And with a 'good to meet you' to Pat, he rattled off.

Father and son watched in silence as the horsebox driver revved and at speed cut a swathe through the aerodrome turf.

Then Pat burst out, "I can't believe what I've just seen."

"I hoped you'd be pleased I'm good at something."

"For God sakes!"

"Yeah, well… I'm sorry."

"Then look as though you mean it."

Duncan spotted his father's fright beneath the anger. Time to attack.

"Perhaps I don't mean it, then. This is my way of dealing with it."

"Don't give me any of your cod psychology rubbish."

"You're on another planet. Why don't you cry or something?"

"We're talking about you, and by the look of that film, you'll be next. So, it stops here and now."

"That's right, ignore me, don't listen, go and read some more war stuff. That's what you care about more than any of us." Duncan felt his tears coming.

"Alright, alright," said Pat moving towards his son, but resisted consoling him. "Go and…" he pointed at the hangar, "clean yourself up a bit."

Duncan turned back to Hannah and locked her up. He closed the hangar door and snapped the padlock shut.

"Car keys, please."

He paused, deciding whether to argue, then reluctantly tossed them over to his father. "What's going to happen?"

"She's grounded. And so are you."

Pat started up the SUV, and Duncan climbed in beside him. "You do realise the only reason you've bought this car is a pathetic attempt to reclaim your masculinity."

Pat clenched his teeth and drove like a madman down the final stretch of the racecourse.

"There you go. Exactly," observed Duncan, while bidding the aerodrome a fond farewell.

Beth's case, due to unfortunate symmetry, was heard on the anniversary of the hit-and-run. Physically diminished, she had withdrawn into herself. Duncan did not know whether she had seen Richard Patterson again, and as for Pat, well…

"You faced the same challenge as the British and American armies advance in Normandy," he told her.

Beth had looked at her husband in bewilderment.

"The bocage. Natural defensive positions. The Germans in their tanks could hide behind them."

"What are you talking about, bocage?"

"Hedges, woman, high hedges. You could claim you couldn't see the man – "

"That hasn't the remotest chance – "

"Let your solicitor be the judge of that. Tell him."

It had been the only time Pat tried to help his wife, after which Beth had refused to discuss it with the family. But now, on seeing Ruth Gifford and her daughter, Kathryn, huddled outside the courtroom, Pat ignored the solicitor's advice and approached them. "If I may I'd like to express my family's deepest sorrow – "

Ruth recoiled as if she had been struck. Her representative tried to cut Pat short, but insisting he meant well, he continued to make what he'd called a personal contribution.

"Go away, please sir," said another man in a wig.

During the exchange, the Giffords remained seated, Kathryn's arm slipped into her mother's. For a second, Ruth had caught Beth's eye. In that moment, Beth saw herself running away from Malcolm's body, back to the car.

> *She scrambled in her pocket for her keys, but they slipped out of her hands, and through crying eyes she couldn't find them. Her mind's eye full of the man's bleeding, broken head, obscured her search.*
> *On her hands and knees, desperately, then a tinkle of light. There! Got them! Door open, but it's the passenger side. She ran round and in. A SHOUT. Someone shouted. Not him, was it? Not the man, his eyes closed, blood coursing. It couldn't be. Don't look. Key in the ignition, hand shaking, steady, steady, there; good, now drive, drive, drive. Someone's coming, someone's chasing? Are they? No. The engine roared, raced, slow, slower. What happened? What have I done?*

"Are you ok?" Duncan looked into his mother's staring eyes. "Sorry, stupid question."

Pat took Beth's arm and gently levered her up, and together they entered the courtroom.

Elizabeth Morag Connor pleaded guilty, adding, "I was there. It was me, I did it."

She spoke clearly. She had finally accepted it. Once more she looked at Ruth Gifford and bowed her head.

After legal arguments, she was granted bail. But Duncan found it impossible to focus. Despite his promise to himself after the Abby debacle, he had not so much as looked at a girl. Now, he could not stop. Kathryn mesmerised him. But it was unthinkable, wasn't it?

In the weeks before sentencing – which included Christmas and New Year, both low key – the family somehow stuck together. A phoney peace, surely: they all knew nothing could be the same again. On a bitter January afternoon, Beth sat in her bedroom, "Today, in 1649, they cut off the King's head."

"For a second there, I thought you were Dad speaking," Duncan smiled.

"When it comes to the Tudors and Stuarts, I know my history, probably better than him."

"Well, they're not going to do that to you." He put his arms around her, and she clung to him. However briefly he felt his mother's strength returning.

"You know you're going to have to look after him, don't you?"

"Not really."

"He can't take it. I don't think he ever will."

"I'll do my best."

Beth patted his hand and then, assuring him she was ok, asked him to leave. Duncan did, but waited outside the door. Alone, Beth walked slowly round the room, stopping and looking as if committing everything she saw to memory. Then, she cried.

She was sentenced to four years in prison.

As he scuffled home after another meaningless day at school, a car drew up on the opposite side of the road. Duncan's name was called. Trevor Ingleby walked swiftly towards him.

"What d'you want? I'm not allowed to talk to you."

"It's alright," he gestured over his shoulder. "My dad's in the car."

A man in a flat cap peered through the windscreen. Duncan spotted the family resemblance, the smiling tic.

"Tell him I'm not going to hit you."

"Ok, no," said Trevor nervously. "I just think it's awkward at school. It's gone on too long, so what I was thinking was, could we shake hands and forget about it?"

They did.

"I'm sorry," Duncan said. "Abby's alright with this, is she?"

"Nothing to do with her. She just chucked me."

"Oh, right, sorry again."

Job done, but Trevor didn't know how to leave. "You're not going out with anyone, are you, at all?"

"No, and I've sort of made it a rule not to with anyone at school."

"Yeah, get you on that. Rumour is Abby's new bloke's married."

Trevor shuffled his feet, "We're hoping you're alright, what with your mother going away."

Duncan nodded. "Thanks."

He refused the offer of a lift and, after they left, Duncan stood awhile. The Inglebys meant well. Some pupils had already spoken to him, so perhaps Trevor's ok would further help. But the truth of it was, if Abby was going out with a married man, so what? Duncan's priorities had shifted.

He could not get Kathryn Gifford out of his head. Her photogenic qualities had appealed to the press: 'grief-stricken beauty' and 'the tragedy girl' had been everywhere. But given the odds, surely his chances were none in a million. Nevertheless, he had written to Kathryn, and she had replied. She hadn't commented on his sorrow for her family and his mother's uncharacteristic behaviour, but rather, wrote about how hard it was without her father, whom she'd loved more than she could say. She said how busy she was going to be doing her GCSEs in the summer, and how she didn't want to let him down. Finally, she had thanked Duncan for writing.

Not even driving distracted him. Martyn had turned up a spare pair of keys for Hannah. Once he had convinced Duncan he hadn't told Pat about the moor – "I promised you I wouldn't" – he persuaded him to come back.

The old crowd showed up, and Duncan rallied. While it was good to drive at the aerodrome again and meet up with some of the drivers, he'd been spoilt. Nothing here could ever match the excitement of the moor. When he called time, the others presumed his mother was preying on his mind. But no, Duncan was racking his brains about how to meet Kathryn.

CHAPTER EIGHTEEN

Beth's first step in prison had been to start divorce proceedings. Unwise, Duncan thought. Take some time – she had it in spades. Pat was furious, but Duncan guessed it was pique that he hadn't filed first.

Duncan would never forget his first visit. Beth was held in a Victorian-built prison in the centre of an industrial city. The slamming doors echoed in the vast alien space; Alsatian dogs incessantly barked; and a warder's laughter sounded like a sneer. He wanted to turn and run, but was trapped among the trail of visitors, most of whom avoided eye contact and seemed as captive as the prisoners themselves. They looped their way round a circular corridor, which looked as though it had not been painted for a century.

Beth shyly thanked him for coming and asked about Pat. After that, silence. But Duncan still had questions.

"Is it because of what happened, or is it about this bloke, that you want a divorce?"

"Oh Duncan."

"Well, I am part of it."

"I'm sorry." She leaned forward, seeking more privacy. "I spend a lot of time thinking."

"And?"

"I don't talk very much, so conversation takes getting used to."

Duncan looked around at the other tables. Everyone else was chatting, especially the little girl in a pink hat describing her first day at school to her mother.

"The answer's probably a bit of both," started Beth. "But if I hadn't had the accident – " she could barely bring herself to say the word " – I'd still be with your father. Whether that's good or bad, I can't say."

"You'd have still gone on seeing this bloke, then?"

"His name's Richard," her tone was admonishing. "Yes. We had no plans to stop."

"Has he been to see you?"

"He was the first," she said, with such pride that Duncan was not sure if she was accusing him of tardiness, or even of neglecting her. He was annoyed, too, that this man he did not know, but who he thought was so wrapped up in his mother's downfall, had stolen a march on him. He was about to ask if Richard had been in the court that day, but he did not want to stop his mother.

"He loves me, Duncan, which is more than can be said for your father. Perhaps I shouldn't say that, but it's true, isn't it?"

"You'll have to talk to him about that."

"I would if I could… The important thing's you're alright, are you?"

"Yeah, I suppose so. I'm just getting used to the idea that my mum's in prison."

"I'm so, so sorry – "

"I believe you, Mum, but you drove away and that's what I can't get my head round."

Beth sighed and Duncan worried he had consigned her to silence again, but then she spoke in a burst.

"Do you think I can? If I knew, I'd tell you. It's right that I'm here, but that won't solve anything. And by the end of it, who knows, but I doubt I'm a recidivist."

"Did you think you'd get away with it?"

Beth flinched. "Duncan, I didn't think."

"You must have. You were thinking about this – Richard."

She sunk into her chair. "This is awfully hard," she whispered. "I wasn't fully concentrating; I was probably thinking about him." For the first time she looked straight at Duncan. "Alright, I was." She ran her fingers through her hair, vulnerable and lost. As much as he wanted the truth, he wanted his mother back more. "I was going too fast, not paying attention, and well – I hit Mr…" She bit her lip. "But that doesn't explain what I did next."

"Doesn't it?"

She raised her voice. "Well, if you know, go ahead. I'm sure we'd all be very grateful."

Heads turned, and one of the female warders made a move towards them.

"I think you do know – "

"I do not," she insisted. "Who d'you think you are, a mind reader or something?"

Beth got to her feet, crying. How many times had he seen her like this in the past months?

"Sorry, Mum."

Duncan stood up and held her.

The warder arrived and asked them to separate.

"Can't you see she's upset?"

"Please do as I ask."

"She's my mother – "

Beth stirred. "I'm alright. Let go."

He did and Beth retreated to her chair, but she remained standing.

"Alright now?" the warder asked her.

"As if," Duncan snapped.

Beth said quietly to him, "Please I have to live here," she gestured to the warder, who leaned towards her. "I'm ok, but I think that's enough."

"Just sit there for me," and the warder lowered her back into her seat, then she took Duncan to one side.

"Listen to me. I can understand how you feel, right?" Duncan didn't reply. "But don't play silly buggers."

"I wasn't. I was comforting my mother."

"I know that, but for you as well as for her, when I ask you to do something, you do it."

Another warder now joined them.

"What's this, mob handed?" Duncan complained.

"Have you been listening to me?" asked the first warder, her tone notching up.

"Yes, I have," said Duncan, and raised his voice. "And while I don't agree with you, or anything to do with this shitty place, which I hope I never have to come back to, I'll do what you ask."

A visitor wearing a Leeds Utd shirt with the player's name, Eric Cantona, printed on the back stood up and clapped his hands in support. A man in a red shirt and braces from the other end of the room laughed and chanted, "King Eric is Man U". The Leeds man sat down again, a sour look on his face.

"He's neither", said a warder blowing her whistle. "Last I heard, Cantona's retiring,".

Both men looked at her in astonishment. She nodded, "Now shut up the pair of you."

"Same advice to you" said the first warder, still looking directly at him, and after a significant pause added, "sir."

Duncan returned to his mother. "I'll go, Mum. Sorry."

Then he watched the warder help her up, and she walked away as slowly as she had on leaving the dock.

CHAPTER NINETEEN
GREECE 2010

In the harbour, the husk of a galleon exploded in a ball of flame, the outline of the port quivering in the vivid light. As the raiding party rowed for the shore, their task complete, a cannon roared so loudly it seemed to shake the island's foundations. Fireworks lit up the dark skies, their tracers falling towards the packed quay. The crowds cheered as the names of the patriots were broadcast through a P.A. system.

From the highest point above the harbour, beside the windmill, Duncan, Beanie, and his American girlfriend, Jenny, enjoyed the re-enactment of the islanders' sinking of a Turkish galleon in 1823. Resistance against the oppressor, Duncan thought, must resonate vividly these days for the Greeks. But as impressive as the annual celebration was, within 24 hours no one on the island was talking about it.

Earlier that day, Duncan dived into the sea beside the old, battered fort where he had spent his first disastrous night on the island. All part of Beanie's cure to wash off the viscous slime that had healed his scars. Duncan, rejoicing in the cool water swam out of the cove and failed to see a photographer striding onto the pebble beach and checking his light meter. He also missed a flotilla of taxi boats carrying models, makeup artists, camera crews, a famous fashion designer and an assortment of assistants pulling alongside the beach jetty. Nor had he spotted in a synchronised schedule donkeys arriving laden with equipment.

After a lengthy breather on a rock, but careful not to let the sun wreak the havoc it had before, he swam back into the cove. At once he was dazzled by an array of arc lights. Treading water and shading his eyes he took in the scene. A small army occupied the beach forcing other swimmers to abandon hope. A gathering crowd of gawkers strung along the cliff path. Naked but for a pair of Beanie's blue swim shoes, he swam closer. The fashion designer looked familiar. As did the blonde female star of a popular TV series, who sat in a canvas chair, her bare feet on a camera box while curlers were removed from her hair. Not only a photo shoot, but the set for film coverage.

Duncan smiled, happy he was done with this world, but he faced a problem. His clothes were on a rock right at the back of the beach. Now it appeared he was in shot. Everything had come to a standstill, a crew stood beside a camera up on legs waiting. Only an A.D was in action running up and down on the pebbles gesticulating to him to clear the cove. Duncan was close enough to the shore to stand, the water covering him below his waist.

"No can do, I need my clothes," he said pointing towards them. A Runner dashed over to the rock.

"Get ready with the towel," advised Duncan.

It wasn't easy to move forward on the uneven surface beneath, but aware all eyes were on him Duncan did his best. As he proudly cleared the waterline a ripple of laughter and applause broke out. Crew and spectators recorded the moment on their phones and rather more sophisticated equipment. The A.D and the Runner stepped forward with the towel, but not before Duncan had bowed to his audience.

"Sorry to hold you up," he said to the A.D. who hastily drew the towel round Duncan's waist.

"We'll have a drink on it later," he smiled with a wink.

Still smiling he had quickly dressed and headed towards the steep flight of wide steps beneath Beanie's flat. Halfway up, a small woman with a bright face and jet-black hair styled into a severe fringe struggled with two overflowing bags.

"D'you want some help?" asked Duncan.

Her hand shading her eyes, she looked him over. "Oh, thank you, if you wouldn't mind."

English, posh, southern, summarised Duncan, taking one bag loaded with tins of paint, hammers, boxes of nails and a wood planer.

"What's in yours?" he asked, feeling the tonne weight.

"Food. Mine's the lighter."

She had done well to climb half the steps.

"We're just up here," she said pointing towards another flight of steps opposite Beanie's flat,

Duncan was regretting his Good Samaritan act.

"Sorry, even more to go," she said, opening a blue-painted door. "I should've got a donkey."

Perhaps she meant her husband. Duncan realised the figure he had seen climbing these steps from Beanie's window was not a figment of his imagination. He knew exactly who he was about to meet. Charlotte, an academic in her early thirties from Eastbourne, had been visiting the island regularly for about five years. She and her husband had rented an apartment, but after sleepless nights agonising, had bought a plot of land and built a house.

Designed in the traditional island style, the house had been carved out of a giant rock and now stood gleaming white on a man-made plateau with a splendid view, above Beanie's place, across the valley.

Duncan, ushered ahead, into the narrow path between the house next door and a high wall, squeezed through an opening and up a step on to a tiled patio, which had been built on two levels. A pair of medium height pillars, topped with spherical ceramic flowerpots, guarded more steps to the higher level. A large wooden table, ideal for family meals and the buffet spread at parties stood beside a small walled garden. A long yellow hose pipe draped over the branch of an orange tree drizzled water into a flower bed. Sitting on a bamboo chair at a marble-topped table beneath an umbrella, wearing khaki shorts and sandals, was Duncan's beaten opponent from the school boxing championship, Tony Caldwell.

He almost dropped his coffee cup. "Well, fuck me, it's you, is it not?"

"Hello, Tony," said Duncan, grateful to put the bag down.

"Anthony, actually, if you wouldn't mind," and then he laughed. "I see Charlotte's put you to work."

"Doing your job, mate."

'What am I?' considered Duncan – on the run from some bad guys, questioned by the police, and with a borrowed couple of hundred euros, less, to my name. Who was the winner now?

Then, Caldwell had been a leaner specimen. Either he had let himself go, or else Duncan's experience on the road, lifting and shifting, had kept his body in shape.

Duncan offered his hand, but Caldwell, absurdly, threw a fake punch that grazed his victor's shoulder – just as well Beanie's remedy had worked.

"I still say your last punch was late," he said.

"You were dead and buried."

"Alright, you won," admitted Caldwell, now pummelling Duncan by the hand. "But I see someone's caught you a shiner." He was peering over the top of his sunglasses, and Duncan, could almost hear him say, 'Look at me now, and you, ragged round the edges.'

"It was a political disagreement."

"Ah, yes, your Greeks can get a tad hysterical."

Nikos would have lapped this up, thought Duncan. As many false assumptions and stereotypes crammed into one sentence as was possible. The colonial spirit alive and well.

Charlotte made more coffee, and chairs were brought onto the patio. A striking little calico cat hovered proprietorially.

"He comes with the territory."

"She," corrected Charlotte.

"Lordy," said Caldwell, shifting round in his seat. "We'll have thousands of the little mites before long."

"Don't be silly, look at her ear."

The missing tip to her ear indicated she had been spayed.

"Otherwise, you'd have got your marching orders, Sunny Jim, or whatever your name is."

Charlotte sighed. "Hardly, she's adopted us."

The cat, bored with their footling conversation, set off patrolling the walls. Caldwell was behaving like someone much older. Duncan recognised that while dealing with students – Anthony it turned out was also an academic – kept some lecturers young, others it crabbed and aged.

"This is us, as you can see," said Caldwell, proudly.

"It's lovely," agreed Duncan, hoping to keep any hint of envy out of his voice. Yes, he coveted the house, but how had this berk managed to sort his life out? The likely answer was Charlotte.

"Tell us about you, Duncan?" asked Charlotte, replacing her cup on its saucer. "What brings you here, helping women with their shopping bags?"

"Just passing through," he said, never presuming he would get away with that. "I'm travelling."

"Oh, island hopping. How lovely. My sister did that when she was a student."

And there it was – Duncan's lifestyle suited to somebody ten years younger.

"Well, actually, I was thinking I might linger just for a while." Charlotte said she could not think of anywhere better, and drew a line under the interrogation, but Caldwell was having none of it.

"But what are your plans when you get back?"

"I'm taking some time out. For several years now I've been running rock bands all round Europe."

Though 'running' was not strictly accurate, it put Caldwell on the back foot and suggested a status to satisfy this couple.

"Oh, how exciting," trilled Charlotte, now regarding him as someone she might like to know. "Which bands?"

Duncan reeled off some well-known names, and threw in several more top leaguers, whom he had met in bars.

"Oh, I love them," said Charlotte, picking up on one quartet. Duncan could not resist saying she might not if she met them.

Caldwell tried another angle. "As I remember it, you shuffled off rather smartish from the old alma mater."

Was this a parody? As far as Duncan could tell he was in earnest.

"You mean, I left earlier than expected."

Caldwell's eyebrows raised. "Rumour was you might have been expelled."

"I was caught with some junior boys, pants round my ankles."

"Good Lord!"

Duncan left a pause, then, "Or would you rather I'd got a girl pregnant? The headmaster's daughter, how's that?"

Charlotte replaced her coffee cup. "Now, boys, the boxing was years ago."

"He lost."

Caldwell sulked. "Thank you, Connor, I can speak up for myself."

Duncan could have sworn the cat, posing on top of a pillar, winked at him.

"Thanks so much for helping with the bags," said Charlotte.

"Not at all." Duncan got to his feet. "You really do have a lovely spot here."

"Thank you," she said purring in tune with the cat, who had jumped down beside her.

"I look forward to seeing the inside."

"Not sure how long we're staying this time, are we, darling?" Anthony coming out from under the umbrella plonked a sunhat on his head, which made him look even more like a throwback to the Raj.

"We'll have to see," Charlotte smiled.

As Duncan made his way back down the steps and out through the blue door, the little cat followed him.

"I'm not surprised you're looking for another place," he told her, "But I'm not the one."

She waited while he crossed the lane and opened the door to Beanie's flat.

"Charlotte's alright, isn't she, just ignore him."

A one-eyed Ginger bruiser mooched towards them.

"This your date?" wondered Duncan.

The little cat looked at him with disdain and pootled off down a couple of steps towards a battered door. Before slipping through the hole in the bottom she gave Duncan another glance as if to say, "If you really think I'd entertain that old scuzzy, you're certainly not for me." And she was gone.

Duncan shrugged at the Ginger Tom. "Sorry mate, you don't cut the mustard either,"

Pretending disinterest, the one-eyed cat slumped onto his haunch and scratched himself.

CHAPTER TWENTY

The day after the galleon was fired, Duncan hung about on the quay, hoping Eleni might surprise him by catching the last boat. By now an experienced, if frustrated, boat greeter, he was used to the chaotic turnaround in the port. This one would surpass most.

As the hydrofoil drew into the harbour, the passengers on the quay predictably surged forward. Then suddenly, a bunch of excitable photographers popped up, and Duncan's focus switched to the fashion-shoot crowd heading towards the embarkation point. Some dawdled, kissing friends goodbye; others waved at well-wishers leaning out of the windows above the café. At their head, the designer, improbably dressed like a movie star of Gloria Swanson's vintage, barked instructions.

"Concentrate. Make sure you get all your kit on board."

Duncan noticed the photographers focused on the scantily dressed TV star rather than her.

By now the hydrofoil had docked and while passengers disembarked down the shaky gangplank, port officials made it none the easier by carrying parcels aboard. Then a siren sounded and an ambulance – the only other vehicle of note on the island besides the dustcart – sped onto the quay, scattering the crowd. Pulling up, two orderlies in scrubs, a man and a woman, emerged and from the back lifted out an elderly woman on a stretcher and dumped her on the cobbles. They leapt back into the ambulance, hit the siren, and reversed. Covered by a thin white sheet, the woman seemed oblivious. Duncan, shocked, but still with an eye out for Eleni, drew near. His way was blocked by Miss Swanson, who had knelt beside the woman. Swanson had stolen the photographers' attention, and they zoomed in.

A couple of Seaways personnel wrestled their way down the gangplank to claim the patient.

Miss Swanson launched into them. "Disgraceful. Dumping the poor woman like this? She could be my mother."

That was stretching it, thought Duncan, but he saw her point.

Taking an end of the stretcher each, the bearers carved their way through the queue for the ticket check. Miss Swanson accompanied them, still complaining. Rather than allowing the bearers free passage, the models and their crew jostled in front. Duncan noticed she did not censure them.

In the scrum, a photographer fell to the ground, but still tried for a picture. The TV star, fearing he was going for an intimate shot, kicked him.

Just as the bearers finally got a foothold on the gangplank, a large crate was passed up to a crew member. The bearers were forced to lift the stretcher above their heads, but in so doing tipped their patient onto her side. She hung on for dear life. The flimsy sheet dangled, revealing her threadbare nightdress.

Miss Swanson was beside herself. "It's a human being you're handling, not a parcel. CAREFUL!"

For a jaw-dropping second or two, the stretcher slipped to vertical, the patient in severe peril, which provoked a cacophony of advice in several languages. But the moment passed, and with the woman and the stretcher horizontal once more the bearers reached the safety of the deck.

The horn blew.

"NO! WAIT!" cried Miss Swanson.

A tall, lean man, close-cropped hair, a sausage bun leaking tomato sauce in one hand, and dragging a case on wheels with the other, raced along the Quay.

"HURRY!" she roared.

The captain yelled from the bridge.

"You're going to miss your boat," warned Duncan.

Swanson, chiding the sausage man, presented their tickets which were torn in half, and they climbed onto the gangplank. Halfway up, she turned.

"And you," she said, smiling at Duncan, "You can keep your cock to yourself."

He couldn't help but laugh. She tottered on board. The gangplank jerkily pulled up, the hydrofoil slipped its mooring, and then in a swirl of water and with another hoot, it was gone.

No Eleni.

Bereft and feeling alone, Duncan joined another queue for the opening of an art exhibition. A crowd in all their finery had gathered outside the austere hall at the harbour's head for a range of paintings, work in textiles, and small sculptures all created by islanders. Through the door, Duncan grabbed a glass of wine, nodded appreciatively at a combo of school kids playing rebetika music, and found Beanie and Jenny beside her exhibits. Her work was clearly in the Pre-Raphaelite style, which Duncan loathed. He said he admired her skilful paintwork, but Beanie shouted out, "The schmuck doesn't dig them. Tell the chick, she can take it."

Around them, people moved away. Duncan had picked up rumours that Beanie had upset many with displays of naked drunkenness, coupled with what was to him wooing of young women: but to them, sexual harassment. These transgressions had happened in the past, but they were neither forgotten, nor forgiven. Duncan reasoned that to Beanie's credit, most would grudgingly accept he had curbed his behaviour and become a member of the community, but only on licence. No doubt it had helped that he now had a partner, especially one who would paint portrait commissions to order. Thankfully, too, for Duncan, the couple's blissful nights had removed to her brightly coloured apartment above the little harbour, leaving the flat to him. Rent added up to a cheroot or two, and Duncan noticed his landlord was often flush after picking up a package at the post office. Any inquiry turned into a literary quiz.

"There are more things in Heaven and Earth, Horatio, than are dreamt of in your philosophy."

"Shakespeare."

"Every sucker knows that, but which one?"

Duncan had gone for the first title that came to mind. "Hamlet?"

"Beginners luck," scorned Beanie.

"First class classical education," Duncan had insisted,

"Stop bullying him," said Jenny, at the exhibition. "There's no rule says he has to like my stuff."

"Well, let's try him on some other poor sap."

Beanie pointed to a couple of works permanently on show by one of the island's internationally known artists. Expressionist in tone, one captured the island's effervescence in dazzling light and richly dense colours. The other in its texture and composition reminded Duncan of the painting Kathryn had sent him. It took him straight back to that lonely road outside the pit village, Malcolm Gifford breathing his last and his mother's flight from the scene. A sliver of regret ran through him, and he shivered.

Jenny, thinking his discomfort was from Beanie's provocation, took him by the arm, "Don't rise to it, Duncan."

He did not have time to explain.

Heads had turned to a ruckus at the door. A scrawny man all in black shouted in broken English, "GREECE FOR GREEKS!"

Wild eyed and carrying a bucket, he charged into the hall. People stood back in surprise and then in horror as he hurled a thick blue substance at the exhibits.

The rudimentary equipment, Duncan initially thought, pointed to an act of performance art. But the dollops of goo ruining the paintings, and the collateral damage to people's clothing, suggested something darker. An attack maybe inspired and timed to coincide with the celebration of the historical fight for independence.

A large Englishman, whose young daughter's work was ruined picked up the empty bucket.

"YOU BASTARD!" he shouted and threw it at the scrawny interloper.

He missed.

"GET HIM!" cried someone else.

Duncan made his way forward, but the man backing towards the door produced a knife.

A second figure appeared.

"GREECE FOR GREEKS!" he screamed and, despite a couple of people trying to restrain him, hurled a second bucket amongst the throng. Guests scattered as it thudded to the floor, spreading its sticky gloop in a wide circle.

Two of them, it occurred to Duncan later, always two.

Both sped from the hall and leapt into a taxi-boat moored by the quay, the driver held at knife point and trussed up on the floor. Arms aloft in a Nazi style salute the assailants drove out of the port, leaving the police led by Andrea Koutsikos, Duncan recognised, helpless.

Guests flooded out of the exhibition, while others set to clearing up the mess. Jenny, her work luckily untouched, commiserated with the artists, whose paintings had been destroyed. Ironically one spattered by spots of gloop was by the famous artist – not the piece that had jogged Duncan's memory. Collateral damage he thought and hoped the picture could be restored. The outraged Englishman fulminated against the lack of security, complaining that the world was going to hell in a handcart. Someone else with a broad Scottish accent told him to "Shut the fuck up; it's the likes of you provoke these people."

The argument continued outside. Duncan later stood on the quay for the second time that evening. His view in the hall had been obscured by the throng, but he was convinced the second attacker was Kafandaris.

CHAPTER TWENTY-ONE
NORTHERN ENGLAND 1998

As winter turned to spring, Duncan mooched in town. No films to see; no CDs he wanted. The shoes he had once spotted were no longer in the shop window, and he could not be bothered to ask inside.

But then, through a doorway mirror, he saw Mrs Gifford quickly followed by Kathryn. They went into a shopping centre. This was meant – a sign! He dodged through browsers, double-decker prams, squalling kids, but where had they gone?

There, in a department store. Kathryn stopped at a perfume counter, but her mother hustled her up the escalator. At a distance, Duncan followed them into Soft Furnishings.

Tricky, he was exposed, no shoppers to conceal him – only eager assistants with helpful smiles who might approach. His nerve was failing him when he spied the Giffords engrossed in an A3 volume of wallpaper samples. Keeping an eye peeled, Duncan feigned interest in a mini conservatory with a charcoal gourmet barbecue stand outside. His patience was rewarded when Kathryn wandered away from her mother.

She sat down on a large cream sofa and sank back into gaily coloured cushions. On a coffee table in front of her stood a bottle of white wine and 2 glasses. Perfect in other circumstances.

Close to her, Duncan's mouth had dried up – someone open that bottle! – but then the word emerged, "Hello."

Kathryn just about smiled, but it quickly turned to a frown. Had she recognised him from court?

Softly this time, he said, "I'm Duncan Connor. I'm – "

"Oh, God!" Her hand flew to her mouth. Duncan worried she would call out.

"Sorry," he said. "Bit of a shock."

"What are you doing here?"

He opted for the truth. "I – well, I saw you outside and I wanted – "

She stood up. "What d'you mean? Outside where?"

"Um, just outside, you know, the centre – coming in."

"So, you've followed me?"

He knew this didn't sound good – not the best start. But he persisted,

"Yes, just from outside, when I saw you."

"Why?"

Encouragingly, her voice had a teasing tone now.

"I wanted to meet you."

"Hello," she smiled a fraction more this time, and walked round the back of the sofa. Duncan dug his hands into his pockets, struggling for nonchalance. "Thank you for your letter. It was very thoughtful." She watched him. "I think."

"Thank you for writing back."

Kathryn moved on as far as a Gentleman's Club armchair. Surely, she couldn't really be interested in that, reckoned Duncan, but she glanced at the price. "Oooh! That's a lot – " She must be playing for time, thinking what to do or say next. "I don't know about this."

"How are you? – " He asked quickly. "I mean, how are you managing to…"

She sighed. "Well, you know… but I don't suppose you do."

"No."

And then she said, "It can't be easy for you, either."

He looked at her in awe. Was he falling in love?

"Kathryn?" said Mrs Gifford. She had arrived quietly and was staring at Duncan. "I know you, don't I? Is this – ?"

Duncan gulped and held out his hand. "Duncan Connor."

"Yes." Mrs Gifford looked at her daughter. "What the hell is going on?"

"It's alright, Mum."

"It is very far from alright."

"He was just talking to me."

"Well, I don't want him talking to you – "

"I realise this is a bit awkward, Mrs Gifford – "

"Go – "

"Actually, Mum, he was being very kind."

"This is not a conversation," Mrs Gifford hissed.

"Well, I don't see why not." Kathryn's hands moved to her hips.

"Perhaps when Mr Connor has departed." Mrs Gifford's eyes bored into Duncan, but Kathryn's expression was equally insistent he stay.

The jolly sales assistant, with another collection of samples, joined the party.

"So sorry," she said breezily, "but we do have it after all."

No one moved.

Then – "Come along," said Mrs Gifford, beckoning to her daughter.

"Well, I'm glad I've met you," said Duncan, nodding at Mrs Gifford, who took Kathryn by the arm and pulled her away.

He stood alone in what felt like a draught. He had been made to feel guilty, but about what? It was not him who had driven into Malcolm. Low-grade stalking? Yes, maybe. But Kathryn had looked disappointed her mother had intervened. A conversation with him was a better bet than a decision about wallpaper.

"Fuck, fuck, fuck." He was sick of feeling like this.

By the time he reached the bottom of the escalator, his mind had somersaulted through despair and back to asking Kathryn if she would like to go for a drink. Or, and he was pleased with this, inviting Mrs Gifford, too. Pray to God she would not accept. He would show her, though; show them both he was a normal bloke.

Except in their eyes, he was far from normal. And in the circumstances, was it ok to fancy someone? He was not a child abuser or a mad murderer.

This is me, Duncan Connor, saying hello to a girl. Ok, not just any girl… but how else does the world go round?

He was halfway back up the escalator when he saw Kathryn stepping onto the opposite side.

Whoa! Was she after him?

He raced to the top and then jumped onto the down escalator as Kathryn got off at the bottom. Taking several steps at a time, Duncan hit the ground and carved through menswear accessories and back to the perfume counter, scoping left and right. He burst towards the exit and nearly knocked an elderly shopper to the floor.

"That's no way to behave," she said, furiously. He apologised and picked up her handbag. She grabbed it. "I'll have that, thank you very much."

He felt a tap on the shoulder and spun round.

"Is this your grandmother?" asked Kathryn.

"No, young lady, I am certainly not. He's a heffalump."

"Sorry again," said Duncan, and, scowling, the elderly shopper walked off, never to know how grateful he was. Seconds later and he would have been through the automatic exit doors.

"Sorry my mum was a bit… well…"

"Understandably," Duncan said. "Where is she?"

"Busy."

They went to an unappealing pub and found a quiet corner.

"Take That or Boyzone?" asked Duncan.

"Oh, please."

"Just testing. How about 'Ab Fab' or 'The Fast Show'?"

"Ooh, now… Both."

"Oasis or Blur?"

"Neither."

"Really?"

"Yes, too boysie," she smiled. "All too boysie. Pulp for me."

Was this code for being a lesbian? he thought.

"So, who do you like?"

"Dusty Springfield."

Not only had Duncan never heard of this person, but he was also in the dark as to their gender. He played it safe. "Who?"

"You don't know Dusty Springfield?"

Duncan shook his head. Kathryn was beaming.

"Most people pretend." She drank orange juice through a straw.

"Go on, then."

"My mum's era really: 60's and 70's. She's wonderful, and still around. You should give her a listen."

Duncan nodded, anything this girl said was fine by him.

"So then, apart from music, what else d'you – "

"Painting," she jumped in, her eyes sparkling. "I love painting, it's all I'm good at. Art's my best subject at school."

"I can't draw at all, I'm afraid."

"It doesn't have to be drawing, or painting. I happen to love painting, but we've got a great teacher, and we do collages and photography, you know, all sorts of messing about."

He loved her enthusiasm; how her eyes widened when she was excited.

"I saw the card at the – memorial. I guessed it was you."

Kathryn blinked. "When did you see…"

"On the road, I went there. It's a lovely – well."

Kathryn stared. "By yourself?"

"Yes, I was trying to work out what had happened."

"Why did your mother leave him there?" Her eyes brimmed with tears.

"Why didn't she get help? That's what happened."

"Yes."

"What do you mean, yes? Don't you know? Haven't you asked her why?"

Duncan pictured Kathryn coming with him to the prison.

"I think she panicked," he said.

"She thought she'd get away with it, didn't she?"

Duncan wished he hadn't started this.

Kathryn was crying. "If you'd known my dad – he was the sweetest, most incredible… You'd have…" She covered her face with her hands.

"It's alright."

She took her hands down; her eyes were bloodshot. "It isn't alright," she said. "It never will be."

Duncan reached out for her, but she withdrew.

"Don't," she snapped. "And don't pity me." Kathryn pushed back her chair. "This isn't right, I shouldn't be here."

"I'm glad you are. You and I aren't to blame."

"Well, I'm certainly not; we're just the ones left."

Did she mean the two of them, and it was up to them to find some sort of future?

"It's pretty crap all round."

"Difference is your mother gets out, doesn't she."

"Yes, but it's still a life sentence."

"And what d'you think it is for us?"

He cursed himself, and then tried to get them back to where they were.

"Picasso or Rembrandt?"

"Whoever you like." She got up.

Defeated, Duncan stood up too.

"Where are you going?" She challenged.

"Well, I'll come with you, I'll come out – "

"No. Don't."

He sat down.

"Bye," she said.

"Please, just one minute," not sure what he was going to say. "I like you, Kathryn, and I know all the horrible things are in the way, but I hope when you feel better you might get in touch."

His hand trembled as he scribbled down a number on the back of an old receipt he had pulled from his pocket.

"Well…" she said but took it and left.

He noticed his side of the table was disfigured by graffiti, the 'M luvs B' variety and, in thick marker, 'Man U R indecipherable'. What was he thinking bringing her to a place like this? The other drinkers, mostly single elderly men, seemed equally unhappy in their lonely swamps. He drank up and replaced the empty glass. Mrs Gifford sat down opposite him. Duncan looked around for Kathryn, but there was no sign.

"What the hell have you been saying to my daughter?"

All the things he had wanted to say to Kathryn, he poured out to her mother. "I think your daughter is a beautiful girl, Mrs Gifford, and you should be very proud of her." Adding, quickly, "I'm sure you are. I can tell she's very talented, lovely, and I know this is a terrible time for her – for you – well actually all of us, but obviously mostly for you and your family, but I feel… no, I know Kathryn's going to come through. And her dad, she told me how much she loved him. He'll be very proud of her, too. She's a fantastic girl, Mrs Gifford, really is fantastic…" Aware he was losing the thread, Duncan stuttered to a halt.

"Your father's a prick," said Ruth Gifford, "but I thought you might be better. In fact, you're much worse."

"Hang on – "

"NO! You hang on. You're a creepy, nasty… You're a very unhealthy young man. Taking advantage of this situation is one of the very worst things I've ever heard, and it's stopping right now."

"What d'you mean? What's stopping, Mrs Gifford?"

"Do not contact my daughter. Do not see her ever again."

"I know it's a bit weird – "

"Shut up!" She was near tears. "Stop it, stop everything."

She got up. Duncan leaned back in case she hit him.

"Just fuck off and die." And off she went.

Duncan watched her go. They were people whose lives had been turned upside down, and the mother was lashing out at anyone who might harm her cub – especially him. The clinical-sounding correctness of 'a very unhealthy young man' had the smack of formality and being written down somewhere officially.

Maybe, somehow, there might be a chink of hope at a family-level truth and reconciliation meeting. If they could manage it in South

Africa or Northern Ireland, then… he told himself now to shut up, he was being ridiculous.

The barman removed the empty glasses and leered, "Hey, you're doing well, mate. I make that two of them in tears."

Duncan thought about Kathryn every day. He bought Dusty Springfield's Greatest Hits CD and imagined she might be listening to the same tracks. He veered from blaming himself for fancying Kathryn, to defending his feelings as caring and compassionate, and accusing Kathryn of moodiness. It was now, ironically, that a boy needed his mother. Days went by and his A-level results were all he had to look forward to. Huh!

The doorbell rang, dragging Duncan from a mid-morning lie-in. A cardboard tube addressed to him, which did not fit through the letterbox. In the kitchen, he took the lid off one end and pulled out another, much thinner tube, wrapped in an elastic band. He removed the band and opened out a painting. On the back, in pencil, he discovered the initials K.G. He stuck the painting on the cork noticeboard, drawing pins in each corner. He saw a bird in flight against a light blue sky and below a road ran into the distance – the brush strokes jagged and colourful, in thick screeches of paint. He stepped back and was shocked to see a figure, unmistakeably his mother, horribly stretched as if she had been the victim of medieval torture. Her face, witch-like with pitch black eyes, wept blood.

He sat down. She had replied in the form she knew best. She must really hate him.

Later, about to rip up the painting, he stopped, rolled it up, slid on the elastic band, put it back in the cardboard tube, and stored it under his bed.

It was time to get on with his life.

CHAPTER TWENTY-TWO

Beth had been transferred to an open prison. Instead of grubby streets and derelict mills, a farmhouse and several fields in bloom led to this place. Outside the entrance, a rose bush stood in the middle of a lawn. Inside, a bright reception hall indicated that management treated their inmates as human beings, there but for the grace of God.

His mother, a dash of colour added to her cheeks, waited for him in a large room surrounded by bookshelves. She might as well have been a branch librarian.

"What a change," said Duncan. "You look so much better."

"And I feel better," she said, and gave him a quick tour of her new domain.

She had read short stories and novels by Annie Proulx, Donna Tartt, Anne Tyler and, lately, Irvine Welsh, of whom she said, "I do like his stuff, but sometimes I think he's showing off."

Once they had sat down, she took a deep breath: "You challenged me before."

"If you mean I asked you some questions."

"Well," this was still an effort for her, "you were right. That day." She looked at him. Duncan waited.

"I was thinking. I did think." She moved a magazine around in front of her until it was straight with the table's edge. "We'd had a Christmas party, well, a lunch. It was my Christmas, you see. I don't think I'd ever been happier."

Duncan remembered their family's own insipid festivities. "Just as well then – "

"I'm sorry, that sounded harsh, but I'm trying to be honest."

"Try neglectful."

"Oh dear, this isn't going very well."

Duncan waited.

"You've no idea how many times I've been practicing this."

"As Dad, would say, that's a waste of time. You must wait until the enemy is in front of you."

"Goodness gracious, you're not the enemy."

"No, I'm not." Duncan smiled. "As Dad would say."

"Alright." Her eyes beseeched him. "Please don't judge me, I've had enough…"

Duncan nodded.

"I ran away because I was frightened that if Richard found out he would, he might…" she tailed off.

"He wouldn't have had any more to do with you?" helped Duncan.

Her lips came together. "Mm."

"But what you did in running off made it so much worse."

"It did. I, you see – I know it doesn't make any sense – " She struggled for the words. "What was I thinking?"

Duncan leaned forward and held her arm. "Mum, it's alright, no more. One thing at a time."

A weight seemed to lift from them both. Beth had admitted what Duncan assumed was the truth. He got up and hugged her. "No warders I hope."

She smiled. "We'd better leave it, though."

They both sat down again. He was so relieved, it felt like he was getting his mother back. Unlike his last visit he wanted to stay longer.

"I'm proud of you, Mum."

"Oh, now, don't go too far."

"And Richard is, he's still…?"

"Yes," she said. "He's still here. Well, you know what I mean."

Duncan nodded.

"It must be love."

"Bloody hell, Mum."

"I don't know what I'd do without him."

This Richard Patterson person must be a good thing. Duncan looked forward to meeting him. They might even get on.

"No need to tell your father."

For a moment Duncan thought she might ask him how Pat was, but she didn't. And in the matter of not saying things, he was well aware he hadn't said anything about Kathryn Gifford. But after all, what was there to say?

"What's next on the reading list?" He asked.

"Well, I was thinking – as I've had a go at some of this modern stuff – so while I've got the time…" she paused. "Time. Now there's a big word."

"In this place, I imagine so."

"Yes, so make sure you don't waste it, my boy," she said. "That would be a crime."

"Promise you," he replied, though it was a demand more likely to come from Pat. He wondered if he'd regret saying it.

Outside the prison the bus chugged up and he ran across the lawn and joined the lengthening queue. Unlike his experience at Beth's original prison, he was happy to see the visitors were chatting to one another. Perhaps the influence of nature and fresh air. He looked back at the building and imagined Beth was already scouring the bookshelves for her next project, the classics. He'd advised her against 'Great Expectations'. He'd remembered a tv serialisation in which Magwitch the prisoner had given him nightmares.

"No," she'd agreed, "You were far too young, must've been him that let you watch that."

Yet another opportunity for her to ask about Pat but seeing as he'd been relegated to 'him', that was unlikely.

"George Eliot's novels are nice and long aren't they?"

"Come on, Mum, you're not going to be in here forever."

She'd smiled, a big smile.

CHAPTER TWENTY-THREE
GREECE 2010

The island was jumpy. No one doubted the attackers were Golden Dawn, whose partners in far-right parties were spreading like a virus in Holland, Spain, Hungary, Germany and the UK. People were scared.

One of them had a knife. What if the next time they had guns? Golden Dawn members were behind every other door, at the next table in the taverna, buying food in the mini market. A woman on the quay ranted that Golden Dawn were right, her house had been taken over by Pakistanis.

Then rumours circulated the pair had been arrested, but there was no official confirmation. After a sleepless night, Duncan walked into the police station to tell Ms Koutsikos everything he knew.

But she was not there, neither was the young policeman.

Beanie cornered him. "Anything to do with you, Connor?"

"One of them I recognised, but I'm not sure."

Beanie nodded. His regular 'Amarillo' breakfast omelette had failed to lift his mood, and his rheumy eye was damper than usual. "Coincidence, huh?"

"Are you accusing me of something?"

"Hey, me?"

"You're still sore I didn't like Jenny's work?"

"You admit it, huh?" He pretended to cuff Duncan. "Hell no, I ain't."

He winked. "Anyone asks, I'm an Edward Hopper fan." He waved at Vassos helping a child onto a donkey while her anxious mother held the girl's hand. "I'm just trying to figure it out, is all."

"What are we talking now?" asked Duncan. "Artistic preferences… world peace…"

"If you like. We're in the birthplace of democracy here, so where does all this darn fascism come from?"

"They chant, 'Blood and Earth."

"Well, you sure as hell can't eat that."

A fisherman had once drunkenly challenged Beanie's right to be on the island. 'Who's going to buy your fish, buddy?' he had replied.

"That's where you're falling down, these bastards don't follow logic."

They read the notice on the Exhibition Hall door. Despite the artists insisting the show continued, the mayor, citing technical reasons – i.e. cleaning – had closed it.

"Mistake," shouted Beanie, addressing the harbour. "Don't give in to these peckerwoods!"

One of the mayor's officials opened the door and Beanie went in to collect Jenny's paintings. A man with a magnifying glass was stooped before the famous painter's glooped work.

"Any joy?"

The man winced, "I hope" he said, but did not look convinced. "Rednecks" muttered Beanie.

The man returned to his task, the floor remained an ugly, sticky mess. There was no sign of any cleaners.

Clothing had become Duncan's number one priority. His top from the infirmary, grimy with Beanie's green salve, was done for. He tried one of his host's t-shirts – incredibly, a survivor from the Woodstock Music Festival in 1969 – but it only reached his midriff.

His finances took a severe hit. He left a shop carrying a bag of basics and ran into the Caldwell's.

They bought him a cappuccino and explained Charlotte's mother was in hospital. She had been in a car accident. Not her fault. Duncan's spoon stopped, mid stir.

"I'm very sorry to hear that," he said, his head suddenly filled with that minor road and Malcolm Gifford's memorial.

"Still with us, Champ?" asked Caldwell needlessly.

Without looking at him, Duncan nodded.

"We'd usually ask a couple of our friends," Charlotte said. "But they're not here." She looked at her husband for his support, but none came. "We just wondered if you'd possibly mind house-sitting, not that we don't trust people, but considering what's happened…"

"Right now, you can't be too careful," grunted Caldwell.

If it were up to him, Duncan knew he would never have been in the frame. He imagined the man groaning: 'For God's sake, no, he loafs about with that ghastly American. They're probably as high as kites.'

When Charlotte put her hand on his to thank him, Duncan could feel Caldwell's loathing.

"And please feed the cat," she asked him.

Later, as Duncan saw them off from the quay, Caldwell removed his sunglasses. "Just make sure, you don't mess this up, Connor,"

"Look after your wife," replied Duncan, and after a deliberate pause added, "Tony."

At the insult Caldwell glared and missed his step on the gangplank.

Duncan waved at a teary Charlotte before she disappeared into the boat.

"Thank you," she mouthed.

The house inside was spotless and a delight. A kitchen slash dining room, a cosy bedroom with a king size bed, inbuilt wardrobes and both a shower and bath on the ground floor. Upstairs a lounge; an office space, his; and a work room, hers, where she sewed tapestries. A4 pages of instructive notes on the kitchen table from Charlotte, signing off with 'Have fun'.

While Duncan was in the shower, the cat slipped through the window, scattering shampoo bottles, soaps, and lotions.

"Well, whaddya know," he said to her later, "It's you and me, cat. Destiny."

Tickling under her chin brought her out in squinty-eyed joy. "A hedonist. That makes two of us," said Duncan, "But just remember, I'm the one in charge."

Curled up on a cushion, she yawned and settled down to keep an eye on her new guardian. Perhaps, Duncan had to admit, the chain of command was not quite so simple. He checked the crammed-full larder, and the fridge was stocked. Eking that out for a while, even between two, would be no problem.

There was a knock at the door.

"Party central, yeah?" said Beanie, plonking a cowboy-booted foot on a stool. "Jen's on her way with a bottle. Promise I'll smoke outside."

"I hate to disappoint you," Duncan replied, "but I've already got company."

Beanie eyed the cat, who was wide awake at the intrusion.

Eleni had texted. Finally. Duncan sadly absorbed the news that Dmitri was still in a coma. He reminded her which island he was on, and Eleni replied with her arrival time, sunny asterisks and kisses.

"The man of mystery has an old lady," said Beanie.

"Not sure she'd like the old."

"Betcha she's gonna love your new crib." He made a lassoing gesture with his finger in the air. "Guess, I'll take the grand tour some other time."

Eleni ran down the gangplank and into Duncan's arms. Her embrace took him backwards on the cobbles and they seemed to float. Then, joining ghosts of past lovers greeting in the twilight, they walked arm-in-arm along the quay. He was blind to Andrea Koutsikos sitting at a table with the waitress and sharing a post-work drink. The policewoman was in tears.

He and Eleni climbed the steps outside the carpenters, nimbly avoiding the trails of donkey shit, turning right up another flight, catching their breath, passing the grocers on the corner. They talked in spurts, thighs turning inwards, kissing, on towards the house, then waiting for a donkey train to go by, her back to the wall, pressing hard against each other, crushed lips. Here, do it here… no, no, wait. Come on, gangly limbs, hand in hand between the high walls, nearly there, up through the blue door, elongated strides mounting the steps, her bag fell, he swept it up, carrying it over his shoulder and in through the front door, the cat looking up then turning her back, clothes shed, pulling, clawing, hot sweat mingling, slipping and sliding, brief laughter… And then together in each other, eye to eye, smiling.

Rats to Robert Louis Stevenson's quote, 'It's better to journey.' This was arriving.

Days and nights passed in a tempest of lovemaking. In the shower, on the fluffy rugs, a mattress on the patio at dawn. Two builders, hoping to make an early start on the outhouse, slid backwards down the steps. Later, the lovers stood in wonder at a single rose left in a vase by the front door.

The cat was settled with a bowl of biscuits and treats, and with a packed lunch for later, Duncan led Eleni along the dusty cliff path and over a narrow humpback bridge. Down at the water's edge, waiters in black trousers and white shirts laid out tables for a big party beneath the trees, a stunning view of the islands in silhouette to the south. They struck on further to a ramshackle harbour that had become a dumping ground for old boats. Relics from the maritime history of the island.

Standing on the stone jetty, Eleni took it all in. "I think I've seen an engraving of somewhere very like this."

They continued inland up a dirt track, and Eleni told how in the Napoleonic Wars the islanders had sailed their boats through the British blockade. "They were brilliant shipbuilders."

"But as I remember it, the Brits still won."

"You can certainly remember that old man. You were there."

Whooping, he chased her up the track.

Above them was a scree, one of the many that gave the island its austere appearance. This unyielding rocky façade was mediated by rich green swathes of grass and tilled terracing where inhabitants past and present had grown crops and reared livestock.

Soon they reached a village, most of the houses second homes or holiday cottages. Others were deserted, or in arrested development: the result of disputed ownership or the lack of finance to complete. A regular feature of the island's landscape.

In a hollow beyond the last house, they stopped for a lunch of bread, black and green olives, cheese, the juiciest tomatoes, and wine. They made love and were convinced the earth moved, but it was the dustcart rattling round making the island's weekly collection.

They climbed a steep gradient, often slipping on the stones, but their reward was at the top. Mouths open, they gazed down at the port and the bluest sea dotted with yachts and boats to the Peloponnese beyond. On this, the island's highest point, Duncan realised for the first time in his life he had found somewhere he never wanted to leave. He kissed Eleni and held her tight.

Caldwell telephoned checking all was well.

"All fine," replied Duncan.

"I'm relieved to hear it." Duncan pulled a face into the receiver. "But" warned the house owner, "I'll see for myself." He would return in a few days, no mention of Charlotte's mother.

The idyll was nearly over. So, there was no time to waste.

Not for one moment did Duncan reflect on his earlier doubts and frustrations; the time Eleni had not been in touch, for which she had never apologised; Nikos' place in her life. All his anxieties had evaporated in this paradise of love and kept him a safe distance from unpleasant reality.

In the morning, he would get up early, swim, and then during a long and lazy breakfast get down on one knee.

CHAPTER TWENTY-FOUR

Duncan's romantic plan misfired. Eleni was so drowsy she skipped the swim, but promised to have breakfast ready. He left for the beach in a pair of new trunks and, swimming along his familiar route, practiced what he was going to say. His head came up above the surface and he saw Jenny sitting on a rock. He tread water.

"Hey Duncan, keep swimming. I'm drawing you."

The subject of a Pre-Raphaelite style painting? Well yes, ok, why not? If it immortalises the day. He backstroked out to sea, did the crawl on return, and put in further sprints.

"Gives me plenty of options," she explained.

Exhausted, he hauled himself up beneath Jenny's rock.

"You're a darlin' boy," she said, and kissed him on his wet hair. "I'm gonna make damned sure you like this one."

"I've got to get moving," he said, forestalling a chat.

She laughed. "You're under the thumb already."

He dried off and rushed back up to the house, passing the cat out on feline business, who ignored him.

Eleni was still in bed. Quelling any disappointment, he cleaned out the cafetière and reloaded it with coffee. He switched on the kettle and caught sight of movement through the window.

Nikos was walking across the patio.

Duncan cut him off at the front door.

"Well," he said.

Nikos, smiling, pocketed his sunglasses. "You know, you need to be careful who you make your friends. They give you away so easily."

Duncan's heart had sunk through the floor. Behind him, he heard the kettle click off.

"He's a good look-out man, but I had a feeling he'd fold under questioning." Nikos took out a cigarette from a packet, his father's brand, and lit it. "Coffee please," he said, drawing up a newly painted green rattan chair and sitting down at the marble-topped table on the patio.

"Make yourself at home."

"I will. And get her up. I've got something to tell you both." Nikos' smile had slipped. He put his sunglasses back on. The door behind Duncan opened. Eleni appeared, wrapped in Charlotte Caldwell's dressing gown.

She went out and sat down opposite Nikos. "I know what this is."

"Would somebody like to tell me?" said Duncan.

Nikos blew out some smoke, "Dmitri's dead," he said.

Eleni's body shook.

"He's buried now, and it's all over, but we have plans." Nikos was on autopilot.

"When was this?" asked Duncan.

"Two days ago, at the hospital, he never recovered," said Nikos bluntly.

"Eleni sobbed. Duncan sat down beside her and put his arms around her.

"What about this coffee?" demanded Nikos.

"All you have to do is add water."

Nikos kicked back his chair and went into the house.

Eleni's head came up and, between gulping sobs, she said she'd had a nightmare about Dmitri. She repeated his name, before covering her face in her hands. "I knew it would happen, but now it has."

Duncan looked across the valley at the colourful higgledy-piggledy array of houses opposite, heard the scuzzy dog barking, and a donkey train rumbling below, but none of it registered.

Dmitri had gone.

He blamed himself. He should have stuck to his guns and thrown Kafandaris and Mazarakis out of his party. They'd have gone, and Dmitri would be alive and well.

Oh God. He hung his head.

Nikos reappeared with a mug of coffee.

"The rest of us might like some," Duncan snapped.

"I couldn't find any cups."

Duncan blinked at him. "You really are a fucking arsehole." He rose from his chair. "Why did you stop me getting rid of those bastards that night?."

Nikos reared, "You're blaming me!"

"I'm blaming us, all of us, we should have protected him."

"Exactly, and what did I tell you. If we'd known about those guys – " he was about to go on but suddenly stopped.

"You knew I wanted them out. I told you," Duncan said quietly.

"Everyone's upset." Nikos, avoiding eye contact, drew long and hard on his cigarette.

It had struck home. The messenger who'd arrived seeming to be above it all was as culpable as everyone else. Duncan was right. They'd all lost a friend, a very good friend, who could have been saved.

By the time Duncan returned with a tray of coffee and glasses of water, Nikos was sitting beside Eleni. They were talking quietly, but they stopped as Duncan sat down.

Eleni smoked.

Nikos checked his wristwatch. "We're booked on the next boat back."

"We?"

"All of us."

Eleni, her hair scraped back from her face, sipped water.

"These plans you mentioned – " began Duncan.

"Everything in due course."

"He was all alone in my nightmare," said Eleni, her eyes filling with tears again. "But he was talking to me."

"It's murder, but there won't be any arrests."

"But they know who did it. Everyone does," said Duncan.

"I want to speak to Ms Koutsikos, please."
At the reception desk, the young policeman with the irregular face smiled.

"She's not here."

"Where is she?" asked Duncan.

The man answered in Greek.

"I'm sorry, my fault, I know, but I don't speak Greek."

The policeman turned round to a map of Greece tacked to the wall. He pointed out a place on the mainland, Duncan leaned forward.

"That's – is that Corinth? She's in Corinth?"

The policeman nodded. "Corinth. Yes."

"When?"

The policeman shrugged.

"When did she go?"

The policeman thought for a moment and then held up three fingers.

"Three days ago? She left three days ago?"

The policeman nodded again.

"Thank you."

As he turned to leave the policeman laughed. "This not, Spetses."

Duncan, not in the mood, stopped. The Policeman still giggling was leafing through the pages of a file.

"You just keep on looking at those photos, you wanker!" For good measure he added the appropriate gesture. Later, Duncan admitted it was not his proudest moment.

Back on the quay, he bumped into Beanie.

"Whoa, pardner, how's it going? I'd sure like to meet the mystery lady, where is she?"

Nikos was leaning against the lamppost by the donkey station, his hands stuck in his pockets. Duncan tried to strike a note of calm but Beanie wasn't fooled. He picked up on Duncan spotting Eleni leaving the bank and like a homing pigeon making straight for Nikos.

"Your eyes are tap-dancing boy, or you've got bees in your pants?"

"You could say. Sorry, look thanks for everything, but I've got to love you and leave you. There's been a death in the family."

"What's that?" Beanie was shocked. "Ah, no. Sure, sure, that's how it goes. Sorry to hear it."

Beanie picked up on Duncan watching Nikos and Eleni threading their way through the milling crowds to the departure point. He carried her bag, his arm around her waist and her head rested on his shoulder.

"Ever seen 'The Dark Corner', an old black-and-white Hollywood picture?" asked Beanie. "Knowing your record – "

"You're right. No."

"All about a bunch of guys double-crossing each other, but there's a good woman at the bottom of it all. Lucille Ball, never better," he gestured towards the dock. "You sure you got one there?"

"I live in hope."

Heading into the harbour was the boat for Piraeus.

Beanie gripped Duncan with both hands. "Stay strong there, fella, and hey, when it's all over, come back, won't you? I'll be here, and by the grace of God, Jenny too."

"Heaven willing."

He meant it. He had come close to this man. Everything he knew about him, the way he looked, his crazy speech, spoke of a comic parody. But did he know him properly, who he was? And now he was leaving. His favourite option, wasn't it? No, not this time. Nikos and Eleni had reached the long queue for the boat.

Looking into Beanie's eyes, he knew he had missed someone: someone, who was more faithful than the two he was joining, someone he may never see again. Were they both thinking the same. What could he say?

"Good luck, Archie."

Beanie beamed, and Duncan ran.

If paradise, heaven or whatever was the bliss Duncan and Eleni had enjoyed for a week, then this was Hell. The hydrofoil ploughing through choppy seas was packed to the gunwales with school kids. Every educational establishment on the island, it seemed, had decanted onto this boat, separating Eleni and Duncan by several rows. Nikos sat at the front and often turned back towards Eleni. Not once did he check on Duncan, beside whom a child vomited into a paper bag, much of the vomit missing. Duncan closed his eyes, cold turkey in a rancid environment.

At the Caldwell house, he had stripped the bed, bundling the sheets into the washing machine, and filled the dishwasher. His belongings all fitted into the clothes bag, and he had left a note on the back of Charlotte's instructions. He had tried to get Eleni by herself, but she had bolted the bedroom door to change. She had no trouble speaking to Nikos or making sure the cat was put out. On the way to the port, he'd asked her to interpret for him with the police, but she'd refused. When he pleaded that Koutsikos had photographs of Kafandaris and Mazarakis, Eleni and Nikos shrugged.

"You're a fool. I told you to stay away from the police," Nikos had said. "They'll have circulated a photograph of you – top suspect in Dmitri's murder."

"Anybody tell you you're full of it?"

"Have it your way. You know best."

Could it be true? Of course not, they'd have arrested him by now. But…

On the boat, he tried to sit beside Eleni, but she took no part in his negotiations with a girl, who insisted on sitting beside her friend and her PlayStation. Nikos and Eleni had known Dmitri for much longer, but he was hurting too. He thought of St Panteleimon and the little flat they shared. Now everything had changed.

In the hustle disembarking at Piraeus, Duncan tried to reach Eleni, but she dived forward to get ahead of the kids. Then an implausibly blonde-haired crew member, a shoo-in for a bad guy part in a Bond movie, charged on board with a box on his shoulder. She had to wait. Duncan caught her up and took her hand. But once on shore, spotting Nikos – how had he got off the boat so quickly? – she shook free of Duncan's grasp

"Wait, Eleni, please wait," he implored her.

She had been crying again, but who for – Dmitri? The end of their tryst? For Nikos, for Greece, what?

"I can't think about anything now. I must see Dmitri's sister."

"Let me come with you."

"No," she said quickly, too quickly. "I'm sorry."

"I love you."

She closed her eyes. "You must go," and she turned away.

"Why? Where?" called Duncan. "When will I see you?"

She hurried towards Nikos waiting impatiently. They spoke, they kissed, and then she ran through the gates leading to a road several lanes wide, on which every driver seemed to be trying out for a racetrack. He peered through the railings, hoping she was safe.

Nikos gestured for him to follow, but Duncan turned away. Two men stepped in either side of him and one gripped his arm.

"Hey."

He was steered in Nikos' direction.

"Walk," came an order from his left.

"Why? Who are you?"

Silence.

Duncan swung with his free left arm and struck the talker's head. The man grunted and let go. But his colleague had an even tighter grip and enveloped him in a bear hug. Duncan lashed out with his feet and they both went down. Now the other one crashed in and pinioned Duncan to the ground.

He looked up to see Nikos. "What the hell's going on?"

"Do as the comrades tell you."

"Comrades?"

Nikos walked away.

Duncan was pulled to his feet, shouting, "Hey, don't just – Hey!"

The two 'comrades' gripped an arm each, and they walked Duncan to a dusty Toyota Corolla.

CHAPTER TWENTY-FIVE
NORTHERN ENGLAND 1998

A day after Duncan received his A-level results, Kathryn rang. She suggested a walk, where and when, and sent him a bus timetable. In case of bad weather, he was advised to wear walking boots and waterproof clothing. She would bring food, but if he wanted to add extra that would be alright. She spoke rapidly, as if she only had limited time.

Not just a suggestion, but a plan. Duncan was thrilled.
But what about the painting? He checked it again, but was still confused. Perhaps the artist would explain it.

Looking on a map, he discovered he was in for a route march. He looked through the outdoor pursuits shops for an impressive pair of hiking boots. Pat, surprised but pleased by his son's exam results, helped financially, and Duncan wore in the boots on training sessions in the park so A) they would not look brand new, and B) they would not chafe. Their first meeting had ended badly, and he was determined to minimise any risk of a repeat. This one had to go well. Call it paranoia, but the nearer he got to the rendezvous he couldn't shake off the lingering fear he'd been lured into a trap and Mrs Gifford was lurking.

But Kathryn was alone at the end of a wooden jetty jutting into a lake.

"Congratulations," she said.

"Well, it was hardly difficult. I just caught the bus, like you said."

"Not that, silly – your A-levels."

He wanted to kiss her.

"I was lucky, phew!" he said, mock-wiping his brow. "And the same for your exams – I thought you said you were only good at art."

She nodded shyly. Now he could kiss her, a passing brush of the cheek.

She looked him up and down. "I'm glad you've dressed for it."

"I'm just following orders, ma'am."

She laughed. A good audience.

She wore a silk scarf, the pattern perfectly complementing her hair; a dark cagoule; light-blue jeans; the last word in boots; and, on her back, she carried what seemed to Duncan a heavily packed rucksack. As they set off through the woods beside the lake, he confessed he was surprised he was there.

"Were you expecting something more challenging? It can easily be arranged," she smiled.

"No, no," he said. "I mean, being here with you. After the painting you sent me."

"Why?" she asked, a puzzled look on her face.

"Well," he raised his arms in the air. "I thought it was – a goodbye. Even more than that."

"Why?" It was turning into her favourite word.

"Well, it – it was a picture of your – the accident, and everything wasn't it?"

"Is that what you think?"

"Yes. Isn't it?"

"Could be."

"But it's yours. Don't you know? You painted it."

"It's yours now – I've done a different one for me."

"I see," he didn't.

"I can hear your mind whirring."

"It is. You see – oh. You sent me, of all people, a painting of your dad's death."

"But I didn't. I mean, it wasn't that. Not for me."

Duncan, in the middle of nowhere with the one girl in the world he wanted, was lost.

"Well, I don't know. My mother was in it wasn't she?"
Kathryn shook her head. "No." And then she said, "Well, alright, she might have been in your eyes, I accept that, but not for me, no. She wouldn't be."
Duncan wondered what the hell he had seen.

"It's an optimistic painting," she said. "That's why I did it."

"Really? Oh."

She looked teary. "God, if you can't see that."

Duncan cursed: upsetting her was to be avoided, and within minutes, here he was. "I'm sorry. We won't talk about it anymore."
She leant against a tree, bent forward, resting her hands on her thighs. "Did you see the bird? It was a bird in the sky."

"Your dad?"

"Yes, flying free." Now her tears came. "It wasn't about the accident; it was what happened afterwards, and he was ok."

"Oh."

"Stop saying 'oh'." She breathed in. "I wanted it to be about forgiveness." She held her arms out to him. "Can you – ?"
Duncan held her gently. She smelled of lemon and fitted snugly against his body.

"That's enough," she said, and pulled a tissue out of her jeans pocket.

"I'm so sick of crying."

He stood back. "It's good for you."

She blew her nose. "Too much of a good thing, then." She stuffed the tissue back into her pocket. "I'm going to run ahead, but you can catch me up."

Duncan let her go and then caught up with her at the edge of the woods.

She smiled. "You're a funny runner."

"Am I?"

"You lollop."

Duncan felt on his guard; she was setting him tests. He wanted to take her hand, but she was holding her rucksack by both straps. They crossed a road and set off up a stony lane. Warm, they paused to remove their jackets, which they stuffed into their rucksacks. Duncan offered to carry hers, but she would not think of it.

They reached the top of a rocky crag above a vast green carpet of ferns interrupted by lichen-stained boulders poking through. A single straggly tree disentangled from the crag and, as if pleading for help, clawed towards the sky. Duncan sympathised. After the art discussion, he decided any reference to the accident would come from Kathryn. It didn't take long.

"Have you seen your mother recently?"

"Yes."

She looked at him. More was required.

"She wants a divorce. She has a lover."

"What? In prison?"

Duncan shook his head. He realised he was tipping into dangerous territory. Malcolm Gifford would surely be alive if Beth hadn't seen Richard Patterson that day. Less said.

Hands on her hips, Kathryn stared hard into the distance. "So, she's alright then."

"I wouldn't say that."

"She's got something to look forward to, hasn't she? She'll get out; there he'll be, a shoulder to cry on. What's my mum got?"

"You."

She sat down on the rock. Duncan moved away.

"Where d'you think you're going?"

"Thought I'd give you some space."

"Liar. You just don't want your head bitten off."

He smiled and took off his rucksack.

"She's betrayed you with this lover."

"That's for the Connor side of things," said Duncan firmly. "I realise for you she's the Wicked Witch of the North, South, East and West, but she's still my mum."

Kathryn waggled her boots. "I don't think she's a witch."

He unzipped one of his rucksack pockets and pulled out a couple of Bounty bars in red wrappers. "It's a well-known fact that blue

Bounty bars outnumber the red ones." He held them up. "But it's also a well-known fact the red ones are far superior."

He lobbed one in Kathryn's direction. She let it drop beside her.

"You'd be no good at cricket."

"Don't try and get round me with chocolate."

"I wouldn't dream of it."

"It also happens to be a fact that I *much* prefer the blue ones."

"Throw it back then," he said, cupping his hands.

"Wicket keeper."

"So, you do know something."

"I know what a googly is too. Dad loved cricket."

She ripped off the wrapping and they both ate in silence. Whatever they talked about and however much Duncan tried to steer clear, there were elephant traps.

"Did your parents send you to a private school to get rid of you?"

Duncan laughed. "They could've, yeah. They probably did."

"Would you send your kids?"

"Never really thought about it. I wasn't there too long. Time off for good behaviour. No, there was a dip in the family finances, and, well – "

"So, you had to join the common herd."

He stood up. "I don't know about you, but I've got a walk to be getting on with."

She pulled on her rucksack, and followed him down a steep gulley between the crags. At the bottom, they passed some rock climbers practicing on the overhangs and crevices, black mats on the ground to break their falls.

"Isn't that cheating?" asked Kathryn.

"Only if you want to kill yourself," said one of the climbers. He was wearing a bandana round his head.

Another kicked away a mat and pointed to the top of the crag. "Go on then, you give it a go."

The others, wearing rugby jerseys with their collars turned up, laughed. Kathryn raised her middle finger and stalked off into the ferns. The climbers looked at Duncan. Each had the mocking sneer he recognised from the privately educated.

"Best of luck there," said Bandana, and the rest chortled.

"Yes," he said. "She's with me, not you."

Kathryn had picked up the pace hacking through the greenery, but the height of the ferns and the uneven terrain was a match for her. Duncan caught her up.

"Oh, I thought you'd stayed to play with your mates."

He laughed. "I'm getting it from both sides now."

"I don't like people laughing at me, 'specially pricks like them. Think they own the place."

"D'you want me to go in front?"

"No chance," she said, swiping away the triffid-like strands that whirled around their legs.

Kathryn's tenacity paid off. They burst through into an open patch of tufted grass and stones, but then after fifty yards the rough ground gave way to a bog. They nimbly skirted the patch and picked up a path._It led them onto a ridge that wound into a gulley about twenty feet wide, between two rock faces. The geography was as changeable as Kathryn's brittle mood. Halfway along she stopped.

"What's the matter?"

"There's something," she whispered.

A dead tree with shocked spindly branches poked out of one side of the rock. Duncan sensed they were being watched and half expected the climbers to sneak up behind them and shout 'boo!'.

But there was no one; not a sound.

"Can you feel it?" whispered Kathryn. "Something bad."

Duncan shivered.

"See."

They hurried towards a wood and when the ground allowed broke into a run. They clambered over a stone wall and sheltered safely in the trees.

"I think something frightening must have happened there," Kathryn said quietly. Duncan leaned in closely to hear her. "And the fear's stuck."

They stayed together. They had circled back towards the lake on the other side of the wood. They could hear distant shrieks from a group of bathers braving the cold waters.

Duncan put his arm around and thought of the road where her father died, and the beach at Dieppe.

"Lots of places are haunted," he said.

"Doesn't help me." Kathryn said and cuddled into Duncan. She looked up at him. "Makes me feel horny though."

She slipped from his grasp and wriggled out of her rucksack, which slipped to the ground.

"What did you say?"

"You heard."

She tugged at a knot on her rucksack, which came free, pulled out a rolled-up rug and flung it open. "Grab that end," she instructed.

"I don't remember this being in the schedule," he laughed.

Kathryn decided it would go best beneath the biggest tree. Duncan agreed the rug was better than the twig-covered ground, and the position was private.

"Come on, get your rucksack off."

But he had a problem. "Thing is, I hadn't presumed – "

"It's not true then that blokes think about sex every 30 seconds?" She knelt on the rug in front of him.

He laughed, "The point is I haven't brought – "

She produced a packet of condoms from a pocket in her rucksack.

"Will these do?"

He got rid of his rucksack and got down beside her. "You're very well organised," he said, cradling the packet in his hand.

A moment's hesitancy when noses might have collided, but Duncan inclined his head, and they kissed.

Then she pulled back and, holding his head between her hands whispered, "D'you mind I'm not a virgin?"

He shook his head. "Neither of us, then."

They kissed again, but once more Kathryn withdrew. "Please, can you go very slowly?"

He nodded, and she moved forward, but he stopped her. "Any more instructions?"

She grinned and kissed him. "You taste of chocolate."

"So do you."

They kissed again pressing their bodies into each other. Kathryn pulled at Duncan's belt while he tried to remove her jumper.

They broke apart.

"Easier if we do our own?" suggested Duncan.

Their clothes came off in a flurry, Duncan's plain black pants in contrast to Kathryn's flowery bra and knickers.

"You're so beautiful," he said.

She smiled.

He lowered his pants. She stretched towards him, and he folded her into his arms, kissing her lips, her face, her neck; his hands eagerly undoing her bra.

She stiffened and slumped back covering herself.

"I'm shy."

He stopped.

"I'm frightened you won't like them."

He held out his arms to her, and she curled into him, still covering her breasts. He kissed and stroked her, whispering how much he wanted her and if she wanted to keep her bra on that was alright with him. She kissed his chest and nipples one by one. As he lay back, she moved on top of him, her hand round his penis. He shuddered and for a moment feared he had come. Perhaps sensing this she let him go.

His hand slipped down towards her knickers, and he caressed her dampness through the cotton.

Kissing again, she allowed him to sit up and he pulled her knickers clear. He cupped her bush in his hand. He burrowed gently into her, but she let out a little cry. "Nails."

He stopped, but she took his wrist and guided him into a slower rhythm. Then, her eyes closed, she arched backwards, giving him full rein with his hand. Then she fell forward onto him, her fingers pressing into his flesh. They stayed still for a moment before Kathryn leant back and unhooked her bra.

Duncan held her breasts in wonder.

"They're perfect," he said softly, and Kathryn smiled and wrapped her arms around his head and pulled him onto them. Duncan kissing and sucking, Kathryn's hold tightening, they gasped in unison. Kathryn, focusing on Duncan's eyes, eased the condom on to him, and he gently got on top. Then he pushed into her and, feeling her open to him, plunged further.

"I love that," she whispered, and shook beneath him.

She held him tightly, restricting his movement. He grunted and she relaxed her hold. Now he established a rhythm, pulling out as far as he could and then going into the hilt. They smiled together, his breathing louder and louder. But then, worrying the end was close, he withdrew.

"Please," she said.

"I want it to last."

She nodded and he entered her again. She murmured, "My favourite."

His rush of excitement overwhelmed him.

Afterwards, they lay in silence on their fronts, his arm curled around her head.

"How long have you been thinking about that?" he asked.

"Since I phoned you. What about you?"

"Oh, way before that."

She laughed and slapped his bottom. "Then you should've been prepared." She rolled him over and got on top. "Who was your first?"

"All these questions – "

"Come on, come on," she said, pulling his ears.

"It was one of the serving maids at school."

She burst out laughing so much she rolled off him.

"What's so funny?"

"Classic," she said. "Posh schoolboy gets off with serving maid. It's like a Catherine Cookson book."

"There's a twist: she was Italian."

More disbelief. "Girls flown in. Remind me, is this the 20th century we're talking about?"

"Only just. It wasn't so funny, it was November and freezing cold."

She looked around. "Outside's your speciality."

"Woods, it seems."

She cuddled into him.

"I love your breasts." He licked her nipples. "Especially, when they stand to attention."

She laughed. "They're not soldiers."

An overpowering urge to sleep came over him and he closed his eyes.

"Hey," she said holding up the condoms. "I've brought a pack of these things, and I don't intend to stop."

Duncan opened his eyes and they both checked his flaccid penis.

"Maybe have something to eat first," he said.

But by the time she had opened her rucksack, Duncan was asleep.

When he awoke, bleary eyed, he found he was wrapped up in the rug.

"Snug as a bug in a rug," she said.

Kathryn, half-dressed, was sitting cross-legged beneath the big tree, a

Tupperware box open, tucking into watercress sandwiches with a side of tomato, and prawn cocktail crisps.

"Come on, sleepyhead," she said. "While you've been lazing around, I've crossed the Zambesi River and climbed the North Face of the Eiger."

"Dressed like that?" he said, throwing off the rug and swaying towards her, balls swinging. She pretended to be shocked. Duncan now assumed an ape-man pose.

"Argh, why do blokes think that's a good look?"

"I didn't hear you complaining before," he said, pulling a pack of peanuts out of his rucksack.

"I have a plan."

"Oh no, not one of your famous plans, Kathryn Gifford."

"Kathryn Louise Gifford, if you don't mind. What's yours? No, let me guess, there'll be half a dozen, so something like Duncan St John McIntosh O'Neill Bora-Bora Connor."

He laughed. "Haven't got one. Duncan Connor, pure and simple. See how deprived I am?"

"Poverty stricken," she said.

Once they had eaten, her famous plan was to forsake the rest of the walk and head to the lake for a swim.

"Skinny dipping," she grinned.

Kathryn lost her virginity after an end-of-term dance at school with a boy called Harry, who was leaving.

"Thoughtful going away present."

"If it had been a disaster, I wouldn't have to face him the next term."

Duncan shook his head. "You girls are so calculating."

"I did fancy him – sort of, but you know it was just to do it," She kissed him. "This was much better."

Kathryn took him in her mouth, but preferred he came inside her.

"Best day in the country I've ever had," Duncan said, entering her. Kathryn squealed.

"Is that a what d'youmacallit? A euphemism?" She slapped his back, "In the c-u-n-t-r-e-e."

"Yes, ok. Can we get on, please?"

Sadly not. The swimming party had come ashore. They were drunk and thrashed through the trees, three men and two women.

"They won't see us," whispered Kathryn.

But she was wrong. One of the women, rather than taking the path behind the wall with the others, was in the wood and heading straight for the couple.

"Peachy arse!" she slurred.

Below Duncan, Kathryn stiffened. He turned his head to see the woman in a bright yellow dress, a leather jacket slung around her shoulders and twirling a stick.

"Can anyone join in?" she asked.

And then, "Er, is that you, Kathy?"

Duncan knew she hated to be called that.

"Hello, Siobhan."

"Ooooh, so sorry," Siobhan giggled. Maybe sobriety had hit, but not tact. "Hey, I was dead sorry to hear about your dad."

"Dead sorry, yeah," replied Kathryn, but the point passed Siobhan by.

"Least they caught that bitch that did it."

Duncan prayed for her to just go. But she didn't.

"Look, thanks, Siobhan, would you mind…?"

"Oh yeah, don't mind me" she said and, picking up on the other swimmers' distant cackles, followed them. "Have fun."

Kathryn sat up and shook. Duncan collected her cagoule, which he put around her. She cuddled into him and cried. "What we're doing's wrong, isn't it?"

"No," he said, firmly. "She doesn't know who I am."

"I don't mean her. Us, we're wrong." Her face was puffy and raw with tears.

"No," he repeated. "And I'm the one who usually feels guilty about everything."

Holding her, he did not feel guilt, but at night, alone, lying awake, he wondered if it really was alright. Joined through a death – a horrible, cruel death – but what if that was all it was? The only thing they had in common. Would they wake up and look at each other one day and find there was nothing? No, please no. He had never felt a connection like this before. But he could not think about Kathryn, be with Kathryn, and even be inside Kathryn, without a whole lot of trouble landing on top of them. Like this. He didn't want to think about it.

Fuck that woman!

"Who was she?"

"Sort of a neighbour. Her mum knows mine."

"She won't say anything, will she?"

"No," said Kathryn. "Probably too drunk to remember."

"I doubt that."

"Well, that's it then." She pulled her clothes out of her rucksack. "We can't do this."

She was on her feet getting into jeans.

"Kathryn, we haven't done anything wrong."

"No?" she slipped on her top. Dressing seemed to underline her shame. But hurriedly packing away her nakedness, concealing herself from him, only made him want her more.

She sat down again. "It's like I'm betraying him." Her eyes searched Duncan's face for reassurance. "It's not, is it? Tell me it's not."

"How can it be?"

"I don't know. Ok, so it isn't."

He kissed her. The kiss developed, until Kathryn said, "Just kissing."

His hands beneath her top cupping her braless breasts, she made little gurgling noises, her nose, wrinkling. Each time with her he learnt more.

"I love being with you, Duncan," she whispered in his ear and kissed it. "And I never want us to stop."

She had been thinking the same things, asking the same questions, they were in the same place. There was no stopping them. The worst had happened.

Or so he thought.

CHAPTER TWENTY-SIX

As summer faded beneath September mists, university beckoned for Duncan. He and Kathryn met as often as possible. Kathryn badgered her friend Claudine to use her spare room while her parents were away. This worked until Claudine suddenly found a 'boyfriend'. Kathryn was convinced she'd made him up. Duncan went to work on Ray: a blanket and sofa cushions round his? But then one look at Ray produced a flat no from Kathryn: "Not with that trog and his mates at the keyhole."

Girls, Duncan groaned, were impossible.

He found the keys to his grandmother's bungalow. Perfect, but neither Ruth nor Pat must find out. While Kathryn had chosen life, her mother had slid into bitterness and pessimism. Pat, too, had sunk into a stupor of self-pity, his mother gone; his wife, who had brought shame on the family, was divorcing him; his son was nowhere to be seen.

Duncan suggested Ruth and Pat might be good for one another. Either they would climb out of the sinking ship together, or drown.

"Good luck with that," was Kathryn's reply. Parents were well off the agenda as they snuck off behind a locked door at Lynette Rankin's 17th birthday party.

The highlight of Duncan's university preparations was finding the best room in the college for Kathryn's visits.

"Our very own bed," she said, bouncing on it, and for the next 36 hours they barely left his room. The only interruptions were the cathedral bells clanging every quarter of an hour outside the window.

She gave him a series of her paintings. There was always the possibility he might be mistaken, but his favourite he took as a celebration of their first time in the wood. This, and some drawings in charcoal of them together, he kept private.

Kathryn re-hung two of them: "They catch the light better here." In return, inspired by his mother's 'library', he gave her novels by Anne Tyler and Elizabeth Taylor. She made him promise to eat properly and work hard.

"You sound like my mum," Duncan only just stopped himself from saying out loud. Kathryn carried an extra parcel home: a teddy bear from 'the girlfriend' she had been visiting for the weekend. Waving her off, Duncan was already counting the days until her return.

In a week, Duncan managed to attend one lecture and a seminar, so the report to his father, who had suddenly turned up, was positive.

"Can't a father take an interest?" said Pat.

Duncan had known; the student next door had been leaving as he strolled into the college from several games of pool.

"There's a shifty looking cove outside your door," Rick had grinned, amused by Duncan's startled reaction. Duncan had been vague about his family, never once mentioning his mother. He was anxious when home life intruded.

They called in at the Student Union for a bite to eat and, to Duncan's relief, bumped into a new friend: Nevin from Aberdeen, whose speciality was Military History. He left them to it and imagined Kathryn reading his letter as dozens – well, maybe one or two girls – swooped: "Ooh, ooh, a letter from the cool university boyfriend, read it out." Or, more likely, he pictured her in a comfortable chair, in a quiet corner, her legs tucked under her, with a big smile, poring over his ardent prose.

Pat decided the cathedral was top of the list for the afternoon. They strolled round the vast Norman building, seeing from the inside the dazzling Rose Window that overlooked Duncan's room. Pat enjoyed the local saint's reputed misogyny: a line drawn at the back of the cathedral was as far as women could tread.

"So, I should think," he said, stoutly.

"Come on, Dad, he was well dead by the time this place was built."

"Well dead? What sort of slovenly language is that for an undergraduate?"

The saint had remarkable powers of resurrection. During the war, and – wouldn't you know it, Pat did – as the Luftwaffe bombers were flying up the river towards the cathedral, it was the man in the grave, dead for over a thousand years, who so the story went produced a sudden thick mist. The Germans lost their way and missed their target.

Saint - one; Luftwaffe - nil.

While Pat, from the top of the highest tower, admired the autumn sunlight casting a rich glow over the city, Duncan was struck by a cluster of people in dark blue uniforms walking round a yard. He was staring into the middle of the gaol during the prisoners' break. He pointed them out to his father.

"Pah!" shouted Pat and retreated down the tower steps.

"You can't ignore it."

"I just don't like it in my face."

"You're in denial. Why don't you go and see her?"

"Because she doesn't want me to. She's made that very clear."

"I don't think that's really true, Dad," said Duncan, crossing his fingers behind his back.

Pat stopped and grabbed him by the arm. "You don't know what you're talking about. Bloody well shut up."

"No, I won't. She is my mother."

"Right," Pat looked at his wristwatch. "Smarten yourself up. 7.30 on the dot." He marched out of the cathedral throwing a last word into the breeze: "And consider this conversation closed."

Pat's treat of a slap-up meal at a restaurant on the city outskirts was an excuse for a pep talk. His son's demeanour had disappointed Pat.

"I don't want you waking up in ten years' time saying, 'Damn and blast it, I missed an opportunity there.'"

"Hang on, I've only just got here."

Pat pointed a fork at Duncan, "You've a tendency to glide, which soon turns into a slide, and what I want is graft, so get stuck in."

Duncan couldn't help but grin at the rhyme and metre of his father's lines, which surely Pat hadn't meant to do, and which undermined his point. As did the meat slipping off the end of his fork and splashing into his gravy. But he was undeterred.

"There are plenty of people who'd give their right arm to be at a university like this."

"I earned my place, Dad."

"They're like schools with ashtrays. It's easy to lose focus," he paused.

"Any girls taken your eye?"

"No."

"Wouldn't be surprising. I mean to say, you are nearing your peak of potency."

He hated it when his father talked in this chummy way.

A waitress interrupted to ask if everything was alright.

"Actually, no, it isn't," said Duncan, standing up. "My dad's a complete twat, and I'm hoping you've got people on alert for this sort of emergency. Please take him away as soon as possible. And see what you can do about barring him from entering this city for the next three years."

"Of course, sir, we do indeed have arrangements for just this kind of thing," said the waitress and she beckoned to a couple of figures in white coats…

Instead, Duncan murmured, "Yes, thanks."

Pat, leering at the waitress, ordered more wine. Knowing the order of service, Duncan's spirits sank. A drunken anti-Beth rant evolving into a dismissal of all women, followed by a tonne of Richard Patterson hatred, who Pat happened to know had the smallest penis of anyone on the coast. Finally, a war story; a cab ride back to his hotel; and a lachrymose farewell in front of sniggering receptionists who would be only too happy to escort the drunkard up to his room. Not.

"Here's twenty-five quid…"

"Oh, in that case, certainly sir, thank you sir," said the receptionist, smartening up.

That would account for half the cash Pat had slipped him earlier.

Duncan ignored the war story until he realised it was the one his grandmother had wanted to tell him about his father's amorous adventures.

Pat had gone to Halifax in Nova Scotia after a girl. One day he was waiting for her beside a memorial that listed the Nova Scotians who had died at Dieppe. He remembered Hannah's young soldier with the battle in his eyes at Waterloo Station. Had that soldier survived the war? Could he be here, in the café opposite, in that office block, perhaps? Was he still smoking? Or gripped by survivor guilt, had he blown his brains out? Pat would never know, but time had shifted, distances shortened, bringing him, the soldier, Hannah, and the memorial together. The Dieppe raid had been the Canadian soldier's first and only time abroad. Now that Pat knew where they had come from, he had to see where they died. As the rain fell, he memorised their names, and vowed he would look them up. The many pilgrimages to the stony beach and the cemetery in Normandy began.

As his father wiped away a teary eye, Duncan thought this was the best of him: he would have liked him in those days.

Something was wrong. Instead of bounding towards him, Kathryn stood waiting. Was Ruth Gifford getting off the coach behind her? No, Kathryn had her period and warned him she was on a short leash. They shared a sandwich, though Kathryn only nibbled. But she did brighten up, Duncan putting it down to his selfless understanding.

She suggested a film. Not what he had in mind. Then she insisted on catching the 6.30 coach home. This was early. Her choices had all the hallmarks of an escape route. His plan had been for a drink and a meal and, until then, to go over to his room. Not so. 'The Big Lebowski'. He could go with that. In the cinema, Duncan put his arm around Kathryn, and they snuggled together.

"That is the best, the very best film I have ever seen, dude," said Duncan, laughing as they bowled into the street. Kathryn agreed. Back on track, he steered her hopefully towards a restaurant he had earmarked earlier.

"I told you, I can't," she said.

"I'm going to treat you – "

"Sorry." A car beeped, and Duncan, in the road, stepped back on to the pavement. Passersby hurried between them. This was awkward.

Kathryn checked the time. "Actually, if I'm quick I could get the 5 o'clock."

"Not even a drink?" sulked Duncan. The mood she was in, the period must be a bad one. Unfortunately, his thought was out loud.

"Just be thankful. Blokes couldn't cope."

"Yeah, course, it's my fault."

"Pathetic," said Kathryn, "I'll say goodbye now."

"Hold on. Let me come with you."

But she walked on.

"Kathryn, what's happened?"

Then she was out of sight.

Bewildered, he passed the cinema they had left so happily minutes before. Outside the restaurant, he watched a young couple, arm in arm, going in. It was over, he concluded, he had been dumped. But why?

As he made for his favourite pub and downed the first of many pints, he did not know Kathryn had cried all the way home.

But days later:

Dear Duncan,

I'm sorry for being such a cow on Saturday, but I was very upset.
I don't think we can go on seeing each other.
I wanted to tell you, but I didn't have the courage. I
know you're just starting out at university, which will be quite a
challenge for you, so it's for the best if you begin with a clean slate.
I know I'm going to find the Sixth form very challenging too.
The gap between university and school is too great really, and when
you think of everything that has gone on… well, it's the right thing.
I know we had a great time, and I shall always ~~treasure~~ remember it.
Please don't think too badly of me.

Kathryn

P.S. 'THE (lovely) BIG L' was a great way to go out. And please don't reply, I do mean it.

He stared at Kathryn's drawing of them in the wood. He fished out her more intimate sketches, held them in his hands, put them back and got them out again. He'd loved them, so delicate and expressive of their feelings for each other, but now he didn't recognise them, or he didn't want to. Could he bear to even look at them? Kathryn was right, wasn't she? He was out in the world, a student, carefree, and she was just a schoolgirl. She may have been, she was… but she'd drawn these pictures with an intensity and such maturity. Something didn't fit.

Duncan let them slip out of his hands and read the letter again. He read it so many times he could tell her biro point pressure on every letter of each word. But it didn't sound like Kathryn. If she'd found someone else, some spotty, nerdy, sixth-form whizz, she'd have said so. That crossed-out word: 'remember' for 'treasure'. 'Well, 'treasure' sounded adult, even a grandmother word, and reducing the change to 'remember' was code for 'I DON'T MEAN ANY OF THIS, I'M BEING FORCED TO WRITE IT!'.

No, the hand of Ruth Gifford was all over it.

Her mother must have dictated, edited, and even frog-marched Kathryn, drenched in tears, to the post box. But how had Ruth Gifford found out? Had the teddy bear alibi fallen through? Or did Siobhan from the lake sneak round? He could imagine the scene…

"So sorry to intrude, Ruth, I know you've had so much trouble, but I just wondered how old Kathryn is?"

"Sixteen, why?"

"Oh, really, sixteen. Oh right, I see, that's alright."

"What's alright, Siobhan? Have you got something to tell me?"

Siobhan, backing away, "Well, it's not really any of my business."

"If it's about my daughter it's very much my business. What's happened?"

And out would tumble the lurid details, Siobhan tidying up her own part.

Door slamming, footsteps down the hall…

"KATHRYN!"

Duncan was having none of it.

CHAPTER TWENTY-SEVEN

His coach crawled. Major road works from now until Christmas, expect delays. His original plan was to surprise Kathryn at the school gates. But already he was too late for that. Probably better. Too public. That left a home visit, which risked Mrs Gifford and the outbreak of World War Three. Unless she was out. They would be alone. Perfect. However, in Malcolm's house, it would feel like trespassing. He wobbled.

He read Kathryn's letter again, the paper heavily creased. Once more, he detected the evidence it was written under duress. What else could *'The [lovely] Big L'* mean but a plea to 'COME AND GET ME'? Emboldened, he was on his way, but his guts played havoc.

It was twilight when he reached the detached house in the middle of a smart crescent. Answer, Kathryn, please, and they'd enjoy a big tearful reconciliation on the doorstep: hugs, kisses, gasps of 'I knew you'd come', neighbours' curtains drawn back, people spilling into the crescent, applauding, cheering. Everyone loves a love story.

"Hello Mrs Gifford, I'd like to talk to Kathryn please."

The door slammed shut in his face.

Duncan pressed his finger on the doorbell and kept it there.

The door opened again. Mrs Gifford was purple. "GO AWAY!"

"I'm asking you politely – "

The door slammed shut once more.

Duncan bent down and looked through the letterbox. The hallway was dark, but a light shone at the top of the stairs, and he glimpsed a shadow.

Kathryn.

He pressed the doorbell again.

The door flung open this time, but Mrs Gifford was so wound up she could barely speak.

"I've called the police," she said, and shut the door.

Duncan opened the letterbox. "Kathryn, please, I don't understand what's going on. Will you come and talk to me?"

Nothing.

"I'm going round to the back, could you meet me there?"

A gravel pathway between the house and the garage led Duncan into a small garden, where a cherry tree stood in the middle of a lawn. At the back, a wooden fence ran in front of a trimmed high hedge, separating the Giffords from their neighbours behind. There was a garden shed, painted dark blue, and Duncan was struck by how everything was neat and ordered. Unlike the Connors'.

The kitchen light went off. He looked in through the window. Then

Kathryn appeared in the hall.

Duncan's heart leapt. "Hello!"

Kathryn remained where she was.

"Can you open the door?"

But Kathryn shook her head.

"What's the matter? Please come to the door."

She turned and, back lit by the hall light, her hair looked lank: she was worn out. Even on Saturday she'd had more spark.

"Is it your mum?"

She left suddenly, and the light went on. Mrs Gifford leant against the worktop, arms folded, a picture of relaxed triumph.

"Mrs Gifford – "

A rushing sound behind him alerted Duncan, but before he could defend himself, a firm hand gripped his arm, another circled his waist, He was pulled roughly away from the window.

"Hey!"

Duncan was thrown against the cherry tree, facing two uniformed policemen. Mrs Gifford watched from the kitchen window.

"Turn around and spread your legs."

One forced him to face the tree and kicked his legs apart. Then hands ran roughly up and down his body, ending with a sharp knee in the groin.

Duncan doubled up in pain.

"Stand up."

"You've just – " but he could hardly breathe.

They grabbed him again and hauled him upright.

"Do as you're fucking told," said the policeman, standing close enough for Duncan to know he'd been chewing gum.

Duncan could just stand. "You can't do that."

"Perving on schoolgirls, bastard, we can do what we like."

Mrs Gifford was still in the window.

"Is that what she told you?"

Chewing Gum acknowledged Mrs Gifford.

The other policeman laughed. "She's old enough to be your mother."

Chewing Gum dragged Duncan away from the tree. His colleague approached Mrs Gifford, who opened the window.

"Ask her why she's holding her daughter prisoner," shouted Duncan.

Chewing Gum's foot clipped Duncan's heels and he sprawled on the grass, his head inches from the concrete path. The policeman popped another piece of gum into his mouth, squatted at Duncan's level.

"Dear me, that's a red card. What you going to do, send me off?" he play-acted. "Naughty, Mr Policeman." He slapped himself on his hand.

Chewing Gum hauled him to his feet. "Address?"

"Why? What for? I haven't done anything wrong."

"Right now, you're trespassing, Even more serious, you're getting on my tits," Chewing Gum said, rising menace in his voice.

Duncan gave an address: Hannah's.

"Occupation?"

"I'm a student."

Chewing Gum spat, "Stuuuuuuuuudunt," he said. "Move."

As Duncan walked down the gravel path, a curtain-twitching epidemic broke out in the crescent.

"Go on, give your audience a bow."

The other policeman followed rapidly.

"Hey, Ryan, this perve's a student." Distaste was once more reflected in exaggerating the word.

Duncan had Ryan down as the 'good cop', but there was a disturbing intensity about him now. He was staring hard at Duncan.

"And that's not all he is," said Ryan. Then he opened the back door of the police car.

"Where are you taking me?"

"We'll call it giving you a lift," said Ryan, still staring.

"I don't want a lift, thanks very much."

In an upstairs window, Duncan glimpsed Kathryn. "Kathryn, please, stop this, tell them – "

Without looking down, she closed the curtains.

"Kathryn!" he shouted.

Chewing Gum sneered and marched him towards the car. "Too late. Your little piece of beaver's going beddie-byes; probably got a man up there to do the job."

"Get in," said Ryan, opening the back door.

Duncan reluctantly did, and Chewing Gum shuffled in beside him. He looked back at the house: all the curtains were shut. He was desolate. And then, with twilight darkening into night, things got much worse.

Ryan, driving fast, told Mrs Gifford's version of the Giffords and the Connors as if it was a children's story.

"And then guess what happened…?" He encouraged Chewing Gum to perform the chorus: "Tell me, tell me…" and "No, really?" with faux horrified expressions.

"D'you know what?"

"What?"

"I 'm going to find out what prison the bitch is in and I'm going round there – "

"Yeah – "

"And I'll – "

"Go on, what?"

" – tear her another arsehole!" roared Chewing Gum into Duncan's face.

There was silence. Perhaps their hideous fantasies had even surprised them.

"There's more," said Ryan.

"More?"

"This arse-wipe's far fucking worse."

"Far worse?"

D'you know what else the Mrs Woman told me?"

"What?"

"She told me," Ryan spoke very slowly. "This cunt – this cunt sitting right next to you – this cunt fucked her fucking daughter."

Chewing Gum looked at Duncan. "No. Really? Fancy that, you dirty fucking, bastard."

"Yeah," Ryan made slurping noises. "What about that?"

"What a nasty fucker you are!" said Chewing Gum, forcing Duncan's arm up his back.

"Let go."

"Say please."

Duncan resisted, but a further excruciatingly painful twist forced it out of him.

"D'you know what I think?" said Ryan looking in the driving mirror.

"What's that?"

"This fucking student needs teaching a fucking lesson."

"Yeah, fucking right, he does. He fucking needs a fucking good fucking."

Ryan swung the car off the motorway and up a slip road.

"Where are we going?" asked Duncan.

"What'd he say?" asked Ryan.

"He wants to know where we're going."

"Tell him he's going to hell."

Duncan was already in hell, and these two were Satan's little helpers.

"Hell," said Chewing Gum in Duncan's ear. "And he should know, 'cos he's the driver."

"Yeah, I'm the driver," insisted Ryan. "What am I? I'm the fucking driver."

Duncan's brain was churning. Had Ruth Gifford called in her private cavalry? But where would she come across these two? They couldn't be police, surely? Could they? They were in the correct uniform, as far as he could tell, and the car – could that be faked?

The boil of frustration in Duncan's stomach at the Giffords had morphed into rocketing fear. Was this really happening? Was he heading for a night in the cells? Or had he been caught up in some macabre gameshow when a grinning presenter would step out in front of the car and say, 'Duncan Connor, you've been had?'

But now a new worry: Ryan turned off the minor road down a bumpy lane.

CHAPTER TWENTY-EIGHT

"You're not really police, are you?"

Ryan repeated at screaming level, "WHAT AM I, STUDENT FUCK?"

"The driver," whispered Duncan.

"What did he say?"

"He said," grinned Chewing Gum, "– and wait 'til you hear this – in his humble opinion, Ryan, he said you're a bit of a cock-sucking twat."

"Did he say that?"

"Yes, my mate, I'm very much afraid he did."

Ryan accelerated on the uneven surface. Trees flashed by. Duncan glimpsed a bend ahead. Dropping a gear, Ryan threw the car into a hard slide, shouting, "I'm the fucking driver!"

Duncan, looking forward, could see his angle was wrong, "Watch out!"

It was as though the trees had leaped in front of them. Ryan slammed on the brakes. Unable to stop himself, Duncan lurched forward, crashing his forehead into the back of Ryan's head. Aided by the brakes, Ryan nosedived into the steering wheel and the horn blared out.

The car crunched to a standstill.

Chewing Gum jeered, "Heed the ball, fucker."

Duncan felt as though his skull was splitting in two. The intense pain made him nauseous.

"Hey mate, that's a good one." Chewing Gum was still laughing, but Ryan was motionless.

Chewing Gum jumped out of the car, leaving his door open. He hauled Ryan off the steering wheel and sat him upright. The horn stopped. Ryan's nose was mashed, blood poured from his nostrils. Chewing Gum slapped him round the face and, now panicky, pleaded, "Come on, baby, wake up for me."

Duncan struggled out into the cold night. The air revived him, his muzzy vision clearing. He could hear the traffic rumbling down the distant motorway.

He took a step back when Chewing Gum spun him round and spat in his face, "You could've fucking killed him."

Duncan wiped away the spit and smiled.

"You think it's funny?"

His head still grinding itself back together, Duncan faced his opponent. Spotlit by the car headlights, he was back in the boxing ring. Only the referee and his supporters were missing, but you can't have everything.

"I do think it's fucking funny."

Chewing Gum threw a punch, but Duncan stepped out of range. The policeman lost his balance and his fist rammed into the side panel between the car's windscreen and passenger door. On either side, his fist would have gone through the glass. He yelled in pain, but tried again, this time swinging round with his left. Duncan ducked. Then, loading all his built-up fear and venom into the punch, he thundered his fist into Chewing Gum's solar plexus. A volley of saliva and gum issued from the man's mouth, and he doubled over. Duncan followed swiftly with an uppercut – his favourite – to his chin, which threw the policeman back against the car, and so provided a perfect target below. Duncan pulled his right foot back and smashed a free kick into Chewing Gum's groin.

With a throat rasping cry, the bully slithered to the ground and vomited. Then… nothing.

"GET UP BASTARD, GET UP!"

Still nothing.

Duncan grabbed him by the lapels and hauled him up against the car. Chewing Gum's eyes flickered briefly and then closed. Duncan let go, and the man slumped to the ground. He tore the notebook out of the policeman's pocket, unhooked his radio and, taking a run-up, threw them all as far as he could into the darkness of the woods.

Duncan, catching his breath, stood over the recumbent body. He undid his trousers and urinated on Chewing Gum, the relief flowing as freely as his piss.

He looked up. Ryan stared at him from the car.

"What's happening?" he asked.

Duncan zipped himself up.

Ryan's face was a corrugated mess, blood still coursed from his nose.

"What's happening?" he repeated in automaton mode.

Duncan told him to move over. Ryan tried to focus and then, dripping a trail of blood, sunk into the passenger seat.

Duncan returned to the stinking Chewing Gum, a revolting combination of vomit and urine, and bent down as far as he needed to hear him breathing. He grabbed him by his shoes and pulled him across the lane into a muddy ditch.

Back in the car, he switched on the ignition and reversed. Slowly, in the headlights, Chewing Gum's body came into view, but he was moving. Like the Creature from the Black Lagoon, he was trying to get to his feet. In case Ryan saw him, Duncan dimmed the headlights and sped backwards fast.

"It hurts," said Ryan. "It well hurts."

Adrenalin was wearing thin, Duncan's knuckles had swollen, and slivers of pain sharked through his head. They hit the road. Ryan sat up and did his best to look behind, but soon gave up.

"You know what?" he said. "You can't half be a prick at times."

"Take a look at yourself, arsehole," said Duncan, checking in the rear-view mirror. Then, slipping the car onto the motorway, he put his foot down.

Ryan pulled down the windscreen flap in front of him and looked in the little mirror.

"Suits you," said Duncan.

Ryan scrabbled through the glove box and pulled out a packet of Kleenex. He tried in vain to stop the blood and whimpered, "My nose is broken."

"Probably."

"Bastard." Ryan adjusted the little mirror to the left and then the right.

"Where is he?"

"Who?"

"That guy… That guy who isn't there."

"He's gone now." said Duncan.

"Gone where?"

"You killed him."

"I – what?"

Duncan laughed. "How many more times, prick? You killed him."

Ryan stared in the mirror. "I killed him?"

"Put up a fight, didn't he?"

Ryan touched his nose and winced.

The city outskirts loomed into view: just a few more minutes.

"I never did… you're lying."

"Don't ever talk to me like that." Duncan demanded.

Ryan sniffled, and then tears flowed, mingling with blood.

"You've got to help me… Please, please help me." He grasped Duncan's arm, who pulled it away, and then smashed his elbow back into Ryan's face.

The policeman's head slammed against the door, and he was silent. At a crossroads, Duncan hit a red light. Facing him, another police car arrived at the back of a two-car queue. Suddenly, the other police car shot into reverse, then, sirens blaring, leapfrogged the cars in front and roared forward. Duncan lowered his face while, at a furious lick, the police car took a turning to the left.

"Wah," said Ryan, and a dollop of blood fell out of his mouth. The light turned green, and Duncan accelerated. Ryan spat and stared hard, again.

"Who are you?"

Had the elbow punch brought him to his senses?

"Who d'you think I am?"

"I don't know, that's why I'm asking."

"I'm your mate, and I'm taking you to hospital."

Duncan checked in the rear-view mirror for the other police car turning and following, but there was no sign.

"What's your name?"

It was like being accosted by a drunk, but Ryan's unpredictability had Duncan on edge. "Mickey Mouse."

"Tell me." He was working with the Kleenex, the few tissues left. His face, already smeared in blood, mucous and tears, now had a vivid bruise on the cheekbone.

"And you're Pinocchio."

Duncan stopped the car fifty yards from the A&E entrance.

"You can walk from here." He pointed at a nurse lighting a cigarette.

Ryan squinted through the window.

"Come on," said Duncan, took the key out of the ignition and opened the door. Ryan remained in his seat, holding up his hands. He said something.

"What?"

"I want you to…" but his mouth filled with blood.

"Get out of the car," said Duncan.

Ryan, his hands in the air "Go on, please, I'm asking you to – "

Duncan got out. Conveniently, he had parked close to a drain. He dropped the ignition key and heard it tinkle in the water below.

He opened Ryan's door and, zombie-like, the policeman slumped out. Duncan held him under his arms and hoisted him out of the car. He stood him upright.

"Walk!" Ryan edged his way along the pavement. "Keep going." Duncan couldn't resist. He kicked Ryan so hard his feet took off from the ground and, unable to shield his fall, he crunched onto the pavement. The nurse and another hospital worker came running.

Duncan ran too, hard and fast through empty suburban streets, his lungs fit to burst.

He looked behind him. No one was chasing. He slowed down. It was so quiet he feared the residents could hear his pounding heart. He rested on a bench overlooking an allotment. The sounds of a party nearby floated on the night air. His head ached; he wanted home, his bed, normality.

What was that?

In the bathroom mirror, the lump on his forehead shone, his hands shook, and tears fell. But it wasn't all bad. Carson, Hetherington, Williamson, Latimer, and Caldwell, he'd beaten every one of them, but tonight they could take a bow – and the captain of boxing. Without them he couldn't have done it. He'd acted in self-defence, and those demonic two had got what they deserved. Hadn't they? But he hadn't stopped there: he'd urinated on the unconscious and assaulted the wounded. The surprise discovery of his boxing skills had been trumped by something darker. His abilities were not, as he had once reassured himself, confined to the ring or the Marquis of Queensberry rules. Pat had told him how soldiers immune to constraint shot prisoners in cold blood, mutilated their bodies and driven by bloodlust, went on killing sprees.

Duncan made excuses, reiterating that it was Carson, who had thrown the first punch and started it; so, had Chewing Gum and Ryan. They made him do it. He resented them, and Mrs Gifford. She had to take her share of the blame. What would that pair have done to him? It didn't bear thinking about. They would have shown no mercy. And Kathryn, what would she make of it all? Questions, questions: they haunted him. But mainly, the ones he'd asked himself that night in the school dormitory, what was he capable of, and could he trust himself to stop?

Downstairs the front door opened. He crept onto the landing, expecting to see his father climbing the stairs. But he wasn't. Another noise… Ryan? And Chewing Gum, but how…? Duncan's imagination hit overdrive, when a woman's voice lilted upwards, and he heard his father's laugh. Pat had found someone, good news. He headed softly down the stairs. He was sorry to break up his father's evening, but he needed his assurance everything would be alright. The state he was in, surely Pat would believe him. He felt like a child again, depending on his parents to sort out the bullies.

The kitchen, the site of many a Connor family drama. The same place he had hovered while his mother confessed her affair. The door was ajar. Then a side light offered Duncan a view of Pat leaning backwards against a work top, his trousers round his ankles, while a young woman kneeling in front of him worked hungrily on his engorged penis.

On the list of things not to see, this was in the top three. Sudden and unexpected, just like the police attack. Only Pat seeing him in the doorway would make matters worse. Duncan returned to the bathroom, quietly tidied up, removing anything that could give him away.

Then he left, briefly stopping to pick up a card from the floor. Mandy, wearing next to nothing, advertised her contact details beneath garish red letters: 'High Life Escorts'. So… he put the card down on the hall table.

He couldn't work out his reaction; impossible while the image of Pat and Mandy was so ingrained. Who was he to judge? His father could do what he wanted, but oh, how he wished he had not seen him.

CHAPTER TWENTY-NINE
GREECE 2010

He took several hardback Harry Potter books off the shelf, weighing each one. Then he hurled them one after the other at the window. The first crashed to the floor, and the next, but the one after that did the job. Glass everywhere.

He shouted through the jagged gap, "I'VE BEEN KIDNAPPED! SOMEBODY PLEASE HELP!"

Sorehead dragged him back. Duncan fought hard, but when the Shopper joined in, threatening him with a shard of glass, the game was up.

"Harry Potter fans, then?" he said, captive in an armchair.

It had taken fifteen minute's driving in the Corolla, which had seen better days, from Piraeus port. Duncan spotted some landmarks more than once, and presumed they had gone round in circles. Why? He had thought of recommending a taverna he knew and catching the floor show. Instead, he demanded to know what was going on and why he had been taken, but the two goons, whom he'd nicknamed the Shopper and Sorehead, had no English, or pretended not to. When he tried to phone Eleni, his mobile was confiscated.

The flat, ten floors up in an apartment block, was bigger than Dmitri's and, compared to Beanie's, luxurious, but it was a serious step down from the Caldwell's. Two comfortable armchairs in the lounge; three chairs for the dining table, with a fruit bowl – satsumas – and a long low sofa. Shelves up to the ceiling, stacked with books.

The Shopper, continually on his cell phone, popped out. Sorehead, after spending time in the bathroom on repairs to Duncan's punch, made undrinkable thick, black coffee.

"I hope it hurts," said Duncan, pointedly splitting open a satsuma. "I don't like being kidnapped."

Sorehead slurped his coffee.

The Shopper returned with milk – with which Duncan swamped his sludge-filled cup –, bottles of mineral water, croissants, bread, feta, butter, jam, and chips. They ate and drank in silence, the Shopper eating most of the chips.

Later, he was bundled into the back of the Corolla. The goons were excitable, yapping and laughing all the way. Their destination was an empty industrial block. Through the lift window, he watched as they zipped past floors of uprooted clumps of machinery. At the top, they picked their way through dusty rooms stacked with plastic chairs – once, Duncan assumed, management offices.

He was shown into a small, curtained room, where a woman in a see-through negligee and scrappy lingerie lay on a mattress. In the lamplight, it was difficult to guess her age, but her face was scarred. From behind the door, the goons sniggered. Duncan turned to leave, but she leapt up and tried to kiss him. He backed away. She sat down on the mattress, coyly patting the spot beside her.

This time he left. Sorehead took his place.

Next door, he pulled down a plastic chair and sat on it.

"She's ill," said Duncan. "It's my guess she needs food."

The Shopper, lying on a sofa, laughed.

"I'm telling you, get her something."

Now he yawned.

Sounds of a scuffle came through the wall and then a shout. Next, the woman screamed.

Duncan rushed to the door, but the Shopper caught him and pushed him back. He fell over the sofa. The noise from the room escalated. But before Duncan could get up, the Shopper was on him, kicking and shouting. Sorehead, in his underpants, ran in and the two of them dragged Duncan across the room and handcuffed him to a radiator.

The woman appeared in the doorway.

"Run," shouted Duncan. "GO!"

Too late. Sorehead stopped her and took her back next door. The Shopper joined them.

Duncan cursed, then listened helplessly to the woman's sobs as they raped her. With each of her desperate cries, he twisted, turned, and kicked trying to free himself. He felt something crack: a bone in his wrist, perhaps, had succumbed to the pressure of the handcuffs, but no. Something in his outer shell, the protective layer that guards us from thinking the worst.

Once that goes, all the snakes in the Garden of Eden slither through the gap, and the worst is not only imaginable, but it happens – right then, next door. As the woman's sobs reduced to whimpers, the tune, 'Three Blind Mice' played in Duncan's head. He shouted out, less in the forlorn hope of shaming the rapists, but more that someone might hear. Just as in the alleyway where the American begged Nikos for mercy Duncan was trapped, an unwilling witness to degradation. Andrew Cunningham, the boy in the music room bent over the back of the teacher's chair, cried for help. But no one dared, not Duncan, none of them. How could they? They were only children. Then they were instructed to sing.

Past or present what use was he? His pain was nothing to the victim's.

Hopelessly, he rattled the handcuffs again.

Then a long silence.

"Hey!" he shouted. "Hey!"

Footsteps, water running. The door opened and Sorehead came in. His face was scratched, and his lip was bleeding.

"Fully deserved," said Duncan acidly.

Next came the Shopper, also scratched, but grinning.

They unhooked Duncan from the radiator, but kept the handcuffs on.

"Where is she?"

Sorehead shrugged.

"What have you done with her?"

The Shopper put his hands together and mimed sleep. Then they both returned to the little room, locking the door behind them.

"Arseholes," shouted Duncan.

He edged over to the sofa and sat down, learning how difficult moving around was in handcuffs. He listened but heard nothing. Through the window, he looked up at the sky. Closing his eyes, he imagined he was floating high above, way up beyond the clouds. Far from this. He thought of Sam Shepard as Chuck Yeager, flying through acres of clear blue space and breaking the sound barrier in Phil Kaufman's film 'The Right Stuff'. Beanie was the Kaufman fan. A film they'd both seen. They'd talk about it together, but not now, no longer. No more comfort from there. How far and low had he sunk from those high notes on the island? In his mind's eye, he saw the poor woman, could hear her cries. He shook his head as if to try and free himself, but there was no escape. Would they always be with him now, and repeat like 'Three Blind Mice'?

CHAPTER THIRTY

Horta and beetroot, followed by beef stifado and white or red wine. While Sorehead and the Shopper tucked in, Duncan stared at his plate, still unable to get the woman out of his mind. After some hours, his kidnappers had returned, taken off his handcuffs, driven him on another tour, and ended up in a taverna.

"After rape, eat, is that the idea?"

Sorehead shrugged and returned to shovelling in his food. Duncan picked up his plate and cutlery and stood up. Sorehead, his mouth full, scrambled to his feet. Duncan sat down at another table. Sorehead wrenched his napkin from his collar and headed for the toilets. The Shopper pointed his knife at Duncan, who ignored him. He looked around at the scattered diners. Athenians passed the window in a world he recognised, but which was out of reach. Two women entered, one going straight to the chef at the open oven. The other woman sat down at a table next to Duncan's, and he stared into the eyes of Andrea Koutsikos.

He could not believe his luck. He introduced himself, but something wasn't right. She was pale, her hands clung to the edge of the table. Didn't she recognise him?

The Shopper watched them warily.

"You showed me some photographs, remember, Kafandaris and Mazarakis, they are the people who murdered Dmitri Hajdari – "

Andrea took a deep breath. "No one will arrest them."

Her companion hurried over and took her hand. "I don't know who you are, but please do not disturb my sister."

Sorehead returned and spoke to the Shopper.

"There was no chance for me; I had to leave." Andrea whispered.

"Terrible things happened, but there is no justice. Don't trust the police."

By now he was tired of hearing it, the Nikos refrain.

Sorehead and the Shopper picked up their plates and wine and took seats at Duncan's table. Sorehead spoke in Greek to the Koutsikos sisters.

Duncan interrupted him, "Whatever these bastards say, they're rapists and they've kidnapped me."

Andrea's sister looked astonished, and then at Andrea and asked.

"Seriously?"

"Ask them."

In Greek, she did. Sorehead and the Shopper both laughed.

Under the table, the Shopper tried to trap Duncan's legs between his, but Duncan kicked him away.

Andrea and Duncan swapped glances.

"I'm telling the truth," he said. "But I couldn't tell you where – these guys drive me round in circles."

She looked at Shopper and Sorehead. "Sounds ridiculous enough – "

"Promise you, it's a deserted site now, some sort of plant – "

"Like your lie about looking for Simon Gray?"

"I'm sorry about that."

"Your sins will find you out."

Duncan despaired. The cavalry was disappearing over the hill.

Then Andrea asked, "What are you going to do?"

He smiled. "Make a run for it. Can you help?"

"What's happening?" asked her sister.

"Nothing,"

"You're no longer in the police, Andrea – "

"But this makes me feel so much better."

Her sister smiled anxiously.

Sorehead winked at Andrea and spoke in Greek.

"He's inviting me back to his flat, but I don't think his intentions are honourable," translated Andrea.

"I'd love it if you castrated them."

"I think we should go somewhere else," Andrea's sister suggested.

"We'll probably have to in a minute."

"Why, what?"

The Shopper interrupted her in Greek, but the sister didn't reply and avoided his eye. A waiter arrived with a pannier of bread, some cutlery, and a tumbler of wine for their table.

Sorehead leered and performed a mime with his mouth and forefinger.

"They're disgusting. Do it now," advised Andrea.

Under his breath, Duncan counted to three, stood up and up ended the table. Plates, cutlery, wine and food slid into the rapists' laps.

Heads turned in the taverna.

Duncan ran.

The Shopper was the first to his feet. Andrea, with penalty-kick ferocity and accuracy, aimed at his groin. He bent double and sank to the floor.

Duncan pelted out the door and down the street. Sorehead, wiping off scraps of food pursued him, shouting in Greek.

A barking dog was the first to take up the challenge, but no one except Duncan was going to lose this race. His captivity had slowed him down. As much as he tried to shift into gear, his clogged body resisted him. So not even the two men outside the bakery, who hearing Sorehead's cries barred his way, were responsible. He came to a standstill.

He felt sorry for Andrea. He had entangled her in his sorry mess; may have even raised her hopes that she did have a future in her chosen profession. Except her evidence hinted at a level of industrial-sized institutional corruption, which meshed with what he had witnessed at the Golden Dawn meeting: some of her colleagues were in league with the Nazis. His struggle was microscopic but nevertheless linked to a wider world that showed no mercy. The one big plus was the Shopper's injury: in tears, he hobbled after Sorehead, and Duncan hoped he would never be able to hurt a woman again.

CHAPTER THIRTY-ONE

Two new custodians, English speaking, woke Duncan. The previous day's excursion to the industrial plant had not been scheduled, and their predecessors, one of whom Duncan hoped was permanently out of action, were now otherwise employed. The routine kicked into familiar gear: one left to do the shopping, while the other went over the rules of the house, which Duncan, bored, knew backwards.

Days later he turned a page in a newspaper and recognised a photograph at the head of a brief news report. He extracted what he hoped were the key words, wrote them down on a piece of paper and asked his captors to translate. Slowly, he pieced the report together.

A woman's body had been found at a seaside go-karting track, next to the beach where he had met Eleni and Nikos. Trussed up in a refuse bin, attempts had been made, the report delicately put it, to remove the person's identity. However, she was Melina Georgiou, a sex worker who had disappeared from her home in Kipseli, central Athens.

Duncan locked himself in the bathroom. A noise like a road drill vibrated in his head. He lifted the toilet seat and spewed into the bowl. If he had slept with her, might she still be alive? Would that have changed what they did? What had she ever done to die like that? And what hell was he involved in?

A knock on the door.

"I'm not feeling well," he said.

Through the frosted glass he saw the guard still there.

"I'm ill," he persisted.

The guard shuffled away.

Duncan turned on the taps and dunked his head in the sink. He cleaned his teeth. Energy used up, he sat back down on the toilet seat. His stomach was an empty hole and by some terrible digestive mistake it felt like he was slithering through it.

He lay down on his bed.

He imagined the refuse bin and Melina's mutilated body stuffed amongst fast-food cartons. How many kids on go-karts had sped by before she was scooped out by the bin men?

At the waste depot, she was unloaded like a Belsen victim. The tipping man was in shock. A colleague, who had been slipped several euros, climbed into the muck and flies. For the second time, Melina was rescued. All far too late. Her grandson, Aeolus, a teenager, identified her. He was drunk when the police knocked on the family's door, but they force-fed him black coffee to get the job done. He could not remember the last time he had seen her; his mother would know, but he's no idea where she was. Melina had stolen a bottle of wine, the shopkeeper chased her, but when a group of kids headed towards his shop, he turned back. But no, Mr Laskaris was not the last person to see her alive.

To stem the horror, Duncan smothered his head in his pillow. Did Eleni know? He bet Nikos did. He didn't sleep.

Next day, the guards told him to pack his belongings into a Samsonite bag.

"Holiday time?" he asked.

They left in an Opal Corsa. One guard drove; his colleague sat in the back beside Duncan. The drive took them by the Olympiakos Football Stadium and then out through the suburbs en route to, he realised, the go-kart track and the beach. Is that where they were headed? On one side they passed the old airport site, on the other the sparkling sea and in the far, far distance the island. He couldn't bear to look that way and switched to watch out for the turn off to Nikos's parents' house, but would he recognise it? What use was it anyway, and where the hell was the man himself?

A bus pulled in front of them to pick up passengers. By now they were getting closer to the go-kart track. Melina's cries returned, rattling in Duncan's brain. The bus moved on again, but the Corsa driver tucked in behind it. A child on the backseat of the bus pulled faces at them. Overtake, urged Duncan, silently, get away from here. But it was no go, the car slowed again and stopped once more behind the bus. The guard beside him pulled out his mobile. Then there it was, the go-kart track sign, and beneath it an array of bright, shiny new refuse bins. Replacements for Melina's 'resting place'? It was possible. But none of the flowers that had been for Malcolm Gifford, no memorials. So, who knew? Gone and forgotten, even the newspaper that carried the story, pulped, or floating in the wind.

Still stationary behind the bus, the guards talked to one another. They knew. They were looking at him. The one next to him said, "You won't have long now.".

What did that mean?

"Long for what?" he asked his voice sounding from somewhere in the distance. "Life?".

Was he going to be put in a bin too?

No reply.

Car rides with two escorts to a destination unknown had already featured in Duncan's life. Didn't they know?

The bus moved, and the car followed. Duncan's heartbeat settled.

Following signs for the airport, they turned off the coast road, passing a patch of rough grass piled high with discarded and broken sofas. Behind a wire fence, another dumping ground, but for speed boats. That's Greece, Duncan thought, incongruous and unpredictable.

They turned off the road, passed a café and parked next door on a garage forecourt. Inside the workshop, several mechanics in blue overalls overhauled a wheelless chassis. A young woman, a mobile phone pressed to her ear, opened the door for Duncan. Impressively synchronised, thought Duncan, could all this be to get him to the airport? See him off the premises. He doubted it.

Nikos sat in the back of the café with a clear view through the front window. The woman on her mobile vanished. Nikos stood up.

He was wearing sunglasses. With his shaved head and decked out in black down to his large Doc Marten boots, which added to his height, Duncan was reminded of the Golden Dawn crowd at St Panteleimon. Nikos held out his hand, but Duncan, putting the Samsonite bag, down ignored it.

"Have you changed sides?" he asked. Nikos stared at him. Duncan stepped into his face. "Fascist."

Nikos took off his sunglasses and smiled.

"What happened to Melina Georgiou?" hissed Duncan.

"Who?"

Duncan raised his voice. "Melina Georgiou?"

"Well, as I don't know this person, how can I say?"

Duncan grabbed him by his jacket lapels. "Tell me, prick."

Nikos was silent.

"Answer!" Duncan threw him back down on his seat.

Nikos, shaken, hastily drank from a glass of water on the table.

Duncan produced the rumpled newspaper from his bag and slammed it down.

"Look at the photograph."

Nikos glanced at it and then away.

"AGAIN!" demanded Duncan, shoving the paper in Nikos's face.

He pushed aside the paper.

"Understand, we're at war," he spoke slowly, "and it's irrelevant what happens to individual people, even you, me, this woman you're talking about."

"This woman had nothing to do with your war. Your goons kidnapped her, raped her, and killed her – Melina Georgiou from Kipseli, and you know it."

Nikos looked out of the window.

"She was found near your favourite beach so carved up they took a while to identify her. They should've asked you."

Nikos shrugged.

"This is where extremes take you, horrible disgusting violence."

"Look at yourself," replied Nikos, riled. "You are the man to talk about violence, hah!"

"Defending myself – and you, you might remember."

"I saw you; you revelled in it."

That stung, due perhaps to a hint of truth.

"And you have people who do it for you!" countered Duncan.

But Nikos had more, "Have you ever crossed the line? Done things you should account for?"

Another nerve hit, and they both knew it.

Nikos nodded, "Not so virtuous are you," a sly smile creeping across his face.

"Maybe, but – "

"No maybes."

"But I admit it, difference is, you don't."

"No slipping off the hook," Nikos stood back, as if the matter was closed.

Five fights after the plucky loser he'd intended to be, he was the champ. Cheered and validated. But would they cheer him urinating on chewing gum, or kicking the defenceless Ryan? Now it was Nikos, of all people, who challenged him. He was guilty, but then what? Until the next time?

"What's going on? Why am I here?"

A waitress arrived with a tray of coffee and a saucer of sweet fruits.

Nikos looked at his wristwatch. "Patience is a virtue."

The waitress smiled at them both and then turned away. Nikos lecherously watched her walk back to the counter.

"And chastity apparently. Are you chaste Nikos?"

"I've had enough of this. Please be quiet."

"Or," continued Duncan, "we know you're not kind, so are you diligent perhaps? The show you're putting on today might suggest as much. What about humble?"

"Stop showing off," said Nikos passing him the saucer of sweets. Duncan declined "Allow me something" he asked, "My free will has been taken away."

"Most people would be very pleased for what we've done for you."

"'We' again. Who the hell are 'we', if that doesn't sound too philosophical?"

Nikos' eyes anxiously flitted towards the window.

"Are we expecting Father Christmas?"

The waitress returned and sat down beside Nikos. She stroked his knee and whispered in his ear.

Nikos put his hand on her thigh, "She says, I'm tense, she wants to relax me."

"Don't mind me," said Duncan. "Though before you go any further you might ask her age."

"Nineteen," said the waitress.

"A friend of Eleni's, no doubt. How is she by the way?"

"Who's Eleni?" asked the waitress. She tried to stand up, but Nikos restrained her.

"Careful, you don't want to end up in a litter bin," said Duncan.

The young woman with the mobile reappeared in the café doorway, clicking her fingers. Nikos quickly removed his hand from the waitress, and without a word to her got up. She sulkily mooched off.

Nikos smiled at Duncan. "Come on. It's your favourite."

CHAPTER THIRTY-TWO

As Nikos and Duncan left the café, a dark blue BMW saloon growled out of the garage. The driver, a uniformed mechanic, jumped out and threw Nikos the keys, who handed them to Duncan.

"Our treat," said Nikos, and opened the driver's-side door. "Go on, you know you want to."

Duncan slipped behind the steering wheel, putting his bag on the passenger seat. Nikos climbed into the back, and from nowhere, a scrawny, saturnine man got in beside him.

Duncan observed the man in the mirror. A cap worn low hid most of his gaunt features. Saturnine. The nickname suited.

"Drive," said the new arrival in a thick accent.

"No introductions?" asked Duncan.

"Correct," said Nikos, "To the airport."

The road was busy: trucks, stonking great motorbikes, and busloads of flight passengers.

"Hey, that's too fast, go slower," instructed Nikos.

Duncan's inclination for speed always to the fore, he slowed, but it was such a waste. The BMW's straight-six rumbled beneath his right foot, itching to be let loose.

"You won't miss your flight," Nikos added.

"At last, you tell me. But if your friend was thinking of coming too, I don't need a babysitter."

"First, we've got some business with a prick doing something naughty," Nikos offered more in a minute than Duncan had heard in days.

"That hardly narrows it down."

"With a woman."

"Still leaving the field wide open."

"Someone he shouldn't."

"On a moral crusade, are you?" Duncan asked. "Doesn't fit to me."

He caught Nikos' eye in the mirror. Was he smirking?

"Who exactly are we talking about here?"

"Something on your conscience?" replied Nikos.

The passenger mumbled something in Greek.

"Sorry, you'll have to speak up."

"He said, if I don't shut you up, then he will."

"I'm driving, so tell him he can walk."

"Too fast again, hold back."

Duncan noticed a pattern. A black Audi S6 lurked ahead, and each time they drew close, Nikos restrained him. Another car overtook and filled the space between then, and Nikos relaxed.

They left the suburbs, car dealerships, pottery shops, diners, and boarded-up businesses, and headed on to the dual carriageway.

With the sun high in the blue sky above the scrubs and dusty tracks leading to the hills, Duncan imagined he was in Arizona – an Arizona he had only seen on film. He thought of Beanie in a B-Movie, on horseback, riding across the range.

Nikos leaned forward, his hand rubbing up and down on his thigh.

"Looks like you could use that waitress just now."

"Shut up – " snapped Nikos. "Do exactly what I tell you."

Olive trees stretched as far as the hills. A train roared towards them behind the concrete barrier separating the road lanes north and south.

"Speed up,"

Duncan did.

"Overtake."

Duncan did. Once again, the Audi was directly ahead.

"Oh I see, it's a willy-waving contest."

"Overtake. GO!"

Duncan, aware Saturnine had rolled down his window, floored the accelerator. Then he saw the compact pistol glinting in the sunlight.

"Whoa, FUCK!"

He lost speed.

"Keep going! Get level!"

"Your man's got a gun!"

"GET LEVEL!" screamed Nikos.

The back window of the Audi burst open, and a rifle barrel sharked through.

"NO!" Duncan had no choice but to power alongside. The Audi driver was a spotty-faced kid, dark haired, with a fringe.

A shot was fired.

The boy instantly cowered over his steering wheel, looking round in terror, his mouth open.

"Keep going," Nikos urged Duncan.

"Who is it?!"

Saturnine raised his gun.

The Audi gunman poked his face through his side window.

Combat Jacket – Mazarakis!

"Jack off, prick!" screamed Nikos. "It's all you're getting, you fuck!"

Everything fell into place for Duncan.

Another shot.

Both cars racing. The Audi turned in Duncan's direction, the boy's mouth still open, screaming.

"Please God no!" Duncan breathed and swerved away.

A third gunshot. Louder. Closer.

Mazarakis at the window again, caught in shock, a bullet through his face, blood pouring, then his body slumped forward.

The young driver lost control. The Audi struck the concrete barrier and tipped onto its side. The driver of a following van tried desperately to evade, but barrelling into it the two vehicles burst into flames. Duncan, clear of trouble, watched in the mirror as more cars crashed into the mounting mayhem, the road quickly blocked by skidding, mangled vehicles.

An explosion from within the melee sent burning jagged shards of metal shooting into the air and spiralling down onto the road. A figure engulfed in flames emerged from the wreckage, stumbled, and fell, consumed by the fire and thickening putrid smoke.

"Rest in peace, Dmitri," said Nikos, his face a blur of tears.

Duncan drove on, regularly checking his mirrors.

A gurgle, it was soft at first, but then louder by the second. Laughter: Saturnine was hysterical. Eyes wide, he pointed the pistol at Nikos, who ducked helplessly and screamed in Greek.

Saturnine pulled the trigger, but the pistol had jammed.

Exasperated, he lowered the weapon, checking it over. Nikos lunged forward knocking it out of his hand and then, clutching him by the lapels of his jacket, rammed him against the door. Pressed together, Nikos on top scrabbled for the handle. The door flew open and for frightening seconds they both might have fallen out, but the door swung back, wedging them inside.

"What the hell are you doing?" Duncan shouted.

"Keep driving!"

That was difficult. Saturnine was fighting back and they wrestled each other, bumping and rolling, knocking the back of Duncan's seat.

"You're going to get us all killed!" Duncan warned, who for a mad second wondered if Saturnine might be a fascist plant. His eyes snapped from the road to the mirror. The BMW charged on.

Saturnine had recovered his pistol, and with-it smashed Nikos across the face, spattering blood.

Couldn't have happened to a better target, thought Duncan, when through the windscreen he saw he was seconds from slamming into the back of a slower car. He swerved and roared past, glimpsing the angry driver shaking his fist. But much worse was immediately behind him. In pain and fury, blood smearing his mouth, Nikos had lost control and with his fists was pummelling Saturnine to a pulp.

Just before the final punch landed – "STOP!"

The command echoed as though from the boxing ring long ago, when Duncan's late right hook had bought him victory. Back then, however brutal, it was sport played within the rules. But this was real.

Was it murder? Another one?

Nikos' punches had reduced Saturnine to a crumpled heap, his head hanging over the edge of his seat, his eyes closed. Still.

"Is he dead?"

Nikos grabbed the gunman by his hair and shook him. Saturnine opened his eyes and muttered something. Nikos raised his fist.

Duncan, keeping one eye steadily on the mirror, said, "Don't."

Nikos let go of the gunman and doubled over, gasping for breath. Saturnine shuffled as far away as he could and sat weeping. After the horror of death, the noise and thunder of the crash, and the unexpected battle in the car, all of which could only have taken minutes – less – a curious calm settled inside the BMW. Duncan though, was still aware of danger.

"Where's the pistol?"

Nikos, wincing, leaned over and dropped it onto the passenger seat.

"Take the next slip road off," he said, his voice weak.

They drove off the dual carriageway and emerged opposite the Swedish superstore IKEA. Surreal, said Duncan to himself, this must be what comes after Hell. He pulled up beyond a bus stop, where Nikos' guard and the woman from the café emerged from the Opel Corsa and an old Ford Escort.

Nikos climbed out gingerly, and holding a handkerchief over his mouth, gestured to the guard who ran over and pulled Saturnine out of the BMW. He dragged the helpless assassin towards the Corsa and threw him in. Nikos motioned to Duncan and made a shooing gesture towards the café woman and the Escort. In different circumstances, Duncan would have found this comical. He collected his bag and got out. Looking back down the road, he saw a rising column of black smoke. In the distance sirens wailed. How many people had been killed?

The guard, carrying a glugging jerry can, sped towards them. Nikos grabbed the pistol and, abandoning the handkerchief, screamed hoarsely.

"RUN!"

They both sprinted to their separate vehicles. Duncan dove into the back seat of the Escort. The café woman had the engine ticking. It was a tough landing; the old motor's suspension crocked. A whooshing sound, as if the air was gathering itself into a spiral, and the BMW burst into flames.

Duncan, clinging to his bag, ducked and the Escort rattled off towards the motorway.

CHAPTER THIRTY-THREE

He sat down on a bench outside Athens airport. A man juggling a polystyrene cup, a sandwich and hand luggage gestured to the pall of smoke. Duncan ignored him. More people gathered. Like the young soldier Hannah saw at Waterloo Station, perhaps his eyes told the story.

Mazarakis's bloodied face; the flying chassis; the young driver in terror – and then he imagined a woman waiting in a room at the airport hotel. They'd killed a Nazi. Was Hannah watching, he wondered? She'd have approved, wouldn't she? It made up for the euros he'd dropped into the Golden Dawn tin at the rally. How he missed that dinky ambulance, it had acted like an umbilical cord between the generations but losing it had broken their connection.

He pulled a package out of his pocket. The café woman had given him a ticket in his name to Paris, a boarding pass, and an envelope stuffed with euros. He had counted to a thousand when someone sat down beside him. She squeezed his hand.

"Come on," she said.

Eleni led him through the crowds, and they sat in silence across a table in a noisy airport cafeteria. She had a plateful of salad from the self-service buffet counter; Duncan, unable to stomach food, chose wine.

"How's Dmitri's sister?"

"Lule, terrible, the whole family are."

Duncan sipped the wine.

"Mazarakis is dead," she whispered. "Nikos messaged me."

"Imagine that" Duncan scoffed. "And some other people besides."

She frowned.

Duncan put down the plastic cup. "Did he tell you he got smashed in the face with a pistol?"

Eleni shook her head, "It was just a scratch, he said."

A scratch? Nikos was downplaying his war wound.

"Really, a scratch?" he repeated, "My bet he'll have lost a tooth or two and won't be up to much for a while."

"You know, Duncan, you have a habit of over playing things – "

"I was there."

"Okay, okay," she relented. "Anyway, you were very brave, you took one hell of a risk."

So, she admired him too.

"No, I didn't. Not when I had no idea, when no one told me. Your boyfriend's a cunning little prick."

Eleni put down her cutlery and pressed her hands against her ears.

"No, you don't," Duncan reached over and pulled one hand away. "You've played that trick before."

"He doesn't want me to know, that way I'm safe."

"There's murder out there – "

"Shut up, don't tell me."

"You're ok. That's all that matters, is it?"

"Nikos doesn't know I'm here."

An overwhelming tiredness passed through Duncan, and he wondered whether he had the strength. Did she expect him to be grateful? He drank some more of his wine and ate a slice of tomato that had fallen off her plate. Tasteless after the succulent food he had enjoyed on the island, or else shock had numbed his taste buds. Everything was falling away. For days she had been conspicuously absent, why had she come now?

"I didn't know where you were."

"Neither did I."

"If I'd known, I'd have – "

"You'd have what? Tell the truth. Not even a note to say 'I'm not coming because I don't love you, I never did, the whole thing's been a big joke, so piss off' – "

Eleni raised her fork in the air.

" – Don't interrupt, I'm nowhere near finished. And this one's the biggest laugh of all, you'll love this: to think I was going to propose to you that morning. Hah!"

Eleni put down her fork. "What morning?"

"The last one, when you couldn't be arsed to get out of bed. Just as well, when I think about it. Thank God for that. Saved me from making a complete prat of myself. What could I have been thinking? Put it down to an aberration."

Eleni didn't understand. "A what?"

"I'd had too much sun. I was loopy."

"If you're not going to be serious – "

"Fucking hell!"

"Stop shouting." She wiped her mouth with her napkin. "I did love you. I still do, and I would've loved it if you asked me."

"Right, taking that at face value," Duncan flipped open his plane ticket. "Come with me now, we'll get you a ticket, we're going to Paris."

"I don't have my passport."

"Of course you don't. You've come to the airport without your passport."

"Stop it, Duncan."

"Go and get it, and then catch the next flight. I'll wait, even if it's tomorrow. I'm like that, you see. It's Paris, Eleni – what do they say? The city for lovers, I know it so well."

"All your girlfriends, I bet you do."

"Yeah, hordes of them, too many to count. We'll look them up, shall we? You can compare notes."

"I'm pregnant."

He laughed, slapped the table. "I think I'm going to need more wine. Make that a bottle. No, a vat."

"You're not funny,"

"No, I'm not, am I? I've had enough, well enough, over enough, and that's just today." He looked at his watch. "It's only lunchtime. Christ, what'll happen next?"

"Stop being horrible."

"I'm having difficulty in believing anything you say."

"It's true, every word – "

Duncan held up his hands and then in despair let them fall.

"It's Nikos'."

"Now that I do believe."

An empty, hollow feeling after drinking during the day; a terrible flatness following an inebriated high lodged in his stomach. But he wasn't drunk. Her news had dug into him and left him breathless. He felt faint. A cold washed through him.

Suddenly Eleni was beside him, other people too.

"He'll be ok," he heard her say.

How the hell did she know? How dare she? He had fallen to the floor, and clinging to her leg, the smell of her a comfort.

"I'm ok, sorry, thanks."

"Maybe, can we have some water please?" a Scottish voice.

"A fellow countryman," said Duncan.

"You don't sound Scottish," said the man.

Stefani, her name on her badge, arrived with a glass of water.

"Thank you, Stefani," Duncan looked up at the man. "I've never lived there."

"I'm from Stirling, I recommend it," the man said. He looked like that rare species, a Scots Tory, in a tweed jacket and a yellow jumper. Duncan guessed he was a salesman in agricultural machinery. "Duncan Connor."

"Well, that's always a good sign, if he knows his name?" the man asked Eleni, who nodded. "Ok, Duncan, nice meeting you." The man bending down, they shook hands, "You're very lucky to have such a capable friend."

"There's the Irish side of me, don't forget," said Duncan. "My grandfather was a dance hall owner from west of the Shannon River."

"Ok," Stirling man smiled, uneasily. "I think perhaps – "

Even in his dimmed state, Duncan recognised the shy not-wanting-to-leave little shuffle that all men did in Eleni's presence. The man gave a small wave and was about to go when he bent down and retrieved something from beneath the table.

"Would this happen to belong to you?" He held the dinky ambulance in his hand.

Duncan gasped, "Where did – ? How – ?" he said taking it.

"I suppose it fell out of your pocket when you…"

The rest was lost on Duncan as he looked from the ambulance in his hand to the turn ups in his jeans, the left hand one of which appeared slightly wider than the other. He reached down with the ambulance and put it in what he presumed had been its pocket. Perfect.

"My God," he pulled out the dinky, marvelling at it.

"Thank you," he said looking up at the man, "you don't know what this means."

"I think I do, I have some childhood keepsakes." He smiled at Eleni and left.

Ducan rolled the ambulance in his palm, he'd had it all the time. He laughed. Hannah did know, she'd been with him. This was something.

"Are you going to sit down there all day," asked Eleni.

"A little longer," he said inspecting the ambulance for any damage.

"What is that?"

He felt reluctant to tell her, why should he tell her anything, she'd told him nothing.

"Like the man said, something from long ago."

Eleni shrugged and bending over picked up her chair which in the rush to get to him, had fallen over. Duncan felt buoyant, "The first part of you I ever saw, I thought it was gorgeous, still do."

She sat down, "Actually, it was my breasts."

"Who's counting?" Duncan looked at her, "How d'you know that?"

"You couldn't take your eyes off them."

He drank again.

"Do you blame me?"

"Get up, Duncan."

He did, slowly and hung onto his chair. "Do you think that chap had any idea he'd come to the aid of an accessory to murder?" he said.

"Tell everyone, go on."

"I'm not sure what an accessory to murder is supposed to look like. Do you? Well, it's me."

Eleni checked the time.

"Can't wait to get rid of me?"

She sighed.

"Tell me some good news," he asked her, sitting down in the chair and rolling the ambulance across the tabletop.

"Put that away," said Eleni, in a tone a mother might use to a recalcitrant child.

Duncan slipped it carefully into his pocket and zipped it up.

"We had a big party for Maria. She got a job."

He had to think. "In Patras, wasn't it?"

"Heraklion, in the end."

"I'm sorry I missed it, otherwise detained."

As he drank the rest of the water, he remembered Maria on the beach, in tears at the hospital. It felt like a lifetime ago.

They got up and left the café.

"Seeing this is the time for returning things, Nikos said you must have lost it." Eleni took Duncan's mobile out of her bag and gave it to him,

"His goons confiscated it."

"Mostly I never know what you're talking about."

"That's because you refuse to listen, or to see." Duncan scrolled through his phone.

Eleni stood in front of a wall-high photograph of a Victoria's Secret model, her head against a skimpily clad crotch. Duncan grinned.

"What?"

"Look."

She turned round.

But the clump of booted feet and shouted commands broke the moment. A squad of armed police, or maybe army, raced across the concourse.

He spun Eleni back to him and hid his head in her hair. He found her mouth and kissed her. The kiss was long.

Eleni stretched her hand down to his cock, "I knew you cared." Then she gestured to the model. "Unless it's her you want." Duncan stepped back, but she clung to him.

"You can't pretend." She had both her hands round him now. "See."

He tried to pull her hands off. "Let me go."

"Not now, not when you're like this."

"You're pregnant." He pushed her off.

The squad were searching the franchise shops.

She came towards him again.

"Eleni, you can't have both of us – "

"I already have." She smiled, her head tilted to one side.

Behind them, a bookrack flew into the aisle and toppled over, followed by a familiar figure running. Police leapt after Sorehead and pulled him to the ground.

Duncan slipped behind a pillar. Eleni followed.

"Go," he told her.

"Who is he?"

"I could get arrested, and it's all because of Nikos."

Police obscured Sorehead who was shouting. Other officers fanned out amongst the gathered crowd, moving them on.

"Go, Eleni. Now!"

The police hauled Sorehead to his feet; his shoes and trousers had been removed. He was still shouting. Had he come to see me off, too? Duncan thought as he joined the passport queue. Eleni, beside the Bureau de Change, forlorn, waved. His wave back turned into a gesture to go. She did, slowly, and after one last look was gone.

A nerve-fraying moment at Passport Control followed. The blue-shirted official checked Duncan's opened passport and closed it to pass it back. Suddenly she snapped it open again at the photograph page.

She looked at Duncan and consulted something beneath her desk. A colleague leaned into the booth and they both stared.

Duncan's mind raced and imagined the exaltation.

'We've got him!'

He was sure they had caught Nikos, and he had folded under questioning. Leant on his 'scratch' wound. Duncan's guilt quotient ran off the scale. Like mother, like son, he was guilty of a hit and run. That young driver, ten to one an innocent – and the others, how many of them? They were counting them in the morgue.

Instead, the official smiled and returned his passport. Duncan's hand was shaking so much he was barely able to pick it up.

"Thank you," he mumbled.

Then, between a specialist chocolate outlet on one side of the duty-free aisle and the perfume counters on the other, he stopped. A uniformed, weapon-carrying patrol approached. The passport official must have pressed a buzzer. Should he put his hands up, make it simple? He did not, he waited, his bag on the floor and… the patrol swept by.

Onto security.

Surely, they would get him now. Another passenger, sweating profusely, suffered a prolonged baggage search, but Duncan sailed through.

The Stirling man brushed by: "I bet you're glad you're out of all that. Got a bit heavy back there, didn't it?"

Duncan watched him head for the Edinburgh gate. Only then did he wonder why he had been put on a flight to Paris. What was waiting for him at Charles de Gaulle? To arrange a guard of honour, or some protection for himself, he texted several of his old road crew friends, suggesting something along the lines of 'How about blurring the edges?' He also asked if anyone had seen his money belt? Nothing came back. He clicked off his mobile, his heart still thumping. He patted the dinky ambulance in his pocket, boarded the flight, and left Greece.

CHAPTER THIRTY-FOUR
NORTHERN ENGLAND 1998-1999

After escaping from Chewing Gum and Ryan, never mind his father's exploits in the kitchen, Duncan lay low in his college room for several days. Time, too, for the lump on his forehead to recede. He kept an eye on the local press and the TV news for any items about 'Lovesick student on the rampage' or 'Police in search for youth', but there was nothing.

One afternoon Duncan's neighbour, Rick, dug him out of his isolation.

"Are you alright?" he asked at the door.

"Hungover," pretended Duncan.

"Someone's landed you a whopper."

"If that's what you've come to tell me, thanks," replied Duncan, and tried closing the door.

"Phone call, I think it's your father."

"Definitely don't tell him," said Duncan, coming out.

"You're weird Connor."

"Thanks. I'll bear it in mind," he said over his shoulder as he anxiously walked towards the communal telephone at the end of the corridor.

What did Pat want?

"Have you been at home recently?"

"What?"

"It's a perfectly simple question, Duncan: have you been here?" Pat was irritated.

"No. Why?"

"Well, the other morning the bath was full of water."

Duncan winced. He had forgotten to empty it. An image of Mandy amidst soapsuds entered his mind.

"You're getting forgetful in your old age, Dad."

Pat started to reply, but a bunch of chattering rugby players passed by Duncan and clattered out the door. Their jerseys reminded him of Kathryn and their encounter with the climbers at the crags. It pitched him into more gloom.

He interrupted. "I'm sorry Dad, I've got to go. Lectures."

"New experience for you, I expect," replied Pat, putting the phone down.

Duncan stood there for a moment, wondering whether he'd got away with it. He gingerly felt his forehead. More recuperation was needed.

Following his call to Duncan, Pat's next was to a firm of painters and decorators. In future, he would do his 'entertaining' in his mother's old bungalow.

Duncan switched from lying to his father to a charged conversation with Richard Patterson. They had both turned up to visit Beth. Richard was large with a beard turning grey at the edges, and he smiled constantly. The man Duncan thought was so good for his mother annoyed him on sight.

The saintly Patterson made out he had rescued Beth from a family he regarded as dysfunctional. Somehow the male Connors behaviour had been responsible for the poor woman's infidelity, accidentally driving into Gifford and leaving him to die at the side of the road. Worse, Richard the shepherd, the gatherer of lost souls, targeted Duncan. He offered him a lift to the railway station. Beth was pleased they would have a chance to get to know each other. Duncan felt obliged.

After a perfunctory exchange about how well his mother had looked and how it was 'nice Duncan managed to visit her', Richard warned him he was unwise to judge Beth.

"I don't," said Duncan.

"Oh, but I'm sorry to say, I think you do," Richard said, entirely missing the irony that he was judging Duncan.

"Has my mother told you so?"

"I'm able to read between the lines – "

"She hasn't then – "

"I must say, there's no need to be so defensive."

"You're making an accusation on no basis whatsoever, and one which is absolutely not true."

"Let me try again," Richard said, still smiling, and sounding like a country parson wooing a disbeliever.

"I'd rather you didn't." What the hell was his mother doing with this pompous ass? The fact her head was full of him when she hit Gifford added insult to injury. "The truth, if you want to know, is that if she hadn't just been with you, it would never have happened."

"Ah," said Richard excitedly. "That is a judgement, right there."

"You bet. And a fact."

"You're a young man who could do with some pepping up."

"Young man?"

"Please do me the courtesy of hearing me out."

"Well, it is your car."

"Yes. I can quite understand how your mother's incarceration has unsettled you, but you're an intelligent fellow, and I'd like to make you a proposition."

"You're under no obligation to me, and neither am I to you."

"Indeed. But whatever my plans for your mother may be – "

"Woah. Your plans for my mother will count for nothing unless she says so."

Patterson ploughed on: "I have no offspring, and so I'm constantly on the lookout for bright young people to teach them the antiquarian books trade – an occupation well suited to someone with your interests. And all being well, in time, that person would take the driver's seat." He pointedly looked at Duncan.

The driver's seat! How could Patterson suggest this? Was he blind to even this irony of ironies? The man was insufferable. Wasn't Duncan's attitude towards him obvious, or was he so thick skinned?

Duncan stared ahead through the windscreen; the railway station seemed further away than ever.

By the time Patterson's pitch had meandered through wages and share options, Duncan understood. To clinch Beth's hand in marriage, or even a permanent partnership, Patterson needed a member of the family on board.

"Thank you for this idea, but – "

"No, no, you haven't been listening. It's not an idea. Once you've finished your degree, it's very much an offer."

"Thank you for making this offer, but you haven't been listening, either. I have absolutely one hundred per cent zero interest in running a second-hand bookshop. As far as I'm concerned, please do not take your prospective stepfather responsibilities too seriously."

"The thought of becoming your stepfather gladdens my heart."

Duncan wanted to punch him in his smug face but instead watched him drive away hoping upon hope his mother would see sense.

Academia barely impinged. Duncan's life revolved around excessive drinking and a half-hearted attempt to win over a girl called Charlotte, whose father owned most of Sussex. She sulked. Oxbridge had taken her brother, but not her.

"He's a rower," explained Duncan. "As long as you can pull an oar, they'll let in any old thicko."

After yet another tutorial interview, Duncan stirred himself to open a book from the reading list, but the effort did not last. Besides, he'd tried to read it before, turgid Henry James. Unsettled by his encounter with Chewing Gum and Ryan, he was distraught about Kathryn's desertion. Tucked away in his room still surrounded by her drawings, he hardly slept and barely ate. One morning he made a decision.

"Don't run away," Pat was exasperated. "Look life in the eye and bloody well get on with it."

That hurt. Duncan lifted his gaze from the water. They were standing on a bridge, the cathedral towers loftily solid above the trees on the riverbank. He had told his father he was giving up his university place.

"I'm not running away."

"What d'you call it then?"

"Well – it's an odyssey."

"Oh, give me strength!" Pat looked ready to tip his son into the river.

"Alright, here's the deal: stay on, get your degree, and then go on as many odysseys as you like."

"I want to do it now, Dad. Think about it, I can always get a degree later."

"Don't you dare tell me what to think."

Each believed the other equally unreasonable.

"I told you the last time, stop faffing about and get stuck in."

"I'm not faffing about."

"It's giving up, that's what it is. That's the word for it."

Duncan withered. He could understand his father worrying, but this full-on attack…

"You've gone off at the deep end. Can't we talk about this quietly, Dad?"

"You're not sixteen anymore – "

"What's sixteen got to do with anything?"

"Shut up and listen to me."

"No. I'm walking away." And Duncan did.

"Come back here."

"No." But he stopped walking.

Pat was right behind him, so red in the face heat came off him. "This is exactly what I mean. The slightest hint of difficulty – which I must say, you have failed to explain – you duck out."

"I'm going because I can't talk to you when you're like this."

"For God's sake, Duncan, be a man."

"Like you, you mean? In the fucking war?"

"Don't swear at me – "

"You weren't there, not like Gran. Second hand, that's what you are. She drove the ambulance. And another thing: this is not your life, it's mine. Thanks for the concern, but it's me going out there to get on with it, not you. And if you want to know, I'm not getting the ferry to Dieppe. I'm going to Cherbourg. I saw a film once with Catherine Deneuve where everyone sings the words. I doubt she'll be there, but I want to see the place anyway. After that? Well, wherever the wind blows, or something. It's a French proverb, lost a bit in translation, but you get the drift… Sorry."

As he climbed the riverbank, he looked back through the trees. Pat still stood on the bridge. Duncan worried what he might do.

"I realised," explained Pat in the pub, days before Duncan's departure. "The route you're intending on this great misadventure puts you plumb in line to visit Caen, a key to the allies' victory during the 1944 Battle of Normandy."

Duncan carefully put down his pint and, anxious not to provoke another eruption, looked across the table at his father.

"Had you there, didn't I?" laughed Pat.

Duncan relaxed and forced a grin.

But despite the jest, he knew his father had not changed nor even listened to what he had said. Their relationship had dwindled into a wary peace.

Pat mulled over the crossword in his newspaper. "*Calm down*: five letters, beginning with A?"

"Abate," said Duncan.

Pat smiled and filled it in. "By the way," he said, "You'll be back."

Duncan looked a question.

"Stay at the university and you'll learn that an odyssey is all about heroes battling the odds and then returning home."

"Not sure Homer is on the reading list."

"Can't think what higher education is coming to these days," Pat replied extending his hand.

Duncan couldn't remember when, if ever, they had shaken hands.

"Thanks Dad. Hope I avoid any battles."

"Good luck."

Duncan quickly drank up and left.

It was the last time they would see one another.

CHAPTER THIRTY-FIVE
EUROPE 1999 – 2004

Watching the propeller churn through the waves and England disappear excited Duncan as much as it frightened him. From the ferry deck, he threw the last 18 months into the sea below. Not that it had all been bad: the thrill of setting up the racetrack and the danger of the moorland road were highlights. All down to Hannah. He smiled and then first making sure the dinky ambulance was safely in his pocket he headed for the bar. From now on, he told himself, life was going to be a whole lot better.

However, Cherbourg had been disappointing. No Catherine Deneuve, but in keeping with Jacques Demy's film 'Les Parapluies de Cherbourg', it rained. Paris though…

He arrived just as he was tiring of being on his own. He fell in with a multi-national stage crew, roadies for topline music acts across Europe, who were bidding farewell to a popular member. A bear of a man, Aksel, was returning to Norway to get married, though none of the crew imagined he would settle for domesticity. The carnage lasted 24 hours, and in drink they took Duncan to be one of them. But at dawn, in a hotel room stiff with bodies, the truth came out. Roused by a fearful hammering and shouted commands from the corridor, Duncan thought he had woken in Bedlam. Amidst the stifling male fug, each crew man groggily opened an eye, and after the merest ablutions were ready to roll.

"Who the fuck are you?"

Everyone took a step back, and Duncan found himself the centre of attention.

"Duncan," he replied. "Duncan Connor."

"Anyone know this twat?" asked Robert, who hours earlier had told him a preposterous story involving a James Bond film shoot in Jamaica, and someone of psychopathic ferocity called the Bastard Bollox!

No time for an answer. They were decanted into a coach bound for Le Parc des Princes. Duncan suggested to Robert, who appeared to hold a senior position, that he would be an ideal replacement for Aksel. Robert reported the same to the coach. Laughter was followed by a caustic, "Hey kid, no one replaces the Bear."

As they disembarked, Ivan, a Czech in the front seat, told Duncan to wait. Dubois, otherwise known as Pee Wee, had been summoned. Five minutes later, a tiny Frenchman in large horn-rimmed spectacles and wearing a red bow tie pulled up in a Renault. Duncan was instructed to drive to Gare du Nord, approximately 15 minutes away. The train he was meeting was due in 10 minutes. If he was late – don't come back.

Time trials on an aerodrome were one thing: driving on the unfamiliar side of the road, and in Paris, another. Worse, Pee Wee issued directions at the last second: "à droit", or "à gauche". A task designed to fail, but Duncan had no intention – the clock was ticking.

"Speak English?"

Pee Wee triumphantly shook his head.

Duncan turned a sharp left, put his foot down and gunned the car towards a brick wall.

"Do you speak English?"

Pee Wee stiffened in his seat. The wall was coming rapidly closer –

"OUI! YES, YES!" yelped the Frenchman.

In the nick of time Duncan skidded to a halt. "Directions in English, and the earlier the better. Yes?"

Pee Wee nodded.

"START!" Duncan backed out of the cul-de-sac.

Pee Wee mumbled.

"LOUDER! THE QUICKEST WAY!"

Pee Wee wasn't reluctant to co-operate; he was plain terrified. He'd been instructed to supervise a madman. A kamikaze pilot. Duncan put his faith in the French capital itself. He promised the Eiffel Tower unconditional love, never to speak ill of the Louvre, or betray Pigalle, so long as Paris delivered him to the station in time.

And thus, Duncan outdrove the Parisiennes and the gendarmes, and cheated death twice, though later Pee Wee, downing several cognacs, would double that number. They reached Gare du Nord before the clock.

Pee Wee welcomed a short, fat, crimson-faced woman stamping down the platform pulling a suitcase on wheels behind her.

"You fairy, Pee Wee." She greeted the quivering Frenchman and then looked up at Duncan, his hand outstretched to take the suitcase. "Is this the streak of piss Ivan told me about?"

"I'm the driver."

"Yeah? We'll see about that. Put your hand away, looks like you're trying to cop a feel." She passed the suitcase to Pee Wee. "Come on, you cretin," she commanded. "Tell him who I am."

Pee Wee's Adam's apple wobbled. The car journey had undoubtedly unhinged him, but much worse, this woman put the fear of God into him.

"Duncan, may I please introduce the Bastard Bollox."

Duncan stared. That was her actual name?

"Duncan?" she sneered. "What kind of poncy moniker is that?"

"I might say the same," replied Duncan, judging it best to front up to this Boadicea, who, standing at exactly the right height for the manoeuvre, grabbed him by the balls. Her hold was less tight than a grab might suggest, but she immobilised him. For anyone passing, this trio, stock-still amidst the busy station, made an intriguing tableau: the fey Frenchman, not sure where to look; the surprised six-foot tall Celt, eyes bulging; and this chunky Anglo-Saxon bruiser, with her hand round his penis. Her hold morphed into a cupping, but Duncan's surprise overcame any reaction.

She beckoned him down to her five-feet level. "If you think for one second, I'll ever suck you off, bear in mind I've got a case full of dildos that would put you to shame."

Pee Wee, as a child might, stifled a laugh.

She released Duncan, leaving him to decide whether he had been threatened or she had made a pass. Later, he learnt he had received a standard Bastard Bollox greeting.

Without entering the hotel, she turned down her one-night booking. Duncan, driving sedately, the Bastard Bollox from time to time caressing his knee, and Pee Wee tucked in the back, toured Paris for alternative accommodation.

But in half an hour, they were back at the original hotel. Ivan was informed the driver would do. Pee Wee held his head in his hands.

Duncan tempered his triumph, silently questioning why he was joining this tyrannical organisation. He imagined it was like the army: a hierarchy, a clear definition of roles, and a target, travelling to a new venue, rigging the set, striking the same and moving on. Failure to keep schedules was out of the question, and tests both mental and physical were continuous. Anyone who faltered was sacked. But here at least was racial harmony, a Palestinian and Israeli were the lighting genii; and when an Orangeman from Ulster joined, the Catholic bit his lip then found their common bond in the work – showing up bigotry for the worthless waste of time it is. In a world of mostly males, the Bastard Bollox prevailed. Her forthright and competitive approach was based on 'anything they could do; she could do better'. Some hated her; some were frightened of her, but all respected her. No one knew her real name, except the Bear, now paddling up a fiord. Allegedly he and the pint-sized one had got together one drink-fuelled night. It was an achievement alone to overcome their sizeable physical differences, but afterwards they had never spoken to one another ever again. Typical of families, in Duncan's view. It did not take him long to realise it, but no sooner had he given up his own family, he had joined another.

Duncan drove: picked up equipment; replacement gadgets; musicians; agents; V.I.P.s; drugs from dealers in airports, train stations, hotels; and several times dragged crew and musicians out of bordellos. A solo cog in an international wheel, but regularly earning the Bastard Bollox's approval. A life the opposite of stuffy classrooms and lecture theatres. He wished his father could see it. An academic career parlayed into a white-collar desk job, or better still, military service was more in Pat's line for him. But why even consider it on a rare day off crossing the Piazza San Marco arm in arm with Larissa from Verona – a violinist playing at a Venetian jazz club.

Duncan's earliest memories of music were through TV shows like 'The Tube', and at three or four years old the opening titles struck him, especially the explosion in the living room. He would wait all week to see that. Now admitting he had been starstruck, he eagerly anticipated the bands on the tour list. But the shine soon wore off. A hero in his underpants, or just socks, quickly paled. Their frailties, insecurities and often brattish behaviour put pay to any admiration.

The concerts became secondary. The real art was backstage: the heavy lifting, the arduous rigging, the delight in transforming a bland arena into a palace of dreams – for a few hours at least. No applause, just the satisfaction of a job well done and on time. Duncan would sneak into the auditorium and marvel at the set, the lighting and all systems go from the technical box. Occasionally, he'd stay for a special effect or a band, but often he would sneak off – as in Venice where Larissa had invited him to sample some real 'music' As a member of this self-contained 'army' roaming the continent, he got used to quick-fire liaisons that burst into flame but were doused by the roar of the departing coach.

When the planes hit the World Trade Centre, some Americans amongst the crew headed for home. They were in Marseilles, a strongly Muslim quarter, and Beef from Kansas, the original doughboy, downed a rich cocktail and foolishly ventured out to, as he put it, "level the score." He got what he deserved and returned via the Gendarmerie, a knife wound to his ribs and a charge of 'causing an affray'.

Andrzej, a Pole, a wizard on the sound desk, and one of the few who'd always kept an eye on the outside world took a dim view of the future.

"I tell you," he spoke in a gruff voice that underpinned his authority, "this is what's coming, there will be war."

"No, no, no one will be that stupid," said Ivan,

"Hah, you must still be in shock to think so. See you think of peace and love, like it was at Woodstock, but next came Altamont."

Everyone recognised both names, the latter being one of the darkest days in Rock history, at the Altamont Speedway track in California when Meredith Hunter was murdered by a Hell's Angel during the Rolling Stones' set, but they couldn't follow Andrzej's reference in connection with 9/11.

"We had progress, didn't we, the hippies and anti-war at Woodstock," explained Andrzej.

"Those wankers," sniggered Robert, but Andrzej ignored him.

"And then at Altamont, you see, it was the reverse. We went backwards, and always the backwards is much, much the bad."

While most scratched their heads, Duncan reached for the little dinky ambulance in his pocket but was careful not to reveal it. He could imagine the ribbing he'd get carrying around a kid's toy. He'd remembered Hannah's warning. Almost the same words as Andrzej. The fear that the backlash is worse each time.

The management recruited replacements and life continued as before, but with a hotter line to any intelligence for security purposes. Sealed inside the rock 'n' roll bubble plus a healthy pay packet, Duncan went with the flow, and time zoomed by. So, too, did the great cities of Rome, Madrid, Berlin, Moscow, St Petersburg, Stockholm, Amsterdam – but he never saw any of them, properly. Hotel rooms, the road, the airports, the jokes, the food… it took a while for him to realise it, but he was going stale. His elevation to the rigging crew – and elevation it was, spending his time high up on gantries – provided a fresh impetus. The prospect of falling from a great height gave his day an extra edge. But even this soon palled and the further he travelled, the more his focus narrowed. He was in perpetual motion, but at the same time he was stuck.

It was after a concert in London that his familiar desire to leave welled up.

Beth was there. "You must be eating your greens," she said, seeing how much he had filled out.

As they hugged, he told her how fantastic she was to survive prison. She, though, was fearful of her reception at home and regretted she had not returned immediately. Since release she had stayed with a friend in the Midlands: "Just the thought of being seen; it'll be unbearable."

"Peoples' memories are short."

"Oh, don't you believe it," she went on. "But the worst of it is me. I'll never get over it, Duncan, and back there it'll be even harder."

"You never know. The waiting is often worse than the thing itself."

"Well," she looked unconvinced. "Let's hope."

"I should come with you."

"Don't be silly, you can't."

"I want to help."

She nodded and held his arm. "I've just got to do this. It's down to me."

She shyly deflected all questions about Richard Patterson. Duncan took this to mean along with his books, the man was history. An afterthought, as an accessory, Patterson should have been in the dock, too.

"Hamburg next? Where the Beatles kicked off." Beth beamed.

"Yeah, but I'm not actually in a band, Mum."

"Yes, you are. Come on, you've talked of nothing else. Where'd these so-called stars be without you?"

Duncan took her hand in his. "And what about Dad?"

"Well, who knows? He's got his own life now."

"Has he met someone?"

She shrugged. "It's over between us."

She left.

As he watched her walk away to catch her train, he cried. If she had agreed or, better still, asked him, he would have gone with her knowing it was not just for her. Maybe going home would help him steer a new course.

He'd made up his mind, he was leaving.

CHAPTER THIRTY-SIX
SPAIN 2004

It was still early when Duncan crawled into the café in San Sebastian in northern Spain. He had washed himself as best he could – using a tiny basin in a cramped space – and, sitting at a table in the window with a cup of black coffee, he took stock. If anyone had told him his leaving party had lasted three days, he could not argue. Neither was he so foolish as to think this level of damage was a special privilege, or a measure of the exceptional way he was regarded by the crew. His departure had taken much longer than he'd thought. Only Pat's shadow had held him back. Was he a quitter after all? A bolter, a runaway, as his father had charged. He tried replacing his father's view with Hannah's anarchy, and her challenge: "Don't look back, boy. It's your life, make up your own mind and get on with it."

Those days and nights of freedom in Paris had been an excuse to drink round the clock, or as the Bastard Bollox put it, "unleash bedlam". Russell Crowe's line in 'Gladiator' is "unleash hell", but nobody had bothered to correct her. She had such disdain for the 'talent' that she regularly treated the crew to amalgams like Julia Grant and Hugh Roberts.

Duncan could remember snatches of the journey to the station where he was poured onto the midnight train. But his mind had only started to clear hours later in the toilet, when he had discovered the money belt in which he had stored three and a half thousand euros worth of savings was missing. The thundering pain in his head and the unsettling disturbance in his stomach was nothing against this. His guts churning over, he had returned to his seat, but there was no sign, the belt had gone. A quick scavenge revealed he had approximately one hundred euros. He had ignored the misty dawn breaking over Biarritz outside the window and tried to piece together the night before – but nothing.

Next, a new hell: an insistent woman, Naomi or Nancy – Canadian, he thought – had demanded he get off the train with her. He had resisted, she got upset, and other travellers had sympathised. He had asked her if she knew anything about his money belt. She had accused him of calling her a thief.

"Please, please," said Duncan. "I've lost a large amount of money. I'm not accusing anybody, but as you can imagine I'm desperate to find it."

All eyes had turned to her.

"Ok," she had said. "I can categorically assure you, you were not wearing a money belt, and never have been."

He had looked at her blankly.

"Don't you remember?"

"Remember what?"

"Thanks a lot." She had slung on her rucksack and walked up the carriage.

Duncan had caught her up in the vestibule. "I'm sorry. I was colossally drunk."

"Did you think I was sober?" She was small, plump, with a sweet open face. "Honestly, there was no money belt."

The train was slowing down.

"Was this – did it happen – were we in public?"

She had smiled. "If you're not coming with me, you might want to find another seat somewhere else."

Duncan had taken this in. "I'm sorry I – "

"Yeah, yeah, I get it; your girlfriend's waiting for you someplace."

The train stopped, and he had opened the door for her.

"You can't remember what you've missed, but don't worry, I'm over you."

She had jumped onto the platform, slammed the door shut in his face and stalked off without looking back. Why would she?

Duncan, hands in pockets, had closed his eyes. He had opened them again immediately.

His phone? Where was it? To his great relief, he had turned up his passport and train ticket. But his whole life was in his phone. The plan had been to enjoy a period of 'recollection in tranquillity' in Spain, then Italy, and possibly Greece. Now tranquillity would have to wait.

In the café, he had begged a piece of paper and a pen from the waiter and tried to remember crew phone numbers. By the time he'd jotted down a few, he realised the party would rage for at least another 24 hours. So no immediate chance to see if anyone had his phone or his money.

He put down the pen and pushed his empty coffee cup aside. He was alone. The moral of the story: as soon as he had stepped out of the tour cradle everything had gone wrong. He thought of home. Even if he could ring them, what would he say? "Fantastic opportunities to look forward to, sun's shining... What d'you mean, I'm always leaving? No, no, I've saved tonnes."

Maybe, in that case, his unexpected quarantine was not such a bad thing.

Then something strange happened.

"Time's fragile, Duncan, it passes so quickly." Pat's voice was clear. "And you damn well look to me as though you're wasting it."

No mistaking his father's same old battle-cry.

Pat stood in front of him, his hands balled into fists pressed down on the café table. His face paler than Duncan remembered, but his eyes as stern as ever. He was talking again, his mouth moving, but Duncan could not hear. A buzz in his ears, like the sensation aboard a plane in descent.

Pat vanished, but he could still hear voices, a female. His mother? He shook his head clear.

Two anxious Dutch women were talking to the man behind the counter in pidgin Spanish. A tall woman with cropped blonde hair, Anita; the other, Helene, with longer dark hair, a satchel slung over her shoulder.

"Are you English?" asked Anita.

Duncan had not landed yet, but heard himself say. "Close enough…"

"We look for a garage, please, our car has broken down."

Helene indicated a Peugeot parked outside the window, stuffed with suitcases and the rear suspension suffering accordingly.

"I've probably been here as long as you have," said Duncan. Their faces fell. "I don't know anything about garages, but I could have a look at your car."

"Oh, please, can you? Thank you."

They had driven all night from Rotterdam and desperately wanted to reach their camp site twenty minutes away, pitch a tent, and collapse.

Duncan was a godsend, and they would never know how relieved he was to have met them. A mechanical problem was reassuringly real: a system, a logic he understood; a clarity he surely needed. Once he figured the problem out, they fixed it. Their toolbox was as professional as you could get.

"We're a team," said Anita.

Helene linking her arm into his and convening a group hug, he welcomed their womanly warmth.

"I think we better get a shower," Anita suggested. "Are you going anywhere?"

The question stumped him. The start of a philosophical debate. Helene followed up with something simpler. "Would you like a lift?"

"Well, what I'd really like… d'you have a phone? I must make a call, but it's to the UK?"

"Yes, of course," said Helene. "Wherever you want."

Beth gasped when she heard his voice.

"Dad, isn't it?"

He imagined her nodding, unable to get the words out, then in a burst.

"How did you know?"

Tears sprung to his eyes. How could he explain? He moved away from the car. His mother was talking again, but he only caught snatches.

"In his sleep, apparently… best way really… where are you?"

He slumped down on the kerb. He could not tell whether his reaction was prompted entirely by his father's death, or perhaps heightened by the 'visitation' – was that the word? – or was it a co-mingling of both, plus the hangover?

"Please come back, Duncan."

Across the road the women had finished rearranging their luggage. "I will, Mum, but there's a problem."

He woke under canvas and smelled food. No question, the Dutch women had said. They were good souls and dynamite cooks. He was their lost pup until Beth relayed him the money for the journey home.

Looking down from the cliff top at a beach sloping towards the blue green sea, Duncan thought of his father in his shed, spectacles perched on his nose, poring over endless pieces of paper, some of which had spilled onto the floor indented by muddy boot marks. Duncan had picked them up and tidied them into a neat pile. Who cared now? Did his father, even then?

A cloud slipped in front of the sun, casting a dull shadow across the camp site. It would soon be time to eat.

Resentment followed. Why had Pat's departing speech been the same old nagging refrain? Couldn't he have been positive or loving? But then hadn't Duncan run true to form: broke, hung over and out for the count? What else could his father have said?

But something else niggled. That morning, it was if he had been at Pat's bedside. He had never paid any attention to the supernatural, but what happened in the café had turned him upside down. He gnawed at it again and again.

He was implicated in his father's death.

CHAPTER THIRTY-SEVEN
NORTHERN ENGLAND 2004

First, Duncan, using the name F. Scott, had made a telephone call. Then he had booked an en-suite room in a city centre hotel in the name of Fitzgerald. 'The Great Gatsby' was his favourite novel; he had read it twice. At Pat's funeral, a conversation with Old Henry, who lived several doors down from Hannah's bungalow, confirmed Duncan's fears about his father's death. Pat had moved lock, stock, and barrel up to Hannah's bungalow, leaving the family home to Beth. Freedom had woken his mother to one reality, and Duncan's hope had come true: Richard Patterson was dumped, locked away in the nightmare of the country road. She had put a stop to one life and, restarting another, had invited neighbours, faithful friends, and relatives to Pat's wake.

Many Duncan knew, except for Angela, a sprightly woman his mother had befriended in prison. She was staying with Beth while they both helped each other get back on their feet. As well as being a good companion, Angela was down to earth, with a practical grasp of domestic appliances, which had never been Beth's forte.

Old Henry had told Duncan he had spotted him and a girl, years before, sneaking out early one morning. The thought of Kathryn cut right through Duncan and as ever plunged him into memories. They'd thought they'd been extra careful by leaving out the back door and hurrying away down the lane. It had all added to the excitement.

"Have I lost you, son?"

"Sorry, I am listening."

"Your Dad said you had ants in your pants. Pity that girl didn't dust you down."

"Oh, she did, Henry."

Henry laughed loudly. Other mourners turned towards them. "Oh, go away with you, Pat liked a laugh, so he did."

Henry, long retired, did odd jobs, mostly carpentry, and had found a kindred spirit in Pat. They had spent hours over jugs of tea discussing great battles from the ancient Greeks to the Second World War.

Duncan had spotted him away from the main wake, taking nips of whisky from a flask.

"We've got plenty in bottles, if you'd like?"

"You're alright, son," the old man had smiled. "This stuff's one off. Cheers," he raised the flask and drank.

"Good of you to come."

"Not a bit of it, your dad, well… we – ah," Henry's voice faltered, his eyes brimming with tears. "It's not right you know."

"Sooner than expected, certainly."

Henry had wiped his eyes with the back of his hand and went out through the French windows into the garden.

The man had every right to be upset, but much later as people were leaving, Duncan realised he was still outside.

"Here you are." He had handed him a glass of whisky.

His eyes blotched red, Henry shook the drink down in one. "Where's your mother?"

"Somewhere around," said Duncan. "Shall I get her?"

"No," said Henry, pulling Duncan into a corner. "I don't know how much you know about your dad's life, but he was a bit of a hit with the girls."

"You can be a bit of a hit with anybody if you pay them."

"So, you know that much then."

Mandy had been a regular companion, but she was only the start. A range of women had found their way to the bungalow. Pat had often hosted parties and it was after one of these he had died.

"Best way to go out," suggested Duncan.

The old man stared into his empty glass. "I didn't stay long," he said. "But there was a fella; he turned up out of the blue. Your father didn't know him. The girls did – some of them, at any rate. They were bad news, son."

"Hang on, who is 'they'? You said 'they'?"

"Oh aye. He had a mate."

"So, what happened?"

"I wish I knew. These two were ugly bastards, the one of them had a bashed-in nose."

Duncan listened as the old man described Ryan's facial peculiarity. Guilt fizzed through him.

Days later, in the hotel room, the guilt still bubbled. He checked his wristwatch. For the umpteenth time, he crossed to the window and looked out over the city. Around the world in hotels, how many other men were waiting for a woman?

A knock. He opened the door and Mandy stood, dressed to the nines, an impish grin on her face. She had shorter hair than the first time he had spied her. "Aren't you going to invite me in?"

He stood back and she sashayed by, her bag swinging off her shoulder. She looked round the room, dumped the bag on the bed and faced him.

"Nice… Might be an idea if you shut the door."

He did.

"I always like to get business out of the way first." She held out her hand.

Duncan walked past her and picked up the envelope from the table by the window.

"Thank you," she said, slitting it open and rapidly counting the contents. "Perfect." She slipped the envelope into her bag and lifting it back on to her shoulder headed for the bathroom. "Relax and I'll just get ready. Got some lovely tricks in here."

"No, hold on," he said.

She stopped.

"Actually, you might like to sit down." Duncan gestured towards a chair.

"Alright," she said. She sat down, slid her bag onto the floor, and crossed her legs.

"My name," said Duncan, "is not Scott."

"Oh, I don't care about names. Call yourself what you like. I do."

"I'm Connor, Duncan Connor." Mandy's mouth opened slightly. "I believe you knew my father Pat."

Her poise slipped and a tear glazed her eye. She reached into her bag and pulled out the envelope. "I'm sorry, I can't do this," she said, and standing up she handed it back to Duncan.

"Keep it, please."

Mandy frowned and wiped her eyes. A smudge of mascara came off on her hand.

"Well, I'll leave it, then," she said, walking over. "A father and son's a new one on me, but I'm not starting now, especially not after – "

"I'd like to talk to you."

"I'm not doing that, either."

"No, I want to talk about my dad. About Pat."

"It's not against the law, you know. I've done nothing wrong."

"Please," said Duncan going towards her. "Put the money back in your bag and sit down."

Mandy paused, the envelope still in her hand.

"It's for your time. Call it a gift from my dad."

She was curious. "Did he, you know – did he recommend me?"

Duncan told her his father had often mentioned someone who had made him so happy. He paraphrased from Old Henry. Mandy sat down again and slipped the envelope back into her bag.

"We did have a professional relationship to start with, but he was special to me. I liked him. I wanted to come to the funeral, but you know…"

She had often been to the bungalow, and they'd spent weekends together, and there had been a trip to the Lake District. "He promised we'd go to Paris."

They had co-hosted his parties, and he had become a part of the agency. She didn't know the financial details, but she understood there was an arrangement.

"He used to say he took full advantage of the facilities." She smiled. "I'm not a jealous person."

"Didn't you ever get bored by the war stories?"

"No, he was the hero of them all."

"He wished," Duncan laughed. "He was born at the wrong time."

"Then I'd have missed him. I really liked your dad. I can't say that about many I meet."

When the subject of the last party arose, Mandy was guarded. Duncan couldn't tell if it was too painful for her, if there was another, more sinister, reason. "I'll be frank with you: Henry told me a little bit, but I want to hear your version."

"He was hardly there."

Duncan took a breath. "The two guys, you know the ones I mean?"

Mandy nodded. "I'm not going to get into any trouble, am I?"

"No, this is absolutely for my benefit. It'll go no further."

"I've heard that before now."

"It's just that I think I might know them. They're police, aren't they?"

"Once, I think," she leaned forward. "They did special ops, they called it. Boasting, probably. Said they like to have fun with people. How did you know them?"

"Well…" Duncan wasn't sure how much to say.

"Come on, you're expecting me to talk"

"They sort of arrested me, but I escaped."

"What does that mean?"

"It was all a bit of a misunderstanding." Mandy inclined her head questioningly. "I was trying to talk to a girlfriend and her mother objected, called the police."

"Are you a creep?"

"No, I don't think so."

"You must've been pretty bad."

"Well, I wasn't. But these two nutjobs turned up."

Mandy nodded. "See, I only knew one of them. I mean, he was a client once or twice, the one with the nose."

"Ryan?"

"Yeah. Mr Ryan, I knew him as."

"What about the other one?"

Mandy pulled a face. "Mr Slipper, that's what we all called him. He had a thing about spanking – heavy duty, if you want to know." Mandy shook her head. "You should've seen the state of the poor girls afterwards… A thoroughbred bastard, he is."

"So, who invited them?"

Mandy shrugged, "One of the girls, I s'pose. All sorts would come. Your dad was a kind of matchmaker."

"A pimp?"

"Ooh, no, don't think of him like that. He just liked bringing people together, but not those two."

"What happened exactly?"

"I wish I knew. They took your dad off."

Duncan had an awful vision of a car ride. "How d'you mean, off?"

"Into another room. They said they wanted to speak to him."

"What about?"

She shrugged. "I guessed it was some girl, or a client."

She fell silent.

"Can you go on, Mandy?"

"Well, they were shouting, and I think, I don't know, they hit him. Maybe."

Duncan slumped back in his chair.

"It kind of did for the party. Most of the girls left, and then they went soon after."

"What about my dad?"

"He stayed in the room, and then I went in to see him."

"And?"

"He wasn't very well. His jacket was off, and he was holding his arm."

"They'd twisted it up his back."

Mandy frowned.

"It's what they do," Duncan explained. "One of the things. Then what happened?"

Her hands briefly covered her face. "Could I have a drink?"

Duncan opened a small bottle of white wine from the mini-bar and poured it into a glass. He placed it on the little table beside her.

"Thanks." She drank. "My name's Linda."

"Ok. Thank you for telling me. That's nice, Linda."

"I don't like talking about this." She put down the wine, got up and went into the bathroom.

Duncan looked out the window. He imagined he had a rifle, and through the telescopic sights he aimed at Chewing Gum and Ryan. A deep breath… 3… 2… 1…

When Linda returned, she had scrubbed off her make up. She sat down again and cleared her throat.

"I gave him the best send-off I could," she said, looking directly at Duncan.

"Thank you."

She held up her hand. "I didn't realise that's what I was doing, mind," she briefly smiled, "He'd become the life and soul again."

Duncan liked her. She was naturally funny. He could tell what Pat had seen in her.

"In the morning, I cleared up a bit, made some breakfast on a tray and when I got back to the bedroom he was gone –I mean, you know, lying there. I'm sorry."

She cried.

The way she had described it reminded Duncan of Hannah's death, her perkiness and then a sudden relapse. Through her tears Linda hoped Duncan didn't think the worse of her. He went over and held her.

"Of course not," he said, "I'm glad you were there."

She nestled into him. They stayed together silently for a while, then she drew back dabbing her eyes with a tissue.

"What did they want with him? Do you know?"

Duncan nodded. "Me, I think."

Duncan beefed up Beth's security. Old Henry was drafted in to fix new locks, starting with the French windows.

"Wouldn't it be simpler to have a dog?" suggested Beth, bewildered by the transformation of her suburban house into Fort Knox. Poot, a black labrador puppy, arrived. The bungalow underwent a similar makeover where Duncan secreted a baseball bat and a strategically placed vicious-looking rat trap exponentially expanded by Henry again. It was capable of doing medieval-style damage. Henry recalled a scene from an old Dustin Hoffman film, 'Straw Dogs' when a bunch of thugs laid siege to an isolated farmhouse.

"Don't make 'em like that anymore." Duncan wasn't sure whether he was referring to the Peckinpah film or to the trap, which Henry keenly demonstrated by releasing a catch and the claw thudded into its prey with lightning speed.

He smiled, "That'll give 'em a stump for life."

In the park, Poot scampered, legs in all directions, snuffling, peeing, approaching dogs and their walkers.

"Hey," said Duncan. "You're far too friendly. You're supposed to be on guard."

Poot wagged his tail and Duncan threw a stick. If stick collecting was instinctive in dogs, returning it was not. Poot, wrestling the stick in his mouth, avoided Duncan's attempts to snatch it back. Only when he found what looked like a cowpat did he drop it.

"Attention span of a flea," said Duncan, and walked on.

He quickened his pace and thought through what else he needed to do.

Before he realised, he had crossed the park. He turned back. A cyclist in bright yellow and black lycra leggings sped past the adventure playground; a cocker spaniel drooped after its owner – but there was no sign of Poot. Duncan whistled and a jack russell cocked an ear, but thought better of it. He shouted several times adding a hopeful "Come on, boy", and then wondered if the dog knew his own name yet. A woman with a poodle had not seen Poot, and neither had a boy with a terrier. The dog had vanished. Duncan checked the slope where the kids drank and lit bonfires, then hurrying by the site of the old bowling green pavilion where he'd kissed Abby Ranson that bonfire night, he ran down to the road. Had the dog been run over? Or, a nagging worry, had someone taken him, kidnapped him? Somebody who was picking off the family one by one. If that was paranoid, he was.

"POOT!" he yelled in fear and desperation.

An hour later, holding the leash limply, he returned. Beth was peeling onions at the kitchen table while Angela cooked at the stove.

"When you take a puppy for a walk, the lesson is: don't go wandering off on your own," advised Beth, without looking up. She called, and Poot ran in straight to his bowl.

Then, some good news, the Bastard Bollox, enjoying a break in Gloucestershire, had his 'lost money belt', and for good measure, his phone.

"Come to mama and collect," she invited. Failing that, she could return it by courier. She had deducted 'commission', which still left a handsome amount. She was vague as to how she'd come by the belt, but any further investigations meant dipping into her web, so Duncan suggested she send it and the phone, he'd pay the cost. He was getting his life back together. To celebrate he took Beth and Angela out for a slap-up meal.

CHAPTER THIRTY-EIGHT

"You said this would never happen," he said smiling. Linda frowned. "The father and son thing."

"Ah, that was only in a business sense."

They were lying in bed in the same hotel room where they'd first met.

"But with Pat hadn't it developed from being business into a sort of, well, a relationship?"

"Mm," she said, her hand stretching down to his groin. "Are you complaining?"

"Certainly not, no," laughed Duncan.

"Remember, you're sleeping with Linda, not Mandy."

"My point, you made the same transition with Dad. And 'sleeping with' that's quaint."

"I'm an old-fashioned girl. Now shut up, I have a question?"

"Uh-huh… don't stop."

But Linda did, "Who gave you the fringe?"

Duncan's eyebrows furrowed, attempting to look upwards.

"No, down here," she said, sweeping back the sheets and tugging at his pubic hair.

"Ow!"

"Definitely been cut." She slipped further down the bed for a closer inspection. "Scissors, no question."

She looked up at him.

"Honestly?" said Duncan, sitting up.

"Here," she pulled a compact mirror from her bag and held it at a precise angle for Duncan to look. "I've seen some weird stuff, but this is *really* odd."

"Hm," said Duncan, observing topiary had clearly been attempted. Suddenly she shut the mirror. "You're getting excited," she grinned. "Talk about up yourself."

"No, that's because of you," he said, pulling her to him.

"Tsk," she said. "What have you been doing?"

The only explanation was the Canadian woman, Naomi or Nancy, on the night train from Paris to San Sebastian. She had taken something from him after all.

"God, you're so lucky," Linda said. "Drunk on a train, she could've lobbed the whole thing off."

"S'pose there are pubic hair collectors. Is it like notches on the bedpost?" Duncan wondered.

"Or trainspotting," she shrugged. "Don't ask me."

"I'd expect you to be the expert on weird."

"Are you asking for some trade secrets?"

They snuggled down together, and Duncan was given an education in tales of freakery, much of it laugh out loud. But Linda was giving up 'Mandy'. She'd done it before, however the money had been difficult to resist. And that's when it had happened: Mr Slipper had rung the agency, and Linda had declined or, in the jargon, had said she was not available. He got the same answer from all the girls.

But when Ryan got in touch, she had agreed.

"Risky," said Duncan.

"I wanted to see if I could find anything out."

"That's my job."

She playfully slapped his hand. "I can take care of myself."

She had gone to a hotel and Ryan let her into the room, but guess what? Slipper was there.

"No way," she told them, and was out the door quicker than you could say Jack Robinson. "Ryan came after me, he was shouting and raving. It was helter-skelter down in different lifts" she laughed.

"I'm glad you're laughing," said Duncan.

"I can now. He catches up with me in the foyer going, 'Pretty please, come back, you know how much I love you.', 'Don't touch me,' I say. 'Get off.' Next thing, he's really gripping hold and he's in my face, saying, 'You bitch, you'll do exactly what I'm paying for.' And I think I've had it here, and he's wheeling me around to the lift. I'm crying, thinking 'when's one of these nice people down here gunna do something? Couldn't they see a woman in distress?' Then this security guy comes between Ryan and the lift. And he says, as nice as pie, like he's asking for a light, 'Excuse me, please.' And Ryan's nicey-nicey back to him, thanking him for his interest, but do one. Now he talks to me. 'Madam,' he asks – I loved the Madam – 'Are you happy with this gentleman?' Well, I'm shaking, aren't I? Ryan's still got his claws into me, hurting. The guy says to Ryan, 'You're old enough and, if I may say so, sir, ugly enough to know when a lady says no, she means no.'"

"Is that what he actually said?"

"Promise you, word for word."

"Brilliant."

"Well," Linda pulled her nose, and they both laughed. "Ryan loses it – 'Mind your own business, shithead.' Security guy's calm as you like. He just keeps saying, 'I am asking you politely, let her go, sir.' And Ryan's coming back to him, and he says, 'she's paid for,' which I am not. I wasn't – there hadn't been time."

"I believe you," said Duncan.

"I just want you to know, I've never walked out on anybody, even when they've been the most disgustingly, repulsive, ugly person ever."

"Professionalism is respected in any business."

"Anyways, Ryan's still trying: 'I'll have you sacked,' he says. So, the guy leans right in his face and says if he doesn't let go of me at once, he says, Ryan will wish he'd never been born. So cool. But Ryan's still hanging on, so the guy just jumps on him, and throws him into the lift so hard Ryan rebounds off the side."

"Lovely," purred Duncan.

"The guy says to me, 'Thank you, Madam, good evening.' Well, I'm so grateful I'd have had him there and then. But he goes up in the lift with Ryan. Next thing, I hear the guy's given Ryan such a beating

Slipper's had to carry him out of the side entrance. And since all this, they've been barred from the hotel and the agency has warned all the girls to have nothing to do with them anymore. So, what d'you think of that?"

"I'm so glad you're alright."

"Ahh," she kissed him on the cheek. "It's a little bit of payback for Pat."

Duncan nodded grimly.

"I think that's the end of them."

Duncan wasn't so sure, but Linda abruptly switched tracks, "With your dad gone, bless him, you need to get your head right."

"What's brought this on?"

"The way you talk about her, you're still in love with Kathryn?"

Duncan was as much taken with the swift change of subject as Linda's clear-eyed assessment "D'you think?"

She got out of bed, "Oh, you can be so annoying. If you were mine, I'd kill you."

He was astonished. "What?"

"Duncan, the answer is YES!"

"Right. Er, will you get back into bed, please?"

"No. Get your arse in gear; the rest will follow."

She found her knickers, pulled them on, went into the bathroom and slammed the door shut.

"That's your lot," she shouted.

Duncan lay back. Of course, he told himself, Linda was right about Kathryn, but still the dark cloud of Chewing Gum and Ryan hung over him.

"It's my break in five minutes, I'm dying for a tab," said Joe, the security guard.

He wasn't the towering six-foot-plus Superman that Duncan imagined. Instead, he was a squat but muscular unit. His eyes boring into Duncan told their story: do not mess.

"That's the way to keep out of fights," he said, pointing two fingers at his intimidating steel blues. "The threateners."

"Pity that guy didn't take the hint."

Joe laughed.

They huddled together in the alleyway behind the hotel, Duncan in no doubt he was getting the onceover. "Thank you for meeting me," he said, declining a cigarette.

"Don't mind me saying," said Joe, "but you don't look the sort to get mixed up with a couple of turds like them."

"What can I say? Something, we unfortunately share. The one with the nose was down to me."

"Respect," said Joe, expelling a lungful of smoke. He confirmed Chewing Gum and Ryan were ex-police, but unofficially they'd retained a link with the force.

"They couldn't be done for impersonating police officers?"

"Who would know they weren't?" Joe continued. "Put it this way: they deal with things your serving officers couldn't or would rather not. Their usual M. O. is such that, well… let's just leave it at unorthodox."

Duncan explained why he'd been at the Giffords, which, though fraught, could hardly be described as unorthodox.

"Known in the trade as a domestic," Joe smiled grimly. "Sounds like they were bored and intervened on the mother's call."

"Playtime," said Duncan.

"Yeah, that fits. Some kid harassing a girl, they'd pass their contribution off as just desserts – same as the cops would at the station."

"I wasn't – "

"Hey, it's how the mother saw it."

"OK… thugs on call – "

"I'm not judging you. Everything comes down to perspective. Immediate justice from their point of view, and a good time had by all. Except they picked the wrong bloke.

"But it doesn't explain the lengths they went to."

Joe looked Duncan up and down. "If you want my help, you've got to be straight with me."

"I am, and I do. I absolutely do want your help."

"You're sure, you'd never met them before, upset them in some way?"

"No," said Duncan. "I'd remember."

"These people are driven by grievance, they sure as hell hold grudges."

Duncan nodded but his answer was still, no, their paths had never crossed.

"Sounds like they went a bit rogue, even for them."

A couple of hotel staff came by. Joe nodded at them. And then Duncan told him about what had happened to Pat.

"There you go." Joe stubbed out his cigarette with the heel of his shoe. "I'm sorry."

It felt odd to Duncan, to say the least, that he had his worst fears about his father's death confirmed by a stranger. He closed his eyes. His memory of Pat materialising in front of him in the Spanish café Duncan now saw as a cry for help. He couldn't tell his torturers about his son's whereabouts because he didn't know. This was agony.

Joe sensing Duncan's discomfort, said, "Come inside a sec." They sat opposite each other in a small non-descript office with a tall grey steel cabinet and a coat hanger on the back of the door. Joe cleared a folded-up tabloid newspaper from a chair and brewed Duncan a cup of tea.

"All roads lead them to me, don't they?" Duncan asked, placing his cup on a chipped saucer.

"Your dad, Linda… yeah, sex with her wasn't uppermost with them that day. Great girl, by the way."

"She is," agreed Duncan.

"How well d'you know her?"

"Well enough…" He caught the gleam in Joe's eye.

"Ah, I see." Joe was still looking at him, waiting. "It's ok, she's sent me in another direction." Joe nodded.

They both smiled.

"Aren't you worried those bastards will want revenge?"

Joe grinned. "They know where I am."

Duncan drew a breath. "This is a big ask, I know, but if I ever need to, can I count on you?"

Joe's nostrils flared, he was like an animal sniffing out friend or foe.

"Why not?" he said, "I hate bullies."

They shook hands, Duncan trying hard not to show his relief. Joe produced a card and, with a biro, scrawled a number on the back. "The unofficial one. Day or night."

"Thanks so much, I'm really grateful." Duncan stood up.

"One thing, when I got nosey boy in that lift, I had him done…" Joe looked up at Duncan. "Then he kind of laid himself out to me, and he said, 'Kill me.' And again, 'Go on, kill me.' He was smiling. It was weird."

Ryan's bloodied face flashed through Duncan's mind. Was that what Ryan was begging him to do when he'd dropped him at the hospital? To kill him?

"Live by the sword, die by the sword," he muttered.

"From St Matthew's Gospel, that."

"Is it?" asked Duncan, surprised.

"Paraphrasing, of course."

"Of course."

"Not just a pretty face, you know," grinned Joe.

They liked each other.

As he walked away from the hotel, Duncan thought hard. Had he met Chewing Gum and Ryan before that night? Had it been so traumatic that he'd blocked it out? If so, surely, he'd have done the same with the horror at the Giffords'. But he could never forget it. The pair were inseparable in his mind. But what about if he'd come across one of them or either of them on their own? Again, he thought not…

Everything was as he remembered it: the same quiet crescent; neat identical houses; his heart in his mouth as he approached the paved path up to the house; the letterbox. He was about to ring the bell when the front door opened. A man in his mid-twenties, tweed cap on his head, stood there pulling on a Norfolk jacket.

"Oh," he said. "Can I help?"

"I'm not sure," Duncan replied. A bleak thought hit him. "I was looking for Kathryn, but perhaps I've got the wrong – "

"Just a mo." said the man, in a rush. "Kathryn!" he called behind him, then returned to Duncan. "Who are you?"

This was the scenario Duncan feared. His instinct was to bolt, but what the hell was she doing with this animated berk? Hadn't she set herself against people like this?

"Er – Duncan."

"Come on in, go through." The man pointed down the hallway.

"Kathryn, it's for you!" he bellowed again, and crossed the threshold. "Bye. Got to dash."

The door slammed behind Duncan. Then silence. Wherever she was, she had heard the man shouting.

"Hello?" There was a shuffle from the kitchen and suddenly a woman appeared, holding a baby. She stopped and stood back. "Oh. Do I know you?"

The relief that she wasn't Kathryn flooded through him.

"Who are you?" she asked, panic in her voice.

"No, you don't know me," Duncan said quickly to allay her fear. "I was looking for Kathryn Gifford, she used to live here."

"Oh."

"I'm sorry to interrupt. I'm trying to find out where she's got to."

"Gifford." She seemed to relax. "Come in."

They reached the kitchen and, once again, Duncan saw the tree and the fence in the garden. This time from the safety of inside.

"Do sit down."

He sat at a table covered in cooking utensils and empty food bowls. The baby's direct stare disconcerted him.

"Gifford," she repeated.

"Mother and daughter. D'you happen to know where they went?"

"The name's familiar… Wait, yes." She plonked the baby into the highchair. "Would you mind – "she indicated.

Duncan got up and gingerly held the baby in place while she flicked through papers in a rack on the wall.

"How long have you lived here?"

"Oh, what'll it be now?" She looked round at the baby. "How old are you, Jeremy?"

The baby gurgled.

"Six months. We brought it from some people called Pope. Helen Pope?"

Duncan shook his head.

"God knows why we've kept them." She handed Duncan several envelopes, all addressed to Ms K. Gifford. "I'm a Catherine with a 'C'," she explained, strapping Jeremy into the chair.

But it was Kathryn's voice Duncan heard. She was there in front of him, fussing with the child. Coming so soon after his father's 'appearance', it unnerved him. What did this mean? Could Kathryn have died like Pat? Just then?

"Are you alright?"

Duncan realised he was staring. "Yes, sorry, I was thinking."

"Quite a thought by the looks of it."

"Yes." He distracted himself with Kathryn's post, which was from catalogue companies: one for footwear, another for painting materials, and the last from the Tate Gallery in London.

Baby Jeremy was agitating.

"You've got a lot on your hands," Duncan said.

"Haven't I, sweetie," Catherine said, smiling in admiration at her child.

"Well, thank you. I'd better be off."

"I'm sorry I can't be any more help. I do know the Popes weren't here very long. He got a job in New Zealand and off they went." They reached the front door. "I'll put those in the bin, if you like."

Duncan was about to hand the envelopes back when he had a second thought. "You never know, I might find her."

"Good luck," she smiled.

Catherine closed the door. Duncan stood in the road. Except for Siobhan, the woman who'd interrupted them at the lake, there were no other links – and he didn't know where she lived. Neither did he wish for a further encounter. There was the girl whose party they'd been to,

Lynette something or other, or Claudine... But what was the point? And that apparition? Did it mean he had sixth sense? Like that Bruce Willis film? Or was he just seeing things?

Walking away, a police car had entered the crescent. He watched the solo driver pass him and then pull up outside the house, exactly as Chewing Gum and Ryan had, years before. He looked up. Catherine, Jeremy in her arms, was in the same upstairs window Kathryn had been that night – the last time he had seen her. Catherine waved, Duncan waved back, and then she was gone.

The police car moved on, and so did he.

Duncan swung along the landing, bag in hand and saw his mother's bedroom door was ajar. In the wardrobe mirror, he could see Angela propped up in bed. She was reading the newspaper.

"Is Angela, ok?" he asked his mother.

"Nothing but a head cold. She'll be alright in a day or two."

"But she's in your bed."

Beth smiled. "How has it taken you so long to work that out?"

"Oh," said Duncan.

"Anyway, I was rather dreading the big speech so thank God."

"Dreading?"

"You know having to spell it out, as if it was some kind of drama. I've had plenty of those, thanks very much."

"How long have you been... er, you know?"

"What? A dyke, a muff diver, a rug muncher?"

"Come on, Mum."

"Well, say it then. It won't bite you."

"Gay."

"All my life, I suppose, but never met the right girl."

"I meant, how long have you been with Angela?"

"Ooh, now, since whenever we met. Chalk it up to the penal system, wouldn't you say?" Beth blushed.

Duncan had a lovesick teenager on his hands. "Anyway, that's enough about us," she said. "We're supposed to be talking about you."

Beth, making up for lost time, had taken up the maternal role once more. She wanted to know his plans.

"This is far more interesting. Did Dad know?"

"God knows. It was none of his business."

"You don't need to be like that about him."

"You weren't married to him."

"I guess neither were you, as it turns out."

Beth held her hands up. "Ok, fair point. Plans, please," she said, back on topic.

Duncan kissed her. "Leaving on a jet plane," he said, slinging his bag over his shoulder and heading out the door.

CHAPTER THIRTY-NINE
EUROPE 2005 – 2010

Happy that his mother had found Angela, and the house made secure, Duncan was on tour again but with a difference. He had been approached by the lovechild of Bob Geldof and Richard Ashworth: Benji Wilson, the cocky lead singer from a band making industry waves, called Heavy Rain. They needed someone to manage a northern European tour. But, beset with problems from the start, it was not the escape Duncan had planned. In Copenhagen, the narcissistic Benji, who already envied Josh, the bass player's aptitude, demanded he was sacked. Josh had taken up with a girl who had knocked Benji back. Duncan refused to get rid of him, and resentment hardened. The tour rumbled on through Oslo, Stockholm, and Gothenburg, but by the time they reached Berlin, it was Duncan who had the problem.

He had not slept all night. First thing, he rang the management company saying he was out. Barefoot, he struggled down to the tour coach, and handed over the schedule to Josh. In shock, the band watched as Duncan sat down on the pavement and wept.

He had managed to get through Pat's funeral, but the guilt in him now was off the scale. Pat must have felt the same bewilderment and fear that Duncan had when Chewing Gum and Ryan had driven him off into the darkness. But, unlike Duncan, Pat was helpless. He could not fight.

Thinking he had mistaken her name, Linda had told him Pat had cried out for Hannah. No mistake, Pat had called for his mother.

Duncan's crying became great racking, heaving sobs. Where the hell were those two bastards now?

The hotel receptionist helped him back inside. A doctor was called, but Duncan refused any medication. He took the view there wasn't a medical remedy for his diagnosis. Pat would have complained he'd gone on the run again, but how far had he got? He might as well have been in Timbuktu for all the difference distance made. Leaving hadn't solved anything. But the solution whatever it turned out to be had yet to appear. He booked another night in the hotel.

The following morning, still feeling as though he was in a fog, he got out of bed, put on his shoes and went for a walk. Kreuzberg, the district was singing with history. Didn't the communists take on the burgeoning nazis here during street fighting in the 1920s? Pat would know, perhaps Hannah too. And wasn't Checkpoint Charlie the famous Berlin Wall crossing point between West and East on Friedrich Strasse?

The only clear thinking he'd managed was the fact that Pat had gone, and there was nothing he could do to change that. The one person he could talk to about it, he couldn't anymore. But what was he looking for: to get off the hook, stop feeling guilty, apologise, seek his father's forgiveness, redemption? These were all big words; he tried to settle for something far less lofty. All he wanted was to feel better. Even that seemed hopeless, but he decided to walk a little further before returning to the hotel.

It was worth it; a miracle happened.

A young French actress, Matild Tabard, sat at a table outside a café, surrounded by a mountain of shopping bags. Using a range of cell phones, she was furiously texting and ringing. The miracle was parked nearby. A gleaming green Maybach. This particular model, the 62S, sported the six-litre v12 capable of nought to sixty in under five seconds. Astonishing performance, Duncan thought, given the bulk of it. He idly priced the vehicle somewhere in the region of 400,000 euros. He sat down and ordered a double cappuccino. Matild's constant noise irritated him, but, once he had connected her to the car, he lent an ear. Her chauffeur had left her in the lurch; a three-hour drive from her apartment.

In a rare break from her telecommunications, she asked him, "You are looking at me because you recognise me, yes?"

Duncan had no idea.

"Well, I'm sorry, but I have no time for autographs," she continued.

"I don't recognise you, no."

Mathild took off her sunglasses. "Is this better?"

"Yes," said Duncan. "I can see who you are." Mathild glowed. "But I still don't know who you are."

Mathild's expression switched to disbelief. A reaction that even outshone Benji Wilson's self-adoration. But from her, it was stupidly sweet.

He had landed on Planet Actor.

"What's happened to the chauffeur?"

"I don't know. I have not seen her since early time this morning, and she is not answering me," she said, impatiently.

"Won't she be back?"

"I have such an important date tonight. It is for my career. I must get home, *l'impératif!*"

She'd been invited to a party hosted by a world-famous movie star, who happened to have a villa across a lake from her apartment.

"You can see I have all the costumes," she pointed at her bags and added. "This man I will marry, too."

"If you're going to marry him, shouldn't he send a helicopter for you, or his own chauffeur?"

Mathild played with the necklace around her neck. "Ok, if we had already met."

Duncan rolled his eyes.

"This is my mission."

"You, and a million others, perhaps."

"Maybe," she agreed, "but they don't get invited to his party."

"How did you?"

"It is work. My agent, she tells, and my father has some say."

"If you'd like, I'll happily drive you."

Matild held up a finger and pointed it at Duncan, as if instructing him to wait. Then she picked up her phone and took Duncan's photograph. "If anything happens to me, my father's a gangster. He will kill you," and added flirtatiously, "If you're good you can come to the party. I take you."

The sun was shining too. Duncan thanked the people at the hotel for their care.

He switched on the engine and eased the Maybach forward. For Duncan, it was his number one restorative, driving something powerful like the Maybach's mighty twin-turbo, with its heated wooden steering wheel, handstitched premium leather across the dashboard, designed by the company who had made Zeppelins. What would Hannah have made of that? It was surreal. Let the journey last forever. Françoise had left her chauffeur's uniform, which Duncan had no chance of getting into, and indeed no desire – but the cap fit, just, and played its part when they purred well above the speed limit. Mathild, lounging in the roomy back, cocktail in hand, gave the alarm, and soon afterwards the sirens jangled into earshot. Duncan adjusted the chauffeur's cap. The police car slowly, but surely, dipped back and out of sight, sirens fading.

"Well, I wouldn't have believed it."

Mathild giggled. "It suits you, keep it on," she said.

The road disappeared beneath him, and Duncan was floating in the clouds with the same feeling of invincibility that protected him in the boxing ring and on the moor. Superficial perhaps, but it was the prescription he needed.

He parked the Maybach in the garage beneath Matild's lakeside apartment and, despite her by now hectoring demand that he escorted her to the party, he had had enough. He wished her well with the famous film star, thanked her for the ride and returned the keys.

Benji Wilson's father, it turned out, had bankrolled the Heavy Rain tour and was a decent human being. Alexander Wilson paid Duncan's wages in full and supplied him with a plane ticket home. Not long after, Duncan noted that Benji Wilson became a front-page tabloid sensation. As an X Factor contestant, he had breezed through to the Boot Camp episode of the show before hitting an assistant director, and in a 'drink and drug fuelled rage' trashed his room. Alexander had met his son off the plane at Heathrow and hounded by the press, transferred him to rehab. Since when, no further sightings. But Duncan had more concerns on his mind.

Andrzej's warning had turned out right, but no one could have guessed it would be a 'War on Terror'. Was this a new concept for the 21st century, or something dreamt up by an illiterate U.S president? But a name hardly mattered when thousands of people died, and countries were destroyed. Pat though would have delighted in the military strategies of Generals like Tommy Franks, who based his M.O. on the German blitzkrieg of 1939/1940. He'd have chalked up new names like Abu Ghraib in Iraq, or Helmand Province in Afghanistan to rival Dieppe. Duncan pulled himself up short. This amount of interest in battlefields, was he in danger of turning into his father? Steering clear of war zones was a no brainer, but nevertheless, a concomitant increase in terrorism from Bali to Madrid and London spread across the globe. The options for risk-free travelling, or "turning aimlessness into art form", as Pat would have had it, were contracting.

Duncan became adept at frugal living or making a virtue of self-denial. He had no choice. But there was something else. It was as though a hand guided him. Since leaving Matild, he had crammed in Rome and then Florence, where he took a job at the Uffizi Galleries guarding the exhibits. He rapidly learned that daily exposure even to some of the finest art in the world palled – except for Caravaggio. He hunted down as many of the originals as he could, attracted to the rich darkness of the compositions, the characterisations, life's mean little corruptions. 'The Card Sharps', one of his favourite's, thrilled him.

Then in Nice, he discovered Matisse. It was on an all-expenses-paid trip with a bored young financier, Albert – who had taken a shine to the itinerant, only to be disappointed Duncan's interests lay in his car: a white soft-top Maserati GranCabrio. While it was a beauty to behold, and a joy to drive, it couldn't compete with the shapes and colours of Matisse's cut-out period. Duncan was mesmerised. Here was art so simply made, it seemed, at the flourish of a pair of scissors. So youthful and playful he was amazed to learn they had been made towards the end of the artist's life. Outside the Musee Matisse, contemplating beneath the trees what he'd seen, and wanting much more, his thoughts strayed to Kathryn. He wished he'd discovered Caravaggio and Matisse with her. How he'd love that. What would she think? What would she say? And an even better question: where was she? What was she doing? He'd love to know. His head thrummed with memories: their first walk, making love, their time together. Had everything that had happened to him stemmed from her refusal that terrifying night? Ever since then he had been anxious something fearful was round the next corner. He hadn't been wrong.

But now what?

During his touring days a gig at the HolyWood Stage in Vouliagmeni near Athens stood out. Duncan had promised himself he would return to Greece. Now was the time. But by abandoning the art galleries, he felt like he was leaving Kathryn behind – again.

As it was, he went from the sublime to the ridiculous. Janni, a seller of cheap t-shirts, 'Greek antiques', and other suspect cargo ran a shop in the maze of streets that ringed Monastiraki station, in the centre of Athens. Standing five-foot tall, Janni was a squat figure, always dressed in a dark suit ("good for business"), the lapels sprinkled with cigarette ash from his three-packets-a-day habit. He wore prehistoric standard trainers, and a pork pie hat squashed on his head. He was a master of the art of ducking and diving in his den of knavery amidst the outcrop of ancient ruins beneath the Parthenon. For the pittance he paid, and the camp bed and room he offered above the shop, Janni demanded Duncan also take on security guard duties. In practice this meant overseeing dawn visits, at least once a week, from the Schneiders.

They sounded like the Hounds of Hell at the door.

Sleepily, Duncan pulled back the bolts and opened the double doors.

"Probably not a good idea to wake up the whole street."

"Better if you were ready on time," growled the senior Austrian.

Bruno and Schneider Minor carried in the first of several metal boxes from their rust-heap of a van. They were suitably dressed in removal men overalls.

"Same old rubbish?" Duncan gestured to the boxes.

"Ja, ja."

"Der Mull, der Mull, der Mull," chanted Schneider Minor in a childish sing song voice, which Duncan learned was the German word for garbage.

He quickly got fed up with sorting through the Schneider's knockoffs. And neither was he happy with Bruno grooming the younger Shneider, who had learning difficulties, in his nefarious ways. Once more, something had to give.

Janni suspected Schneider was also supplying a rival. A trap was laid, and a fraught encounter followed when Janni showed up at his rival's backdoor to find Bruno and Schneider Minor unloading boxes. Janni's enthusiasm for the business dwindled; he was homesick for Ithaca. But not before one more delivery from a new source. Duncan opened a cardboard box from a man in a sailor's hat who did a passable imitation of Uriah Heep, the creepy sycophantic character from Dickens' 'David Copperfield'. Out spilled a load of Nazi insignia, mini model swastikas, a helmet or two. Even a pile of brown shirts, and CDs from right-wing bands.

"Special order for a collector," explained Janni.

That did it for Duncan, but where to go?

One afternoon off, he caught the tram up the coast. He hopped off at a spot not only offering a beach but a go-karting track; exactly the place to consider his next move. After he had wheeled round the circuit and dipped into the sea, he fell asleep – future planning no further forward.

He awoke and saw Eleni.

His proper Greek adventure began.

CHAPTER FORTY
NORTHERN ENGLAND 2010

After the chaos he'd left on the road to Athens airport, the rain lashing down as he reached his mother's door perfectly matched Duncan's dismal mood. Still fearing the arm of the law or someone sinister, he had passed through Charles de Gaulle airport without interference and regularly checking he still had the little ambulance caught the earliest flight home. The Channel had always been Britain's first line of defence and, absurdly, he reassured himself that if neither the Armada, Napoleon nor Hitler had managed the crossing, then he was safe. Julius Caesar and William the Conqueror had not entered his calculations.

Beth was in distress. Angela had left, and not for the first time. Duncan, without a shred of evidence, found himself convincing his mother that Angela would be back, which only led to her doubting whether she wanted her.

"I thought it was only younger people who had this trouble," Duncan said.

Beth, a crumpled handkerchief in her lap, blinked. "Go on, then," she admonished. "It's been years, Duncan,"

Where to begin and what to say? Greece's fraught financial situation was as good a start as any, and as he delved into the minutiae, as far as he knew it, he was relieved to spot a distant look in his mother's eye.

Without ever intending to, he suggested, "Talk about it later."

"Welcome home." She kissed him.

He unloaded a box of Belgian truffles bought at Charles de Gaulle, and a print of a Matisse cut-out. His mother spent the rest of the day deciding where it should hang. Duncan shuffled up to his old room; a perfect haunt for a teenager, but he had long outgrown it. A photograph of him and Hannah the car at the aerodrome had bleached in colour. He sat on his bed. The tube containing Kathryn Gifford's painting poked into view. He unrolled it, then instantly shut it again and shoved it back in the tube. Any reference to a death on the road was to be avoided.

Days later, Angela was back. But only to collect her things. Duncan made his mother a cup of tea, and then went upstairs to plead or remonstrate – he wasn't sure which. He found Angela barely dressed on the bed, eyes closed, fingers strumming herself.

"What took you so long?" she murmured.

First it had been his dad, and now… Angela opened her eyes.

"Oh God." She tried to cover herself.

"Stay as you are, I'll…"

Duncan popped his head around the kitchen door and suggested Beth went upstairs. He grabbed Poot's lead and, with the excited dog now grown to guard-dog size, left the house. It was a relief to avoid his mum; his lack of a plan had come under scrutiny.

"Get in touch with the University Admissions, say you want to continue your degree. After all that's what you told your father you'd' do."

Absolutely not, thought Duncan. That was so far off his map.

"Well, what *are* you going to do? Life's flying by and you're just sitting there."

It was true, he was 'just sitting there'. An unwelcome echo of his father's line.

"Since you got back, you haven't been yourself, Dunc. You seem very furtive."

"Maybe it's a family trait."

"Alright, I asked for that, but I am concerned. You will tell me if something's worrying you, won't you?"

The decision he made, he told his mother, was to move to the bungalow.

"Like father, like son," Beth retorted.

"Well, no, I hope not, not exactly, it'll give you and Angela more space."

He pretended to himself moving to the bungalow was a step further away from Interpol, or whoever else might be calling. Greece was never far from his mind: the island, the boiling hot mornings, swimming, and even Beanie's cheroots. On the other hand, he would wake at night disturbed by gunfire and burning bodies.

As he opened the bungalow's front door, a noise came from inside. Duncan tensed. Someone else was here. He paused in the hall. Another sound, from the kitchen. He readied his bag as a weapon and strode through the door swinging. A man, lying full length on the floor, headphones clamped to his ears, was prodding the skirting boards.

"HELLO?"

The man turned round in surprise, cracking his skull on the table lip, which dislodged his headphones. Henry Blofeld's plummy-voiced commentary on 'Test Match Special' filled the room. Yet another seagull had landed on the square at Lords Cricket Ground.

"Bugger," the man said, rubbing his head.

Beth had asked Chas, Old Henry's son, to give the place the onceover and he was checking for wood rot.

"Any sign?" asked Duncan.

"Nowt so far, nah."

The likeness was startling: Chas was the same size and shape and continuing the odd-job family tradition. For the sake of another body around the place, Duncan thought up some minor repairs.

Then he took a deep breath and went into the room where Chewing Gum and Ryan had tortured Pat. Before he died, Old Henry had refurbished the bungalow, but Duncan knew too well how places retained an aura. He had thought of suggesting his mother sell the house, but the prospect of explaining why stopped him. Once more the lesson: life was no more than constant re-engagement with the same old crap. Uncomfortable, he left the room never to return to it.

Beth arrived with a bundle of literature from universities, his alma mater on top.

"I can get all this on the internet."

"Well, you haven't, and you don't have to now," she said, plonking them down on the kitchen table. "Angela and I are taking off for a week or two, don't know where. We'll see where it takes us."

"Careful, I remember doing something like that once."

Beth slung her bag over the back of a chair and sat down.

"Why do I get the feeling there's something you're not telling me?"

Duncan shrugged.

"You're not yourself, you're blinking a lot."

As a child he had a twitchy eye and had been nicknamed 'Blink'.

"Come on," she urged. "Given my record, there's not much going to shock me."

There was nothing he could say – not Dmitri's murder, his own captivity, and certainly not his part in the incident near Athen's airport. Admitting one would lead to the rest, and the last he could never share with Beth.

"I know you don't believe me, but I am thinking about the future."

"I'm sure you are," she said, not convinced. "When we get back, I want you to have an action plan. Get to it."

But he did not. He regularly tuned into the BBC's World Service and one night heard that two men had been charged with the horrific murder of a sex worker in Athens. He got drunk and, in the morning, the university bumf was still there – he was lying on it. But he found it impossible to think about the future. He was delighted the murderers had been charged, but what if the investigation widened and they linked them to the cell that killed Mazarakis?

Chas arriving for some heavy-duty work with a hammer drove him out of the bungalow. To clear his head, he walked into town.

In a record store, he saw the man flicking through a vinyl rack. His hair was greyer, but that puny frame had not changed. More bad memories cycled before his eyes. Bile rose in Duncan's throat.

"Wilkinson?"

The man squinted at Duncan.

"I don't know you, do I?" The voice was the same, but croakier.

"It is you."

"Are you drunk?" Wilkinson covered his nostrils with his hand overtly.

"You stink."

Duncan wanted to hit him, but Dmitri's voice echoed in his head: "I don't believe in revenge. Where does it stop?"

"I am Mister Wilkinson," he emphasised, taking his hand away from the rack. "And whoever you are, I'm finding you unpleasantly aggressive."

"Are you still teaching?"

"No, no, I'm not, if you must know. I'm following my passion. I'm a conductor now with a local orchestra," he said proudly. "I haven't actually taught for some time."

"Thanks for small mercies."

"Oh dear, oh dear," Wilkinson mocked. "What can the matter be?"

"If you had been anywhere near a school, I'd have reported you for child abuse."

Wilkinson turned pale and he steadied himself against the vinyl rack.

"I've still a mind to," added Duncan.

"I promise you I've never touched a child in my life. Now please get out of my way." He tried to edge past, but Duncan stepped in front of him.

"Andrew Cunningham. Twelve years old, remember? Overweight. You called him Fat Boy."

Wilkinson opened his mouth, and then closed it again, his bony fingers raked through his thinning hair. "I'm afraid not, no, I don't."

"You humiliated him – "

"Not me – "

"Yes you, to discourage the rest of us from misbehaving. In front of a class of eight-year-olds you brought him in and made him bend over a chair, and you caned him until he was crying."

"You must be mixing me up with somebody else – "

"Crying for his mother."

Wilkinson twitched.

Then you stood him up and kicked him so hard he fell on the floor. Then you yelled at him to get out and threatened us with the same if we didn't behave. Fucking Nazi, aren't you?"

"Now look here – "

"You sat down at the piano and played 'Three Blind Mice'.

Duncan let that sink in. Wilkinson, his eyes darting, was breathing heavily.

"You gave me nightmares for weeks. What effect it had on Andrew is unimaginable."

An urgent rapping on the window, and a woman and two men peered in, the woman indicating her wristwatch. Wilkinson raised his hand shakily to them.

"Friends of yours?"

Wilkinson tried to move again, but Duncan stood in his way.

"If you'll excuse me – "

"Invite them in, and I'll tell them what you're really like."

"Please – "

"For kicks, you terrorised small kids."

"You're terrorising me – "

"Not nice, is it? And the orchestra, I'm sure they'd like to know."

"Like to know what?" The woman from outside had come in. Wilkinson gulped. "What's going on? Is there a problem, Maurice?"

She looked at Duncan.

"You could say, yes. Your friend here – "

"I won't be long," interrupted Wilkinson. "I'm just coming, I have to…" his voice trailed away.

"If, you're sure?" The woman looked suspiciously at Duncan.

Wilkinson nodded.

"We're just outside."

Wilkinson waited until she left. "Could I have your name, please?"

"Duncan Connor."

"And what d'you want me to – er…?"

"Admit it."

"But what if… I have no guarantees you won't take this further."

"No guarantees, you're right. The school had one towards me, didn't they? In loco parentis, but you broke it, and to Andrew."

"Mr Connor, please, I'm sorry if anything I did caused you pain. I apologise."

"Anything you did – " Duncan was disdainful. He raised his voice. "Anything… You did it!"

Wilkinson shivered; he was close to tears. "Please, I beg of you. I've said I'm sorry. I truly am," he whimpered. "I shouldn't have. No, I shouldn't. Please, Mr Connor."

Duncan had him penned in between a stack of Billie Holiday anthologies, and racks of Mozart recordings. He slowly stood aside. Broken, Wilkinson had difficulty walking. Dmitri might have offered him a hand, but Duncan could not find it in himself.

The woman opened the door for him, "For heaven's sake, Maurice, what's the matter?"

Wilkinson was weeping.

For years Duncan had imagined this moment, wondered if it would ever happen. And now it had.

Once his anger had drained away, he felt empty. Except there was some residue. Hadn't he kicked someone so hard they'd fallen over? Someone ten times more guilty than Andrew Cunningham ever could be, but someone as defenceless as the humiliated boy. Ryan, at the hospital.

Did this make Duncan the bully? Put him in the same category as Wilkinson, or as Nikos with the American, Richmond? However spirited Wilkinson had been with the conductor's baton, he was old and frail. Now Duncan, no doubt, had added fear of what might happen to him during his declining years. Was this recompense for Duncan's sleepless nights often spent shivering outside his parent's bedroom door? Would it finally rid him of the tune 'Three Blind Mice'? What about Cunningham, would he have been grateful? By the time he got back to the bungalow, he was inclined to think the answer was no. It wasn't only other people who were at fault.

When might he have to pay?

CHAPTER FORTY-ONE

The old university city had not changed. Duncan once joked to some American tourists that the cathedral was a model; the real one was at the next stop down the line. They had hopped onto a train. He stood at the top of a cobbled street and looked across the river. Still there – not even the Luftwaffe could shift it. Below, through the trees, he saw the bridge where he'd told his father he was leaving. Now here he was back again…

But some things had changed.

Born under Thatcher's yoke, Duncan had come to something like consciousness around the time stale Tory rule under John Major stuttered to an end and gave way to the fresh air of Tony Blair's new dawn, but he had not taken much notice. Now back and much more politically aware, he noticed alright. He resisted putting this down to Nikos's influence but rather settled for the strife that had befallen the Greeks. The UK electorate had swung right, and the entitled, born-to-rule mob were back in power, albeit tempered by the Liberal Party.

But beneath mainstream politics, something else was happening. National discontent, fuelled by a belief that politicians could not be trusted, was more widespread than he ever remembered. Perhaps it was not surprising in a country pulling itself out of a financial meltdown and a parliamentary crisis over MPs' expenses. In addition, Britain had been infected. Opportunists lurked in the wings, ready to take advantage of any crack or division between the public and their elected leaders. A city trader, Nigel Farage, the head of the UK Independence Party, was busy stoking up anti-EU sentiment using the ancient excuse, and well tested strategy of blaming foreigners for a country's ills. He had been banging his drum for some time, but now people were listening. UKIP's appeal was popular on the right and Duncan saw plenty of their members were a natural fit for Golden Dawn. Posing as patriots, these liars and chancers would say and do anything that promoted division and spread poison.

In a charity shop, he found a pinstriped suit with theatrically wide lapels. It reminded him of the frock coat Janni had given him in Athens. He bought it and wore it for his appointment. Whether or not Beth would have approved of his sartorial flourish, her persistence had worked; he had rung the University admissions department.

He was early and, looking himself up and down in a shop window, his eye caught sight of a black and white photograph of Henry Fonda on the film set of 'My Darling Clementine'. Arms outstretched, the actor balanced on a chair, the two front legs off the ground. Duncan smiled. What he would give to be back at Beanie's now.

He entered. The shop was a jumble of artists' equipment: paint, easels, canvas frames, stationary, greeting cards, and prints for sale. Either the business was not focused, or it was just a mess. Adding to the amateurish vibe, a child with fair hair, wearing a t-shirt a size too big for him, sat beside the till. He was playing on a computer.

Duncan leaned over the jungle of goods and picked up the Fonda photograph. The boy at the till, whispering 'Yes' to himself, had been joined by a woman with black hair tied up in a bright yellow scarf carrying boxes from the back. She looked harassed but managed a smile.

"Yes!" shouted the boy.

"No," said Duncan paying for the photograph, and smiled as the boy glanced up at him. "Good game?" he asked.

"It was," replied the boy, disgruntled, and shaking his head he returned to his computer.

Duncan and the woman together pulled faces. He was leaving when he spotted a poster advertising an art exhibition opening that evening from 6pm 'til 8pm at the College Gallery. He stopped.

The poster featured several expressionist works. The vivid colours and the vibrancy of the light provoked memories for Duncan. Amongst the number of artists featured, the name Catie Bassett jumped out at him.

It was five o'clock when Duncan left the admissions meeting. Subject to departmental negotiation, he could resume his studies, or else begin again as a first year. The registrar, David Maclean, and Duncan had been contemporaries as students, but had not known each other. No wonder. Maclean, a stuffed shirt, was a walking, talking example of everything Duncan loathed. But job done, he had enough information to keep his mother happy.

Duncan's mind was elsewhere. Surely no two artists painted in the same style? And Kathryn becoming Catie was barely a stretch. He dived into the same pub he had years before, when she had left him for the coach station. Confirmation yet again that life was circular. Maybe the answer was to break the circle. Refusing to return to the university did just that. He looked up at the clock. Yet the rational, boring, no-fun voice rattled in his skull: Bassett, Bassett. Only one reason for the surname change. Leave her to it. Duncan drank up. Go home, he told himself.

The Gallery was housed in a glass extension jutting out from the college building into a lake dotted with lilies. Music tinkled as the evening sun dipped low behind the surrounding trees, creating their bulky reflections in the water. Hot from the walk, Duncan slipped off his suit jacket and joined a growing crowd. Offered "red or white wine, sir?", he chose a large glass of white.

He remembered the last exhibition opening he had attended on the island – not a good omen. Though this time, he did not rule out real performance art. Fine art students, heavily made up and in costumes influenced by Otto Dix and Georg Grosz paintings, circulated with trays of vol-au-vents and the tired old fruit and cheese combo. Were they reluctant recruits, like he had been at his parent's bonfire party? Or perhaps a complement or even a challenge to the exhibits, he wondered.

A voice rang out and Duncan jumped. Not another attack, no, but an alpha male calling for order.

"Ladies and Gentlemen, I'm enormously – " deliberate pause to allow the kerfuffle to die down, as no one could miss a word of his important speech. Obediently, the crowd formed a semi-circle in front of him. "As the Master of St Wilfrid's College, I'm enormously proud to welcome you this evening to this exciting exhibition by artists who, for some years now, have had an association with the city or the university, or both. Indeed, I am proud to say they are destined for great things. We're delighted to have them all here before they step up the ladder and out of our reach." He consulted his notes, "And so, without any more from me, introducing from my left to right: Aynsley Finch, Bunty Nicholson, and – er – Catie Bassett."

Duncan edged his way through the crowd, and suddenly there she was, only yards in front of him. Her hair was shorter, her body plumper but wearing a colourful top, a short black skirt, dark tights, and buckled boots, she looked radiant. The Master, a man as domineering as his voice, passed her the microphone he hadn't needed and ushered her forward.

Catie cleared her throat nervously, "Excuse me… Oooh!" She exclaimed at the volume "Sorry – "

A student in a red cloche hat and a pale blue tango dress adjusted the mic.

"Thanks," said Catie, and looked at her notes. "I'm delighted to see so many people here, but like the others I'm pretty terrified."

While the crowd murmured encouragement, Aynsley, who resembled Rik Mayall's character in the TV comedy 'The Young Ones', shrugged. "They'll either like it or they won't." He folded his arms. "Suits me."

Bunty looked up shyly. Duncan recognised the woman who had served him at the shop.

"Because I have quite a long association with this place," continued Catie, "there are several people here who've known me from before. So be gentle, won't you."

The audience laughed, one or two clapped, Catie confidently looked around. "I am very happy to say how grateful I am and, as well, we all are…"

She and Duncan were eye to eye. She stared. He smiled, but her composure slipped. Her expression turned to alarm and her notes crumpled in her hand. She looked away. Duncan willed her to turn her head so he could raise his glass, or somehow ease her back on track, but no.

"I – er, Bunty, d'you think – "

Bunty took the microphone, but before she could speak, Aynsley grabbed it, and upped the volume.

"Ok, right, to those who don't know I'm Aynsley Finch, she's Bunty, you already know Catie. Let's cut the crap and get on with it." He tossed the mic to the Master, who juggled it but held on. Aynsley pointed towards the paintings and shouted, "Mine are over here on the left."

The crowd clapped and crammed in. But the Gallery could not accommodate both the number of visitors, which was still growing, and provide enough room to view the paintings. That was openings – the very worst time to look at any art. Duncan tried to read Catie's printed introduction on the wall, but too many heads got in the way.

What he really wanted to see was whether any of her drawings of him were on show. Or were they surely, like he was, long away in the past. He was happy to see her section already peppered with red sold stickers. But not to see what he took to be the large abstract of her mother sitting in a garden beneath a familiar cherry tree. He smiled to himself, he'd been wrong about her paintings before, but nevertheless he cautiously looked around to see if Ruth was present, but someone else thrust his hand forward.

"How do you do?"

He had a handsome face, fair hair swept back, revealing a high forehead and bright blue eyes. Put him in a flying jacket and he would be perfect casting for a World War 2 fighter pilot. Duncan looked for the man's name badge, but a flower drooping from his buttonhole hid it.

"I'm sorry to interrupt your evening, but I don't believe we've met."

"Right. Duncan Connor."

"I'm wondering whether you collect?"

"Possibly, but whether the funds are available, that's always the question."

"Perhaps I can be of some help there." He leaned forward and reached inside his slim black folder to produce an Arts Council brochure on how to pay in instalments. "Have a look, have a think. I'll be around all evening."

Duncan took the brochure, and, in the exchange, the badge slipped into view.

Duncan retreated to a cubicle in the gents. He sat down and considered. Bassett, confident and in his prime; so now what? Catie had seen him, so stealing off into the sunset would not do. He stood up. Bassett be damned: get out there, tell her how lovely she is and what a great talent she has. Apologise for surprising her during her introduction and then whatever happened next…

Duncan checked himself in the mirror, put his jacket back on, and took the wrong way out.

"Hello, stranger," came a familiar voice behind him. "You're not leaving without saying hello, are you?" He turned. Catie and her wing woman, Bunty, were taking a break in the corridor.

"No," he smiled at her. "Certainly not."

She kissed him on the cheek with such ease and openness he relaxed, but the baton was his.

"I'm so sorry for stealing your thunder back there. I didn't mean to."

In a familiar gesture her hand went to her mouth. "Don't remind me, I think poor Bunty got the worst of that."

"Hello again," said Bunty. "You're to blame, whoever you are."

By now Duncan was sure Bunty knew who he was, but introductions were made.

"I'm not sure what to call you now. Mrs Bassett, or – " Catie and Bunty exchanged looks before laughing.

"Oh no, Catie's much better," she said.

"All right, Catie, with a C, you're looking – well, you're great." He found it difficult to match her calm.

But Catie beamed.

Bunty nudged her. "See you in a bit." She waved at Duncan and returned to the gallery.

"Not so bad yourself. Like the suit, that jacket."

They both smiled. "I don't want to keep you. This is an important night – "

"It's alright – "

"But can we catch up? I mean, would that be alright?"

"Yes, please, of course," she said, handing him her card. "I need to."

"Thanks."

Duncan leaned forward and kissed her cheek; she grasped his arm.

"And what I've managed to see of it…" He gave her a thumbs-up sign.

She smiled "Thanks, that's, well… Thanks."

"Feels light, airier, like the Mediterranean."

"Well, I went to Rhodes once, does that count?"

"Certainly. And I've still got all the early work."

"So, I should think!"

"I'll call, text…"

He left, her words "I need to" repeating in his ear. He looked back and, through the glass, caught an anxious expression crossing her face. Surprised, he stood still. She saw him. Her smile returned and he waved. Bassett joining her held out his hand, but, folding her arms, she walked behind him back into the gallery.

CHAPTER FORTY-TWO

Beth wanted a full report. She'd come up to the bungalow, thought Duncan, to have a better chance of catching him unawares.

Then: "What else?"

He looked at her vacantly.

"It's been two weeks, Duncan. More. I can't believe that's all you've done."

"Right, ok. I threatened an old teacher I'd report him for child abuse."

"What?" She asked, "Who? Not against you – ?"

"No, not me, exactly…." He didn't want to get held up on this.

Beth eyed him suspiciously. "What does that mean?"

"It's done, mum."

"Why've I never heard anything about this before?"

Duncan could have kicked himself for even mentioning it. "Something that happened, God knows, years ago, and like I said it's sorted.

"Go on," Beth looked resigned to more drivel.

"I looked up an old mate, Ray, remember him, who believe it or not he's now a solicitor. Anyway, he wouldn't give me a job in a month of Sundays."

"What sort of job? Connected to the abuse thing?"

"No connection And I met an ex-girlfriend."

"This is all bull."

"As you can see, I helped Chas with some of the shelving –"

"Enough. When you're ready to tell me the truth, call me."

"It is the truth."

"Tsk."

"How was your holiday?"

"I only fell out with Angela once."

"An unqualified success, then."

Beth laughed. "I've never been happier."

"Good, you deserve it, Mum."

"Don't say that," she said, softly. "You know I'll never think so."

"Yes," he said. "I do know that."

"Really?" She had picked up a scent. "What do you mean?"

"Well, things happen, don't they? And you learn from them."

"Hopefully, yes, but there are things I'd dearly love to change."

"Me too, Mum."

She got up. "I don't appreciate this, Duncan, you're not being at all fair."

"Where are you going?"

"Home. I don't like it when you talk in riddles."

"Hang on, not every shit thing only happens to you."

"Maybe not, but I'm well ahead as far as this family is concerned."

"And we never got a choice about that, did we? Like, it wasn't something you could keep to yourself. We all had to know, along with the rest of the world."

"I know, and I'm sorry. We all suffered. Is that what you want me to say?"

"Not really, we've had all that."

"What, then?"

"Please don't go around bearing the blame, thinking you're the only one. You're not. That's all this is."

"I'm your mother, if something's happened, I want to know."

Duncan shook his head, and after she had left in tears, he was still shaking.

"I don't understand it," she had said. "Are you still punishing me?"

"No."

"How can I believe you?"

"It's the truth, I'm not lying, Mum. I haven't told you any lies."

"We're just going round in circles."

"That's life."

"What?" Beth had become exasperated. "You haven't told me anything!"

If she knew he had been talking to Ruth Gifford's daughter… He pulled out Catie's card. He found it impossible to think about the future; despite what he'd told his mother, he was still dealing with the past. He tapped the card several times on the kitchen table. How long should he wait before he contacted her? The normal rules of dating, whatever they were, hardly applied. It was how he had described it at the gallery: a 'catch up' between ex-lovers for whom a decade had passed. How little he had achieved bit into him again. According to his Google search, she'd had exhibitions in Liverpool, Manchester, and Edinburgh, and on the continent. Well, he'd played the continent. How many gigs in how many countries? None of them counted. It's not a competition, he told himself, and anyway, where did this 'show me your medals' attitude come from? She wanted to see him. She 'needed to'. So, why delay?

By the time he picked up the phone all he could think of was the look on her face as he'd left the gallery. It had sliced through him, but signified what? He was prepared for her to say, "It was nice to see you again, but actually, I hope you don't mind, can we just leave it at that?"

On the contrary, he sensed she had been waiting. As ever, her organisational skills were top notch. She chose the pub. She had been there once before and had wanted a special occasion to go back. They did food, so depending on how things went that was an option.

So far, so good… But the task now was to dampen expectations. He had never forgotten her, even when he was with Eleni. Was he ever with Eleni? He could never take her away from Nikos. But there were similarities between the two women. Both had drawn him into some of the worst experiences of his life. No blame attached; he was the common denominator. They had also given him some of his best days. Thinking about it, perhaps they were the ultimate duo.

Duncan arrived early and had an agonising wait. With enough time to convince himself she had changed her mind, he realised he had downed a pint. When his mobile pinged, he was grateful at least she had rung, but it was Chas calling the next morning off. Duncan got rid of him pronto…

She had arrived. He stood up, the proudest man in the pub. He had rigged himself out – a smart new pair of trousers, plus that jacket – but it was Catie who'd pulled out the stops. A skirt pleated; a cashmere top; a lovely long flowing cotton scarf; little earrings that sparkled; and, from the gallery night, the same boots. She joined him, but neither could speak. After a welcoming kiss, they stood grinning at each other.

"Bit late, I know, but I've bought you the post," he said, finally, offering her the letters from her old address.

She was bemused for a moment, then she laughed and put them in her handbag.

"Brave of you to go back there?" A question in her voice.

"It was," he agreed. "I was looking for you." He could tell she was pleased. "Drink?"

The locals treated the place as their front room. The barman conspired in this fantasy and, on the nudge of a glass, served them and ignored the strangers. Once Duncan might have objected, but not tonight. No fuss, please.

"Well," he said to Catie. "How are we going to do this?"

"You first, please."

"Edited highlights?"

"Yup," she said and sat back.

Duncan upped the music tours part of the history, which interested her, but when it came to Greece, as with Beth, he talked about political aggravation, leaving sizable gaps. Her poise on arrival had slipped. She laughed nervously, spilled her drink, and fussed over it too much. Her mobile rang twice and, annoyed, she declined both calls, eventually turning it off. She took a toilet break, which lasted forever. And then it was her turn.

"I've only got one thing to tell you," She said, and took another sip from the drink he had bought her.

"You've been nominated for the Turner Prize?"

"Then it's two things," she laughed. "The first is, Bunty liked you."

"That's good, I liked her. And I'm guessing that's important."

She nodded. "I want you to promise me something, Duncan. Please don't interrupt until I've finished."

She looked so serious; he feared she was ill. Might she be dying?

"I should have told you years ago." She covered her face with her hands and continued, but Duncan could not hear her. "I know I'm breaking the rules, but – "

She dropped her hands; tears were in her eyes.

"Sorry," she said, dabbing them. "D'you remember when we saw 'The Big Lebowski'?"

He nodded.

"I lied. I was pregnant."

She searched his face for a reaction.

"I've taken a vow of silence," Duncan said, rapidly trying to fit this information into a chronology.

"I'd come to tell you, but I chickened out."

He nodded again.

"My mother got me to write a letter – "

"Ahh."

"I wanted to tell you the truth, but she didn't agree. I was sixteen, remember."

He was back to nodding.

"You've probably forgotten it."

He shook his head vigorously.

"Why are you looking so pleased with yourself?"

"Because, minus the pregnancy, I'd worked all this out for myself, and I thought it was entirely your mum because of your dad and my mum. Everything."

"Makes sense, but then you go and fucking well turn up."

"Well, I would, wouldn't I? And that was never to be forgotten, I can tell you."

She looked at him, hard. "But you still don't really get it."

Duncan frowned.

"The pregnancy, clever clogs. That's why Mum had kittens. Once I'd given birth, you had the right to be around and all the rest of it."

"Wait a minute," Duncan looked at her, and she blushed.

"Oh, shit," she said. "Are you going to be ok with this?"

Duncan felt their table slide sideways, but it hadn't. Everything was exactly where it should be, except for his world, which was about to change for good.

"You had the baby?"

She nodded. "His name's Marcus. Duncan, you're a dad."

A dad, he said to himself, and thought of his father.

No, I'm the dad. Me.

"Please say something." Catie's eyes watered again.

"I'm a dad."

She nodded.

"And I've been that way for what?" He was speaking, but he was on auto pilot. "Ten years?"

"Actually, he's eleven."

He nodded. "He's the boy in the shop, isn't he?"

Catie described him.

"So, I've seen my son. And he's seen me."

"What d'you think?" she asked fretfully. "It's not too much of a shock, is it? Sorry, I don't mean – of course it's a shock, silly thing to say…"

"Honestly, truthfully? I've got absolutely no idea."

Of all the things she might have told him, he had not expected this.

CHAPTER FORTY-THREE

A boy.

Duncan thought back to when he was eleven. He ate, drank, slept, and played football in the park. He could tell you the reserve left back for most teams in the top league. But what hooked Marcus? Locked into headphones and a computer, he was connected to a world Duncan knew nothing about.

"Father," he said aloud to the bathroom mirror.

"Mother…"

As if Catie and Marcus weren't enough, what about Beth?

"Hey Mum, I'm a dad. And here's the kicker: his mother's the daughter of the guy you killed in the hit and run. Yeah, you've got it, you and her, happy grandmothers. Won't that be fun?"

All flippancy aside, propped up against the stacked pillows on his bed, the path ahead was strewn with obstacles. The bungalow ceiling seemed to press down on him. His moods swung in quick time. Anxiety for the future was only natural. He had been a one-man band for so long, and then suddenly, now look. How would he cope? The instinct to leave snaked in, but this time he really would be running away. Or perhaps he'd put the dark ages behind him and for the first time be on the brink of finding harmony and intimacy. Surely what he needed.

Slow down, he told himself. He was jumping the gun, taking things for granted. He and Catie had both come a long way from the wood by the lake. These days she had to think for two. He was not her priority. Maybe she'd take a long hard look at how he was fixed and head out of the door. He'd be desperately sorry, but he couldn't blame her.

So, forget doom or happiness; best foot forward and take it step by step. He had a son. It was brilliant news. Celebrate. He did, by long distance. He sent Beanie the Henry Fonda photo via the island post office. He included his address and brought him up to date.

"Number one, I was having him," Catie had explained. "And anyway, as far as my mother was concerned, abortion was never an option. This was all happening so soon after Dad's death, she couldn't bear it."

"Even though I'm the father?"

Catie eyed him. "Are you wishing I'd had an abortion?"

Duncan had answered, emphatically. "Not at all. How can I think anything just now? You're going to have to give me time with this."

She had. What stuck in his craw was that she had not told him before. He understood the fix she had been in, the reasons, but even then. After all this time… Wait a minute…

Her fingers had tapped on the table. "Don't even think it, Duncan Connor," she had said. "Marcus is yours."

There it was, his two-name accusation favoured by Miss Coleman, repeated by policewoman Koutsikos, still with the power to cut into him. He was guilty.

"Yes, course. I'm not doubting you, promise I'm not."
It had been the one moment in the evening when things threatened to sour.
His dream before the pub had been Catie coming back with him. Then, the only hindrance was Jonathan Bassett. He had thought about the pilot lookalike since the meeting was arranged. Did he know about it? Did he know the Duncan Connor back story?

They had got married when she was twenty-one. She had done a foundation course at a local art college, which had opened her eyes to new technology and different fields of work. She was a good student, but she found it difficult to devote enough time to her studies. Marcus didn't need the attention so much as her mother. Ruth had been falling off a cliff, literally. There had been one suicide attempt, but salvation came in the form of Julian, a divorcee and an expert on ancient Britain. He tutored Ruth at a life-long learning centre. At first shy and fragile, Ruth had run a mile, but tender nudges from daughter and long walks around Neolithic sites with Julian had restored her.

Catie had thrown herself into art and the arms of the Oxbridge-educated, well-funded Bassett, a dealer several years older than her. He had an eye for talent in all senses of the word. Duncan was unclear when Kathryn became Catie. He detected Bassett's influence. They had been married within six months, Ruth and Julian in attendance, and Jonathan's pukka mother. His father had not been invited. As Clorinda Bassett elegantly put it, "My husband is with his whore."

There had been no time for a honeymoon. They had had a shop to open two days later; Bunty Nicholson's baby. She was another Bassett art find – and Catie the junior partner. A risky venture, but as Catie said, "So was life, so what the hell."

One morning, she and Jonathan had rolled over in bed in one mind: "Not working, is it?"

They had embraced and broken up with one stipulation. Jonathan retained his professional interest and, through his expanding contacts, promoted her work. She had bitten his hand off. And here they were.

So now what? Welcome to grown up time. When would she have told him about Marcus – if ever? What if he hadn't been to the university that day? Hadn't gone into the shop, been to the gallery? It wasn't just the sight of him that had brought her introduction at the exhibition to a standstill, but that the time had finally come. Surely there must have been many a moment with the squalling child or the distressed mother when she would gladly have reached out, "Here, he's yours, have a go."

Shining knight Jonathan had little to do with child rearing. His skill was providing the money, and anything left over was for the shop. Catie had ruefully confessed it was still a basket case. Whatever Duncan brought to the table; it would not be his wallet. He also had to admit that, while Catie had told him the truth, the version of his life he had trotted out for her was far from it.

She had kept her distance, only thanking him for a lovely evening and adding, “Don’t forget us, Dad”.

Beth, with career-strategy reminders, was his most frequent caller.

He was yet to throw his mother this curve ball.

His mobile pinged. The message was cryptic.

‘Lotz to talk about. E xx’

Eleni was flying to Edinburgh to see her aunt. His instinct was to ignore her, but his mind instantly filled with the road to Athens airport splattered with wrecked cars, the flames and smoke billowing into the sky. Exaggerated images, more bodies, usually Mazarakis’s driver burnt to a cinder. Then, typically, he allowed himself the lovely memories of Eleni in bed; the little cat: a time when nothing could go wrong ever again.

But it had. And now they were done, surely?

CHAPTER FORTY-FOUR
SCOTLAND

The National Gallery of Scotland's restaurant had a fine view across the gardens towards Waverley Station. Edinburgh, the Athens of the North, appropriately, had never looked better. Holyrood, standing on the rock, cast a shadow, but Princes Street was bathed in a bright glow. Only whinnying bagpipes struck a false note, a stereotypical soundtrack to a bad film set in Scotland's capital. The tartan-kilted Rob Roy myth had never impressed Duncan, who, anyway, assumed it had been cleared out by the 'Trainspotting' generation. But so long as tourists, and particularly Americans, visited 'the old country', the romanticised vision of the feudal clan system and happy Hogmanay was still a money spinner.

On the train north across the border, he had examined his motives. Was he ducking out from Catie and Marcus? Or was he holding two pasts side by side and asking 'either, or'? He was anxious. What about Nikos? Had they married; was this her 'lots to tell'?

Then in she came, walking towards his table. Keeping watch at the window, he wondered how he had missed her. But she had come from the gallery. Her aunt, the elderly woman waving at them and paying close attention to him through the window, was an amateur painter, and they had spent an hour looking at an exhibition. Eleni, breathless, kissed him. A waiter hovered. They ordered, and then she was straight into it.

"Nikos is in custody."

"Oh…?"

She took his hand across the table. "It has nothing to do with Mazarakis."

The tumult in Duncan's stomach that had arrived alarmingly quickly eased, but he was still unsettled. How could it not be about Mazarakis? And even if it really wasn't, how soon would it be?

"You know, you shouldn't worry about this anymore. We don't. Their bodies were burnt to nothing. They wouldn't have bothered with an autopsy, I mean, not properly. What was left?"

"I don't care about Mazarakis. I do care about the driver."

"Why? He was one of them."

"I must say, you're full of information this time."

"Well, I have more," she said, pulling out a packet of cigarettes.

"Hang on, you can't smoke in here, and anyway – "

"Who says?"

"It's the law."

"Tsk, what a country."

"What about the baby?"

She paused, the cigarette packet sliding into her pocket. "There is no baby."

Duncan leant back.

"I promised I wouldn't cry," she said, softly. Duncan reached across the table for her, but she withdrew. "No. That'll only make it worse."

Nikos, she said, had been arrested on a trumped-up charge. They were treating him as a danger to the state.

"But they've got nothing specific?" Duncan asked.

"Nothing. They're as corrupt as anything. It's worrying me so much, and I lost the – " Her sentence was drowned in tears.

Duncan got up and walked round to sit beside her. "I'm so sorry," he said. "I'm really sorry," He put his arms around her.

"I'm being silly," she said.

"No, you're not."

A waitress arrived with plates of food, and then a waiter bought some water and fresh napkins. Duncan mouthed 'thank you'.

Eleni smiled through her tears. "You must eat your sausages."

"It's why we're here," he replied, and returned to his seat. He picked up his knife and fork and plunged in. Eleni wiped her eyes and drank some water.

"You're right, they're delicious."

Eleni smiled, "I'm right about most things."

"D'you think?"

She raised her eyebrows. "Of course. Now you must tell me, Duncan, about you. What's happening?"

He scratched around, explaining how he had met up with an ex-girlfriend and she was making a real go of it as an artist. Eleni lapped it up, perhaps as much as anything else to take her mind off her own difficulties.

"Anyway, it turns out she has a son, and he's mine."

Eleni gulped down another piece of sausage. "So there really was something in England all the time," she grinned. "I knew it."

"But I hadn't, not until now."

She dropped her knife and fork, threw her arms in the air and cried, "This is brilliant, how wonderful."

Then it was her turn to run around to his side of the table, hugging and kissing him. The restaurant staff must have wondered what on earth was going on.

"I'm so excited. What's his name? Does he look like you? What's he like?"

So many questions… Duncan was speechless. He had to admit, he could never predict Eleni. Once he had persuaded her back round to her side of the table and filled in any Catie gaps, she challenged him.

"But she has told you now. How could she tell you before? You weren't even there, Duncan? How could she?"

"Is this female solidarity?"

"No. How stupid can you be?"

"Wait a second, what about when it happened? Come on."

"She was sixteen, a girl. D'you know what it's like to be a girl, sixteen, and pregnant? No, you don't, and you never will. And it was you – " pointing her fork " – you made her pregnant. You're responsible, blaming her all the time."

Duncan sat back marvelling at her. "You go right home. And tell her from me, if you like, you want to be with her and your little boy. It's what you want, isn't it."

It was not a question.

"If she'll have me."

"That's better, that's showing some respect. You people and your penises."

"You didn't complain."

She smiled shyly.

Later, waiting with her at the bus stop, she asked, "You don't want me being with Nikos, do you?"

"No, never ever."

"I know it."

"And it's not because of any jealousy." He took her by the shoulders.

"You've helped me a lot, probably more than you could guess. My turn now. He's a psychopath, Eleni."

She winced. "I'm not sure about that."

"Ask him about Melina Georgiou, and if he denies anything to do with her, pack your bags."

"Melina – ?" Eleni was alarmed. "Isn't she the woman – ?" Duncan moved her away from a couple of American tourists and some girls on a shopping spree in Princes Street. "Are you telling me Nikos has been with that person?"

"I don't know about that, but – "

"Well, then," she said, abruptly. "Duncan, you are not being fair."

Her bus arrived, filled with travellers and luggage bound for the airport. A teenager sat on the front seat, biting his lip, his bag on his lap. Duncan smiled at him. The next generation, their turn now for adventure.

Eleni climbed up to the top deck, Duncan followed. In tune with the dark clouds from the southwest scudding across the Pentland hills Eleni's mood was sombre. Was she finally open to accepting the worst about Nikos?

He drew a line from his captivity and Melina's murder, through to Mazarakis's killing and Sorehead's capture. Eleni listened.

Her head in her hands, she said, "Maybe it's justice I lost the baby."

"No, no. Don't think that." He put his arm around her. "When you get back, go and see Nikos's father. He knows his son better than anyone."

"He will be so sad. His mother! Oh, God."

"Never mind about her, it's time to think about yourself, Eleni." She managed a smile and nodded.

They got off at her stop near Murrayfield Stadium, crossed the road, and waited again, this time for his bus back to Waverley.

"We're always leaving," she said.

"I'm used to it." He smiled.

"Let's never lose touch."

"Promise."

"And do exactly what I told you with Catie."

"We've both got things to do, haven't we?"

They embraced.

"Good luck, Duncan."

He watched her walk away, her head lowered, doubtless heavy in thought. In wishing she had left Nikos sooner he wasn't thinking of himself. Rather, he regretted landing the world on her shoulders. But he was bound to, he felt it was his duty. Dmitri had gone, so he was the only one who could. Suddenly Eleni turned round and waved. She stood for a moment and then, still waving, walked backwards. Duncan thought he could see her smiling, more than she'd ever done on the bus. Then she turned to the front again and this time, as if she had come to a decision, lifted her head up and walked on swiftly.

Unlike at Athens airport, it had been a proper farewell.

CHAPTER FORTY-FIVE
NORTHERN ENGLAND

"When can I meet Marcus?"

He could feel Catie's sigh of relief down the phone. They were going to a fair at the weekend. She had told Marcus that Duncan had returned from abroad, but no further details.

"What did he say?"

"Whatever," she said, trying for a boy's voice.

Duncan laughed. "I'm glad you're laughing, but we have to prepare ourselves."

As soon as he got off the train from Edinburgh, Duncan planned to tell his mother.

Only there was a hold-up. Beth and Angela had some friends round for tea, except there were no cups in evidence. Several empty bottles of wine and vodka stacked up. Duncan was ushered in like the prodigal son, and the jolly time continued. At the first chance, he followed his mother out to the kitchen, saying he had something important to tell her, but another time.

"Not likely. Tell me now. Is it about a job?" she asked, excitedly.

"No."

"Well, then, what is it?" She sounded disappointed. "Come on, sit down." she pulled out a chair.

The sounds of whoopee continued from the front room.

"The thing is – "

"Looking at your face, this is serious."

"It is a bit."

Beth was sobering up fast.

He took a deep breath. "I've got a son."

She laughed, incredulous.

"I've got a son, Mum, and he's eleven years old."

"Bloody Nora. How did that happen? No, stop right there. I don't want the gory details."

Duncan leaned forward, took her hand in his. "Well, there is more."

"Twins!?"

"His mother is Kathryn Gifford. Well, she's called something else now, but that was her name before, when…"

"Kathryn Gifford." Beth lowered her head, repeating the surname.

"The boy's name is Marcus."

Beth withdrew her hand from his and, avoiding looking at him, sighed. Duncan could not guess what she was going to say next.

She leant back, stared at the ceiling and whispered, "Let's have a cup of tea."

He popped up and filled the kettle.

"Keep talking."

Well, how d'you follow that? He told her about meeting Catie again and the moment when she had told him.

"And how did that make you feel?"

"Shocked, you name it, but look, this conversation's really about you."

"I suppose it is, but if you had to go and get a girl pregnant, I'd rather it hadn't been this one."

"Of all the girls in all the world," said Duncan. "But she is." He held up his hands.

"I'm not taking against her," Beth paused. "Does the mother know you're back?"

"I really don't know. Catie's the one in charge now."

"She may well be, but you'll both be hoping the grandmothers will be very happy." She slapped his knee. "Smart move to tell me when I'm half cut."

"That was your idea."

The next hour included some tears from Beth, and recriminating remarks like "typical of your mum to rain on your parade, isn't it?", and Angela coming to the rescue with, "Come on Beth, that's your role in life. At least you didn't kiss him in the playground in front of the Year 4s."

"D'you want to bet?" said Duncan. Knowing this was only round one, he hankered to leave. Let Angela take his mother's strain.

But as he headed for the bungalow, he was sure of one thing. Eleni had ended, and something else had properly begun again. From the train he had not told Catie where he had been, and she had never asked. There were more important things now.

To his dismay, Chas was working late. Duncan was in no mood for any carpentry discussions, but Chas had a different topic altogether. Duncan had had a caller.

"Well, not so much a caller, as such…"

Oh, God, here we go. He'll take another hour, thought Duncan, eager to crack open the bottle of wine Angela had lobbed him. "Bit late to wet the baby's head but – " she had said.

"He was sort of hanging about and looking in, so I called him over. 'Could I help you's,' I says. He asked if you lived here. Well, to be honest he only got as far as the Duncan, and I gave him the Connor, so to speak," Chas said proudly.

Duncan paid full attention. "What was he, an official-looking bloke of some kind?"

Chas blew his cheeks out. "Nah, I wouldn't say that. Scruffier, to be honest with youse. Anyways, so I told him you lived here, but like you were out, and I couldn't be sure when you'd be back. I mean I didn't knaa you'd be back tonight – "

"And what happened then?"

"He was odd, like he was waiting for me to say summat. But there was nowt I could've tell't him."

"What sort of age?"

"Er – forties, yeah, mebbe forty-five, summat like that. I says to him, any message? Can I say who called?" said Chas.

"And?"

"Well, nothing. He said nowt, just went off."

"Was he in a car, or was there anyone else with him?"

"Definitely no car, that I saw like. I didn't see no one else, so no, I diven't think there was."

"Can you describe him? Any features? What about his face?" Duncan scratched his nose asking this.

"Not really, he was like your normal run-of-the-mill bloke… anyways, now you're back can we talk about this alcove in the front – "

"Tell you what, Chas, I'm completely knackered."

Chas took the hint, but it was another ten minutes before he'd tidied up and lumbered off.

Chewing Gum had made a visit designed to chill. It was spooky. Catie had come back into his life and as if on cue these two turn up.

But was it spooky? Hadn't it always been like this? For so long as Kathryn/Catie had been a light in his head, so had they been the darkness. Ever since that night, these two opposing forces had driven him. The reason he preferred to leave than stay. On the island he had asked himself, was it him or them? Now he knew it was a bit of both, he could no longer run. He had to stand and face it.

He needed help.

"Bad timing," said Joe the security guard on the phone. "I'd like to, but…"

He was laid up with a broken leg, but not a professional injury. He had crashed spectacularly, as he put it, skiing. It turned out Linda was looking after him.

That works, thought Duncan, pleased.

"Look after yourself," said Joe.

Duncan ran through his home security. Then, fearing the threat was imminent, he spent the night in a chair, baseball bat at the ready. A French film shot in Zurich that was showing on TV for the first time kept him awake. Mathild Tabard, playing a Lolita-esque part, outshone the material. Now if David Lynch had directed it... But Duncan was only half watching. He was already in a Lynchian nightmare himself.

In the morning, he had just enough time to hide the bat and remove old Henry's foot trap before Beth and Angela bowled in through the door, mustard-keen to discuss fatherhood. Angela had once lived with a man who had a daughter.

"You're lucky this chap's a boy, 'cos girls – Oh," she said, pulling a long face. "They're a different kind of palaver."

"Yes, I've had some experience of the older variety."

"And don't we know it. That's why you're in this mess," said Beth, who had been poking around since she arrived. "How are you going to pay for all this work?"

"That's a different conversation, Mum."

"No, it's the same one, the one we've been having for some time. She's going to want support, Duncan. What are your plans? D'you still have feelings for the woman? There's a whole raft of – "

"Whoa," went Duncan and Angela in unison, and held Beth by an arm each, preventing her from flying into orbit.

His mother had prepared a list, pages long. Angela weighed in with the perils of puberty, and Duncan, wilting from the lack of sleep, was relieved when Chas arrived. He suggested Angela took over negotiations about the wretched alcove. She was thrilled.

"I'm sorry," said Beth, once they were alone. "This has been a bit of an avalanche for you."

"One thing at a time. First thing's to meet Marcus, then Catie, and then her mother."

Beth shrivelled. "One minute I'm fine with that, the next… it's terrible, and I'm back in prison again. I knew you had something to tell me, but I could never have guessed…" Her voice trailed off.

This confirmed he was right not to tell her the full Greek story. It would only put her in a tailspin and back to the state she was in after Gifford's death. He remembered her cries in the night. More than ever, he understood Beth's remorse, even shared it. Partly. He thanked her for the list; it was a plan. As for his own plan, the one he could not tell her, the frustration was because of the lack of it. Chewing Gum and Ryan had to show their faces, and then he would know what to do.

He hoped.

CHAPTER FORTY-SIX

Fair day.

Duncan, considering a pair of black jeans to wear, was interrupted by a knock on the door. He crept into the lounge, but before he could check who it was through the window, something dropped onto the mat: a delivery note. He rushed to open the door, and the courier returned with the parcel.

Duncan carried it into the kitchen and, wary, put it on the table. He turned it over, saw the address on the bottom, and joy swept through him. He tore off the wrapping, scissored through bubble wrap, and pulled out a framed painting. The second painting he'd ever received through the post. He propped this one up on the work top, leaning it against the wall. A watercolour of a swimmer, powering through the sea towards the rocks, caught in a ray of light. Jenny had called it 'Duncan in Transit'. How prophetic. She had signed it, and there was a card too.

> *"Hey Old Pard'ner, thanks for the Hank Fonda. Heh heh!*
> *I'll be damned, what joyous news! And don't you forget now, there'll*
> *always be A welcome for you and your folks on this 'loaf of bread'."*

Beanie loved the American writer, Henry Miller's description of the island. Jenny had added, her fingers were crossed he liked the painting. He did, he really did. Not in her usual style, it had expressed his hopes with Eleni. All dust, but now he was on the brink of a new adventure, the gift was still timely.

He had cried the day he left Beanie on the Quay, and he did again now.

Marcus, the only child driving on his own, whirred around the dodgems track. Catie, in blue jeans and a dark puffa jacket, proud but anxious, stood watching. Her son, a determined look on his face, showed neat handling.

'That's my boy,' thought Duncan, as he slipped his arm around Catie's waist and kissed her on the cheek.

"Oh," she said, delighted by his embrace. "I wondered who on earth it could be."

"Better than some random bloke, I hope."

She looked him up and down and smiled. "Glad you've made an effort."

He didn't tell her his mother had 'appearance' on her list.

"I'm thirty!" he'd complained as she'd swept the hair out of his eyes.

"Then you shouldn't need to be told," had been Beth's reply.

All talk of mothers, except for present company, were better off the radar.

"Not so bad yourself," he said, and she kicked him playfully.

"Hey, we're supposed to be responsible parents." He looked at her in pretend shock.

The power died and Marcus's car came to a stop.

"Here goes," Duncan breathed out, but the boy was gesturing he wanted another go. Duncan jumped onto the track, shouting, "So do I."

"Boys!" Catie said, happily digging into her purse.

Marcus thumbed-up, and off they went. Duncan, aware the worst thing to do would be to knock Marcus flying, started cautiously. A thump from behind so hard his hands shot off the steering wheel changed that. Marcus sailed by grinning. They chased each other round, exchanging the full range of bumps. He saw Catie was relaxing, too.

But he didn't see that someone else taking an interest was a man in a blue suit. Greyer, leaning against the dodgem control box: Chewing Gum.

At the end of the session, Marcus ran to his mother's side.

"Did you enjoy that?" Catie asked, and Marcus shyly nodded. "Well," she said, "Marcus –"

Uncertain, the boy looked up at Duncan.

"Meet your dad."

Duncan, smiling, stuck his hand out. "Hello, Marcus."

The boy slowly came forward and took it. "I've seen you before."

"Yes," agreed Duncan. "In the shop."

Marcus looked up proudly at Catie as though he had put one over on his mother.

"What shall we do now?" wondered Catie. "A cup of tea, perhaps?"

"Ah, but Mum, you said I could go on the rollercoaster."

Catie looked at Duncan: his first fatherly decision.

"Why not?" he said, taking the boy by the shoulder. "But you're on your own up there."

"Are you scared?"

"Yup."

Marcus suddenly squirmed out of Duncan's grasp and ran backwards in front of him shouting, "Scaredy, scaredy, scaredy…"

It was off-putting, but Duncan pretended to cuff him, and Marcus ran off laughing. Duncan could see Marcus was small and immature for his age.

"You're born for this," beamed Catie.

Duncan showed her his hand, his fingers crossed.

While Marcus whirled around on the rollercoaster, Duncan told Catie he had put Beth in the picture.

"How'd she take it?"

"She'll get there."

"I'd like to meet her."

"Good. One day," he said, and she slipped between his arms. "She's terrified of meeting your mum – like I am, to be honest."

"Yeah, you should be," she said, laughing.

"Thanks. What did she call me? An unfit person or something?"

"A very unhealthy young man."

"And the rest."

Catie nodded. "She's much different now. It's never going to be easy, but…"

He pulled back from her.

"Hey, I was enjoying that."

"Me, too," he said, indicating the rollercoaster was slowing down. "But maybe we should take things slowly."

"Never took you for a spoilsport."

He laughed, put his arm around her and kissed her head.

Marcus rudely rejected the operator's helping hand and jumped down from the ride. The happy-go-lucky-boy from before had gone missing. One of two things had happened, or maybe both: the rollercoaster had thrown him about, and unwilling to admit it he was feeling sick; or he had spotted his mother and Duncan cuddling. Now, head down, he scuffed along behind them doing an excellent impression of a gooseberry. Duncan suggested they take turns at the rifle range, but he refused.

He accepted a stick of candy floss but had to be reminded to say 'please' and 'thank you'. When Duncan pointed out the House of Horrors, Marcus threw away the remains of his candyfloss and said, "Why would I want to go anywhere with you?"

"Come here at once," said Catie.

Duncan was sure, as adults, they were to blame. The sun was out, and the fairground was filling up, so if they could just get this right...

He turned round. Marcus had run off, with Catie following. "Leave him, Catie, he'll come back."

"Suddenly you're the expert."

She ran looking left and right down the alleyways between the stalls. Duncan joined her, but Marcus had vanished.

"I'm sure this is deliberate. He's probably hiding somewhere."

"Why?" Catie was crying.

He held her. "He's punishing us, I think he saw us – "

She shook him off. "He's too old to behave like that."

Duncan wasn't so sure. On this form Marcus was going to take some handling, but first things first. Get him back. They walked on calling out his name.

"What did you say to him?"

"So, it's my fault?"

"No, I didn't say that – "

She quickened her pace, getting ahead of him.

"We should check back where we were – "

"Good idea," she called out. "Go on, I'll try this way."

Duncan had turned towards the dodgems when he heard a cry. Catie was running, shouting and pointing. Far ahead, Duncan saw two familiar figures dragging Marcus towards the car park.

Here it was.

Duncan ran. He gained on them. Marcus was putting up a fight and slowing them down. Duncan could catch them, he had to. He ran harder.

Then he lost them… Out of sight. He ran on…

There!

But they had reached a car, a Volvo estate. Chewing Gum bundled the boy forcefully into the back and got in beside him. Ryan, behind the wheel, reversed.

Duncan got close enough to see Marcus, screaming in the back window, but the Volvo skidded forward across the gravel, churning up dust, and bolted.

Same M.O., thought Duncan, except this time it wasn't him in the car, nor his father in the back room of the bungalow, but his helpless child carried off beyond his reach. While Hannah had faced the nazis, these evil monsters were working their way through the next generation of Connors.

"It's on me," he uttered, grinding to a halt and struggling for air. Then his guts heaved.

"I saw them," A woman with a child ran up. "They're in a car – "

Duncan was bent over, his hand across his mouth.

"Here's the number plate," she pushed a piece of paper into Duncan's hand.

He took it. Catie arrived.

"Are you the lad's mother?" asked the woman. "You should be taking more care."

Catie ignored her and flipped open her mobile.

Duncan stood up straight. "What are you doing?"

"Calling the police."

"He's got the registration," the woman pointed at Duncan. "I gave it to him."

Other people gathered round.

Duncan pulled Catie away, "They *were* the police."

"What? No…"

"Where's your car?"

"Jonathan's," she said without thinking. Catie's mobile rang. She fumbled, then, "Marcus? Hello darling – I want to talk to my son – Who are you? Let me talk to – " She handed the phone to Duncan. "They want to speak to you."

All he heard was laughter. Sweat trickled cold down his back. The phone clicked off before he could speak. Duncan hit re-call, but it rang straight to Marcus's voice mail.

"Explain."

He returned the phone to Catie, "Where's the car?"

"Explain, Duncan," Catie repeated furiously.

"Get in the car first."

A v6 Mercedes – good for Mr Bassett, thought Duncan.

Catie dropped the keys. Duncan picked them up. "I'll drive."

They got in, "Give me the phone back," said Duncan and pushed the Mercedes into gear. "They'll call again."

She returned it, "Tell me where we're going?"

He drove out of the car park. "I'm taking you home."

"What? Why?"

"Don't get caught up in this, Catie, they're major, dangerous – "

"What d'you mean, don't get caught up? He's my son – "

"Mine, too."

"What are you going to do?"

"Deal with it."

"Stop the car. Stop. Explain."

"It's all about me. They want me."

“They’ve got Marcus!” Catie swiped at Duncan, connecting with his head. “STOP THE CAR!” She screamed.

Duncan skidded to a halt.

It took ten minutes for Catie, through tears, to grasp and then believe Duncan’s story of that night he’d called at the Gifford’s. She blamed herself, her mother, Duncan, and herself again. Then she used a Kleenex to dab his cut where her fingernail had caught him. Duncan gargled with mineral water from a bottle to wash out his mouth.

Her phone rang.

“I talk, you listen…” Duncan was instructed.

For the next several hours they zigzagged within a twenty-mile radius from one arbitrary stop to the next and waited for another call.

“Can they see us?” asked Catie looking round.

“I doubt that very much, they’re just playing silly buggers,” answered Duncan, bowling the Mercedes up to top speed.

“Wooooh,” said Catie.

“Maybe you’ll be safer in the back.”

“I don’t like the way you’re keeping me out of this.”

“I’m not,” he said stopping the car.

“And I’m not sitting in the back.”

“Ok,” he agreed. “We’ve got to be one hundred percent together.”

“I know, I know,” she gestured. “Keep driving.”

Duncan did.

“I’m just frightened sick,” she said.

The phone rang. Catie answered, “I can’t hear you.” Her finger in one ear.

It was her mother.

After the fair, Catie had secretly planned they would all meet, but Ruth hadn’t been told when exactly or where. Not surprisingly, Catie had clean forgotten.

“Sorry about… I’m in a car. Mum, it’s no good, I can’t hear – I’ll text.”

She ended the call. Duncan admired the way she had managed her mother. He stretched out his hand and held her knee. She put her hand on top and through the tension they briefly smiled at each other.

Duncan was filling the Mercedes with petrol when the next instruction arrived.

"In somebody else's car, with somebody else's wife. Tsk, tsk."

"C-minus for accuracy."

"Same woman, naughty cunt. Get here by 9pm or else the kid – " The line cut out.

Duncan was relieved Catie hadn't heard the threat to Marcus, but the destination was what struck him, and over-rode everything else. He got back in the car, he knew where he was going, but why there? Why that place?

Catie was looking at him.

"We'll get him back," he promised her.

"Like you know."

"I do."

But he didn't, he was frightened. Was this what it was like to be a grown up?

"Who are you, Duncan Connor?"

"I think we're about to find out."

CHAPTER FORTY-SEVEN

In the falling darkness, the fields tapering behind them finally disappeared. Duncan looked for familiar sights. The tall lime kiln in silhouette; the road that bent to the right passed the wood yard. They climbed into the hills. A lonely bothy at the edge of a deep gulley. The diversionary signs were in place; a race was imminent. But up ahead – what?

Onto the moor, bleaker than ever.

They drove up to the racetrack and crossed the starting line. Memories tumbled through Duncan's mind. The nerves, the tension of that first day, the opponent he beat, the one in the black and gold helmet whose face he never saw.

Suddenly it hit him.

"I'm the driver. I'm the fucking driver," Ryan's words echoed.

Him!

Then, later at the Gifford's house, his stare… He'd recognised Duncan, and for revenge driven him down a dark country lane. But Duncan had bettered him again, and his mate. Ryan had borne the mark ever since. Literally. Joe the security guard had said it. They never forget, and now the threat had multiplied.

Duncan felt the strands of his life pulling together. They had always come in twos. He imagined a hellish warehouse, where goblins stitched sadistic strains into squads of horror twins and sent them out on diabolical duties. But this was no fairytale with him cast as St George slaying his demons. It was really happening, and he could not fail.

He scanned the horizon for headlights. No sign. He checked the rearview mirror – just like Ryan to sneak up behind him, but no. They were ahead of the clock but had received no further instructions. What to do? What could he do? He knew full well, he was in their hands.

Catie's voice cut through. "I need a pee."

He pulled up. Catie disappeared into the bushes. A picture of Beanie balancing on his chair in the infirmary came into his mind. He'd called it his Henry Fonda impersonation stress test. How far could he push the chair back against the wall before he crashed? Duncan gripped the wheel, his stomach turning over.

Catie opened the car door. "He's here."

Duncan frowned.

"Marcus. I can hear him, come on."

Over the years, the racing marshals and spectators had tramped down routes through the bracken between the bends in the road. In the moonlight, Duncan and Catie crept down one of these paths.

They both heard Marcus's cries.

"Oh, I can't bear it, what are they doing to him?"

"Let me go in front," said Duncan, and went ahead.

"Hurry," she tucked her hand into the top of Duncan's jeans. In single file, the stony path took them between two trees. Duncan accidentally kicked a rock. It rolled free and noisily rumbled down towards the road. He cursed. They stopped and listened.

Marcus was quiet.

On they went.

Duncan saw him first. They had roped Marcus to a wooden cross in the middle of the road. Beneath him lay a lumpy tarpaulin which covered, or hid, what Duncan could smell were petrol drums. So close to the hairpin bend, and leaving next to no room for a car to pass on either side, their wicked intention was clear. The horror of Duncan driving into Marcus and unleashing hell stared him in the face.

"Where are the bastards?"

Catie rushed forward.

"Wait. No," hissed Duncan. But she had gone.

Marcus shouted.

Duncan held his breath.

Catie clambered up on the drums and on up to the rickety cross.

Suddenly Marcus and Catie were floodlit.

Catie pulled at the ropes binding Marcus, untying the knots. Lamps slung from trees beamed through the dark; another tilted upwards from the ditch, pointing at the cross. Macabre; the tableau had the feel of a horror movie set. Chewing Gum and Ryan were filming it – were they? From where? Duncan was still grasping the sickening prospect when a shot rang out.

He scrambled for a stone, threw it, but he missed the nearest lamp.

A bullet pinged off metal.

He raced out into the road. Catie waved him back, Marcus was free.

Another shot fired at the infernal construction.

Mother and son leapt on to the road and collapsed in a heap.

WOOMPH! The petrol exploded. Catie, in pain, staggered to her feet and shouted, "Get the car! GO!"

Duncan ran slip sliding back up the path, dire fears pulsing through him; Chewing Gum and Ryan shooting; a bullet hitting Marcus; Catie's leg broken in the fall? All the worst.

He stalled the car. "You're fucking it up, you're fucking it up."

In the rearview mirror he caught sight of a figure moving. Someone was on the back seat. He spun round. A young woman wearing her full-length ARP pattern 43 blue coat. On her head her dark blue peaked cap, tonight worn at a jaunty angle. Leaning forward her face glistened in the light from the spreading fires. Hannah was on duty.

"Bless you," she said.

Duncan smiled; this was even better than the dinky ambulance. He counted to three and then calmly started the engine. He drove the Mercedes round the hairpin. Flames licked into the night, illuminating Catie limping out of the undergrowth, and beside her, Marcus.

"Are you ok?"

They bundled into the back as Duncan put the car into reverse.

"The flames saved us – they couldn't get near."

"Did they hurt you, Marcus?"

The boy was shivering.

Catie her arms around him, hugged him close. "He's ok."

"I'm frightened mum."

"You're safe" said Catie comforting him. "Promise you."

"Sorry I ran away."

"Shh-shh," Catie told him. "It's alright."

"Who are they? What do they want?" Naturally he was full of questions, but any answers would have to wait. "They're still here," added Marcus.

"Where?"

"We heard a car," explained Catie. "They're stuck."

"So are we," cried Duncan in frustration, slamming on the brakes.

The hillside above them was alight, cutting off any retreat. The soaring flames created a firewall, the heat hotter by the second. The only route was forward. The cross had burned down and most of the petrol drums had been ripped to tatters by the explosion. They'd have to squeeze through the fiery debris. Duncan's further fear was a severe ditch at the side of the road, easy to fall into. Only his best drive ever would do. Beat any race on the aerodrome, better than Paris – even than Athens. He had to go and go now. He pushed into first gear and hit the accelerator.

Aiming for a combination of tarmac and the grass knoll he sped towards the fire, flames flickering on the road. The remaining petrol drum chose this moment to roll out into their path. Gritting his teeth, Duncan steered the car clear, only to subside into the ditch, his right-hand wheels grinding fruitlessly into the turf. He swore and switched to reverse. With the engine roaring, the spinning wheels caught traction and slew the Mercedes back onto the tarmac. Flames licked at the window. Marcus screamed, his mother holding him. Duncan rammed through the gears and accelerated. The car leapt forward, almost airborne, and then back down onto the road. He had skidded clear, but dangerously close to the outer edge and the river below. Duncan spun the wheel and pulled the car back into the middle of the road. Above the smell of burning fire and fumes, he caught a taste of the rocky river's chill water.

"So far, so good," Duncan said, driving on.

"Yeah," Marcus, impressed, agreed.

No time for pride, as each bend brought them face to face with the fire, which aided by dry brushwood and bracken, streaked down the hillside.

Duncan took one more hairpin. "I think they've gone."

Four bends to go, at a guess, and the river would act as a fire break. But getting there…

Ahead, tyres rumbled and screeched. Duncan stepped on it, and rounding the next bend, saw the Volvo scramble up out of a gravel pit and hit the road, turning down towards the river.

"Shit!"

His instinct was to run the Volvo over the edge. He took the next bend quicker than he should, but a touch on the wheel corrected the direction and he screeched into the straight. Catie and Marcus were thrown across the back seat.

"Strap in tighter," he yelled

"Are you sure, Duncan? They're going."

He was back in the boxing ring again, punching to kill. "So are we. I'm not letting them get away."

The drop on the valley side appeared deeper than ever. Suddenly, all he could see were flames. The car seemed to be floating. He worried the windscreen might melt; they'd hurtle down and smash into pieces on the wet rocks. But no, the tyres held their course, and they were through the next bend, safe.

Concentrate, he told himself, concentrate!

The Volvo was in range, the boot door raised, and Duncan saw Ryan facing them in the back.

Why was Chewing Gum driving?

Ryan had a pistol.

Duncan dropped back. He switched the headlights to full beam to blind Ryan. He wished he hadn't._Chewing Gum's arm came round from the front, grabbing for the gun, but Ryan resisted him. The car slewed left and right, across the road. Chewing Gum returned to the front and the Volvo slowed for the bend. Duncan drew closer. Ryan aimed out the back.

"Get down!" shouted Duncan.

Ryan reversed the barrel, put it in his mouth and blew his head off.

"Fuck!" He prayed his passengers hadn't seen it.

The Volvo was out of control. He imagined Chewing Gum wrestling the steering wheel to keep the car straight – "Baby, baby, what have you done?!" – and realising he had run out of road, screaming like the Mazarakis kid.

Braking hard, tyres bit, but it was too late: the Volvo burst through the rusted barrier and careened into mid-air before tipping downwards. It clattered off a rocky outcrop. A wheel wrenched loose and the car, spinning into a nosedive, finally crashed to a stop, the front end smashed and wedged into the river.

After all the noise, the terror and the violence in seconds there was nothing.

Silence.

Duncan steered the car over the bridge and pulled up, facing the fallen Volvo.

They all got out of the Mercedes and stood at the side of the road.

"Dad, it's raining."

"No, it's the fire brigade," said Catie.

But it wasn't them either, not yet. The moor racers, camped along the lane next to the bridge, were organised to the last. They sprayed hoses attached to a water tanker, damping the fire. In the distance, but getting closer fast, sirens howled; blue lights flashed.

Life was still in repeat mode; except this time something had been broken. Duncan had seen Ryan's body slither from the mangled chassis and smash against a jagged rock. For a moment, he saw the thug as just one more car crash victim. He quickly corrected himself. Ryan and Chewing Gum, who was lying lifeless against the splintered windscreen, had reserved themselves a special place in Hell.

Suddenly, he was crushed in the thick arms of a man gnarled by time and experience, but still recognisable by his rich accent.

"Come here," said Mick Cochrane. "Connor, I should've guessed you'd be at the bottom of this." He released Duncan and held his arms up.

"What the hell is going on?"

"Well, here I am, and I'm happy to say, no mistakes. I followed your advice back there. Kept us alive."

"I was worried about you," confessed Mick. "That guy you beat, he went looking for you. Famous for it."

"Now you tell me."

"I didn't know where you'd gone. When you beat him in that race, it was against all the odds. Turned out a bunch of ugly people lost a lot of money."

Duncan listened closely.

"They took their pound of flesh" explained Mick, "I've got the scars to prove it,"

"Shit, I'm sorry,"

Mick shook his head, a proud man.

"Well, he found me, him and his mate," said Duncan, and put his finger to his forehead. "Boom."

Mick was astonished and looked up at the rock. The paramedics were shifting Ryan's body onto a gurney.

"What, you – ?" gasped Mick, with what Duncan took for barely concealed admiration.

"No, no. The driver, self-inflicted."

Mick pulled Duncan up to his face, grinning, "Expect you on that grid, next race."

"Hey, give him to me," said Catie.

They embraced.

Surely Athens had been enough, but no. How well he'd cope with all he'd seen would be the measure of him. Like his grandmother, he now had his own story. He hoped he'd inherited her fortitude.

Catie ruffled their son's hair. "And hasn't this little man grown up?"

"That makes two of us."

Duncan crouched down to Marcus; his pale face smudged with dirt and stained with dried tears.

"Where did you learn to drive?" the boy asked.

He pointed to the hillside "Right up there."

Marcus nodded. All he'd suffered hadn't hit him yet, but it would. Something they'd have to work on together.

He looked up at Catie, "We've been the long way round haven't we?"

She nodded.

"What d'you think? Shall we give it a go?"

"Well, Duncan Connor…" She looked back up the road, the way they'd come. "I'm thinking about it."

He stood up. He was on his toes. Her use of his full name, as ever, sounded like an admonishment.

W.H. Auden's lines came back to him.

'this land is not the sweet home it looks,
Nor its peace the historical calm of a site
Where something was settled once and for all:'

He thought of his father. Pat had been right. His odyssey was over.

But had he come home?

Acknowledgements

Many thanks for their notes and encouragement to The Literary Consultancy, Doug Johnstone, Alan Mackay, Rod Wooden, Alan Maislen, Martin Ellis, Martin Dillon, Iris Charamis, Roger Green, and Francoise Harvey.

Thanks to Sarah Sturm for helping navigate the rights of use for the lines from W.H.Auden's poem 'In Praise of Limestone'.

Special thanks to Chris Andrew for the attention to detail, and to Tessa Green for putting up with me.

Formatting and Marketing by Chris Andrew.
Cover image by Tessa Green.
Graphic Design by Ryan Fenwick.

Any errors are the sole responsibility of the author.

ARP 43 PUBLISHING

www.ingramcontent.com/pod-product-compliance
Ingram Content Group UK Ltd.
Pitfield, Milton Keynes, MK11 3LW, UK
UKHW021903200825
462066UK00006B/27

9 781036 927264